'Why do people like that always carry bags across their shoulders?' wondered Eupheme. The man they had been watching was now looking at a slow passing goods train. He was standing in an odd, knees bent position, holding his camcorder to his eye. His car coat was now more rucked up, the strap of his shoulder bag twisting the material around his body.

'Or maybe it's us. Why don't we?'

'Romance, sex, treachery and a frightful accident, which all adds up to a gripping story. Llewellyn's brilliant dialogue brings his characters vividly to life in this acutely observed and genuinely funny book'
Mail on Sunday

'A bewitching debut . . . gentle humour and skilful characterisation . . . great subtlety . . . Llewellyn has genuine charm and a tremendous gift for gilding the commonplace'
The Financial Times

'Hugely engaging story . . . A fun book, with verve and wit. Think of TRADING PLACES written in the clever style of Ben Elton and you're close'
The Times

About the Author

Robert Llewellyn was born in Northampton. He had a basic education and left home and school at a tender age to become a hippy. He dabbled in shoemaking, nude modelling and tree surgery before stepping onto stage at the age of 24. He wrote and performed in hundreds of sketches, plays and songs for stage and TV. In 1988 Robert wrote a prize-winning play at the Edinburgh Festival which in turn led to a job on the BBC comedy show *Red Dwarf*. He lives with his partner and their two children in London and the Cotswolds.

The Man on Platform Five

Robert Llewellyn

CORONET BOOKS

Hodder & Stoughton

Copyright © 1998 by Robert Llewellyn

The right of Robert Llewellyn to be identified as the Author
of the Work has been asserted by him in accordance with
the Copyright, Designs and Patents Act 1988.

First published in Great Britain in 1998
by Hodder and Stoughton
First published in paperback in 1999
by Hodder and Stoughton
A division of Hodder Headline PLC
A Coronet Paperback

10 9 8 7 6 5 4 3 2 1

A CIP catalogue record for this title is available
from the British Library

ISBN 0 340 70790 9

Typeset by Palimpsest Book Production Limited,
Polmont, Stirlingshire
Printed and bound in Great Britain by
Clays Ltd, St Ives PLC, Bungay, Suffolk

Hodder and Stoughton
A division of Hodder Headline PLC
338 Euston Road
London NW1 3BH

ACKNOWLEDGEMENTS

One of the primary inspirations for this book has been the many thousands of *Red Dwarf* fans I have met around the world. Often lumped together as 'nerdy science fiction buffs' or 'anoraks', they constantly defy glib categorisation. I have never met a more varied, intelligent and colourful cross-section of humanity. Out of the many thousands encountered, only one was actually wearing an anorak, and that was on a very hot day. He seemed a little strange, but nothing to be alarmed about. The man wearing the yellow dress also springs to mind, and the woman with the cardboard Kryten head. There was the guy with the H on his forehead who stood a bit too close and wanted me to sign an autograph on a part of his body that should remain private, so yes, some of them are a bit odd, but they are all very charming really.

Although writing is a solitary activity, there are all sorts of people involved outside my writing shed whom I'd like to thank. My agent, Sarah Leigh, and before her Mark Lucas, both of whom made me rewrite and rewrite until I was going barmy. Also huge thanks to Carolyn Mays at Hodder for putting up with my prattling and reading the manuscript so carefully.

My old friend Charlie Dancey for his help on computer programming, Mel Yates at the Cheltenham branch of Sainsbury's for the background on supermarkets, and Kashif Merchant for keeping my computer working against the odds.

This book is in memory of my father, Reg.

rllewellyn@online.rednet.co.uk

Chapter One

'There are three hundred and seven distinctively different types of underarm odour,' said Gresham Hollingford. 'And he's got the complete set.' She laughed quietly at her own ingenuity and flicked a few pages of her magazine.

The victim of this insult stood only a few feet away, saved from the cruelty of the barb by stout Virgin Rail double glazing. He was standing on the platform close to the window of an InterCity 125, temporarily halted in Milton Keynes station on its journey from London Euston to Manchester Piccadilly. Owing to reflections caused by the bright March sunshine, the victim was unaware of the presence of three women staring at him as if he were an exhibit in a zoo.

'He doesn't look dirty, poor thing, just a bit dull,' said Gresham's half-sister Eupheme Betterment. Eupheme and Gresham shared a father but not a name. Their father was married to Gresham's mother, but had 'known' Eupheme's mother during the engagement. Hence the closeness in age – three months apart, the closeness in height – Gresham was an inch taller, and the immense desire both women had to be as different from each other as possible.

'Anyway, what on earth is he doing?' asked Eupheme.

'Train-spotting,' said Christine Hanks, the third and worst-dressed member of the party.

'No, surely not,' said Eupheme.

'I think so. I think that's what they do,' said Christine.

'Oh, that's so sad. Isn't it? It's really, really terribly sad. Why do they do it?' asked Eupheme.

'I don't know,' said Christine, adjusting her position to get a better view of the man. 'It seems a lonely sort of thing to do, doesn't it?'

'But he's got a video camera,' said Eupheme.

'Maybe he records all the trains.'

'You mean he sits at home and watches videos of trains going through Milton Keynes station?' said Eupheme disparagingly. 'Come on. He must be doing something else.'

'What else could he be doing?' asked Christine.

'He might be an art student.'

Christine laughed. 'Have you ever seen an art student who looked like that?'

'What d'you think, Gresh?' asked Eupheme.

Gresham sat motionless, looking at her page in *Premiere* magazine. Her page, a whole page, not a little column or a small mention, but a whole page, with a huge picture. She had heard everything Christine and Eupheme said, but she didn't want them to know.

'What?' she asked when she became aware that their stares were finally pointing in her direction.

'We wondered why he had a video camera,' said Eupheme.

Gresham looked around for someone with a video camera in the train carriage. She knew this would annoy them.

'No, out there, silly,' said Christine. 'The man with all the different armpit odours.'

'Saddo,' said Gresham as though it was obvious.

The man they were staring at on the platform of Milton Keynes station was holding a Sony TR200 Hi8 camcorder. Gresham knew that much – colour viewfinder, Ni-cad batteries, autofocus, power zoom and a very ingenious clip-on base unit to use during editing. The man wore tinted glasses in vaguely

Easy Rider-style frames and a beige quilted car coat with a Velcro fastening strap below the chin. This strap was done up tight. It was a cold day, but not that cold. The strap pulled the coat into an awkward shape, making an ugly garment look downright unpleasant. He wore light blue pressed slacks which clashed with the beige car coat wonderfully, expressively almost. On his feet were soft grey lace-up shoes – they had white, expanded vinyl acetate soles that looked as if they would stay white through a nuclear winter. Gresham's brow creased as she stared at the shoes. They were repulsive. She realised that it was possible to make a product she actually found physically repulsive, like looking at vomit on the pavement. The uppers were an ugly shade of grey. A deadening light grey, the colour of an individuality vacuum. The colour of these shoes, she thought, sucked the life out of the surrounding area. Not only that, they clashed yet again with the trousers. Then the socks, nylon towelling effect, looked like they were a bulk purchase from somewhere like Millet's and came in a washed-out shade of chrome yellow. Gresham shook her head slightly. These socks made the final statement in the ensemble. This man appeared to have no idea what was on his body, no thought, no self-respect, no self-image. A void, a mist, a non-being. Numerous badges adorned the collar of the coat. Here was the stamp of originality, of individualism. It was kept in check, high up around the neck of the coat. Small chromium shapes with red and blue paint, some representing objects like cars, trains, planes and cameras, some simply geometric shapes bearing the initials IFFAI and BTEIG.

'What a sad, sad spectacle,' said Gresham, turning back to her copy of *Premiere* magazine. The very flattering picture of her sitting on a folding canvas director's chair, her name embroidered across the back-rest in red and gold, had made her month. In the picture she had her head thrown back and to the side, looking at the camera with a beautiful but deliberately vacant expression. Saying, 'How could I make a film, I'm so pretty and dumb?' Her auburn hair hung down long and loose, standing out from the mottled grey backdrop of the studio.

'Train-spotters,' said Christine again. 'More of them.' Gresham and Eupheme followed her gaze. Christine was staring at a platform in the other direction. Since another train had departed, three more similarly dressed white males were revealed. One, a heavily built fellow wearing stretch fabric training slacks and a white vest, was laughing uproariously, his taut belly vibrating slowly as his overstressed diaphragm worked hard to move the bulk hanging below it.

'Imagine that on top of you,' said Gresham.

'Please, Gresh,' said Eupheme, nodding painfully towards a sizeable businessman sitting in the seat across the aisle from their table. 'He can't help it.'

'What d'you mean can't help it?' said Gresham, louder than before. 'He's utterly gross.'

'Some people really can't help their weight,' said Christine.

Gresham smiled at her, eyebrows raised almost imperceptibly. 'Clearly,' she said. 'Look at me. I'm not a great wallowing slob. I'm not on some sad diet. This is the way I am. That bloke is so fat it's genetic. He can't do anything about it. Born to be a porker.' She half laughed at her own joke.

'You're lucky. You're slim and very shapely,' said Christine.

'Of course I am,' said Gresham. 'I'm a Hollingford. We're lean, we're mean.'

'I'll vouch for the last bit,' said Eupheme quickly. There was a pause, then, 'Sorry, Gresh, didn't mean it.'

'Isn't your mum or dad fat, then?' asked Christine innocently.

'Not in the least,' said Gresham. 'Father hasn't gone up or down in twenty years. Mother has allowed her arse to spread a bit, but she's still thin as a rake.'

'She's also very unhappy,' said Eupheme. 'She's had an awful life in many ways.'

'Oh, she's unspeakably neurotic,' agreed Gresham without hesitation. 'That's what makes her so thin.'

'My mum blew up like a balloon after she had me,' said Christine. 'She's never really gone down again. It suits her now, though. She's sort of matronly.'

'She's very nice, your mum,' said Eupheme with a kind smile.

'Your mum's thin,' said Gresham, looking at Eupheme critically. 'Except in the ankles. You've got her ankles, thick and shapeless.'

'Thank you,' said Eupheme. 'Thank you very much.'

'And her face, of course, that's a bit bloated, but that's the booze,' said Gresham, remembering that the last time she saw Eupheme's mum the woman could barely walk, let alone speak. 'Your ankles are a shame, though,' she said with genuine concern. 'I mean, you won't get the face, unless you become a complete alcoholic, but no amount of dieting is going to change those ankles, Pheme. They're hereditary, you're stuck with them.'

Gresham watched her half-sister's face smile on one side and twitch on the other. It was a strained look which used to give her satisfaction. Somehow it no longer did.

There was a near-painful click as the train's public address system came on, a moment's silence as all the passengers looked up at the ceiling of the carriage, and then, 'Ladies and gentlemen, we would like to apologise for the present delay which has been caused by a minor engine malfunction.' The accent was West Midlands, Black Country. 'Another engine is waiting in the sidings just up the way a bit and as soon as that's linked up, we'll be off and on our way. We are very sorry for any delay or inconvenience this may have caused our customers. Thank you.' There was a cough and some muffled talking before the Tannoy was switched off with another painful click.

'Oh, brilliant,' said Gresham, badly imitating the accent. 'I didn't even want to go to this meeting and now I'm going to be late.'

'We're going to be late for our meeting too,' said Christine without a hint of competitiveness. 'What's your meeting about?' she asked innocently.

Gresham stared at Eupheme with an expression of genuine shock on her face. 'She really doesn't know who I am, does she?'

'I do,' said Christine squeakily. 'You're Eupheme's sister.'

'Half-sister,' said the half-sisters in unison.

'I mean she doesn't know *who* I am,' said Gresham, flopping the copy of *Premiere* magazine open at the right page in front of Christine and sitting back with her arms folded. Christine started to read.

Uncle Roger, her first feature starring Richard E. Grant and Nona Wilfred, star of the recent cult *No Ending*, looks set to launch Gresham Hollingford, 28, on the fast track to becoming Britain's number one woman director. Hollingford's short film *Down on Me* received a BAFTA while she was still at National Film School, which sent her to the top. According to friends there's no stopping her. 'I am driven,' says the drop dead gorgeous daughter of architect Sir Roger Hollingford. 'I hate bad films. There's a lot of them around and they make me mad. I want to make good ones, ones that millions of people want to go and see. That's the way to revitalise the British film industry, not with some pat statement from an arts minister and a few quid from the lottery.'

'Gosh, you're a real celebrity, aren't you?' said Christine with genuine admiration.

A thousand cruel retorts sprang to Gresham's mind, but she couldn't use them on this dull woman. It would be like kicking a dog that had just been run over.

'The only thing that really pisses me off about this article is that they are still going on about *Down on Me*. I mean, I was a kid when I made that. Just because I'm the youngest person to have won a BAFTA, I mean, get over it. It's such a shit film anyway, I can't bear anyone looking at it. I've asked the BFI to burn the bloody thing.'

'Why do people like that always carry bags across their shoulders?' pondered Eupheme. She had heard Gresham but was bored with all her old stories. She was looking out of the window again. The man they had been watching was now looking at a slow-passing goods train. He was standing in an odd, knees-bent position holding his camcorder to his eye. His car coat was now more rucked up, the strap of his shoulder bag twisting the material around his body.

'Or maybe it's us,' said Eupheme. 'Why don't we?'

'Why don't we what?' asked Gresham.

'I always carry a shoulder bag on the same side as the strap. I'd never think of wearing it across my body like that.'

'You've got tits,' said Gresham. 'Well, you've got what pass for tits. Let's be honest, Pheme, I've got tits. You've got a slight swelling on your upper chest.' She smiled happily and snatched back the copy of *Premiere* magazine, leaving Christine looking a little dazed.

'No, that's not it,' said Eupheme, the smile and twitch still in operation. 'There's loads of men who don't carry shoulder bags like that.'

'Your bloody hippie sculptor boyfriend does,' said Gresham. Her mental image of Richard Markham was of a scrawny hunch-backed hippie she'd once met outside Chelsea Art College on the King's Road. He seemed to be wearing jumble-sale clothes, and she was sure he had a hand-woven Greek shoulder bag with an astrological symbol worked into it slung across his narrow shoulders.

'He does not. It just shows how long it is since you've seen him,' said Eupheme. 'He's had a haircut, and he doesn't use a shoulder bag. Christine and I stayed there last summer.'

'It was gorgeous, his house and everything,' said Christine.

Eupheme continued looking at the man on the platform. 'It's something else,' she said. 'It's saying something. D'you remember that man we saw on the train in Italy, Chris?' Christine shook her head. 'You know, on the train to Pisa, when we were catching the plane home.'

'Oh, yukky,' said Christine. 'He was really smelly. I mean he stank. It made my eyes run.'

'Oh, please,' said Gresham.

'It was awful.'

'This man was travelling with his mum. It must have been eight-five degrees and he was wearing an anorak thing, with the zip done right up. He had stuck-down hair and spots and he really was a state, and he had a bag over his chest just like the man out there.'

'So?' said Gresham.

'So, it's just weird. Isn't it? I was just pondering what made them like that. Nerdy, anoraky, sort of sweaty, bad-haircut men. Is it universal? Could you find men like that in America? In Germany? China? You know. They're so strange. How did they turn out like that? That's all I'm asking.'

'They were born like that. Born to be sad,' said Gresham. 'Deal with it.'

'I didn't know you were an actual film-maker, though. I thought you were an actress,' said Christine, still looking at the *Premiere* article. 'You know, when Eupheme told me you worked in films, because you're both so pretty, I imagined you were a bit like that Helena Bonham Carter. Do you actually shout 'Action!' and all that?'

'Christ,' said Gresham quietly. Christine seemed unperturbed.

'Have I seen anything you've done?'

'I doubt it,' said Gresham sullenly.

'It's because they feel insecure,' said Eupheme. 'The whole thing with the zips and buttons done up, it's all to do with containing and protecting. It must be.'

8

Gresham knew her dreadful sister was going to have one of her bloody awful theories. She looked at the man, who was now staring off into the distance, his camcorder hanging down by his side. The stiff breeze blew through his hair, throwing it back off his face momentarily.

'He's actually not that bad-looking,' said Eupheme quietly. 'Underneath it all.'

Gresham slapped her hands down on the table. 'I don't believe you're still droning on about him!'

She spoke loudly. Her confident, public-school-educated voice carried the length of the first-class carriage.

'He's not that bad,' said Eupheme. 'Look at him.'

'No thanks,' said Gresham, wishing the train would move, wishing she was anywhere but stuck on Milton Keynes train station with her dreary half-sister and her even more dreary friend.

'His hair is a disgrace, but he really is quite nice-looking.'

'Well, go out there and get off with him for goodness' sake,' snapped Gresham.

'I don't want to get off with him,' said Eupheme. 'I'm interested in him, that's all.'

'I've never understood you,' said Gresham. 'How you could find anyone so totally dull as that man in any way interesting is utterly, right, utterly beyond me.'

'You shouldn't judge people on appearances,' said Christine harmlessly.

'Yes you should,' snapped Gresham. 'That is exactly how you should judge them. That's the truth. They'll tell you lies, try and hide what they are with words, but let me tell you, if you're a film-maker, you know. Image is everything.'

'Why does film-making give you that special skill, then, Gresham?' asked a sweetly-smiling Eupheme.

'Why d'you think?' screeched Gresham. She saw that Eupheme had controlled her twitch and was now just smiling. She ran her hand through her hair. 'Is that guy going to have a lot of money?' she said, pointing out of the window. 'A strong artistic drive? A desire to help people? Anything at all to redeem him? I think not. He's a sad-act child molester who still lives with his mum.'

The businessman sitting across the aisle from them shook his head slowly to signify disgust. Gresham didn't care to acknowledge this and continued unabated. 'He probably works in a park, raking up leaves and dirty magazines, sitting in his shed with his Thermos of tea, watching little kids play on the swings. He's a sad act, Eupheme, a tosser. What more is there to know?'

'You can be so loathsome, Gresh,' said Eupheme.

'For God's sake,' said Gresham, 'your charity should know about people like him. You're supposed to be protecting kids, aren't you? They should chemically castrate all men who still live with their parents after the age of twenty-five.'

'That's a bit drastic,' said Christine. 'My brother still lives at home and he's thirty-seven.' Gresham and Eupheme stared at her in silence. 'Well, he isn't very well paid. He works with disabled kids in a special unit at the hospital.'

'You see!' said Eupheme. 'That's just typical. You'd have had Christine's brother castrated for nothing, poor bloke. You haven't got a sympathetic bone in your body.'

'Thank God,' said Gresham with an award-winning smile.

'Loads of black men still live with their mothers,' said Eupheme after a moment's pause.

'Oh, here we go,' said Gresham. 'Generalised theory number one thousand and seventeen.'

'Remember Wayne MacDonald?'

'Yes, I remember Wayne. Three mobile phones, four BMWs and ten inches, as I seem to remember he introduced himself.'

'Lives with his mum in Streatham.'

'He never does!'

'That's what I'm saying, you can't judge by appearance, Gresh. You really can't, and you shouldn't judge anyway. You never know what's behind someone's unusual manner. That man out there is like that for a reason, a cultural reason, a social one.'

'Oh, no. Stake-holding! New Labour, community artists, murals, playgroups, single-mother benefit workshops. I'm going to be sick. Boring!' said Gresham.

'He's been made like that by the world around him. Look at it.' Eupheme started to gesture towards the view out of the window with her hand but she hit the glass. 'I wonder how you'd have turned out if you'd been born in Milton Keynes.'

'I'd have got out of Milton Keynes as fast as possible,' said Gresham. 'I'd have made a name for myself, got rich, married a chinless wonder and had a great time. I would not have been wearing a grey quilted car coat standing on the train station looking at bollocking trains.'

'Please, miss, watch your language, I'm trying to concentrate here,' said the florid-faced businessman. Christine immediately started to blush, Eupheme flicked a glance at him and looked away, Gresham sneered and without looking merely said, 'Piss off.'

'Hey, now, now,' retorted the businessman. 'I don't have to hear that, young lady.'

'Oh, go away, will you,' said Gresham, turning on the man, her beautiful fine-featured face set in an angry scowl. 'We're having a private conversation here. If you don't want to listen, sit somewhere else.'

'Gresham, please,' said Eupheme.

The businessman stuffed some papers in his briefcase and slammed the lid. He stood up and stormed off down the aisle.

'Wanker,' said Gresham, flicking her magazine.

'Well, your language is a bit on the rich side, if you don't mind my saying so, Gresham,' said Christine.

'Yes, well, I do mind you saying so, ever so much,' said Gresham, imitating Christine rather accurately for once.

'What's up with you today?' asked Eupheme with a mixture of anger and genuine concern.

'What d'you think?'

'I don't know what to think,' said Eupheme. 'I very rarely know what to think when you're around.'

'You talked me into coming,' said Gresham angrily.

'I just thought it would be nice to go on a train together. I don't see you much.'

'Nice. Yes, it would be nice. God! I can't believe I've been so stupid,' said Gresham, running her long fingers through her luxuriant hair. 'I let you talk me into catching the bollocking train instead of flying, and then the damn thing breaks down in Milton Keynes. Not in a pretty valley with cows in a field, but Milton Keynes.'

'It's not that bad,' said Eupheme. 'At least you don't have to live here. Not like him.' She nodded towards the train-spotter.

'Actually, that's what's narked me,' said Gresham. 'Having to talk about him! You're like a walking copy of the *Big Issue*. It's boring talking about stuff like that. He's boring, Pheme, he's a no-hoper. I wish you could see that.'

'He's not a no-hoper. There's hope for everyone,' said Eupheme flatly.

'Oh, what are you now, a Christian? Your Buddhist phase was bad enough.'

'Look, all I'm saying is, given the right encouragement and the right environment, men like him could be completely different. They'd even contribute in positive ways to society.'

'The society word. Ahhh!' Gresham stood up and pulled her coat off the rack. 'If you use the "S" word again I'm leaving.'

'Sit down. For goodness' sake, stop showing off,' said Eupheme.

Gresham sat down, feeling like the younger sister again. A feeling she despised. 'He's not going to change, Pheme,' she said. 'That's all I'm saying. He wants to stay like that. He's happy like that, sitting in his little bedroom playing with himself while his mum cooks his tea. That's who he is.'

'It's not. That's who we've made him.'

'What d'you mean we! I didn't do anything,' said Gresham defensively.

'Yes you did, you're part of it. You're one of the people he's intimidated by. That's why he wears his bag over his shoulder. You set the tone, you and your friends, film-makers and designers and pundits and journalists. It's your fault he's like that.'

'Pundits? What's a pundit? you hippie lecturer,' sneered Gresham. 'He doesn't even know we exist. He has no inkling that there is anything called a fashion industry, a film industry, music industry, even a bloody charity industry. He's interested in trains and camcorders and ... and tossing himself off.'

'He's powerless, disenfranchised, marginalised,' said Eupheme, leaning over the table to bring her face closer to Gresham's. 'He doesn't need to be. That's all I'm saying.' She sat back, pulling her chin in and making herself look older.

'Look, people are born like that,' said Gresham. 'It's genetic. His dad was probably a train-spotter. They have no hope, they have no drive, no ambition like we do. That's why he's out there and we're in here. He'd be lost in here, he couldn't keep up. If I was out there I wouldn't write down the serial number of a train. I'd throw myself under it.'

'Why d'you make films?' asked Eupheme. 'So people see them and think about new things. Change their views.'

'Rubbish. Wake up, Pheme. I'm not going to feel guilty about him. It's not my fault he's got no life and reads science fiction until he's half blind. He's a wanker. Laugh at him, that's what he's there for.'

'Oh, that's awful,' said Christine.

Gresham turned on Christine. 'You're right, Pheme, she actually does sound like Larry Grayson sometimes.'

Christine looked hurt. She stared at Eupheme, who shook her head as if to deny the accusation quietly.

'And you sound like a concentration camp doctor,' said Eupheme. 'How dare you take away people's dignity with such high-handedness. You really are a prize bitch.'

'Tell me about it,' said Gresham with a big smile. She knew her teeth were perfect – cruelty wrapped in such a charming frame, as her mother had often proudly pointed out.

'All I'm saying,' sighed Eupheme, 'is that that man out there has hope, I really believe that. Like all children have hope. Christine and I know that from our work.'

'He's a waste of space, a hopeless saddo. Forget him and get on with your life.'

'I could change him,' said Eupheme.

'I expect she could, she's terribly persuasive,' said Christine, clearly not realising she was stepping into a battle arena of primal depth. 'She gets money out of the most mean and greedy people I've ever met.'

'But for a couple of simple twists of fate,' said Eupheme, 'he could have been someone even you, Gresham high and mighty Hollingford, even you would fancy.'

'Oh, rubbish!' screamed Gresham. 'That is utter bollocks, Pheme.'

'You see what I mean!' said the red-faced businessman. He was standing next to a short and very neatly turned-out Indian train guard. 'She's been effing and blinding all the way from Euston,' said the businessman.

'The gentleman has made a complaint about your language, miss,' said the guard, immediately identified as the man with the Black Country accent who had spoken on the public address system.

'Has he? Fascinating,' said Gresham sarcastically.

'You should be thrown from this train,' said the businessman. Everyone looked at him, and he muttered to himself.

'I have to ask you to tone down your language, miss,' said the guard with a nervous smile.

'Yes, yes,' said Gresham, impatiently waving her hand at the men and continuing to read the magazine.

The businessman harrumphed and walked off. Eupheme turned around to the guard, who was standing behind her shoulder.

'I'm really sorry about this,' she said. 'My friend has been very upset lately. Can you apologise to the man and I'll make sure she's quieter.'

'Oh, thank you, miss,' said the guard, clearly relieved that he wouldn't have to do anything.

'That was so embarrassing,' said Christine.

'Look, he can't handle the fact that I'm attractive and I've got a brain,' said Gresham. 'He wants me to be a lap dancer at Stringfellow's or an ugly bluestocking who's clever. He can't handle the mixture. No men can. It's his problem. He'll never change, just like that sad act out there. God, the world is packed to the walls with tragic men.'

'What is your problem, Gresh?' asked Eupheme. 'Are you saying you're engaged to a tragic man?'

'Of course, they're all tragic in their own way. We live in a nation of tragic hobbyist males.'

'What's up? Has Stanhope turned out to have clay feet?' asked Eupheme, her head on one side as always when the social worker in her came to the fore. Gresham's anger welled again.

'No! Nothing,' she snapped. 'Everything's brilliant. I'm just stuck here with you, that's all.'

'But you're overreacting, Gresh. You're flying off the handle at the slightest thing. Something's upsetting you.'

'You are, you divot,' said Gresham angrily. 'You get on my nerves, that's all. With your pious, dated nonsense about dignity.'

'It's not pious, and it's not nonsense. The whole of history is proof that with time and energy, people develop. It's obvious, Gresh, otherwise we'd all still be in caves.'

'Yeah, but people are born like that.' Gresham pointed out of the window. 'That's what I'm saying. That's what annoys me. It's such a waste of time trying to "do something about it". He was born like that.'

'Yes, but he could grow up to be anything, given the right environment. Everyone accepts that,' said Eupheme wearily.

'Okay,' said Gresham, throwing down the gauntlet as she had done on so many occasions in her childhood. 'If you think you could change him, go and bloody do it and stop whining on.'

'I'm not whining, I'm just saying . . .'

'Go on and do it, then,' said Gresham.

'What?' asked Eupheme.

'Transform him,' said Gresham. Eupheme looked puzzled for a moment. 'Tommy the tosser,' said Gresham, pointing out of the window.

'Gresham, don't try and change the subject.'

'You're trying to change the subject,' said Gresham.

'I'm not,' said Eupheme, smiling annoyingly.

'You are. You're all mouth,' said Gresham. 'You claim people can change, but where's the proof, eh? I tell you, men are sad tossers and there's buckets of proof all around. The businessman, that sad act out there, your piss artist of a boyfriend, my blinkered, narrow-brained future husband. Where's the proof from your argument? Eh?'

'You judge everyone so harshly, don't you? I dread to think how you see me,' said Christine, laughing and looking at Eupheme. Her smile was short-lived. Gresham turned and looked her up and down as much as the train seat would allow. Then said, 'Lower-middle-class with a half-baked education, a smattering of useless qualifications and a hopeless romantic dream that you'll meet a nice man one day and have a family. I imagine you keep cats.'

Christine was silent.

'You snotty bitch,' said Eupheme, eyes half shut with furious hatred.

'Change him,' said Gresham with a proud smile.

'What are you on about?' asked Eupheme.

'Don't pretend you've forgotten. You said you could make me fancy that, out there.'

'Oh, I could, Gresham. I know you think he's stuffed. But if I really put my mind to it, I know I could.'

'Well, go on, then,' said Gresham with her special smile. 'Do it. Get off the train, start work. There he is.'

They looked out of the window at the man, who was now changing a battery on his camcorder with fiddling incompetent fingers. 'A prime candidate,' said Gresham. 'The prince of saddos, the hunchbacked archbishop of train-spotters. He's all yours. Transform him into a relatively attractive man. Go on. I bloody dare you.'

'If I had the money, I could do it.'

'The money?' asked Gresham.

'Yes, to buy him some clothes, get him a haircut, spend time talking to him.'

'Oh, bloody hell. It would take money, would it? Is that all?' laughed Gresham.

'Time, understanding, patience and some money, yes. That's all.'

'Okay, I'll pay for it.'

'What?' said Eupheme, the colour draining from her face.

'I said I'll pay for it, if it works. If you can make him even mildly attractive, interesting, useful, I'll pay you whatever you spend,' said Gresham, knowing she was pushing Eupheme beyond her limits.

'Well, I . . .' said Eupheme predictably.

'I rest my sodding case,' said Gresham triumphantly. 'You see, when you're actually faced with the reality of your pious nonsense, it's all "Well, I . . . er . . . um". It's all a big wank, isn't it Pheme? Your whole bloody life.'

'All right,' said Eupheme, suddenly standing up and slipping on her coat, 'I'll do it.'

'Eupheme. Don't be silly,' said Christine.

'Stay out of this,' said Eupheme, without moving her eyes from her half-sister.

'I don't understand,' said Christine. 'What are you going to do?'

Gresham stood up, facing down Eupheme.

'I really think you should think this over, Eupheme,' said Christine slowly. 'It's just silly. Leave the poor man alone. We'll be going in a minute.'

'Only you've got to get him cooked up in time for my engagement party,' said Gresham.

'All right. When is your dreadful engagement party?'

'The twenty-seventh.'

'The twenty-seventh of what?'

'Next month. April.'

'But that's really soon!'

'It's the tenth of March today, so it's about seven weeks' time,' said Gresham, her smile widening by the minute.

'Seven weeks,' said Eupheme, clearly thinking it over.

'Yep.'

'Okay. Seven weeks it is. If I win, you pay for whatever I spend.'

'Whatever,' said Gresham. The two women shook hands. Christine buried her face in hers. 'I don't believe it,' she said. 'It's so silly. How d'you know that she'll tell the truth? Even if she falls in love with him, she won't admit it and you'll have to spend all the money for nothing.'

'Oh, no. She'll tell me, won't you, Gresh?'

'I'll be painfully honest, don't you worry.'

Chapter Two

'Excuse me, can you tell me when the next train to Manchester is passing through?' asked Eupheme.

'I don't work here,' said the man in the beige car coat. In that first sentence he gave himself away to her ear. Midlands accent, slightly slurred, pouting his lips to pronounce the words which made them sound unpleasantly wet.

'No, I realise that, I just thought you might know. I can't see a station guard or anything.'

'I don't work here. I don't know.' He was smiling but not looking at her.

'I see,' said Eupheme. 'How would you think I could find out? What's the best way?'

'I don't know,' said the train-spotter. He clutched his battered shoulder bag close to his chest. He looked up and down the platform as if for help. He was breathing through his nose. It made a loud noise, a sort of whistle.

Suddenly Eupheme was crisply aware of her educational advantage, her grasp of world affairs, her high level of social ability. It was all so cruelly unfair. She felt her throat tighten with anger and sadness. She was so much better adapted to the world than this peculiar man with the whistling nose. And that was nothing to do with birth or genes or any of the other pseudo-scientific rubbish used to justify cruelty and ignorance.

It was because she had a rich dad and he didn't, it was because she went to good schools and he didn't. That was why he was on Milton Keynes railway station and she was passing through.

He was an outsider with very little to recommend him. She was an insider, she was sought after, she had a clearly defined position in the world. She looked good; in fact, as far as anyone had told her, she looked wonderful. She rarely wore make-up — admirers always expounded on her natural beauty, strength of features and powerful, captivating eyes. Eupheme was a success in her world and she knew why, because it was after all who you knew, and Eupheme seemed to know everyone. Through her work at the charity and her social life, her address book was legendary. Although she came from an unclear background in terms of tradition, thanks to her father Eupheme had received a wonderful education. Bedales school in West Sussex, expensive and exclusive, her fellow pupils bearing the names of pop stars, media celebrities and household products. They knew who her father was because she told them, and the fact that he wasn't married to her mother gave her a certain notoriety which she liked. Her name was unusual, pronounced 'Yoofeemee'. She explained by rote how it was the middle name of her maternal grandmother, Constance Eupheme March Betterment, who had been, possibly, Queen Mary's lady-in-waiting.

Eupheme spent her holidays in exotic locations around the world, she spent weekends at wonderful country houses, went to parties that by any standards were fabulous. Through all this privilege she struggled never to forget where she actually came from, a small and rather dingy flat near the seafront in Hove.

Her mother, Grace Betterment, once beautiful, now ravaged by years of neglect and alcohol, still lived at number 15B. Eupheme hated the smell of drink on people's breath, her mother's breath in particular. Her bedtime kisses were ruined by the clinging stench of alcohol and cigarettes. Her mother's bitterness at being 'the other woman' had been a central feature in Eupheme's life; her fight for Eupheme's love had been never-ending. Eupheme grew up very fast with a mother like Grace; she had to, reassuring her mother that everything would be all right from a very early age.

Although Eupheme was allowed into the Hollingford family home whenever she wanted, Grace Betterment would have been extremely unwelcome and never set foot in the door. Gresham's mother almost adopted Eupheme, but the 'other woman' was never mentioned. She had played with her half-sister from the age of eight – they grew up together, always getting on, always fighting. The argument over this man on the platform was just the latest in a lifelong list of bitter disagreements. Eupheme's whole political outlook seemed to be defined by the seesaw emotional whim of her stunningly beautiful half-sibling. If Gresham said this man was a no-hoper, Eupheme knew in the pit of her stomach he was something very special.

This was the background Eupheme Betterment was standing on as she stood beside the hunched-over train-spotter; this was the gulf she would have to bridge. Her accent, picked up over the years from her social peers, would be to the average ear cut glass, top drawer, pretty damn posh. But Eupheme never traded on her accent. She knew there was more to people than met the eye, she knew people were sometimes judged unfairly. She wasn't about to start down that path now. Eupheme felt more than capable of the task before her – she was sympathetic, empathetic, she knew how outsiders felt. Even though she'd always been accepted warmly, she just knew how difficult it could be to fit in.

The man in front of her was possibly six foot tall, although it was hard to tell as he had an unpleasantly stooped posture. On closer inspection Eupheme could see he had a truly appalling non-haircut which looked as if his mum had done it with a 'K-Tel Trim 'n Tidy' haircutter, £19.99 from a telly sales advert. Eupheme's eyes had finally locked on to his hands. She decided he had nice hands, quite clean-looking, nicely shaped fingers and a good size.

'I don't know,' he repeated, then he pointed up the platform. 'There's a timetable there, mounted on the gantry.'

'Oh, where?' said Eupheme, although she could see the timetable clearly.

'On the gantry, the one, two, three, four, five, fifth one down. Near the passenger exchange tunnel.'

'Is a gantry one of those big metal things?'

The train-spotter nodded and smiled. Although he had three teeth missing from further back in his mouth, he had, Eupheme thought, a nice smile, a gentle smile.

'Now, I know you're going to think me terribly stupid, but I am hopeless at making head or tail of timetables. You couldn't come and decipher it for me, could you?'

'Sorry?' said the man, glancing at her momentarily. Up to now he had been very easy to watch as his eyes had been firmly locked on the rail tracks disappearing into the distance.

'The timetable. I won't understand it. I'd be very grateful if you could come and help me with it.'

'I don't know,' said the train-spotter. He looked up the platform towards the other train-spotters, who had emerged from the passenger tunnel and were talking and looking at a video camera one of them was holding.

'Huh! Graham's finally brought his camcorder, I see,' he said, laughing falsely and breathily with each word and making the sentence last an absurdly long time. 'Must get a shot of that.' He lifted his camcorder viewfinder to his eye. 'Thank God for a digital zoom, that's all I can say.'

'Is that your friend?' asked Eupheme, straining to see where he was filming.

'Graham? You must be joking. He's barmy.'

'Is he? Oh dear.'

'Must be, for buying the Sanyo. I'm sure it's the Sanyo. Yes, it looks clanky enough. Wonder it hasn't fallen apart already! I bet he's got the Sanyo PX 5 S-VHS. I told him not to bother with it. S-VHS is so clanky, nothing like as good as Hi8. It's second-hand. It'll be kaputski in a week. Ha!'

'D'you know all those men, then?' asked Eupheme.

'Oh, yeah.'

'Who are they?'

'Who?' he said, clearly confused.

'Yes. Who are they all? What are they doing?'

'They're spotting.'

'Spotting.'

'Yeah, they're really regular. I'm not.'

'You're just part time, then?'

'Just shooting some footage for their club meet next weekend.' He hadn't taken his eyes off the other men standing on the platform. 'That's Graham with the Sanyo,' he said suddenly, 'then there's Mick, in the vest. He's out in the daytime now. Day release. He's from the funny farm.' The train-spotter did a funny voice when he said funny farm, then laughed quietly. 'The other one, the old man, he's Stan. I don't really know him. He used to work here so he knows the layout better than anyone. And Dave is somewhere, probably gone over to the branch line to see what he can muster.'

'So they're good friends of yours, then.'

'Uh, well, I know them,' said the train-spotter. It seemed he'd never thought about it before. 'But I said to Graham that he should get the Canon Hi8 E2. It's a far better camera with a huge range. It's brilliant. Had I the funds, I'd buy it in a flash. Mind you, even Hi8 is behind the times now. Would that we could go digital. Downloading on to hard disk is so much easier, I've heard tell.'

'So, you're interested in cameras, then.'

'Yes indeedy doodly.' He laughed again. Eupheme imagined 'indeedy doodly' to be some sort of in-joke.

'Video cameras?'

'Camcorders.'

'What make is yours?'

'Says its name on the hand strap, dopey. It's the Sony Hi8 TR200.' He pointed at the name emblazoned on the strap.

'Looks very professional,' said Eupheme, staring at the small black box.

'Well, it's at the high end of the domestic range, or the low end of the semi-pro range. Three CCD, forty-eight times zoom, edit control socket, variable-speed shutter, built-in stereo microphone, time code facility. It's not a bad bit of kit when all's said and done.'

'So, using the camera is your hobby, then?' said Eupheme after a desperate silence.

'Yes. Well, I'd quite like to set up my own suite, an edit facility suite that various videographers could come and hire. We've got the room at my house, there's no doubt about that.'

'Why don't you do it, then?' asked Eupheme, studying him closely. His eyes were anywhere but on her.

'It's all a question of funds. Some of the top video edit equipment costs an arm and a leg. I'd have to save till doomsday.'

'D'you live near?' she asked.

'What, Milton Keynes?'

'Yes.'

'Not on your nelly,' said the train-spotter.

'Oh, are you from London?'

'London! Not on your nelly. I live in Northampton.'

'Northampton,' said Eupheme.

'Yes.'

'Is that just outside Milton Keynes, then?' she asked, trying to conjure up a map of the Midlands and failing.

'Outside Milton Keynes? That wouldn't please many Northamptonians. It's thirty-eight miles north-west, on this line. Where did you say you were going?'

'Manchester.'

'Oh, easy, then. You'll run through her on your way to Birmingham New Street, unless you take the Nuneaton spur which takes you more over the Market Harborough way, but you can still see the Carlsberg brewery chimney when you pass over the Far Cotton ridge. The brewery is in the centre of Northampton, you can't miss it. Situated on the River Nene. Mind you, some people say Neen, not Nen as I did. It's spelt N ... e ... n ... e but it's pronounced Nen. Northampton was nearly the capital city of England once.'

Eupheme felt her mind slip into a lower gear as she listened to his voice; there was something about the monotonous delivery which made her back relax and her forehead feel fuzzy. It wasn't totally unpleasant, but she found the feeling slightly frightening. She had never met anyone before who didn't try to be stimulating, someone who didn't pepper their language with little hooks, explicit references to try to hold the attention of the listener. She wanted to get away, leave this dull man on this dull train platform and find something bright to look at. Something that smelled sweet and rich.

She glanced over her shoulder at the stationary train. Very rapidly her eye was caught by the faces of Gresham and Christine at the window, Christine looking anxious, Gresham laughing herself puce. Eupheme pursed her lips and swallowed. Her half-sister could be so cruel. She seemed to get such pleasure from other people's suffering. What simple twist of fate had placed her at the diametrically opposite end of the world-view spectrum? Why did she feel so much for other people and Gresham feel nothing? She had questioned her motives, she had worried about being a do-gooder, about intervening in peoples lives where she might not be wanted. She had read sociology and anthropology at Exeter, then gone on to complete a Certificate of Qualification in Social Work at the London School of Economics. She knew the implications of intervention – she was a professional, although she never actually practised. Somehow, unlike her student friends, Eupheme never took up a social work post, finding herself drawn to charity work instead.

'Have you been to London, then?' she asked again desperately searching for a way forward.

'Yes indeed. Many a time. I've been up for various exhibitions — Earls Court, Olympia, the Royal Horticultural Hall.'

'Oh, you like gardening.' Eupheme momentarily brightened.

'No.'

'But you mentioned the Royal Horticultural Hall.'

'Model exhibitions. Top ones in the country. Railways, cars, planes. A complete range of the modeller's art under one roof, as they say in the trade. Very big exhibition, some of the biggest layouts in the country there, every year, in October.'

Model railways. How could it be true? Eupheme thought. She was looking at a grown man. She'd heard stand-up comedians doing material about strange men who still played with toys, but she'd never met one. She checked herself — she really was standing on a train platform talking to a loony. She felt a huge desire to run.

'Yes, I was very keen, as a young man. Don't really have the time for it now.'

'Oh, so you don't play with trains any more, then,' Eupheme said, hopelessly gripping the tufts of weak grass on the slippery slope of her plans. 'Why's that?'

'Pressures of work, et cetera.'

'What work do you do?'

'Deputy manager, dry goods. Besco, on the Wellingborough Road. D'you know it?'

'In Milton Keynes, is that?'

'Wellingborough Road in Milton Keynes!' He looked around for confirmation of her stupidity. 'Not on your nelly. No, Northampton. I live in Northampton, as I said. What are you, deaf or something? I just came here on my day off.'

'And are you married?'

'Married! Not likely. I can't with my mum.'

'What's wrong with your mum?'

'She's got arthritis.'

'D'you still live with her?'

'Of course. Poor old bat, she couldn't do much on her own.'

'So, you live with your mum, you come train-spotting on Milton Keynes train station on your day off from working in a supermarket in Northampton, and you go to exhibitions of train sets.'

'Model railways. Yes. You've got it in one,' smiled the train-spotter.

'There goes my argument,' said Eupheme under her breath.

'I'm sorry?' said the train-spotter.

Eupheme looked over at the stationary train. She could see Gresham laughing even more strenuously. Now jumping up and down and pointing. Christine looked confused, smiling against her better judgment. This time, however, was going to be different. Eupheme knew she'd backed down too often before. She knew this was special, this moment was meant to happen. She felt herself standing solidly on the platform. She knew she was stronger than Gresham, she knew she could do things, make a difference, change the world. Even if only by degrees. She grabbed the train-spotter by the arm and pulled him along.

'I'll buy you a cup of tea,' she said. 'I've got something I want to talk to you about.'

As they passed the front of the train, Eupheme could see some engineers looking at the engine. They hadn't even uncoupled it from the carriages. She felt that as long as she kept the train in sight she was okay.

In the Casey Jones burger bar the train-spotter blew on and supped his paper cup of tea noisily. Eupheme found out that his name was Ian, and he lived in a terraced house near the Allen McAfie shoe factory with his mother, Doreen. She was seventy-seven, Ian was thirty-one.

'Thirty-one and three-quarters, to be precise. Why d'you want to know all this?'

'I'm a journalist,' improvised Eupheme. 'I'm writing something about men like you.'

'What paper? The *Sun*?' asked Ian with a strange smile Eupheme took to be lecherous.

'Um, no. The *Independent*,' said Eupheme, thinking she would probably pass as an *Indy* journalist a little more convincingly.

'Oh, right. Never read it,' said Ian. 'Don't get much time to. I'm usually to be found reading one of the leading trade journals. Videography, electronics, computers and such.'

'Look,' said Eupheme, as she watched the broken train engine being towed away, 'why don't you give me a ring some time.' She offered him her card. 'I'm working on a project that I think you'd be interested in, and I could maybe help you with your video business. I know a lot of people in that line.'

He looked at her card for a moment. 'Eupheme Betterment,' he read out loud, pronouncing her name 'You-pu-heh-meh'. 'Is that really your name?'

'Yes, it's pronounced Yoofeemee,' she said, slightly offended. 'Just give us a call and maybe we can talk some more.'

'Eupheme Betterment.' He sniggered. 'It sounds a bit funny. Are you sure it's your real name?'

'Yes, I'm sure it's my real name,' she said, trying to smile. 'What's your second name?'

'Ringfold.'

'No, seriously,' said Eupheme.

'Ringfold.' Eupheme's mouth hung open incredulously as Ian continued. 'It's a name connected with the shoemaking trade in point of fact. A ring folder being someone who pulled the uppers over the last with a wire hoop, or ring. The upper leather was thus folded and stitched, pegged or stapled into position. Hence Ringfold. Northampton used to be one of the world centres of the shoemaking trade.'

'Oh, right,' said Eupheme.

'Not as interesting as Betterford.'

'Ment,' said Eupheme. 'Betterment.'

'Yeah. I've just never heard of it before. Where does Betterment come from?'

'I don't know. My family are from Dorset.'

'Ooo, arr-ee, iy, oh,' said Ian in an impression of a children's record about Farmer Giles and his pig. 'D'you mind if I get a shot of you on my camcorder?' he asked suddenly. 'I can down load the image on my PC and paste it up on my web page as an MPEG.'

'Well, if you must,' said Eupheme, not knowing what he was talking about.

'I suspect I'll get loads of e-mail from people who've heard of your name. Are you a famous journalist? D'you know lots of celebrities and TV personalities?'

'Well, I suppose I know a few,' said Eupheme, now noticing a new engine reversing towards the stationary train. When she turned back, Ian was pointing his video camera at her face and the little red light was on.

'Can you just do an ident?' said Ian.

'A what?'

'An ident. Say who you are,' he said, staring down the viewfinder.

'What? Now?' said Eupheme, her self-confidence suddenly evaporating.

'Yes, just say, 'I'm Eudine Bettering or whatever. The shorter the better. Then when I download it, the MPEG file won't take up too many K.'

'It's Betterment, actually. Eupheme Betterment.'

Ian switched off the camera and looked into her eyes for a second. He seemed more confident now.

'That's perfect. Thank you.' He checked in his viewfinder, absorbed by the camcorder and seemingly unaware of Eupheme's stare. There was something about the shape of his face that attracted her. His forehead, although covered by a raft of thick, remarkably dull mousey hair, seemed somehow refined.

'You can find my website here,' he said, writing with a very short ballpoint pen on a tissue napkin. In very neat, rounded lettering he wrote:

http//www.rednet.homepages.ringfold/tlvid

'I don't understand,' said Eupheme, looking at the hiero-glyphics.

'It's my website, on the Net.'

'What, the computer thing?'

Ian snorted, nodded his head and looked around the neon-lit eatery. He sneered in a way that reminded Eupheme of Rik Mayall in the BBC sitcom *Bottom*. She then realised that that was where the sneer originated from.

'That computer stuff,' he said, laughing nervously. 'I thought all you journalists used the Net.'

'Oh, yes. Well, my researchers use it,' said Eupheme as grandly as she could.

'Well, you should get them to find my web page. It's pretty interesting on the whole.'

'Okay,' said Eupheme, who by now was completely baffled as to what she was talking about or why she was talking to this man in the Casey Jones burger bar on Milton Keynes train station. Something glimpsed out of the corner of her eye made her jump. It was the train. Moving.

'Call me,' she said as she stood up and ran for the door. She dashed across the platform, her long coat billowing in the rush of air. The train was moving slowly as she ran along beside it. She saw the Indian guard who had accompanied the irate businessman standing looking out of an open window. He opened the door for her and helped her in. She tumbled on the floor as she leapt aboard.

'I really shouldn't do this, miss. I could lose my job,' said the guard, slamming the door shut.

'I'm very glad you did, though,' said Eupheme, feeling elated. She gathered herself together and started to rise, only then seeing the slender tapered ankles of Gresham Hollingford who was standing, arms folded, looking down on her with the nearest thing to pity she could muster.

'Looks like you're on to a winner this time, Pheme,' she said, her teeth glistening in the dappled sunlight that played through the moving train window.

Chapter Three

One week later Eupheme walked out of the board meeting in the offices of the International Children's Trust with office manager Kevin Waslick. She gently put her hand on his arm and pulled him to one side.

'Can I have a quick word?' she said. He looked utterly delighted to have the opportunity for any sort of contact with her. Kevin did not keep it a secret that he held a torch for Eupheme, but as usual she did not seem to be in the mood for some light-hearted flirting.

The International Children's Trust was no laughing matter. Since its founding in 1972 it had built and refurbished over three thousand schools in rural Africa, India, Pakistan and the Philippines. The trust, as it proudly liked to boast, had been directly involved in the education of over two million children. It had been at the forefront of campaigns to eradicate child prostitution and child labour, had linked up with other international aid organisations to help with child health programmes and had been publicly supported by everyone from Princess Diana to Scary Spice.

The news at the monthly board meeting was uniformly bad. Income had plummeted since the inception of the lottery. The trust had received £300,000 from the lottery commission the previous year, but it was far from clear whether they would do so again.

The receipt of bad financial news was nothing new to Eupheme Betterment, who had always rubbed along awkwardly between a world of extreme wealth with her father and dire although genteel poverty with her mother. Eupheme had very clear memories of her mother in tears in their little kitchen in Hove as she tried to work out a way to pay the gas bill, and only days later of her father complaining about the fittings in his new yacht.

As chief fund-raiser of the International Children's Trust, Eupheme had her work cut out, which was accepted by the board. She had to try to be very convincing about her plans for the year. They thrilled to hear of the money that the brewery in Manchester was willing to throw at them in sponsorship of an event, but finally despondent when Eupheme took them through the figures of ten recent high-profile benefits. They had all made a very small amount of money and a very large amount of noise. They were good for profile, rubbish for fund-raising, was the essence of her message. They had decided to delay a decision until the next meeting, a typical fudge, to Eupheme's mind, so nothing had been done and the problems were mounting. Eupheme had found the meeting unusually hard because a new background project had somehow taken over her life.

'I know it's a hassle, Kevin, but I'd be really, really grateful if you could go into your computer Internet thing and find this,' she said, handing Kevin the napkin she'd received on Milton Keynes station. 'I don't understand what it is, and I quite understand if you don't want to. But I'd be really, really glad if you could help me.'

'No problem,' said Kevin.

'Oh, that's so nice of you,' said Eupheme, glancing at the peculiar-looking Mr Waslick. She had to suppress her dislike for his bright red hair and freckled skin. It didn't mean anything and she shouldn't judge people, but Kevin Waslick looked like a sex offender to her. His legs were too thick and his hands were too small. She almost shook her head trying to throw off these terrible thoughts and decided to be extra nice to him to make up for it. 'I know you're busy, Kevin, and you're absolutely vital to this office. People don't understand what you do and how pivotal your role is here.'

'Tell me about it.'

'It's fantastic what you do. You've transformed the place, believe me. I tell people what you do but I just get so confused. It's so technical. It's like this web business, I just do not understand it. Am I really hopeless?'

'No, you are anything but hopeless, Eupheme,' said Kevin as he sat down at his large desk by the window. Eupheme had surmised that as Kevin was essentially a nice man, even if he was possibly a pervert, he would respond well by being put in a position where he needed to reassure her.

'But I've got no right to remain ignorant about this stuff. It's a form of snobbery really,' she said as she watched his huge computer beep itself awake.

'Eupheme, calm down. What you do here is the hardest and most vital job of all, for goodness' sake. If you weren't so successful at fund-raising, where would we be? Out of a job.'

'Yes, and some children would be out of a school.'

'Of course,' said Kevin, screwing his face up. Eupheme had caught him out again, as she did every day. She watched his skin-blemished, small hand move the mouse around on a mat that displayed a picture of Wallace and Gromit.

She heard the cattiness in her last comment, almost as if it had been played back to her on an internal Dictaphone.

She apologised. 'Sorry, I shouldn't have said that. Thank you, Kevin. You're right and I've got to learn to accept praise when it's rightly offered.' She heard the last statement as well, and suddenly it didn't sound as she'd intended. She kept hearing herself being proud and snobbish and clever and snippy, basically horribly like her half-sister.

'Now, let me see.' Kevin looked at the letters written neatly on the tissue. He didn't seem aware of Eupheme's internal war.

'The three w's stand for World Wide Web, that's the Internet, if you like, but it also stands for this particular link to the Internet. The bit that says rednet is the service provider, that's like the phone number you call, and when you call it this computer just talks to that computer which is huge, and that computer is linked to millions of other huge computers all over the world. Then this bit is your man's name, Ringfold. That's a bit weird, isn't it? Is it his real name?'

'It's something to do with shoemaking,' said Eupheme quickly as she stared uncomprehendingly at the screen.

'Okay, then that last bit, well, that stands for something else.'

'What?' asked Eupheme.

'Well, it's like a postcode or something.'

'Oh, Kevin, I really need to understand,' pleaded Eupheme.

'Look, I don't know anything about the bloody Internet, except it's occasionally quite useful,' said Kevin.

Eupheme soon lost interest and looked out of the window. The offices of the International Children's Trust were in a converted Georgian building overlooking Highbury Fields in Islington, North London. The house had been left to the trust by a wealthy old widow who, in her youth, had worked in Africa, mainly with children with leprosy. They only had to pay the barest upkeep costs, the trust being acutely aware of accusations that charities absorb a lot of donated money in administrative expenses.

Kevin Waslick was part of the new-broom economy drive that had swept through charity land. He had a large computer with a big colour screen and from this machine he virtually ran the whole set-up. All the letters, reports, leaflets, posters, accounts, everything was contained in his small humming box which sat under the desk.

'So what do we do?' asked Eupheme.

'Well, I could log on and see what his website is all about.'

'Does that mean we can actually talk to him?'

'Yeah, sort of. We could send him an e-mail.'

'Oh, I'm so stupid, I'll never understand it all. E-mail. What's that?' Eupheme stood with both hands on her forehead.

'All right, all right. Stay calm,' said Kevin. He reached his freckled hand out towards her but withdrew it again, obviously thinking better of it. She decided not to notice. 'Look, I'll just do it for you.'

He started typing and moving his mouse around. There followed the sound of a phone dialling, then some high-pitched squeaking like a fax machine. A small box appeared on the screen with a flashing cursor on the left-hand side. Into this Kevin copied out the letters Ian Ringfold had written on the napkin. He clicked the 'okay' button on the screen and a little clock appeared where the arrow was. Suddenly the screen changed – it went red, then blue, then a picture emerged. It was a small colour photograph of Ian Ringfold smiling, standing on a sunny train station. 'Welcome to Trains, Lies and Videotape,' read the neat banner headline across the top.

'Uh-oh,' said Kevin Waslick.

'What?'

'Who is this guy? Mr Super-Nerd. Look at him.'

'I know, I know. It's dreadful. What's all that writing below the picture about?'

They read it together.

welcome to Ringfold world. the most famous site on the web for trains, lies and video jpegs, mpegs and sound files. this site has been visited 4509 times.

Calling all spotters and rolling stock enthusiasts, there's plenty of info on euro rail spotting opportunities this summer plus data on the new didcote siding and steam days. Links to other great spotter sites worldwide. Bulk train gifs, fast download times.

Warning, journalist babe on the loose wants to interview spotters! wey hey the lads!

'Why is the word babe highlighted?' asked Eupheme.

'Well, if you click on there it will take you to another page or reference, I think,' said Kevin, who was moving his mouse around nervously.

'Please click on it, then,' said Eupheme.

'It does say babe, Eupheme,' said Kevin. 'Could be a cheesecake shot or God knows what. 'There is a lot of sad stuff on here, as you can see.'

'Kevin, I beg you, please do the clicking thing,' said Eupheme.

Kevin sighed and did so. 'If it's some hard-core porn thing and anyone else in the office sees, it was you who wanted to look at it, right?'

'It won't be. Surely it won't be,' said Eupheme.

The little clock appeared then the background changed until there was a mostly dark screen. In the centre appeared a small colour picture of Eupheme. In the frame that surrounded the picture was the title 'babe MPEG'.

'Oh my god!' said Kevin.

'Please be quiet,' pleaded Eupheme.

'It's you.'

'Please, Kevin. Now, what's an MPEG?' she asked.

'It's a system where video images can be digitally compressed and sent down phone lines. Are my eyes deceiving me? That is a picture of you?'

There was a bar underneath with a small arrow at one side. Kevin clicked the arrow. The picture moved jerkily; the sound, however, was smooth and clear.

'It's Betterment, actually. Eupheme Betterment.'

'Well, well. Journalist babe,' said Kevin with a wide grin.

'How on earth did he do that?' asked Eupheme, utterly baffled by what she could see in front of her.

'You know this guy?' asked Kevin. 'You actually know this man? Hold on.' He adopted his favourite and overused vaguely Valley Girl thick Californian impression. 'I'm, like, what's happening here and you're, like, seeing some train-spotter and I'm, well, I'm hanging out here in the hope that we could get something on together. You know, I've bought a new shirt from Paul Smith and now I'm wondering why I bothered. I may as well be, like, an anorak, Pheme. I'm, like, destroyed, you know, totally.'

'I'm not seeing him. I met him a while ago, that's all. Honestly. I was just intrigued. How do I write to him? To tell him to remove that awful thing. Do I really look like that?'

'Wey hey,' said Kevin. He looked up and smiled. Eupheme did not smile back; she was furious. How could this little nerd do that to her? She looked ridiculous.

Kevin turned back to the computer. 'Okay, I'll set it up for you.'

He clicked a few things closed and a clear white box opened up.

'There,' he said. 'Write your letter there and when you've finished, click that box in the corner that says "send" and you're done. I'll make some coffee.'

Kevin got up and walked towards the small kitchen. 'Journalist babe, wey hey!' he said quietly.

Christine walked into the office with a Pret à Manger bag containing her lunch. 'Sorry I'm late,' she said. 'It's such a long walk to my bank. Anyone want an almond croissant?'

'Christine, come here a minute,' said Eupheme.

Christine walked over to her, clutching the large lunch bag in front of her.

'You know the train-spotter? The man from Milton Keynes?' said Eupheme quietly. Christine nodded with her mouth open, ready to hear devastating news. 'What's happened?' she asked.

'Nothing. I just don't want you to say anything to anyone, okay, ever. Please.'

'I won't.'

'Please. Anything. And no one can know. Not even Kevin.'

'I won't say anything.'

'Good. Thank you, Christine. You're really wonderful.'

'Have you stopped, then?' asked Christine.

'Stopped? No, of course I haven't stopped. I haven't even started yet.'

'Oh, Pheme,' said Christine, using her worried voice which annoyed Eupheme. 'It's a bit on the barmy side, you must admit.'

'Oh no. Don't say that. Surely you can see how important it is. You saw how rude and arrogant Gresham is.'

'Yes, I did. She is awful.'

'Well, she's not, she's unhappy, I think. I feel sorry for her. I'm trying to show her as a way of making it clear that she could change too. She's going down such a dangerous road. She's so aggressive to everyone and that just leads to isolation and misery. Marrying that man, it's not going to help her or make her life happier.'

'I don't see how changing the train-spotter's going to help her,' said Christine, taking a bite out of her diet chicken sandwich.

'Well, if Ian can change, and she really sees that, she'll realise she can change too.'

'If you say so.'

'Oh, please support me, Chris. I need help to do this.'

''Course I will,' said Christine. 'What are you doing now?'

'I'm writing him a letter.'

'Really? What are you saying?'

'Chris, please don't take this wrongly, but I can't write with you watching.'

'Oh, sorry.'

'No, I'm sorry, it's my fault. It's just really difficult to type with someone standing by your side.'

'All right,' said Christine, who then returned to her desk and concentrated on her enormous lunch.

Eupheme typed:

Dear Mr Ringfold,
   You may remember we met last week on Milton Keynes
railway station. I am very interested in your 'web' site and
would like to meet you to continue our discussion. Can
you catch a train up to London for an all expenses paid
lunch at a top London restaurant? Please contact me at
any of the following numbers or addresses.

She clicked on the 'send' button as Kevin had instructed. The
letter disappeared and a small message box appeared and flashed
once. It said 'Message sent successfully'. Eupheme looked at the
screen in bewilderment. She had never come to terms with
computers, she realised. In a way she still felt they were there
to be used by the likes of Christine. They were typists' tools,
beneath her in some way. She knew she was wrong. She started
to ponder about learning to use one herself when a message
popped up on the screen. It said, 'You have e-mail. Do you
wish to read it?' There was a yes and a no button below the
message. She clicked yes. The clock appeared, spun its hands
a couple of times and then a letter appeared in a little box.

   dear eupheme, thanks for letter. yes please to top nosh
   offer. i can make tuesday as i'm on night shift monday.
   meet at euston, 12.15. platform 5 usually with the 8.10
   from leeds. might be platform 6 though as they tend to
   change around due to cleaning roster. send confirmation
   to iringfold@online.rednet.co.uk

Eupheme had to read the note a few times just to be sure she
was making sense of it. It really was a reply to her letter. It had
appeared a few moments after she'd sent hers. She was imagining
that maybe in a week she would hear from him. Not in fifteen
seconds. She checked her watch – 3.15 in the afternoon. He had

to be sitting at his computer, nothing else to do but reply to her letter immediately. Why was she having anything to do with him? Everything in his life was so dull. Who cared which platform the train arrived on? How could he begin to know such a thing?

She looked up to see Christine munching her third almond croissant. Christine stared at her, looking worried. Eupheme hated her for it, not realising that her lips twitched as lips sometimes do when their owner is deep in conversation with herself.

Eupheme stopped her lips moving and stared at the screen again. She suddenly noticed a box above the letter from Ian which said 'reply'. She clicked it and was immediately presented with a blank screen. She wrote a short confirmation note and clicked the box that said send. The message disappeared. Another little box popped open and asked her if she wanted to save the messages. She moved the arrow to the no box and clicked. The screen returned to the picture of her face. She clicked on the small arrow beneath as she'd seen Kevin do.

'It's Betterment, actually. Eupheme Betterment.'

She noticed as the image talked a small white box move along a grey bar beneath the picture. It seemed to monitor the movement of the picture above. She moved the small arrow on the screen until it was over the box, and then clicked as she'd seen Kevin do. She slid the box along the grey strip. When she let go of the mouse, the picture changed to her face in mid-word. She looked ugly – eyes half closed, mouth open in an O shape. Technology was so cruel, she thought. The human eye would never see that. She angrily clicked the mouse all around the screen. Different boxes opened and closed, the little clock spun and disappeared, then reappeared and moved as more boxes and files flipped open. Suddenly the screen went still. No matter what she did with the mouse, nothing happened on the screen. A small box opened dead centre. It had a picture of a bomb with a fuse on one side. On the other it read, 'A total system error type 001 has occurred'.

Kevin was returning with two cups of coffee.

Chapter Four

Margaret Ringfold's thin, liver-spotted hand gripped the edge of the bath tenaciously. As she had told Ian repeatedly, she didn't trust anyone any more. 'I've been dropped into the bath on too many occasions to trust people,' she said.

Ian knew only too well that Margaret Ringfold was a nervous woman. The warm water, however, was a great comfort, and as she slowly, degree by degree, lowered herself into the bath, she began to relax. Her face lost its anxious grimace and returned to something resembling normal.

'There you go, Mum,' said Ian. 'See, I didn't drop you, did I?' He spoke in his special singsong voice, the one he'd heard the nurses use when they cared for his mother.

'Thanks, love. You can go off for a bit now if you want,' she said, closing her eyes and breathing a large sigh of relief.

Ian took great care to look only at his mum's face when she was in the bath. Although in truth he'd seen her naked on many occasions, it didn't seem right to stare. He was used to it, after all, it was something that simply had to be done.

The home help bathed her in the week. It wasn't as if he was always doing it. But on a Saturday night after *Blind Date*, Ian would help her up the stairs, help her take her clothes off and help her into the bath.

He lay silently on his bed, comfortable and happy. He could

45

have switched on the Compaq computer, switched on his US Robotics 36.6 kps modem and surfed the Net. He could have booted up his Zip drive and played F18 Hornet version 5, a hyper-realistic flight simulator war game set over Iraq, Korea or Cuba, depending on your mood. However, something made him want to savour the moment of peace.

He had spent virtually every night of his life in the back bedroom, except for brief breaks during his yearly childhood holidays to Bexhill-on-Sea.

The room was not overcrowded with furniture – a three-quarter-size bed, a work table with video editing equipment, a small bedside table and a large wardrobe.

Leaning against the wardrobe and reaching up to the high ceiling was a Cromwellian pike, a twelve-foot wooden pole with a fearful-looking steel spike and disembowelling blade attached to the end. This pike supported a chest plate and helmet from the same period – a complete costume from the British Civil War between Cromwell's Parliamentarians and the Royalist supporters of Charles I. Ian used to go to every 'meet' of the Sealed Knot society, but this had been curtailed by new working practices at the supermarket. Weekends had suddenly disappeared.

Along the floor to the side of the pike was a large box which contained a metal detector, battery pack and headphones. He had spent many a happy afternoon in the fields on the outskirts of Northampton sweeping the electronic pad over the ground looking for bounty. He had found an Elizabethan coin once, which he took to the Northampton Museum. They were mildly interested but said they had thousands of coins from that period and no room to display them. For the previous two years, the metal detector had been stored in its box. The card advertising its sale was still on display at the supermarket. He hadn't been flooded with offers.

On top of the wardrobe were three suitcases, one filled with drawings and paintings he'd done as a boy and his early attempts at creating his own newspapers, the *Cyril Street Gazette*. He had drawn all the pictures and wrote the text in pen on lines he'd drawn in pencil.

In the second, slightly larger case was a Triang model railway set, 'The Mallard' steam train and three coaches, neatly packed in its original presentation box. A present from his mum and dad when he was twelve. It was almost as good as new, very rarely used and still boxed. The dream of owning the model railway, he remembered, had been far more intense than the experience of actually receiving it.

In the bottom case was a fairly extensive collection of what Ian classified as 'soft core' pornographic magazines. *Mayfair*, *Men Only*, *Fiesta*, *Penthouse*, *Escort*. Ian had no taste for the more 'raunchy' titles such as *Hustler*, *Rustler* and *Shaven Haven*. He did use the magazines as a masturbatory aid, but only in the sense that he'd study the pictures carefully then put the magazine away, go to bed, switch off his light and go through the motions of very gentle love making in his mind. He was always in love with the woman, usually in a rather exotic setting, like a hotel on a sun-kissed beach, or next to an exclusive swimming pool, watching the woman he loved climb out of the pool wearing only a wet T-shirt.

He had on two occasions since meeting Eupheme tried to imagine her in one of these dreams; it had proved impossible. He had had to resort to the time-consuming business of climbing on the chair and sliding the big suit case open enough to extract the most recently purchased copy, then creeping back to bed to peruse it at leisure, firing up his loins and imagination ready for the lights-out treat.

'Ian, love, I'd better get out now,' called his mother softly.

'Okay, Mum,' said Ian, snapping out of his breast, nipple, buttock and pubic hair-infested dream state. He entered the bathroom carrying his mother's special towel, a large light blue bath-wrap he had got on discount from the store. His mother didn't like him wasting his money.

'I haven't told you, Mum,' he said as he heaved her gently out of the bath. 'I've had some promotion.'

'Oh, well done, love,' said his mother through grunts of pain. 'What have we got to call you now?'

'Deputy manager, dry goods.'

'Deputy manager, dry goods! And that's promotion!' His mother's face was a picture of toothless anger. 'You've been there donkey's years and that's all they can do for you. That Mrs Philips needs her head examined, wasting the talents of a bright boy like you. I don't know what the world's coming to, I really don't.'

'It's good, though, Mum. I get a leg-up with my pension scheme, a pay rise.'

'A pay rise!'

'Yes, well, it's moderate, something like a one pound sixty p in the hour increase, but it all adds up.'

'Oh, Ian,' said his mother. 'You're just like your dad. No ambition, no drive.'

'I'm not like Dad,' said Ian flatly as he helped his mother's arm slowly into her nightie. She had always goaded him with this. Everything he had done in his life had been an effort not to be like his dad.

Ian's father, Dennis Ringfold, had died when Ian was fourteen. A softly spoken, neatly dressed man in his mid fifties, white hair combed over his balding pate, solid, scarred workingman's hands with clean fingernails. That was how Ian remembered him.

He had been found in the basement of the shoe factory he worked in, quite dead. He was hanging by his ankles from a large hook set into a stout beam wearing nothing but red women's high-heeled shoes and ten-denier tights. There was no suspicion of foul play by a third party as the door had been locked from the inside. The autopsy reported that he had died from a heart attack presumably brought on by being in a sexually aroused state while hanging in an inverted posture for too long. Death by misadventure was how the coroner recorded the event. Dennis Ringfold's report was placed in police files under the heading 'Unintentional Auto-Erotic Fatalities'.

After the funeral they received several visits from a social worker, a sympathetic young woman whom Ian quite liked. He was very confused about his father's sudden disappearance and couldn't seem to find out exactly what had happened. His mother had told him it was an accident at his father's workplace. The social worker called her visits 'sessions' and asked Ian's mum if she had ever noticed any of this sort of behaviour in Ian. Margaret Ringfold was fiercely defensive of her son, claiming he was like her side of the family. Ian would never do such a thing. Ian demanded to know what sort of thing they were talking about. As his mother sobbed, the social worker explained as best she could. Ian was very confused but not altogether negatively: his father had been caught doing the secretive things Ian had up until then thought he was the only person on earth to do. His pre-pubescent sexual fantasies had been varied, but this one incident, instead of sending him off on a spiral of perversion, flipped him back into a very safe, narrow sexual furrow. He wanted to fall in love with a woman and get married, properly. And not do anything else. He wasn't going to be like his dad and pretend to be married while he did other things in a shoe factory basement. He was going to be different.

From that day on, however, Ian was under the watchful eye of his mother around the clock. He was rarely allowed to play alone, never allowed into his mother's room alone, especially not near her underwear drawer. If she had sat back and observed Ian casually, she would have noticed that never had a young boy shown less interest in his mother's underwear, but the trauma of her husband's unexpected demise left its mark.

As her arthritis worsened and her heart became a cause for the doctor's concern, Ian grew up seemingly well balanced. She was slowly forced to relax her grip. Nothing untoward happened – she didn't find him hanging by the neck wearing odd clothes, there was no sign of any aberrant behaviour. She failed to remind herself that in twenty-eight years of marriage there had been nothing in her husband's behaviour that ever gave her the slightest suspicion that he would end up hanging upside down in a Northampton shoe factory basement wearing a pair of tights.

'Your father was a good man,' she said. 'He worked hard, just like you, watching people with half his skill climb the ladder past him. That's the only similarity you have to him. You look nothing like him, you sound nothing like him. You're you, Ian.'

'I know, Mum.'

'You're a good lad. You look after me which is more than can be said for a lot of your generation. Always gallivanting off who knows where.'

'Actually, I am doing a bit of gallivanting, Mum. I'm going off to London tomorrow to meet a woman.'

'Oh, are you?' said his mother, trying to hide her alarm.

'A young and very attractive lady called Eupheme Betterment. She's interviewing me in an exclusive exposé sort of thing. For the *Independent*.'

'Independent what?'

'It's a newspaper, Mum. Blimey O'Reilly, where have you been?'

'Oh, I can't be doing with it all. So you like her, then? This Irene girl.'

'Eupheme, Mum. Yes, she's all right. Bit on the tense side for my liking, but very attractive when all's said and done. So I'm off down to the big smoke tomorrow, Mum.'

'What on earth for?'

'Well, she's doing her interview.'

'What for, a job? You're not going to live in London, are you?' she said, clearly alarmed.

'Hardly. She's writing a shock-horror exposé.'

'What about?' she asked cautiously.

'Well, I'm not altogether sure, but it's all above board, Mum. Don't worry.'

'You've not told her about your dad, have you?' Ian's mother was now very worked up. He knew only too well that once she had something half decent to worry about it would remain the main topic of conversation for many a long day.

'Mum! For goodness' sake,' he said. He spoke as calmly as he could. 'She's writing some sort of article thing about chaps who do train-spotting. It's nothing at all to do with unintentional auto-erotic fatalities.'

'Don't say that, Ian.'

'As if I'd tell her about Dad. Mum, really.'

'You look tired, Ian,' she said, putting a small hand on his cheek affectionately. 'I don't like you gallivanting off all the hours God sends. It's not good for you. You work so hard in that supermarket. They don't appreciate you.'

'It's all right, Mum. It's a bit on the exciting side when all's said and done. As far as I can tell she knows shed-loads of celebrities, so who knows, I may even get to fill up my autograph database.' He lowered his mother slowly on to her old bed. 'I may as well make hay while the old sun shines, Mum.'

'You take care, my lad,' she said as her head hit the pillow. 'I don't want you swept off your feet by some young madam only to land heavily. You know what women are like, Ian, I've told you before. Once they get their hooks into you, my lad, there's no knowing where you'll end up. You're such a nice lad. They'll see that in you and take advantage.'

'I know, I know, you always say that,' said Ian, smiling. 'But Eupheme isn't interested in me in that way, Mum. I'm not likely to engage in lip-to-lip kissing with this particular young lady. She's very much in the career-woman mould from what I can gather. I'm sure she's already got whatever hooks she has at her disposal firmly into someone else.'

Ian returned to his room and turned on his Compaq

computer, deftly used the mouse to open up the TV tuner section and found a German satellite station that was showing a topless game show. He put a CD in the CD player – Pulp. He found the track entitled 'Common People', his favourite. He clicked the highlighted play button. The song came across the digital speakers with a crisp, clean resonance, making him feel relaxed. Everything was sorted out, the washing-up done, Mum in bed, the bathroom cleaned, the laundry folded, his work clothes laid out ready. He sat, lit by the bright pink and green colours playing on the Sony SP seventeen-inch monitor. A very beautiful young woman pulled her top off. He lay back on his bed, folded his pillow to enable him to keep his head up, checked that he had the CD and TV tuner remote to hand, and truly relaxed. Ian Ringfold was, when all was said and done, happy. Very happy.

Chapter Five

Tuesday afternoon at 12.30, as arranged, Eupheme was standing by Platform 5 at Euston station. She had rushed there from her flat on Clapham Common using a cab, which she would never normally do. She kept the receipt carefully in her huge overstuffed leather shoulder bag. This bag contained four final reminder notices from the various gas, electricity and water boards that ran services to her flat. Although to call it her flat, as she was always doing, was a slight misrepresentation of the truth. The flat belonged to Geoffrey Hammond, an old college friend who now worked for the diplomatic service in Washington, DC. His family had pots of money and he had bought the flat as a base in London. He was never there and allowed Eupheme, for whom he clearly held a torch, to live in the property rent free. She was supposed to pay the bills, though. She would pay them, she knew she would, when she got a moment.

She glanced through her bag as she waited, then closed the flap as she realised it was hopeless even to think of doing anything about it there and then.

Feeling very unsure of herself, she was prepared to run the moment she saw Ian if she decided she couldn't cope. Her pre-planned escape route was to dive into the ladies' toilet off the main hall and lock the door, ring Christine on her mobile and give up the whole project.

She could see down the ramp to the platform as the train pulled to a halt. Businessmen in grey and blue suits ran badly up the ramp, their thighs rubbing together as they moved. They were all carrying small cases and macs; they all looked uncomfortable.

After a while a tall man started to emerge from the dowdy-looking crowd. It was Ian Ringfold and he was wearing a suit, collar and tie and was carrying a small holdall hooked over one shoulder, not across his chest. She smiled and he smiled back and waved awkwardly.

'Hi, there,' he said, a little out of breath. 'Only just made it. There was some trouble with electrics at Nuneaton, I think. Looked like they were going to ditch the whole loco and bring us in on buses. Those p-3460s are notoriously unreliable tractor units.'

Eupheme smiled and ran her hand through her hair. As soon as she actually met this man the very idea of trying to do anything about changing him had become an endless white wall of impossibility. Only when she was alone was she convinced it was possible. The notion had taken over her waking thoughts. She spent hours happily planning events and activities that might stimulate a change in him.

'Let's go for lunch,' she said at last.

'Okee diddly doodly,' said Ian, laughing nervously. He walked just a little behind Eupheme, which she found difficult as she kept having to turn around to talk to him.

'Are you terribly tired from your night shift?' she asked.

'No, I'm used to it. I get back at five thirty, go straight to sleep. Mum wakes me at eleven usually. Had to get up a bit earlier today, though.'

The word Mum had made Eupheme's heart skip into a new rhythm. He lived with his mum, he worked in a supermarket. He actually was one of those men who hung around the swings in the summer and looked at children. He must be. Gresham was right, she was always right. Eupheme looked at him carefully as he got awkwardly into a cab. He didn't look like a child molester to her, but then what did they look like? She knew from her work that the most dangerous thing in protecting children was to rely on clichés.

'Ah, excellent, I've never been in one of the new Fairways,' he said as they settled back into the seat.

'Is that a train?' asked Eupheme as brightly as she could.

'Not on your nelly, it's this taxi.' He slapped the seat next to him. 'This is the Turbo Fairway, two point five litre diesel, forty-five miles to the gallon in the urban cycle, turning circle of about eighteen feet. Bloody amazing bit of kit when all's said and done.'

'And you've never been in one.'

'Not this model, no. Oh, I've been in the old one point eight. Still had the turning circle but no power and a very dirty engine.'

'I thought all taxis were the same.'

'No way, José. There's been nineteen different models since the first petrol-operated cab came on line in 1906. This one, as I said, the Fairway, has a Range Rover chassis and independent suspension, anti-lock brakes and electronic ignition. State-of-the-art bit of kit when all's said and done.'

They spent the rest of the journey in uncomfortable silence. Uncomfortable for Eupheme; Ian seemed very content. His bag on his lap, hands resting neatly on top, he stared out of the window and seemed fascinated by everything he saw.

The taxi pulled up outside the Pacific restaurant just off Piccadilly Circus. Eupheme had wanted to impress him. She thought the Pacific fitted the bill – big, noisy, young, energetic and usually with a smattering of celebrities.

She paid the cabbie, making a mental note of the amount. She was going to have to keep meticulous records, with receipts for every last penny.

The doorman opened the door for them. Ian seemed to be pulling odd faces all the time, but never looking at anyone. He could be slightly barking, she worried, as they descended into the cavernous eatery. She stole a few looks at him as they entered; she wanted to see his reaction. His eyes merely skirted around the room, as if he wasn't meant to look.

A smartly dressed Australian man with a sleek ponytail showed them to their table once Eupheme had informed him of her name. He took Eupheme's coat, but Ian wanted to hang on to his bag. As he sat down, Eupheme noticed that his suit was a very cheap one; the material bulged and shone in all the wrong places. Its collar was just the wrong shape, and there was only one button on each cuff, cheap plastic buttons. It reminded her of Russian suits, the very worst materials put together in the very worst style with the very worst workmanship available.

'That's Toby Naunton,' said Ian suddenly. 'Isn't it? That's Toby Naunton from *Brownhill Avenue*.'

Eupheme looked around. She spied a minor actor whose face she vaguely recalled from the cover of a TV listings magazine.

'I think it might be. Yes. Now, Ian, let me tell you, the salads here are very good.'

'Hang on a minute,' he said, and he fished around in his bag. He pulled out a camera and a small book. 'Won't be a tick.' He got up and walked over to the bar where Toby Naunton was standing with a few vaguely recognisable faces. Ian stood in front of him and offered the little book. The truth dawned on Eupheme like a badly overlit contra-zoom. Ian was asking for this man's autograph. The actor smiled flatly, signed the book, and then Ian gave his camera to one of the men by the bar and posed next to Toby Naunton as the flash went off. Two hundred pairs of eyes glanced to see what was going on. Ian shook the actor's hand and walked back to sit down with Eupheme. She stared at him with her mouth open. Her heart thumped in her chest. She had never, even at the hands of Gresham, been so utterly humiliated. Hundreds of people could have seen what happened, and also noticed that the saddo came and sat back at her table. She picked up the large linen napkin to cover her mouth; she didn't seem able to close it.

'He seems really genuine,' said Ian, tucking his napkin into his shirt collar. 'D'you watch *Brownhill Avenue*?'

'I . . . I don't think I've caught it,' said Eupheme. 'Sitcom?'

'Sitcom! Not on your nelly,' he said, and started looking on either side of him as if he were surrounded by cohorts who were in on the joke. 'It's only Britain's number-one daytime soap. I always make a point of catching it when I'm on nights.'

'Oh, I see. Oh, well, that explains it. I don't watch much daytime TV.'

'I can lend you tapes if you want. Still only VHS, I'm afraid. Would that I had a top-of-the-range digital CD recorder.'

'Serious bits of kit?' asked Eupheme with a cheeky smile. She needn't have bothered as Ian didn't pick up on it in the least. He still hadn't looked at her.

'The absolute business,' he said.

'Ian, can I ask you something?'

'Fire away.'

'Why did you get that man's autograph?'

'Why?' said Ian. He repeated the word to himself a few times to try to understand the question. This was clearly the first time he'd been asked such a thing. Eupheme nodded while he sat and thought about it for a while. 'To add to the collection,' he said finally. 'I have about eight hundred.'

'Eight hundred autographs! Who, soap actors?'

'Well, yes, and sportsmen, car designers, comedians. I've got the complete cast of *The Fast Show*, *Men Behaving Badly*, *Red Dwarf* even, and let me tell you, that took some getting. But I've also got international figures.'

'You mean politicians?'

'Get off! Don't want them messing up my autograph books. No, for instance I've got Bill Gates, Microsoft supremo. He was here a year or two back to plug Windows 95, his so-called break-through software. I've also got, and this was a bit of a coup' – he pronounced the silent P much to Eupheme's silent annoyance – 'Nicholas Negroponte,' he continued, 'who some would claim to be the man behind the Internet. He was giving a talk here about virtual living. Really brill, although a lot of it went over my head. Some real boffins there. Would that I had their brains. I've got Richard Branson, he was very nice. All manner of people.'

'And what do you do with them once you've got them?' Eupheme asked, desperate to understand what she was seeing in front of her.

'Collect them,' said Ian, as though it were the most obvious thing in the world. 'Well, I catalogue them, scan them and enter them into a database on my desktop. I use Hypercard, so that each signature is logged by date, place, time, occupation of signee, et cetera. Then if I've got duplicates I'll swap them for other people's, often over the Internet. That's how I got Jim Clark.'

'Who's he?' asked Eupheme, noticing a waitress coming towards them.

'Jim Clark? Blimey, where have you been? He was only international Formula 1 champion.'

'Was he? When? I've lost touch since James Hunt.'

'James Hunt! Blimey, where have you been? No, years before, 1963. He was killed during practice at the Hockenheim circuit in Germany in 1968. Wonderful driver by all accounts. I could never have got his autograph being as I wasn't born, so I swapped an Elvis Costello and a George Michael for a Jim Clark. To me he's more valuable, you see.'

'Ready to order?' asked a young Australian girl with slicked-back blond hair.

'Blimey, are you all Australian here?' asked Ian.

'No, mate,' said the woman with a winning smile. 'The bloke behind the bar's a Kiwi.'

'Bit like being in *Home and Away*,' said Ian.

'I'm having the chef's salad,' said Eupheme. She smiled and looked at Ian. He studied the menu very intently.

'Um, do you do a sort of chicken and mushroom pie?' he asked finally.

'We have the chicken tarragon envelope with deep fried goat's cheese. That's real nice,' said the waitress.

'Goat's cheese! Oh, yuk city. Sounds like smeg.'

'Sorry?' asked the waitress, looking at Eupheme with a confused expression.

'Why not just have a chicken salad? It's very nice.'

'I hate salad. Can't see the point,' said Ian. 'Ummm ...' He said 'um' very loudly. People at nearby tables stopped their conversations and stared at him momentarily, trying to work out whether he was retarded and deserving of their concern.

'What about a big steak? As long as it's imported beef. Don't want to go doolally in here.'

'We do an *entrecôte de boeuf*,' said the waitress.

'Not too herby, is it?' asked Ian.

'No, I don't think so, but then it depends what you mean. I like a few herbs myself.'

'Okay, I'll risk it for a biscuit,' said Ian. 'And can I have French fries?'

'We do chips. They any good?' said the waitress chirpily.

'I thought this was supposed to be a posh place,' Ian mumbled. He laughed to himself, blowing air through his front teeth. 'Chips! Blimey.'

'Chips is the posh name for them now,' said Eupheme kindly. 'Ever since McDonald's have called them French fries, no one ever says that any more. The term French fries is naff now, Ian. Has been since about 1978.'

Ian nodded with his mouth open. The waitress smiled.

'And a large bottle of mineral water.' Eupheme mimed the size of the bottle.

'Coke for me, thanks,' said Ian. 'Unless you've got Fanta.'

The waitress shook her head. She wrote down their order and took the menu away.

ROBERT LLEWELLYN

'So, Ian, listen,' said Eupheme, rubbing her face to try to stimulate her brain to find a way into her subject.

'D'you think she was a model?' asked Ian.

'Sorry?'

'The waitress. She's very beautiful. I wondered if she was some sort of model. Calendar model, or something.' He laughed as he said this and played nervously with a fork. Eupheme had no idea how to respond to such a question so she ignored it.

'I wanted to sound you out about a project I'm working on.' She looked up at him. He was smiling but his eyes were looking over her shoulder. She turned around to see who he was looking at. She saw immediately. It was the actor Nigel Planer.

Eupheme and Nigel had had a three-week fling when she was just out of college. He looked a little slimmer and leaner than when she'd last seen him. As soon as he saw her he smiled broadly and immediately walked over to see her, leaving the man who was talking to him stranded in mid-sentence.

'Pheeeeme!' he squeaked. She stood up to greet him. He embraced her harder than she expected, held her slightly longer than she would have thought publicly acceptable. 'Bloody hell, how are you?' he said as he finally let her go and held her at arm's length.

'I'm fine,' she said. 'Really good.'

'Brilliant. God, I think about you a lot,' he said. She watched his eyes stealing a glance at her breasts.

'Oh, yes. As if,' she said. 'Well, I've watched you enough. Every time I turn the telly on, there you are. Every time I catch the tube, you're all over it.'

'Noooo,' he said coyly.

'Excuse me,' said Ian, standing much nearer than Eupheme thought necessary. 'Can I have your autograph, Mr Planer?'

Nigel's smile disappeared. He didn't look at Ian, just took the autograph book.

'Of course. What's your name?'

'Oh, I don't want a dedication, thank you, just a simple signature will be fine. Thanks. Thanks a lot, Mr Planer.'

The moment was supremely painful for Eupheme. She realised then and there that this agonising second would stand out in her memory for ever.

'There is one thing you could do for me, though,' said Ian, with a broad grin. 'It would make an ardent fan very happy.'

'No, I'm sorry, I don't do Neil any more,' said Nigel, and turned his back on Ian.

'Okay, that's fair enough. Thank you anyway.'

Nigel watched as Ian sat down, looking closely at the autograph.

'He's with you?' he asked quietly.

'It's a long story. Call me some time. I'm still at the same number.'

'I will, I absolutely promise,' said Nigel. 'I'll do anything you want.' There was a twinkle to his smile.

'I might hold you to that.'

Nigel walked away — interesting, well connected, witty, clever, his complex history making him fascinating if sometimes difficult company. All in all, incredibly appealing. Eupheme sat down and her vision was filled with Ian in his cheap suit. Dull, uninteresting, poor, stupid, slightly fat, dubious personal hygiene, terribly dressed, clearly hopeless and unlikely to improve. Dull, dull, dull.

'That was a bit of a coup,' said Ian. 'Meeting him. I've been a fan for many a long moon. Would that I had the signatures of the complete *Young Ones* cast. Now that would be worth a pretty penny. D'you know him, then? You actually know him?'

'Yes, I know him quite well.'

'Blimey, I had no idea you hobnobbed with stars, but then you are very glamorous yourself.'

He said this in such a matter-of-fact way that Eupheme had the strangest feeling. She tingled with delight. She was glamorous. It had never occurred to her before. She suddenly wanted to tell him about all the other famous people she knew, but she checked herself.

'So, what's this project, then?' He was scanning the room and thumbing his pen nervously.

'Ah, yes,' said Eupheme. Nigel's sudden appearance had thrown her equilibrium, not that she was drowning in the stuff beforehand. Everything became awkward in Ian's company. She knew that her intended plan was nearly impossible, but a rock-solid determination spurred her on. She knew Gresham and all her dreadful crew were wrong, they had to be wrong, history had proved them wrong, nearly. People could change, for the better. Or worse, for that matter, but they could change.

'I'm doing this extended piece.'

'Piece of what?' he asked with a strange giggle. Was he actually insane or just mentally deficient? The thought hit her hard and stayed there. She swallowed her panic.

'As I said, an article for the *Independent*. Newspaper,' she added after noticing his blank stare. 'It's all about whether men, like you, you know, men who don't do ... well, what some people call normal. I don't mean normal. I mean, you know, men who have hobbies. It's really to see if I, if we, can change you from what you are into, well, a more sophisticated-looking, and sounding ... well, a more sort of contemporary-looking type of man.'

'Sorry?'

'Look, it's very simple, Ian.' She knew it wasn't simple. She kept wanting to go back to the beginning and start again with him. 'When I first saw you, on Milton Keynes station, you were videoing trains.'

'That's correct.'

'Now that is considered, by a great many people, to be an odd thing to do.'

'Is it?' He seemed genuinely surprised. 'I thought it was a fairly popular pastime, judging by the hits on my website, but then what do I know.'

'Yes. It is. Maybe, but, well ... um ... Listen, the cliché is that men who do that live with their mum and are a bit weird.'

'I do live with my mum.'

'I know, and it's fine, it's just that some people think it's odd for a man your age to live with his mum still. I don't, I think it's fine. Your mum is very ill and needs looking after and I think it's wonderful that you care for her. That's very touching, and this is what I want to clarify. That things are more complex than people give credit for. That you can't always judge by appearance. So what I want to do is explode the myth, show the world that men like you are marginalised, and that there are going to be more and more men like you around as there are less and less heavy manufacturing, engineering jobs, and more and more lightweight service industry jobs so more and more men are going to find hobbies which occupy the parts of their minds which, um, which used to be used to create bridges and viaducts. I'm rambling. Sorry.'

'I don't understand,' said Ian, with a smile. Eupheme let her head drop forward and sighed.

'Well, no, I do understand in a way,' he said. 'You think I do train-spotting because I really want to be a train driver but I can't get a job because there are so few jobs driving trains around.'

'Well, yes, I hadn't thought of that,' said Eupheme, grasping for the ray of light through the dull, low clouds.

'That's not strictly the case. I never wanted to be a train driver in the first place. I quite wanted to be an astronomer as a boy, but didn't have the maths, basically. So no, I don't really know what you're on about, but I'll do whatever you want if it means I can increase my autograph collection. What other celebrities do you know?'

'Ah, well, this is the thing, you see, Ian. If you did what I wanted, you wouldn't want autographs of famous people.'

'I wouldn't?'

'No, you wouldn't. You probably would meet some relatively famous people, but you'd feel at ease with them.'

'Oh, I doubt it,' said Ian, pulling his chin in and looking ridiculous. 'I'm always shaking like a leaf after I get an autograph. You've seen me today. It's really a bit on the nerve-racking side meeting famous people.'

'Okay, so that's something to work towards, isn't it? Imagine being very relaxed in the company of famous people, being almost one of them, someone they know.'

'Oh, blimey. I've dreamt that, let me tell you. I once dreamt that Sting came to my house and I had to make him tea.'

'Sting!' Eupheme's hopes were raised. He knew about Sting, a relatively modern pop icon. He was not as naff as she had supposed.

'Yes. He was great on Live Aid,' said Ian. 'Mind you, not as much fun as Comic Relief. I enjoy that more.'

'Have you been involved in Comic Relief, then?' She knew the team that ran the Comic Relief office. Maybe he knew them, maybe he dressed like this as a deliberate fashion statement. Jarvis Cocker working in a supermarket. It was just possible.

'We do stuff at the supermarket every year. Yes, we all dress up in daft clothes. It's madness for one day. It's brilliant. I dressed up as a pink rabbit and just went loony in the carpark. We raised nearly eighty pounds last year. I made a video of some of the staff looning about the carpark, sent it in. We thought Jonathan "Woss" might put it on but they didn't show it.'

'Okay,' said Eupheme. Every time a door opened, another eight slammed shut and were bricked up, plastered over and hidden behind a nudie calendar. 'But you're prepared to go along with my project, are you?'

'Well, I think so. How long will it take and what about my job? That's what my mum told me to ask you.'

'Your job?'

'Yes, I have to work three twelve-hour shifts a week, some days, some nights.'

'Three twelve-hour shifts! Bloody hell, that's slavery. What ever happened to the forty-hour week?'

'I don't know. I only do thirty-six.'

'Oh yes,' said Eupheme as she worked out the maths.

'Yes, some Sundays, two a month to be precise, so I get four days off in a block, but not regular days. It takes some getting used to, but I do get some fair-sized chunks of leisure time.'

It had never occurred to Eupheme that he might not have all the free time she needed.

'What time have you got to be back at work today?'

'Oh, tonight, eight thirty. Storeroom and shelf stacking, cleaning and basic prep. Eddie is on tonight, though, so it should be a laugh and a half.'

'Who's Eddie?'

'He's the coloured bloke who does nights. Bit thick in the head, but dead funny.'

'Ian, you don't say coloured. You say black.'

'Do you?'

'And you also don't say leisure time. Goodness, you've got a lot to learn. Okay, well, after lunch we'll go on a bit of a shop and haircut outing.'

'Haircut! I've only just had this done,' said Ian, patting the dull brown mop that was combed dryly over his ears.

'Who did it? The council?' said Eupheme, the speed of her comeback making her feel witty.

'Huh, that's a Julian Clary line. D'you know him?'

Once again, Eupheme's hopes were raised. He'd heard of Sting and Julian Clary. He seemed to know a lot about things other than trains and video cameras, and yet he made those things instantly dull.

'Your hair,' she said, trying to picture what he would look like with a decent haircut, 'is so dull it absorbs interesting things around it, sucks them in like a black hole in space. Your hair is so powerfully dull it almost hurts to look at. That's why you need a haircut.'

He was silent for a moment, playing with his napkin and scanning the room. Eupheme worried that she'd gone too far. She was just about to apologise when he said, 'I wish I understood why you're doing all this.'

'Because . . .' Eupheme looked for a lie. 'Because my editor doesn't believe it's possible.'

'Doesn't he?'

She used his response as a lesson. 'She. No, she thinks that someone who is essentially naff, no offence, is always going to be naff.'

'Naff. Is that what I am?' said Ian, crinkling up his nose and exposing his rather yellow teeth. Eupheme noticed with slight disgust that three small beads of sweat had appeared on his forehead.

'Well, no, of course you're not, but that's the way some women, some people, see you.'

'Chef's salad and *entrecôte de boeuf*,' said the waitress as she placed the large plates in front of them. She poured a tall glass of sparkling clear mineral water for Eupheme and a short glass of sugary Coke for Ian. 'Enjoy.'

After a bout of muffled complaining about too many herbs and the thickness of the French fries, Eupheme cut her losses and got Ian out of the Pacific restaurant as soon as she could.

She was impatient with him as she walked him around to Old Compton Street and finally into the basement premises of one of the most exclusively hip, young, trendy, cutting-edge hair stylists in London – Jack's.

'Have you got an appointment?' asked a woman with a shaved head and nine nose rings. This was the reason Eupheme no longer felt comfortable there. She had stopped using Jack, choosing Nicky Clarke instead. She put it down to the approach of her thirtieth birthday. However, she had decided Nicky Clarke wasn't right for Ian. She wanted to push him further into fashion and then reel him back. She had to; he was lagging so far behind to start with.

'No,' said Eupheme, ignoring the girl and catching the eye of a young man in leather trousers who was reading *Loaded* magazine. 'Bert's free, though.'

'Yes, well, you need to make an appointment,' said the bald woman. Eupheme noticed that Ian was staring at the nose rings with his mouth hanging open, absolutely no sign of embarrassment.

To Eupheme's relief Bert threw the magazine on the floor and walked towards them. 'It's all right, Babs,' he said, 'I'll do her. Hi, Pheme, how's it hanging?'

'Got a bit of a job for you, Bertie boy,' she said, motioning towards the smiling Ian.

'What is he? A stalker? D'you want me to give him a clump?' said Bert, balling his fists in all seriousness.

'No, I want you to give him a haircut, you silly man,' said Eupheme.

Ian was guided to a chair by Bert as if he were a sack of overdue refuse.

'Hi, I'm Bert, I'll be cutting your hair today,' he said, staring in horror at the blob of hair as he sat Ian down.

'Can you do anything?' asked Eupheme.

'I can try,' said Bert. 'Who did this to you?' he asked Ian with seemingly genuine concern. 'The Mafia?'

'My hairdresser,' said Ian. 'He's a Greek chappy called Michael, has a shop on the Wellingborough Road.'

'Never heard of him,' said Bert as he held up the dank locks. 'Well, it'll have to be washed and conditioned. What d'you normally use? Fairy liquid?'

Ian sank into himself, nervously allowing a young girl to put a coverall black cotton coat on him and lead him away. Eupheme smiled to herself and sat down. She flicked through various men's style magazines as the young girl washed Ian's hair. She looked at handsome male models in dark suits standing in model poses on old shipping wharves, their eyes perfect, and of course perfectly dead. Ian did have special eyes. She looked over at his awkward slumped form, sitting in the hair-washing chair wearing the black coverall, his hands clasped tightly on his lap, his eyes shut. His chin was elegant, his neck quite long from this angle, and with his wet hair pulled back from his face, she knew she was on to something. He really was a good-looking man. He had good bones, hard to see under the blotchy skin and podgy, badly fed exterior. Eupheme's heart skipped a beat. It was strangely intoxicating to be in control, to make someone do what she wanted, to change them into someone she wanted. As this thought appeared, she checked it. She didn't want to want him. Was it possible she did? She looked at him again, allowing, or thinking she was allowing, any feelings inside, deep down, to well up. None did. No, she didn't want him like that. She wanted to make him different, better. It annoyed her that he didn't know he could be special, it annoyed her that he dared to be satisfied with such a seemingly dead-end life. But then who was she to decide which was better — a suave, sophisticated contemporary man or a train-spotter with a bad haircut and a camcorder?

She could hear all the different arguments in her head. She turned them into round-table talks on afternoon Radio 4, hosted by Jenny Murray. Eupheme was there, bright and industrious, full of reasons and explanations and proof that she, Eupheme Betterment, had changed the life of one individual that society had registered as scrapheap fodder. She was sitting opposite Emma Freud, Jeanette Winterson and Julie Burchill, who all looked at her with a mixture of contempt and admiration. In the dream they had all met Ian and couldn't believe he had ever been any other way. She proved that with education and encouragement even the most hopeless case could be turned around.

'Your friend's nodded off,' said Bert. Eupheme stood up, put the magazine article about infidelity down, realised she had been staring for rather a long time at a very erotic picture of a man and a woman in designer underwear embracing, and looked at the dozing form of Ian Ringfold. He had fallen asleep with his head leaning back into the sink. The girl had tried to wake him but he was out like a light.

'Can you just turn him round there and cut his hair while he sleeps?' asked Eupheme, making spinning movements with her hand.

'Will you take full responsibility?' asked Bert. 'I don't want him waking up and stabbing me with my scissors or something. He's safe, isn't he?'

'Don't worry, he knows what's happening, he's a lamb. Honestly.'

'He just looks a bit like one of those blokes who ends up shooting eighty people in a McDonald's before he tops hisself,' said Bert. Eupheme smiled in pain.

The haircut caused quite a stir in the trendy trimmery. Apparently no one could remember anyone sleeping through a big cut before. Thick slabs of Ian's hair fell to the ground. Bert held up his sleeping head every now and then and checked how he was doing. He hacked off hair like a man possessed, then, when he was finally satisfied, he applied copious gobbets of gel, rubbing it vigorously into Ian's scalp. This action seemed to rouse Ian from his slumber. He rubbed his eyes, sat up and looked in the mirror.

A different face looked back at him, a different man.

'There you go,' said Bert. 'That's a bit of a change.'

'It is, isn't it,' said Eupheme. 'Who'd have thought it?'

'What? D'you like it?' asked Ian incredulously.

'It's fantastic,' said Eupheme, almost wanting to embrace him. 'Don't you think it looks great?'

'I don't know,' said Ian, bringing a hand up to touch it. 'Have you dyed it or something?'

'No!' said Bert. ''Course not. Just washed and conditioned it. Thrown a bit of gel at it. You've got such thick hair I can't style it without a bit of help.'

'It looks wet,' said Ian. 'Mum hates me going out with wet hair.'

'Oh, bloody hell. Hark at him,' said Bert, putting his hand to his cheek.

'How much is that, Bert?' asked Eupheme, pulling out her wallet quickly, hoping they could get out before Ian made a scene.

'Babs will sort you out.' He pointed to the bald woman.

As they climbed the wooden staris back on to the street, Ian's mouth was stuck in full open position.

'Forty-five quid for a haircut!' he squeaked. 'Forty-five quid!'

'It's all right, it's my project, I can claim it all back,' said Eupheme, glad she hadn't gone to Nicky Clarke's for a hundred-and-fifty-pound job and feverishly hoping she would get to claim it all back.

'My Greek bloke charges me four pounds. I can't believe you just gave them forty-five quid to make me look like a cheap pop star.'

Eupheme stopped in her tracks. She stood in the doorway to Jack's, spotting Clive Anderson walk past the Prince Charles Theatre on the other side of the street. She felt momentarily blessed that Ian didn't see him.

'Is that what you think you look like?' she asked.

'It looks like it belongs to someone out of Take That or Boy Zone,' said Ian, finally feeling the short hair on the back of his lily-white neck.

'I'm amazed,' said Eupheme.

'Why?'

'I'm amazed that you've even heard of Take That.'

''Course I've heard of them. Blimey, I watch *Top of the Pops*, don't I? If I'm not working. Mind you, I think ninety-nine per cent of the music is rubbish, especially all the coloured stuff.'

'Ian, what is it with this coloured business? You mean black music.'

'Oh, don't tell me I've got to like that awful noise to be one of your contemporary man-type personages.'

'No, you don't have to like it, but you have to know what it is.'

Eupheme's face folded in disgust as Ian did a bad rendition of rap music, with some very offensive Jim Davidson-style accents as he said 'Hey, mon', precisely like no rap artist had ever done. Thankfully it was quite shyly performed and therefore unnoticed by the multi-ethnic, multi-gender-oriented Old Compton Street pedestrians.

'Just stop,' said Eupheme. 'Will you just stop, please, Ian. What you're doing is so fundamentally wrong, ignorant, stupid, offensive, I just don't know where to start explaining. It's racist for a start.'

'It isn't. My best friend's coloured.'

'Black!'

'All right, black. Eddie, my mate at the supermarket's black. He's almost my best mate in the whole universe.'

'Don't say whole universe either. That really is so naff,' snapped Eupheme.

'I like black people,' mumbled Ian. 'Just don't like the music much.'

'Okay, let's just leave it for now. I want to go and buy you some clothes. Just try not to say coloured again.'

'Okay.'

They walked in silence for a while, Ian's eyes darting towards the shop windows containing pornographic videos. He spotted one featuring two naked men in a passionate clinch.

'That man was a woolly woofter, wasn't he?'

'I beg your pardon?' said Eupheme.

'The hairdresser bloke, Bert, a woolly . . .'

'I assume you mean he was gay.'

'Wey hey, Ben Doon and Phil McCavity.'

Eupheme stopped, held Ian's podgy arm firmly with her left hand and used the open palm of her right to punctuate her remarks. 'I'm sorry, Ian. This really has to stop now.

Let me explain. When you're with me, okay, when you're with me, you do not used the words "coloured" or "woolly woofter". Okay?'

'What should I say, then?'

'Black and gay.'

'Black and gay. Not coloured and woolly woofter, black and gay.'

Isaac Julienne passed them in the street. Isaac Julienne, a delightful, witty, talented and charming man, almost brushed shoulders with Ian as he passed. Eupheme had met him at several parties, usually when she was with Gresham. Isaac Julienne was a black, gay film-maker. Eupheme watched him walking away. Nothing in his demeanour indicated he'd heard Ian practising his politically correct terminology. It would have to be on Old Compton Street, possibly the one street in London that on any given day would contain more gay black men than you could find in the rest of the country.

They walked down Piccadilly and turned right at New Bond Street, past a few shoe and jewellery shops, and stopped finally by DKNY, the huge, imposing high-fashion store, ninety per cent entrance and very few clothes. Eupheme glided in without registering her surroundings. Ian stood just inside the door, intimidated by the size and glamour of the place.

'What's up?' she asked when she finally retraced her steps back to where he was standing.

'What is this place?' he whispered.

'DKNY,' said Eupheme. 'It's a clothes shop. We're going to buy you a suit.'

'I've already got a suit,' said Ian, opening the dull grey jacket he was wearing.

'No, that's not a suit, that's a tragedy,' said Eupheme.

'Yes, but this place is wrong,' said Ian, not moving.

'This is the best clothes shop in town, for Christ's sake,' said Eupheme confidently.

'Well, it's wrong for me. It's teenagers' clothes, it's pop

star clothes, footballers' clothes. It's wrong for me, that's all I'm saying.'

'Footballers' clothes,' said Eupheme, scratching behind her ear. 'Well I never.' She paused for a moment, then looked up the street. 'Okay, we'll try somewhere else.'

She wasn't depressed at this change in her carefully laid plan. Ian was showing an interest and a knowledge of styles and looks that extended far beyond anything she had expected.

They walked up New Bond Street, passing the sculpture of two men sitting on a bench.

'Churchill and Roosevelt,' said Ian.

'Sorry?' said Eupheme.

'Sitting on the old bench-a-roochie.'

'I beg your pardon,' said Eupheme, still completely in the dark as to what he was talking about.

'The statues on the bench.'

'What, the old men?' she asked.

'Old men! Blimey O'Reilly. Just two men who saved the old Western world.'

'Who are they?' she asked. She had passed the sculptures on a thousand occasions and never given them a second look. She considered them slightly naff, a place where Japanese students with bottomless budgets posed for a digital snapshot before spending many more thousands of pounds in Versace and Gucci.

'Churchill and Roosevelt,' repeated Ian.

'How d'you know, where does it say?' she asked, looking for a clue.

'Well, that's who they look like, and Churchill is smoking a cigar. I'm a bit of a Second World War buff when all's said and done. My grandpop was involved, RAF ground crew. I've got his old uniform in my collection. Would that he was a pilot.'

'Try not to say "would that he was", or "would that I could".'

'Sorry,' said Ian without taking much heed. 'It's just that

had he been air-crew I'd have had more for the old archives. Aerial photos of bombing missions, maybe a pair of fur-lined flight boots. Now they'd be worth a pretty penny in this day and age.'

'Okay, that's enough about your collections,' said Eupheme, feeling the fuzzy head coming back. 'And try not to say "this day and age" and "pretty penny".'

'Blimey, what should I say?'

'Try saying nothing and listening, okay? Just for a bit. Now this is Ermenegildo Zegna. They make very nice suits. Do they appeal?'

'Yuk-a-roochie,' said Ian.

'Try not to add "a-roochie" on to the end of everything.'

'Sorry,' said Ian, then muttered 'a-roochie' under his breath.

They crossed the street again and Eupheme dragged a now-silent Ian into the Nicole Farhi store. She looked through the rows of beautiful loose-fitting suits. She held the jackets up in front of Ian. Nothing was right. They left the store and, just as Eupheme's spirit was beginning to stare down the hole of despair, she spied the Donna Karan shop.

'Aha, of course, Donna Karan,' she said as they dodged traffic to cross the road once more. 'You see DKNY is the youthful kind of street arm of the Donna Karan company, but Donna Karan proper, well, that's a totally different thing. This isn't like DKNY at all. Do you understand?'

'And I'm not allowed to say all the things I say and you go on like a wet Sunday with your DKNY business. It's not fair in the end.'

'Please don't say things aren't fair. Now we'll find you a suit,' she said. They walked towards the entrance. The door was held open for them by a large security guard.

'Blimey, what is this place, a bank?' whispered Ian under his breath.

'Follow me and, please, try not to be too embarrassing,'

said Eupheme, who headed confidently into the granite-and-mirror-clad interior and down a huge flight of steps. As she descended she was faced with another huge mirror. She checked herself. Not too bad. Then her eyes locked on to Ian. He stepped slowly down the stairs looking around him like a five-year-old in a Disney exhibition. He was almost dribbling. His suit was a disgrace – the way the cloth rucked up around his crutch was quite disgusting, and the creases looked grubby even if they weren't. She tried to wipe the image from her mind – grubby men, her greatest fear. She knew some people had a hard life and found it difficult to keep clean; homeless people, poor people from the Third World, but Eupheme found body grime pathologically repulsive.

Once down in the menswear section of the store, Eupheme looked around with a sigh. Along the walls an array of beautiful suits were displayed starkly on their hangers. Her eye was caught by a simple, beautifully cut dark suit. She felt the cloth, deliciously soft.

'This,' said Eupheme, like a TV presenter, 'is a suit.'

'Quite nice,' said Ian. He nervously fingered the security tag and price label. 'Gordon H. Bennett. Look at that!' he suddenly said loudly.

Eupheme glanced at the price. Even her heart skipped a small beat – twelve hundred pounds. 'It's perfectly all right. It's all on expenses.'

'But that's enough for a sizeable desktop PC set up including monitor and digital scanner. That much money for a bit of an old suit! It's daylight robbery!'

'Ian, will you please shut up and try the suit on.'

Eventually Eupheme got him to try on the suit with a dark blue shirt. He was shown into the changing room and Eupheme wandered around looking as casual as she could about the process. She glanced in the mirror again and quickly checked her ankles. They really weren't fat; they were actually rather a nice shape. She decided she had good legs and Gresham was stork-like and ungainly.

She checked the door to the changing room. No sign of life. The assistant who had showed Ian into the room with barely hidden disdain was standing annoyingly close. Eupheme had previously decided not to try to cover for Ian, just to 'butch out' the situation.

'Your friend is taking his time, isn't he?' said the assistant with a smile that was meant to be friendly but didn't read correctly. She looked like a lazy shark, six foot plus and deeply intimidating.

Eupheme felt her face flush. Being in this shop with Ian was more embarrassing than she'd imagined. He stood out so much.

'Yes,' she said, her mind racing. 'Well, I'm his stylist. He's an artist. He's, well, really out there. You should see his stuff, though. Well, that's why we're here, he's got an exhibition in LA and his agent has sent me out to get him at least halfway cool. You know, 'cos he's really into the whole nerd thing.'

'Amazing,' said the tall woman. 'What's his name?'

'His name!' said Eupheme, realising there and then that she had just happily dug a rather awkward hole for herself.

'Yeah, I wondered if I'd heard of him. My boyfriend's a painter, totally, totally mad. You know.' The woman flicked her hair over her shoulder in a way that annoyed Eupheme.

'Yeah, right,' she said, hating the conversation and willing Ian to emerge. 'No, his name's Ian. Ian, um, Ringfold.' Her mind was cornering fast to try to predict every possible outcome.

'Fantastic,' said the lanky sales assistant.

'What, have you heard of him?'

'No, it's just a brilliant name. Did he make it up?'

'No, that really is his name.'

'Brilliant. Oh, here he is.'

Ian stood before them, a different man. If you could

ignore the grey shoes, Eupheme thought, which was admittedly difficult, the transformation was staggering.

'Wow, Ian, look at yourself,' she said, dragging him by the cuff to the huge wall-mounted mirror. They stood side by side, Ian taller but stooped, looking uncomfortable in the stiff new fabric, Eupheme checking herself out at the same time. Her legs were okay, not as long as the sales assistant's, but then *she* looked like a cross between a woman and a gazelle. Eupheme was wearing a black crushed velvet frock-coat and thick leggings, a pair of Charles Jordan lace-up boots in a mountaineering style and a simple silver jewelled brooch her father had given her. Dressed as he was, Ian didn't vibrate with such intense discomfort beside her. She felt relaxed in his company for the first time. She looked at his face in the mirror; he looked back at her. This was, she realised, the first time they had ever had eye contact.

'It doesn't feel right,' he said. 'Feels all fake. It's not really me, is it?'

'I think it is. You'll get used to it.'

'Everyone will look at me and think, "Huh, I bet he thinks he's someone".'

'You are someone.'

'No I'm not. I'm just me.'

'Ian!'

'It's better that way. I never wanted to be anyone.'

'Everyone wants to be someone,' said Eupheme, not hearing herself. 'And everyone is valuable, important. That's a terrible thing to say, "I'm not important". You are. It's a cry of despair to say you're no one. Look, that's what this is all about. I want you to show all the people who are so damn sure they *are* someone that *you're* someone too.'

'I don't get it,' said Ian moodily. 'Why can't I just carry on the way I was? What's so wrong with what I wear? It can't be that important.'

'It's not,' said Eupheme, running her hands through her hair in an effort to quell the wave of tension that washed over her. He could blow it. He could refuse. She was going to have to work hard. 'It's not that important except that what you wear tells people about you. People judge you instantly. You say you don't care about what you wear, but you do. You chose your wardrobe and it says "Please ignore me". It says "I am worthless and should be nearly invisible. If you do notice me please ridicule my lack of taste."'

'Is that really what people think when they see me?' said Ian.

'Yes. Well ...' Eupheme's intelligence occasionally came to her rescue. '... I don't suppose everyone who sees you thinks that. But certainly a lot of people do.'

Ian looked at himself in the mirror in silence for some time. 'I can't believe I'll ever feel comfortable dressed like this. I'd be scared to get it dirty.'

Eupheme laughed and held his podgy, shapeless arm. 'Just live in it. It's a suit that needs living in to look good.' She took out her credit card. 'Now, I'm going to pay for this suit. I don't want to hear any more comments about how much it cost. Okay? Nothing. It's my suit, you can wear it, that's an end to it. Okay?'

'All right. If you're sure.' He turned and scuffed slowly back to the dressing room, his grey shoes screaming out to the god of style for forgiveness and redemption.

'I must do something about those shoes,' said Eupheme.

She carried a Donna Karan bag containing Ian's old suit which came from Suits R Us of Kettering Road, Northampton. With a relatively short walk along Bond Street they arrived at the Russell and Bromley shoe store. Eupheme chose a pair of shoes that looked similar to those worn by Jonathan Ross in an old copy of *Hello!* she'd been looking at – a black leather ankle boot with a chisel toe, slight heel and a large strap and decorative buckle across the front.

'These are in full calf grain uppers and leather sole. They

come in at two hundred and twenty-five pounds,' said the assistant.

'Are they machine-welted?' asked Ian as he stretched the beautiful-looking leather at the point where the upper joined the sole.

'They are mainly hand-constructed, the very best craftsmanship.'

'Yes, well they won't be hand-welted, not at this price,' said Ian matter-of-factly. The assistant looked towards the manager, who was on the phone behind the counter.

'No, I think you'll find they're cement construction,' said Ian. 'Which is fine these days as the modern porous epoxy cements are quite ridiculously strong, but somehow they don't have the same feel as a welted shoe. What about a steel shank?'

'Oh, I don't think so.'

'Doubles the life of a shoe,' said Ian. 'As long as it's correctly used. If it's badly put in it'll rip the shoe to bits. I would guess that the heel counter and toe puff are of a fibreboard variety as opposed to the skived leather type. Do they have side linings?'

'They are fully lined,' said the assistant.

'No, I mean side linings.' Ian wrenched the shoe around rather roughly. 'That's an extra strip of skived leather placed between the upper and the lining along the side, here.' He pointed to the side of the shoe. 'It just means the shoe holds its shape for about ten times longer. That's all.'

'All the shoes here are of the very finest quality you've ever seen,' said the assistant, hiding the snide comment under a smile.

'I should jolly well think so for two hundred and twenty-five quid,' said Ian. He stood up in the boots. They made him taller, made the suit look wonderful, but he walked in a most ungainly manner.

'They feel a bit funny,' he said softly, standing right in front of Eupheme but looking clearly over her head. He spoke discreetly. 'I don't think they're worth the money.'

'Don't mention the money,' said Eupheme quietly.

'All right. But I don't think they're very good shoes. We should go to the Tricker's shop on Jermyn Street. D'you know where Jermyn Street is?'

'Oh,' said Eupheme, puzzled. 'Yes. I know the shop. How come you know so much about shoes? Are you a shoe-spotter too?'

Ian laughed, a series of shuddering hisses coming from between his teeth. 'Shoe-spotter,' he said. 'That's funny.'

'Well, how do you know about Tricker's shoes?'

'My dad worked in the Tricker's factory once, in Northampton. Mostly he worked at Allen McAfie's, but they went to the old wall yonks ago.'

'Try not to say yonks,' said Eupheme, attempting not to get annoyed. 'Your dad worked here, then,' she went on, nodding. 'Is he retired?'

'No, dead. He died when I was fourteen,' said Ian flatly. He put his hand up to stop her condolence. 'He was old, that's why he died. Mum and Dad had me a bit late, as they liked to say. Dad worked at Allen McAfie's for years, but not here, in the factory, in Northampton, on the welting machine. They really were the best machine-made shoes ever. They had wonderful old machines in that factory. Beautiful work they produced. But Tricker's are very good. Cheaper than this pair and much better.'

'Let's go to Tricker's, then,' said Eupheme.

She almost skipped as she walked back down New Bond Street and crossed Piccadilly. True, Ian looked a sight in his wonderfully trendy suit and his awful grey shoes, but she didn't care. He had shown not only interest in the project but had come up with a positive suggestion. The boots she had tried to get him to wear were wrong. They said flash git, new money, quick shag and forget you. Actually they said rich, interesting, clever, funny and rather exciting, but she tried to forget that. That wasn't what she was trying to achieve; she wanted secure and confident, mature and reliable, witty and sparkling.

The Tricker's shoes, a black lace-up Derby ankle boot, were easily purchased and looked wonderful. They cost one hundred and eighty pounds, so Eupheme had made a saving. Ian stamped his feet outside the shop.

'Now these make sense,' he said.

'Okay. You don't look altogether too bad,' said Eupheme as they wandered along Jermyn Street. 'Now the real work begins.'

Chapter Six

Gresham walked up the Georgian steps through the cold mid-March air, two weeks to the day since she had been stuck on the broken train at Milton Keynes train station. The memory of that event had already receded into unconsciousness owing to the heavy workload she had undertaken. Added to that there were all her film's financial backers, busy meddling with her creation. She spent all her waking hours in anxiety that she might hear yet another piece of bad news from them.

She entered the building and checked her watch. She was late again, 9.10. It was impossible to get there on time.

'Hi, Gresh, your sister just rang,' said Sally the receptionist as Gresham walked up to the fax machine to see what had come in overnight. Sally was sitting behind a modern purpose-built desk in the former drawing room of a Georgian house just off Curzon Street in Mayfair. The house belonged to Allied Fountain, a worldwide film distribution and entertainment company.

'Half-sister,' corrected Gresham. 'What did the sad bitch want?'

'She wants to bring someone to your engagement party. She wants you to ring her.'

'I haven't got time to piss about ringing her, I've got a film to cut!' said Gresham, running her hand through her thick hair in a way not entirely dissimilar to her half-sister's habit. In the past Gresham had heard people comment that this must be a genetically inherited habit. However, Gresham was always quick to disabuse them of this assumption. The explanation was simple – Eupheme had tried to copy her, and had copied her badly as always.

'Should I ring her, then?' asked Sally quietly.

'Yes, tell her to bring who she likes.' Suddenly Gresham stopped, then, without turning to look at Sally, she said, 'Did she say who this bloke was?'

'No.'

'Why would she ring if that sad old hippie Richard was coming? Christ, you don't think she's bringing the train-spotter.'

'She didn't say anything about that,' said Sally.

'Oh my God. She's mad enough. Oh God! I don't want him at my party, he was so cheesy! Yuk. Ring her and tell her I'll call her when I get the chance but she can't bring anyone cheesy.' Gresham climbed the elegant stairs of the old house and entered what had once been a rear bedroom. It had long since been converted into a film editing suite.

'Morning, Greshington,' said Simon Langham, her film editor. He was spooling his way through a reel of film, its image flickering on the screen before them. Light and airy with a high ceiling, the room was a delightful place in which to work, unlike the darkened spaceship-like caverns used by digital TV editing companies. Simon was a hands-on film man. Three stand-alone canvas bag bins with high frames above them held miles and miles of film clips, different takes from the many hundreds of scenes that Gresham had accumulated during the shoot.

'I know I've got to watch her,' she said, bouncing up and down on her chair. 'I know this is the day.'

'She's not that bad,' said Simon as the face of Nona Wilfred was frozen on the screen. One of the reasons the film got off the ground was that Gresham had managed to secure the services of this trendy actress from Hollywood. The relationship seemed full of promise before the filming started. Nona and Gresh, Gresh and Nona, they were seen everywhere together, but as soon as the camera rolled the two women fell out and Nona's performance suffered.

'Oh, you just want to shag her,' said Gresham.

'Well, only a bit. I mean, I wouldn't climb over you to get to her.'

'You try and climb anywhere near me, chum, and I'll bite it off.'

'You've such a way with words, Gresh.'

Simon was the only man Gresham had ever met, other than her father, who wasn't intimidated by her. They had worked together on three projects and somehow had never fallen out. 'It's a mystery to everyone who knows me,' he said to Gresham one day. ''How can you work with that bitch?' they ask and I say, 'Underneath the bravado there's one very scared lady', but really I know underneath the bravado there's a very dangerous tough-arsed broad.'

The phone rang. It was Sally on reception.

'There's a fax for you. D'you want me to bring it up?'

'No, I'll come down, I need the exercise,' said Gresham, and stood up to leave.

'You're going to have to watch her some time,' said Simon, gesturing at the still-frozen face on the screen.

'I know, I know,' shouted Gresham, angry that she'd been caught out. She stormed down the stairs. The prospect of sitting in the edit suite all day watching a woman whose every nuance, speech defect and attitude annoyed her beyond reason was not a pleasant thought. As she reached the bottom landing, she heard a young man's raised voice.

'I see the way these bastards live. Film-makers. She's not a fucking film-maker, she's a party girl who's found a hobby! You should see the way they treat me. They think the crap they produce is important!'

'For goodness' sake, Pete,' she heard Sally say weakly.

'They're slags, all of them. They've all got family money behind them, and all the women shag their way to the top.'

Gresham smiled. An otherwise miserable day had handed her a golden opportunity to burnish her reputation. She thundered down the remaining stairs, her elegantly long legs trimmed with a pair of very large black boots. She stood in front of the young man, who it was instantly clear was a mere cyclist courier. His radio cracked an incomprehensible message. Gresham smiled calmly.

'You can only shag your way to the middle, um ...'

'Pete,' said Sally helpfully.

'Pete. That's the one thing you can count on in this business. I've never screwed anyone I work with. They've all tried, even some of the gay ones, but it doesn't work, believe me. Where's my fax, Sally?'

Gresham smiled at Pete, who was struck dumb. She had known all her conscious life that virtually every heterosexual man found her very beautiful. She knew she had wonderful teeth, truly wonderful teeth that her father had spent a staggering amount of money on. She saw the confusion on his face. First impressions are everything, she thought; she knew all about this young man in a few seconds.

Sally gave her the fax. Gresham turned and started to walk towards the staircase, knowing he would be looking at her backside. As she walked up the stairs she turned and struck a sexy pose.

'Oh, and Pete, my dad is stinking rich, my future husband is even richer, and I earn shed-loads of money on my own account. Isn't it rotten?'

She spun on her massively overbuilt boot and disappeared.

'Bitch,' said Pete as he left the building.

'Bastards!' said Gresham, flopping back into the chair next to Simon Langham's. 'I knew they'd do this.' She held up the fax. 'The wankers. I said I wanted another three months and they give me, what, one and a half! I said I wanted a low-key press launch with no celebs, they want a huge high-profile launch and only let very few key press people see it before. It's not ready to be previewed yet, anyone can tell that!'

'When d'they want to show it?' asked Simon.

'First week of May!' said Gresham. 'May the fifth! A Tuesday! That's barely three bloody weeks before my wedding. I wanted to screen it after the sodding honeymoon! Shit!'

'Well, that's probably why they've done it,' said Simon. 'And Tuesday's a good day for a launch. Very high-profile. Marvellous.'

'You soft prick, how can you say it's marvellous!'

'Oh, we can get it done by then. True, my wife will leave me, my children will forget who I am, we won't be able to sleep, I'll go bald and you'll go grey, but we can do it.'

'You're such a softy, Simon,' said Gresham. 'You always let people walk all over you.'

'I let you walk all over me.'

'Yes, well, everyone does that. That's why you'll never get anywhere. You'll be stuck in this editing room all your life and when you lie on your deathbed you'll wonder what it was all about. Now let's cut this bloody awful scene down as short as we can get it.' Gresham looked at Nona Wilfred's face cruelly frozen mid-blink on the screen – internationally recognised, globally envied, hugely expensive to hire.

'God, she's crap,' said Gresham.

'Coming to your wedding?' asked Simon.

'Of course she's coming to my fucking wedding.'

Chapter Seven

'We are basically, as you can see, in big trouble,' said Sir Peter Adelphi from his chair at the end of the low table. It was the regular monthly board meeting of the International Children's Trust. Unusually, the entire board was present — Sir Peter, retired merchant banker, in the chair, Yoni Chiata Fairchild, a Zimbabwean barrister, Carol Sarler, journalist and charity organiser, Kevin Waslick and Christine Hanks, who ran the office, and Annie Pinnock, ex-model and active event organiser. Eupheme sat looking at them and felt a wave of depression gently wash over her. This was her life. She had dedicated so much time to running this charity, but never really saw any of the results of their work and spent most of her time with people like the ones sitting beside her.

'Pox-ridden lottery,' said Kevin, which basically summed the whole thing up. Eupheme knew it didn't need a spin doctor to explain the figures — the computer-generated graph Blutacked to the wall showed the change so starkly there was no other explanation. Funding had been on a slow but steady increase, and suddenly, as if a switch had been thrown, in November 1994 there was a massive and calamitous drop. The same chart could be seen in charity offices all over the country. Some of them had a little peak about a year later when the Lottery Commission threw a derisory sum of cash at them, but that was it. They were on their beam-ends and about to bite the dust.

'We've just fallen out of people's consciousness,' said Yoni Chiata Fairchild. 'No one knows we're here any more. That last series of adverts really didn't help.'

There was silent consent around the table. This was, Eupheme remembered, the self-same committee that had okayed a series of pictures painted by eight-year-old refugee children to try to pluck the heartstrings of the affluent. It had uniformly failed to do so and they had spent almost their entire publicity budget on the production of the images. The whole thing had been a complete disaster.

'I know everybody is opposed to the idea of a benefit,' said Annie Pinnock. 'But I've been checking and there are actually a lot fewer around at the moment. The big names aren't asked to do as many as they were a few years back. If you did a really big scale benefit you know, Albert Hall, Prince of Wales Theatre, you raise money but, much more importantly, you raise the profile. A couple of big names and you raise your flag above the parapet and people take notice.'

As Annie spoke, Eupheme couldn't help remembering that this was the woman who was chiefly responsible for the Labour Party's enormous 1991 pre-election shindig at a Sheffield football pitch. The huge gathering where Neil Kinnock, then leader, thanked the party faithful for winning the election that they promptly lost hopelessly the following week.

'It looks like the only option,' said Kevin.

'What d'you think, Eupheme?' asked Sir Peter. She raised her eyebrows.

'Well, we've got to do something. I am worn out trying to find different ways of fund-raising. If we could time it right, get the right combination of names on the bill, it could be the gig of the year.'

'I've checked around all the sources I know,' said Annie.

'There is nothing opening, nothing big, no other benefit on the night of Tuesday the fifth of May.'

Everyone looked through their diaries. It looked good.

'The fifth then,' said Sir Peter after lengthy and, to Eupheme, pointless discussions. 'I'll be there.'

An hour and a half later the committee had talked itself out. There was nothing more to say on the subject. They had actually made a decision at last. It was down to Eupheme to get the whole thing off the ground. She walked back to her tiny desk, festooned with unanswered mail, posters, leaflets, a box of unsold charity Christmas cards, faxes, half-opened envelopes and old sandwiches still in their Pret à Manger plastic packing.

She sat down and looked at a Barclaycard brochure. She was actually looking at a glossy photo of an Italian hilltop town not unlike Cortona near where her boyfriend Richard Markham was presently making sculptures, or more likely getting drunk. Richard and Eupheme had been lovers for nearly five years, on and off, mostly off. Richard was theoretically her only lover – she didn't count the odd drunken encounter she'd had at university. He hated London and she didn't want to live halfway up a mountain in the middle of Italy.

She and Christine had visited Richard the previous autumn. The visit had been a disaster. She shouldn't have taken Christine but she didn't want to go alone. Richard was wonderful-looking, intelligent, a real artist – he actually earned his living from his work, he was successful. He was a wonderful lover. She thought she was in love with him, but he drank. He drank and drank, mostly Amoretto, a sweet, almond-based liqueur. He swigged it from the bottle as he worked his plaster, or chipped at his rock. The smell made Eupheme reach; she couldn't bare his rasping breath. She had begged him to stop, to get help, to come back to London and live with her. She knew loads of people who were in Alcoholics Anonymous. She had seen the transformations, the rebuilt lives. She explained to him that most of the people she knew were high-achievers, famous people; the list of names was astounding. Richard just smiled and shook his head as if to signify that she didn't understand his drinking. He then pointed to the staggering view out of his window, asked her to listen to the crickets and the cockerel outside his door, and told her he'd wait for her.

On the way home after a tearful farewell, Christine had gone on and on at Eupheme about staying, and what a wonderful man Richard was and how she'd never meet someone as talented and creative as him and she should be grateful. But how could she tolerate the drinking, and more to the point why should she? The whole thing was left unresolved, as was the mess on her desk, the mess in her flat, the horrendous mess in her huge bag which she lugged with her everywhere. Everything in her life was a mess except the ideas in her head. They were crystal clear, she knew about them, she could argue people into the ground with her ideas. She knew she was right. She didn't believe or hope she was, she knew.

Kevin started typing and his computer made its familiar noises. Eupheme put the brochure down and smiled at him.

'So,' said Kevin Waslick, turning around to look at her. 'How was the train-spotter?'

'Sorry?' said Eupheme

'Your Internet mate, the bloke with the video clip of you.'

'Oh, he's fine.' Eupheme was confident that a blank wall would stop Kevin pursuing the matter.

'Looks like you've got a message from him,' he said with a big grin. Eupheme got up and looked at the screen.

dear eupheme i will be on 4.15 train today as get off work early. gets in at 5.20pm on track 8 which is platform 7 unless diversion at nuneaton is still in place in which case it will be track 12 which is platform 10. ian.

'Oh, bloody hell, that's just what I need,' said Eupheme.

'Are you having a scene with this guy?' asked Kevin.

'What!' Eupheme snapped. 'A scene? No! And what's more, it's none of your sodding business.'

'I'm sorry,' said Kevin quickly and genuinely.

Eupheme checked her watch, grabbed her coat and left the office. She ran past the long row of elegant Georgian townhouses that faced Highbury Fields. Although it was mid-March the trees still gave no indication that spring was near. She caught the Tube from Highbury station to Euston, ran up the escalators and across the concourse to Platform 7.

Chapter Eight

Ian sat on the electric-powered InterCity express from Birmingham New Street to London Euston. He was reading *What PC* magazine. A new video card had been introduced on to an already bursting market. With a desktop set-up running at 350 megahertz and above, and with this video card fitted, he realised he could input, edit and output near broadcast-standard video to his heart's content using a very small set-up.

He'd been looking forward to this time, forty-five minutes on the train with nothing to do but absorb the tasty chunks of computer information laid out so excitingly within the thick, glossy pages of *What PC*.

He'd had a hard day in the supermarket; five delivery units had arrived during his shift. It wasn't so much the physical work – there wasn't much of that anyway what with the breakthroughs in small-scale fork-lift technology – it was the mental strain of keeping check on the panoply of stock. The sheer array of products in the dry goods arena was mind-boggling. The reams and reams of computer print-out that had to be checked against what was actually physically in the giant storeroom were very taxing. As the roller pallets were arriving like heavy rain, Ian was rushed off the old feet trying to keep up. The fact that the store turned over somewhere in the region of forty million pounds a year meant that an enormous quantity of product had to be processed.

By 1.30, although the shop wasn't overly busy, Ian was still dashing about trying to work out exactly how many tins of McDougall's stir-in Madras Curry Sauce they were actually holding. Eddie helped him out, finding a missing box of the product which had fallen off one of the pallets. Even with a system as well organised as this, a tiny natural error like gravity intervening could still throw things out of whack.

He could feel the tension in his neck still as he sat on the train. He looked at the prices of colour laser printers and shook his head. Still a top-of-the-range product there, price-wise.

The train started to enter London. Ian sighed. He didn't like London – too big, you never knew where to go to get things. In Northampton you always knew where all the relevant shops were – computers, peripherals, cameras, blank videotape, magazines, stationery, books, video hire. He could get all and any of his leisure requisites, as he liked to describe them, with his eyes virtually shut. He knew he could buy another PC magazine in London to read on the train home, a journey he was also looking forward to.

His mum didn't want him to go to London either. They had stood talking in the little Cyril Street kitchen the previous evening, as she slowly washed up and he wiped and put everything away.

'You'll be the laughing-stock at work, my lad,' she said, hearing that this woman he was seeing was going to write an article about him. 'You don't know how cruel women can be, do you?'

Ian had an inkling that women could, on occasion, be rather vicious. There had been a time when he had witnessed some unpleasantness at work between the women who operated the checkouts. During a very uncomfortable tea break, one of them was sitting in the corner of the brightly lit staff canteen weeping while the others sat huddled with each other cruelly and loudly criticising her. As team leader for their section, as well as dry goods manager, he knew he had to intervene. He listened to the firmly held opinions the women were expressing about the outcast. They underlined the common sense of their point of view; in fact they had a very profound political point underlying their dislike of her, but it was completely beyond Ian. He simply could not see what all the fuss was about. He begged them to be tolerant but was frightened by the hard set of their faces. He didn't understand why they were so upset – the woman hadn't killed anyone, stolen anything, she hadn't lied. It seemed she had flirted with Simon, who was Ian's opposite number on fresh produce. Simon claimed not to be aware of anything and the matter was dropped. Not only that, about three weeks later Ian noticed that this self-same outcast was sitting happily chatting with the same bunch of women. Somehow it had all been resolved and he'd done nothing. He worried that this event shone a dim light on his management skills. The women's work certainly suffered during the disagreement, but he felt it was right out of his league. Consignments, even when one box fell off the pallet, were easier to deal with.

A woman sitting across the aisle from him on the train was comforting a wriggling two-year-old. He looked at her without embarrassment. She was busy trying to stop the toddler crying and took no heed. Ian sat back and tried to have a thought for a moment. Not a dream about hardware, pornography or video transfer on the Internet, but a thought. He thought about women – the one opposite him with the child, his mother, Eupheme, the girl on the deli counter at the supermarket who always hid her name badge whenever he went near her. They were, he had to admit in this thought he was having, a mystery. He didn't dislike them – generally speaking he found many of them hugely attractive – but as he sat with his eyes shut on the train, he admitted that he was baffled. They really did talk another language; they seemed to get angry about things he couldn't quite believe were important.

His eye was drawn back to the Evesham Micro power tower, a super-fast 240 megahertz computer with a two-gigabit hard drive, Sixteen megabytes of RAM, built in, and video in and out facility. Would that he had the funds.

The toddler across the way started to cry and eventually his mother put him down on the floor. He began to make his wobbly way along the rocking train floor. Ian smiled at the child and then the mother. The child noticed and burbled some noise, walking towards Ian happily. The mother started to lean forward. Ian put out a hand, naturally, without thinking, to catch the child should he fall. The mother was out of her seat by the time Ian felt the grip of the child's hands on his suit.

'It's okay. I don't mind,' said Ian, smiling at the happy, gurgling toddler.

'I do,' said the mother rather fiercely. She picked the child up, roughly and sat him down on the seat next to her with overly deliberate movements. Naturally, just as Ian expected, the little toddler's face folded up and he started crying again. Ian felt enormous empathy towards the child. He wanted to pick him up and comfort him; the child wasn't doing anything wrong, he was just exploring. He seemed happy to wander around. He couldn't go anywhere — all the exterior doors had time-delay locks that were only released if the train was stationary. Surely everyone knew that.

Ian frowned and looked back at the picture of the Evesham Micro power tower, but he couldn't concentrate on the desire to have it. The urge to comfort the child and tell the woman she was a stupid bitch was far more powerful.

'He wasn't doing any harm,' he said, almost as surprised as the young mother that he'd let the words out.

'Is it any of your business?' asked the woman.

'I'm sorry, of course not, it's just that he was so happy toddling off. The little chap just wants to explore a bit,' said Ian.

'Got children of your own, have you?' asked the woman, her lips running thin and tight across her teeth.

'No,' said Ian with a slight shake of the head.

'Well, then,' said the woman.

The toddler was looking at Ian through his sobs. His mother turned on him. 'Will you shut up, Joshua,' she said through clenched teeth.

Ian turned the page in *What PC* and tried to concentrate on an article about scanning and optical character recognition. He eventually managed to quell the confusion of feelings he had about the child and ponder the possibility of running celebrity autographs through a scanner so the computer would automatically put their names next to the signature to facilitate a faster database build.

The train pulled into Euston station, according to the liquid crystal display on Ian's watch three minutes, thirty-five seconds late. Not bad all in all, he thought. He had got out of his seat before the train had stopped because he didn't want to watch the young mother and little Joshua get off, the mother struggling with her giant laundry bag and old pushchair. He knew his help would be unwelcome, so he thought he'd steer clear.

Eupheme was waiting for him at the top of the stairs. She was dressed in brown from head to foot – a brown frock-type coat, brown leggings, brown boots and a rather revealing, very tight brown top. He noticed that she certainly did have something in the way of boobs up there, but it was remarkable how she kept them out of sight. All the more intriguing really, he thought as he joined her. She looked tense and uncomfortable and was obviously going to say something. He had no idea what; he had come to learn not to expect a 'Hello' or a 'How are you?'

'Yellow!' she said when he stood in front of her. 'You're wearing a shirt with a yellow collar.'

He was indeed wearing a yellow shirt underneath his Donna Karan suit. He hadn't actually noticed the colour, but he could see Eupheme was right when he looked down at his chest. He was sporting training shoes bought from Shoe City in Northampton High Street, £9.99 a pair. His mother had bought them for him.

'Am I?' he asked. 'It's just what Mum put out for me.'

'Does she buy your clothes for you?' asked Eupheme.

'Most of the time.'

'Okay, okay,' said Eupheme. 'Forget it. It's not important. Look, I don't have that much time. I didn't realise you were coming down today.'

'That's what you said,' said Ian. 'I had a reminder on my Claris Organiser, beeped me when I booted up last night. I had to ask Mrs Philips if I could leave early. There wasn't much happening, it's not a busy afternoon, so I wasn't down for overtime. A lot of the oldies come in because they've just had their pension money. My mum usually shops today, but she can't this week because she's gone to visit her aunt who lives in a home outside Rushden. She's ninety-eight my great-aunt she is. Not my mum, my mum's not ninety-eight. Blimey O'Reilly, she's not that old. I never go and see my aunt because she just lies still, hasn't said a word since the mid-fifties apparently, the nineteen fifties, not when she was in her mid-fifties. She's not that barmy. It was when her husband died. I never met him. Men always die younger than women. Have you noticed?'

They walked through the concourse at Euston and went down the short flight of steps to the cab rank.

'The thing about this suit,' Ian said as he slid about on the seat in the back of the cab, 'is that it makes it very hard to sit down. It's got something to do with the density of the weave, I imagine, because there seems to be no friction. If you ever sit on a smooth-surfaced seat, you slide around. Like this.' He slid back and forth on his seat like a spoilt three-year-old who couldn't sit still. 'I've never had that trouble with a polycotton.'

'Ian,' said Eupheme, 'Haven't you got anything interesting to tell me?'

'Um, I heard from an Internet buddy in Utah in the Midwest of America that they executed a child murderer there on Friday. By firing squad. The chap actually wanted to be shot, apparently.

He was on Death Row and chose shooting rather than lethal injection. They used six Winchester SLRs at a distance of eight metres, that's about twenty-five feet or so. He was sitting in a chair with a target tied around his neck so they knew where to shoot.'

'Okay, that's a bit more interesting.'

'Is it?' he asked, smiling.

'Well, it's more interesting than your aunts and your slipping suit. All I'm saying is, if you're not sure what to say, shut up. You'll appear much cooler that way.'

'Oh, right.'

'More like Tom Cruise.'

'I don't think much of him. D'you know Val Kilmer?'

'Yes, excellent, you'll seem more like Val Kilmer.'

'What, you do know him!' Ian's heart skipped a beat. Imagine having Val Kilmer's autograph. Now that would be worth serious spondulications.

'No, I don't know Val Kilmer, but if you want to be like him, you've got to stop being boring. Val Kilmer would never talk about his ninety-year-old aunt.'

'I've only seen him in *Labyrinth*,' said Ian, not really taking in what Eupheme was saying.

'Is it new? I've not heard about it.'

'Don't be daft, it's been in the video shops for ages. It's a science fantasy film, all goblins and elves and witches. He plays a knight. Loads of my mates are into fantasy role-playing. Dungeons and Dragons.'

'Is that a film?'

'No, you big wallet. It's a fantasy role-playing game. Haven't you ever played Dungeons and Dragons? I can't believe it. Where have you been?'

'Why did you call me a big wallet?'

'A wallet. Haven't you heard of that yet? Blimey, everyone uses it. It's female wally,' said Ian with a laugh.

'That's almost amusing. Did you make it up?'

'No, my mate Eddie said it. I thought it was funny. You big wallet. It's funny, isn't it?'

'What a shame,' said Eupheme.

They got out of the cab on Harley Street. Ian stood on the pavement awkwardly as Eupheme paid the cabbie.

'In here,' she said, walking up the steps of an immaculate Georgian terraced house.

'The dentist!' said Ian. 'What's wrong? Got a toothache?'

'No, I haven't,' said Eupheme, opening the door when the buzzer sounded. 'We're here for you. Tom De Groot is one of the best orthodontists in the business. We're here to clean up your teeth.

Ian lay in the dentist's chair obediently as Tom De Groot undertook a close inspection of his mouth. His voice was slightly muffled by his mask, his eyes shielded by reflective glasses, his hands shielded by delicate rubber. His metal tool prodded at Ian's teeth one by one.

'Two, three, four okay. Five missing. Six, seven, eight. Aha. Seven okay, eight loose filling. Well, a few problems, Ian, but nothing a good clean and a bit of repairing won't solve.'

'Is there anything you can do about that gap?' asked Eupheme.

'Well, a bridge cap is about the only answer,' said Tom, pulling down his face mask. 'The teeth both sides are in pretty poor shape. We can cap them and build a tooth between them. Cost a few bob, though.'

'Price is no object,' snapped Eupheme. 'How long would it take.'

'I can cut those two teeth down now, a quick root canal job on that one, take an impression, I should say in a week we could fit it. Quite a bit of drilling to do. D'you normally have an injection, Ian?'

'Oh God,' said Ian.

Half an hour later they emerged from the dentist. Ian's face felt as big as a football, although Eupheme assured him it didn't

THE MAN ON PLATFORM FIVE

show. The temporary caps felt like dry chalk in his mouth, and the dentist have given his teeth such a brutal cleaning that he felt as if he'd been chewing Brillo pads all afternoon.

'Your teeth are really nice,' said Eupheme as they climbed into another taxi and made another very short trip across the Euston Road and up a side street. Within three minutes the taxi pulled to a halt beside a church building set back from the road. They got out of the cab. Ian clutched his bag to his chest and looked around nervously.

'Why've we come to a church?' he asked. His mind had already raced through a handful of nightmare scenarios – his ritual castration and murder on the altar, cackling witches eating his entrails, the entrance to hell opening up in the floor, Eupheme as a green-faced devil maid.

'It's a gym,' said Eupheme.

'Is it?' Ian walked towards the front door gingerly. The unmistakable staccato beat of techno dance music hit his ears as he approached.

'It's one of the nicest gyms in London,' said Eupheme. 'Come on.'

Ian tried to get his bearings by looking at nearby high buildings. 'But it's so near where we've just been,' he said as they entered the brightly lit lobby. 'Why didn't we walk?'

'No time,' said Eupheme.

Ian looked at her and laughed. 'But we'd have got some exercise and we wouldn't have had to come in here. Hu hu.' His laugh, he knew, only half masked the fact that he was nervous.

The aisle of the church had been converted into a very swish multi-gym. Hugely well-built men were slowly moving around, straining as they exercised with vast dumb-bells, barbells and mechanical pulls.

'Jake,' said Eupheme, 'this is the Ian I told you about.'

Ian turned to face a man whose head did not match his body. It looked as if it belonged on a slender man of about forty-five years old. But the body was well over six foot tall, the neck was thicker than Ian's thigh, the arms were nearly as thick as Ian's waist, and the legs were thicker than one of the pillars that supported the postmodern entrance to the Wellingborough Road Besco, which suddenly felt like a homely and safe place to be.

'Hi, Ian,' said Jake in a voice an octave higher than one might expect of a man his size. 'Okay, if you want to get your togs on, the changing rooms are downstairs. We've got quite a strict hygiene policy here so if you're feeling a bit world-weary, you might want to have a quick shower while you're down there. Plenty of towels. I'll see you up here in a minute or two. And you're doing a step class, Pheme, is that right?'

The dressing rooms were clean, tidy, fresh-smelling and nothing like the places Ian used to get awkwardly changed in when he was at Trinity High School in Northampton, the last time he'd been in anything like this. The school changing room always seemed to have odd-shaped pieces of mud on the floor which had fallen off sweaty boys' rugby boots. He took all his clothes off except his red underpants. He sniffed his armpits and decided that he didn't really need to take a shower. He pulled on a pair of thin, droopy training trousers and a T-shirt than read 'My Mate Went To Leeds And All I Got Was This Lousy T-Shirt'.

He put his clothes in a locker and pulled out the key. He walked up the stairs, trying to force the pin that the key hung on through his T-shirt. Suddenly his head banged into something hard. He jerked back and looked up. The hard thing he had walked into was the stomach of a smiling black man with extraordinarily well-developed muscles.

'Sorry, sorry,' said Ian.

'Hey, it's okay,' said the man as he carried on downstairs. As he passed, Ian got a waft of some smell, a wonderful spicy clean smell.

'Bit herby,' he said to himself in a dreadful Afro-Caribbean accent, and entered the gym.

He spent nearly ten minutes on a running machine with a computer-generated running track on a screen in front of him. Every few seconds a computer-generated runner would overtake him and disappear around the bend. The image would be accompanied by the virtual runner's footfalls and heavy breathing. After being overtaken for the twentieth time, Ian hit the red panic button Jake and shown him and held on to the security bar as the track slowly ground to a halt. He let his head drop down as he tried to get his breath. He felt a large lump of burning pain running up the centre of his chest which he assumed was where his lungs were.

'D'you smoke Ian?' asked Jake, looking at the read-out and making a note on a clipboard.

'No. Never have,' said Ian between pants.

'Bloody hell, you've got no excuse, then.'

'I've just had an injection at the dentist, though,' said Ian, thinking this might assuage Jake.

'No, that's nothing to do with it. You're just slob-like, mate. Come on.'

Jake worked every muscle in Ian's body, although not for long because they didn't last long. Leg press, leg curl, bench press, back curl, side dips, pull-downs, squat jerks, the works. The crunch came when he attempted the crunch. Ian lay on his back, knees raised, fingertips pressing on his temples. Jake held down his feet.

'Lift your head up. Come on Ian, up, up. One. That's good, you've done one, go for another. Come on, Ian, lift your head, don't use your arms, just fingertips on your temples. That's it, feel the pain in your stomach muscles. Come on. Try again. That's two. Great. Only forty-eight more to go.'

In between the stomach-crippling exercises, Ian caught glimpses of Eupheme in another room, separated by a glass screen. She was wearing what looked like a swimming costume with tights underneath. She was jumping up and down on a plastic box with about twenty other women. Music could be heard.

'Come on, Ian, forty-three more. Come on,' said Jake as he held a hand for Ian to touch with his head. Ian's stomach muscles were burning with pain; he was white with exertion and there was sweat pouring down his forehead.

'Oh God. I can't do any more,' he whimpered. He couldn't stand. Jake held out a hand. When Ian grabbed it, his body was lifted into the air as if by a powerful hydraulic machine. Without a pause for breath, Jake's rock-like hand was moving him towards a wall bar.

'Chin-ups!' said Jake. 'Now these are fun. I do these for a hobby.'

Ian's arms, thin and white, were shaking with the effort. Jake was holding him by the waist and supporting at least three-quarters of his weight. It was very quickly apparent that the thin white arms really weren't up to it.

'Have a little break,' said Jake. 'I'm just seeing what we've got to do to get you into shape.'

'I just can't do it,' said Ian, sounding as if he were close to tears.

'You are one out-of-condition geezer, there's no denying it, Ian, me old mate,' said Jake, giving him a friendly wallop on the back. 'That loose-knit sack of flab you call a body is in a fucking state, mate. Let's face facts. You haven't gone to seed, you've wilted, mate. No definition, no bulk, except for your stomach and your arse, no upper-body strength, no leg power. It's a wonder you can walk. What are you, a computer whiz kid?'

'Well, sometimes,' said Ian. He was just about to explain about the supermarket when Eupheme came running up, flush-faced, hair soaked with sweat, wiping her neck with a towel.

'How d'it go?' she asked, looking at Jake.

'You say I've got six weeks,' said Jake. Eupheme nodded. 'Well, he's got to come three times a week, two hours a session. I've done it before. It can be done, but it takes a lot of willpower. Diet is vital – masses of supplements, bulk starch, tons of pasta, fish, fruit, as much as he can possibly eat. Early nights, no alcohol, no cigarettes, no wanking.'

Jonathan Ross walked into the gym, not instantly recognisable because of his glasses. Ian, a hardened star-spotter, wasn't thrown. He stared at Jonathan Ross without any pretence of cool.

'Afternoon, Jake,' said Jonathan.

'All right, Jonathan,' said Jake, barely giving him a glance. Jonathan looked at Eupheme, clicked his fingers and pointed at her. 'It's Eupheme, right?'

She smiled and nodded, saying, 'We met when you did the International Children's Trust appeal last Christmas.'

'Of course. How's it going?' He was slowly making his way towards the changing rooms.

'It's good. Yeah, not too bad,' said Eupheme. 'Actually, we're doing a big benefit at the Albert Hall at the beginning of May. We're looking for a compère.'

'Be delighted to help if I'm free, Eupheme.' said Jonathan, now virtually disappeared. 'You've got my number. Bell me with the details.' He ducked down and was gone.

'Wow,' said Ian, face alight with joy, 'that was Jonath . . .'

'So you think you can do it?' Eupheme said quickly, turning to Jake, who looked a little confused as Eupheme continued, 'That's good. I'll sort out with Ian how much he can do, and then we'll have a chat about it.'

'Okay,' said Jake, scratching his head with his enormous hand. 'Well done, Ian, mate. Long way to go but you're a trier.' He shook Ian's limp, sweaty palm.

Ian and Eupheme went down the stairs. Ian was desperate to get in the changing rooms and procure Jonathan Ross's autograph. He'd seen it at a collectors' fair in Leicester once, but he'd certainly been nowhere near getting it himself.

'Okay, Ian, how d'you feel?' asked Eupheme, leaning on the door of the women's changing room.

'I'm ever so tired,' he said. 'I feel like I've got flu.'

'Well, look, are you going to be able to come three times a week?' She looked into his eyes, then before he could reply said, 'You're not, are you?'

'How can I? I have to work. Money doesn't grow on trees. Well, not for me it doesn't.' He rubbed his right thigh which felt particularly painful.

'You haven't got any holidays due?' She knew it was hopeless. He shook his head. 'So what could you do? Two times a week?'

'No way, José,' he said. 'Maybe once, but Mum's going to want to know what's going on. She doesn't understand where I got the suit from. I think she thinks I'm running with some bad sorts.'

'Tell her you're doing it for a journalist in London and it's all paid for and above board and it's only for six weeks. Look, Ian, how can I explain? You see, there's a deadline. I want you to be aware of this. I know I haven't told you, but there's a deadline.'

'What does that mean?'

'It means that in just under six weeks I'm taking you to a rather sprauntsy party, an engagement party.'

'A what?'

'A party that people who are getting engaged to be married have.'

'I know what it is, but why d'you want me to go? Is it like a stag night?' he said, running through some instant stripper fantasies.

'No, nothing like a stag night. Look, it's very stylish, swish, sprauntsy, it'll be full of what you would call "top people". I want you to blend in at that party as if it was the most natural thing in the world for you to go.'

'Who's going to be there?' he asked with a tragically over-bright grin.

'Look, okay, loads of famous people,' said Eupheme. 'Loads of rich people, and even some rich and famous people, but I don't want you to get their autographs, right, I don't want you to get your picture taken with them, I want you to be cool.'

'Oh, that's so unfair. To miss an opportunity like that. The likes of me never gets the chance to go to a top people's party. You know that. I stood outside the Leicester Square Odeon and saw Tom Cruise and Nicole Kidman when they opened *Far and Away*. I could see inside but I never even thought that I'd ever be allowed inside.'

'Ian, please. Listen to me. Are you prepared to go through quite a tough time in the next six weeks? Training here, reading a lot of stuff I'm going to give you, watching quite a few films, learning how to talk properly?'

'I can talk properly.'

'No, you've got an ugly accent.'

'Have I?'

'Oh, I suppose it's not that bad and we could get rid of it quite easily. I know someone who can help. I also want you to stand a little better so I want you to go to an Alexander teacher. You're all hunched over, but I know you could look very nice if you stood well. You can't go like you are. People will see through you in seconds if you start talking about taxi designs, model railways, train-spotting, video cameras, timetables or your hundred-year-old aunt. We've got an enormous amount to do in no time at all. Are you willing to try?'

'Well, I suppose so.'

'Look, afterwards you can tell your mates on Milton Keynes train station that you were at one of the most top, drop-dead posh parties in London. You'll see more stars than you can remember. You can talk about it afterwards. It's just while you're there, Ian, rule number one, don't go up to anyone and ask for their fucking autographs.'

'All right, there's no need to use blue language. Jake was bad enough.'

'Please don't say "blue language". That's so naff. Say swear words. And please don't say "ever so" and for pity's sake don't say "no way, José".'

'Well, please don't swear so much,' said Ian, sulkily.

'And don't do that sulky little-boy-lost stuff. That looks so cra ... I mean stupid. Ian, please try, and I will too. Sorry I swore. It's a bad habit.'

Jonathan Ross came out of the men's changing room wearing training clothes and running shoes. He smiled briefly at Eupheme and climbed the stairs. Ian twitched a little.

'No autographs, Ian. Starting now.'

'Oh, but it's such a waste.' Ian was feeling actual emotional pain as he watched the celebrity legs going up the stairs.

'Go and get dressed. We're going to a café to drink fresh fruit juice and look at style magazines. I want you to learn a few things tonight, then we're going to a movie.'

'A film? Which one?'

'Call it a movie and I don't know which one. Whichever one has come out most recently and isn't utter rubbish. We're only seeing it so you can have an opinion about it later.'

'What, you mean I can talk about movies at the party?'

'If the subject comes up, yes. I'll give you a list of permissible subjects.'

Chapter Nine

'I saw a movie in London last night,' said Ian as he painfully pushed the long row of supermarket trolleys towards the front entrance of Besco's Wellingborough Road branch. 'It was called *Leaving Las Vegas*.'

'Is that the one with all the nude beanies?' said Eddie, his lazy eye inspecting a drainage cover while the other wandered over Ian's face.

'No, you're thinking of *Showgirls*. I wish we had seen that but Eupheme said it had terrible reviews.'

'What, didn't Barry Norman like it? Hu hu.'

'And that, after all, is what it's there for,' said Ian, imitating the Spitting Image puppet that imitated Rory Bremner who imitated Barry Norman. 'Anyway, *Leaving Las Vegas* was strange because the bloke wants to kill himself, and then he meets the girl, who's very attractive by the by, and she falls in love with him and then, well, then you think she'll save him, but he just dies anyway. So it all seems a bit pointless.'

'What, the geezer dies at the end?'

'Yes, drinks himself to death,' Ian said, miming drinking from a bottle, doing quite a realistic glug-glug movement. 'Nicolas Cage it was, won an Oscar for it many a long moon ago.'

'Oh, you've spoilt it now,' said Eddie, slamming the trolleys together. 'What's the point of me seeing it if I know the ending?'

'Sorry, Eddie. As I say, it's not a new movie. It's quite an old movie. I have to say movie. Calling it a film is naff, apparently.'

'You always do that. You always spoil endings, guy! Come to think of it, you always spoil everything. How come a bloke like you gets to go out to top London cinemas and have hair styled by stylists and that, and gets suits and all. No beanie ever comes up to me for anything except a trolley.'

'Eddie, you'll meet Miss Right one day, mate.'

'Get off. Wouldn't get married if you paid me,' said Eddie, walking away and hoiking up his baggy jeans.

'I bet you will,' said Ian. 'You'll meet Miss Right, you mark my words, Eduardo. Now round up those trolleys and bring them here pretty quick sharp, my good man.'

'Yeah, all right,' said Eddie. 'Don't go on. We all know you got promotion.'

'Eddie, me old mucker, it's not as if I've been shot to the top of the organisation. Blimey, I've been here eleven years on a more or less static pay package. I've managed to go from Provisions Manager to Deputy Manager, Dry Goods. That's all. I'm still on the floor with the real people.'

'Yeah, yeah. Okay, Mr Martyrdom,' said Eddie, disappearing around the corner of the massive building.

'Ian, could you give me a hand?' said a woman's voice. 'My pound coin's got stuck.'

Ian turned to see Mrs Dagmar, his old English teacher from Trinity High School. She was a regular customer at the store, retired, white-haired, but to Ian still Mrs Dagmar, a teacher. He wiggled the coin deposit mechanism expertly and removed the pound, reinserted it and freed the trolley.

'There you go, Mrs Dagmar,' he said with a bright smile. 'All shipshape and Bristol fashion.'

'Thank you, dear. You well? How's your mum?'

'She's fine. Bit of trouble with the old hip, but she gets along.' Ian pushed the trolley towards her gently.

'You take care, love,' said Mrs Dagmar. 'Say hello to your mum.'

'Thanks, Mrs Dagmar,' said Ian. He watched her walk away into the shop, the smile falling from his face, which surprised him. He scratched his ear, realising that although she'd known him for twenty years, since he was a kid, she had already forgotten him. He was that easily forgettable. He wanted to tell her about the film he'd seen the night before. He wanted to tell her that now he was starting to do other things, go to London and go to restaurants, meeting Nigel Planer and Jonathan Ross. He wanted to tell her he had a suit hanging in his wardrobe at home which was from a shop called Donna Karan and had cost more than a month's wages. She wouldn't be interested. No one would be interested.

Things outside were interesting to Ian. Model cars, trains, video cameras. Things outside. Magazines about model aeroplanes, new scanning technology and faster modems for his PC. That was interesting. The central Besco computer at the company headquarters in Reading, two hundred and sixteen million calculations a second, the biggest commercial computer in the country, made in the jolly old US of A, of course, but still, quite an achievement. Every till in every Besco store was sending millions of instructions a second to this beast, and it was crunching it all up and producing such pure streams of data that no store ever ran out of a product. Besco's ordering and distribution system was award-winning, apparently. It was marvellous.

However, all these interesting things, although he knew about them, never felt like they went inside him. What was frightening and uncontrollably appealing about meeting this strange woman on Platform 5 at Milton Keynes was that he felt the interest start to seep inside. He kept finding himself thinking about the little toddler, Joshua, the boy he had seen on the train. He seemed so unhappy, like a lot of the children he saw in the store, sitting uncomfortably in their mothers' shopping trolleys, crying and bored and wanting the brightly coloured sweet packets that were hung on every isle corner, specifically to appeal to children.

'Ian, Mrs Philips wants to see you,' said June, the senior deputy manager. She wasn't Ian's immediate boss. She had no official jurisdiction over him in his capacity as Deputy Manager, Dry Goods, but that didn't stop him feeling as if she did. His boss was Mrs Philips, he knew that, she knew that, but on the floor of the supermarket June's word was law. He turned on his heel, ready to go, when June smiled. 'When you've finished removing the roller pallets, Ian, don't leave those there for customers to walk into. And where's Edward?'

'I've sent him off collecting, in the carpark, June,' said Ian, trying to feel that by using her first name he would appear to be on a par with her. It didn't work.

June walked out into the bright morning sun, looking around the huge expanse of carpark for the elusive Eddie. Ian pushed a gaggle of roller pallets into one orderly row and propelled them through the busy store, past the beautifully displayed fresh produce section and through the two large rubber doors that separated the public space from the storeroom. Leaving the pallets in the designated empty pallet storage area, he walked past the vast stacks of washing powder, kitchen roll and baked beans and through another set of double doors. He turned left and went up a flight of echoing stairs, along a corridor and up to the open door into Mrs Philips's office. She sat behind her desk looking through a sheaf of papers.

'June said you wanted to see me, Mrs Philips,' said Ian after tapping lightly on the open door.

'Ah, Ian, sit you down, sit you down,' said Mrs Philips, gesturing to a small turquoise office chair. 'Yes, I've been meaning to have a word for a while. You're happy working here with us, aren't you?'

'Oh, yes. Very happy, Mrs Philips,' said Ian politely.

'Good, good, and I can see you thriving as deputy manager. Dry goods are looking wonderful and we've actually increased the throughput there, so that's all down to you, Ian. Top marks, mate.'

Ian smiled. Mrs Philips was the only woman he'd ever met who used the word mate.

'I've been having words with head office, you see, and we've been putting our heads together as it were, and we were wondering how you'd feel about another bit of promotion.'

Mrs Philips smiled, sitting back in her bigger turquoise chair with her white-shirted arms folded. She was wearing a corporate scarf tied neatly around her neck. Mrs Philips was branch manager — no one called her by her first name except June, the senior deputy manager. However, as she always told everyone, she considered herself very hands-on. She had on two separate occasions been seen stacking shelves, and on one particularly busy Friday night there she was on Till 15, bleeping goods through the scanner like an old pro.

'You're not above getting your hands dirty and I like that in a man,' she said. 'A lot of the young men who work for the company just want the flashy company car and lots of seminars in posh hotels outside Leeds. But you're not that bothered about all that rubbish, are you, Ian? You love retailing. I can tell. You love the look of a well-stocked shelving unit. You're like me in that regard.'

'I suppose so,' said Ian, trying to sound enthusiastic. He still didn't understand what Mrs Philips was getting at. He'd just had promotion to assistant manager, dry goods, and that was proving to be enough of a headache.

'And you like people. That rubs off, you know. People like you and I like customers to like my staff. That's what I'm here for, to make our customers happy, to make them feel safe while they shop. It may be crazy out on those mean streets, Ian, but here in Besco's they are safe to make purchasing decisions in their own time.'

'I've never thought about it like that, but that's very true, Mrs Philips,' said Ian. He tried to imagine Mrs Philips in a kitchen, cooking, wearing an apron. He found the picture wouldn't emerge. He wondered about where she lived. One of those pebbledash bungalows on Lumbertubs Lane with an old privet hedge and two Leylandi either side of the small front door. He'd done a paper round in the area when he was still at school

'I've heard good things, Ian, good things,' said Mrs Philips, leafing through some papers that Ian assumed must appertain to him.

'I am very happy here,' he said, hoping it was the right thing to say. In truth he was increasingly unhappy there; he'd been there too long. He'd looked at some of the bigger stores, outside the ring road. They were at the really exciting cutting edge of bulk retailing. This store was all well and good, but at only eighteen thousand square feet of retailing space it was still a bit on the small side for a supermarket. And only five thousand square feet in the storage department meant they were forever receiving shipments.

'I know you are,' said Mrs Philips. 'I can tell, and I have to say that's partly down to good management, but I'm not here to blow my own trumpet, I'm here to blow yours.'

Ian suddenly had a very strong mental flash, a vivid all-colour pict file picture of Mrs Philips kneeling on the floor of her clean, sunny kitchen, sucking his penis. It was initially revolting, and then suddenly immensely attractive.

'Well, thank you,' he said, not sure why he said it.

'The company are looking for a new Midland's area delivery manager, Ian. I've put you forward as someone who could hit the ground running as it were.'

'Blimey,' said Ian, trying to work out if Mrs Philips was joking.

'It's a big responsibility, a wonderful pay increase of course, company car and a greatly improved pension package.'

Company car! Did she say company car? Ian's mind raced with the news. He couldn't drive, but that was almost secondary. A company car! Would that it were the classic Volkswagen Golf VR6.

'Don't say anything now, Ian. Go away and think about it. It's an important decision. We need someone as ... well, I was going to say sedentary, but I mean reliable as you, but you make sure you're happy with the move. It'll take you into another world.'

'That's very exciting, Mrs Philips.'

'Call me Jane,' said Mrs Philips.

'I certainly will give it my undivided attention, um, Jane,' said Ian. He stood up. He couldn't believe her name was Jane. He'd been there all those years and it had never once occurred to him that she might have a first name. Jane sounded young. It made him think of orange squash on a hot day. Jane was a girl's name, not that of a woman in management. He shook hands with Mrs Philips. He glanced at her lipsticked mouth and for a millisecond in his vivid mind's eye saw something happening that was revoltingly attractive. He left the room and walked back down the concrete floor of the corridor.

After eleven years in virtually the same job, promotion made Ian experience a sudden rush of natural endorphins. He almost floated down the echoing stairway and into the staffroom. It was empty – no one to impart his news to, none of the checkout women having a smoke between shifts. He wafted down the stairs and into the storeroom, through the large double rubber doors and into the rear of the delicatessen section. The store was bustling. The young girl behind the counter who always covered her name badge when she saw Ian was serving a customer with ready-made onion bhajis. Ian smiled. She smiled back at him and turned to face him. Her name was Kirsten, and she was very pretty.

'Hello, Kirsten, everything all right?'

'We're running low on hygiene gloves,' said Kirsten in a thick Birmingham accent.

'I'll sort that out for you,' said Ian. 'No problemo.'

He walked through the store. He knew where he was, he knew how the systems operated, there were no mysteries for him in this building. He knew he could deal with the responsibility that would soon be his.

'Area distribution manager,' he said to himself. 'Wait till I tell Mum.'

Chapter Ten

Gresham woke up in the dark, her limbs aching. As she moved, she heard the squeak of leather upholstery. She looked around. She was in a car – a large car that still smelled new. She was in Stanhope's Range Rover. On her own, in the pitch dark.

He had picked her up earlier that Friday evening outside the Mayfair production offices and they had driven through appalling M40 motorway traffic, Stanhope saying nothing to her as usual, just blathering endlessly into his phone, swearing at people all over the world. As they crawled along the elevated section she had fallen asleep. Woken by cold and stuffiness in the car, she was utterly disoriented.

The interior light came on as she opened the door, its faint glow showing her that the car was parked on a gravel drive in front of a very large house. As she stepped into the cold night air, a bright security light was triggered by her body heat. She knew immediately that she was outside the front door of Landgate House, home of the De Courcey family for eight hundred years, so they claimed. Gresham thought it was a dump, built as it was in the uninteresting Oxfordshire flatlands that surround the Thames. There was a ruin of the original castle at one end of the house, used for three nights a year by an awful Shakespearean theatre company who did dreadful productions of *A Midsummer Night's Dream* with a thirty-eight-year-old woman playing Puck. Gresham had only had to sit through it once, but that was enough. She crunched across the thick gravel and walked over the drawbridge. Although Landgate was just a house, it did have a moat, fed by the Windrush which went through the land and powered the family mill at the other end of the long drive. She tried the door, a huge oak original, pitted with holes said to have been caused by Parliamentarian musket balls during the Civil War. It was locked. Without hesitation she hammered on the ancient wood with both fists, then got hold of the large ornate brass bell-pull and wrenched at it with all her might. After about thirty seconds, she heard a voice, muffled behind the door.

'Who is it?'

'Me! Gresham. I'm freezing!'

The sound of bolts being undone accompanied some shouts and whispers from behind the door. It swung open and Gresham was immediately engulfed in a wealth of warmth and the rich smell of furniture polish. She looked around the large hall as she stormed inside. No one there except servants and Stanhope's awful younger brother Piers.

'Where's Stanhope?' she demanded.

'Crashed,' said Piers calmly.

'He only left me sleeping in the Range Rover. What a prick. Am I really going to marry that man?'

'Apparently,' said Piers with a sly smile.

'And you can piss off, you little toad,' said Gresham as she passed him on the stairs. 'Which bedroom is he in?' She aimed this question at Mrs Tifford, the servant who had opened the door.

'The green one, ma'am,' said Mrs Tifford, making more mental notes of the scene than she would be able to convey in one sitting.

'Green one, right, which one is that?' said Gresham testily.

'It's okay, Mrs Tiff, I'll show her.' Piers slowly climbed the stairs, his feet clad in yellow socks, a family tradition. The De

Courceys were the only boys at Eton who could wear coloured socks. You could always tell a De Courcey, and much as Gresham decried their stuffy manners and old-money charm, she secretly hoped that one day she would bid farewell to a handsome son, off to Eton wearing yellow socks.

Gresham followed Piers along a wide corridor. Large, dark paintings of men on horses adorned the red silk walls; a hand-woven carpet ran its length, covering huge, ancient, creaking floorboards.

'How's school, then, twathead?' asked Gresham.

'Not bad, nearly finished,' said Piers, barely pronouncing any consonants, his words flowing lazily together behind his protuberant front teeth. If he kept his mouth shut Piers was quite a good-looking boy, but out of the De Courcey boys he had inherited the clearest example of the family's genetic identity. Huge buck teeth, no chin, hollow chest, gangly legs and strangely large genitals.

'Got loads of essays to write. Bit of a bore. How's your film?'

'Awful,' said Gresham. 'I've been looking at it all day trying to work out how to cut that useless American bitch out. Trouble is, it's supposed to be her story, so it's a bit tough.'

'You mean Nona Wilfred,' said Piers. 'I've always found her rather attractive.'

'She's so cheap. She's a tramp, a tart. She'd shag anyone, even a little faggot like you.'

'Oh, Gresh, you really are the limit,' said Piers with a slow laugh. Gresham thought he must be stoned. His eyes were red-rimmed and he could barely walk.

'Here's the red room,' he said.

'Mrs Tiff said he was in the green room, you pillock.'

'Oh, yah. Sorry. We walked the wrong way.'

'What is it with you De Courceys?' asked Gresham as she took Piers by the arm and marched him back down the corridor. 'You're so thick. How come you've got so much money?'

'Ah yes, well, that's easily explained, Gresh,' said Piers. 'You see, I'm doing history A-level. Fr'instance, did you know we're all Normans?'

'I'm not,' said Gresham.

'Aren't you? No, don't suppose you are. You're a bloody pleb, but the De Courceys, Normans through and through. Came over with Billy the conk apparently, killed a load of Saxons, stole their land, money, gold, castles, anything and everything.'

'And you've still got it,' said Gresham.

'More or less,' agreed Piers.

'Roll on the revolution,' said Gresham.

'Green room.' Piers pointed to another door. 'Fancy a spliff before you crash? I've got some wicked South African grass. Apparently it's quite cool to have it these days.'

'No, I do not fancy a spliff. I fancy a shag.'

'Oh, don't know if I should oblige on that score.'

'Not you, toerag. Your dong-brained brother!' said Gresham with a laugh, thinking that maybe one day it wouldn't be such a bad idea to curl up with the amorous Piers, once he'd filled out a bit. He was rather good-looking if he kept his teeth inside his face.

'Fair enough. Sleep tight,' said Piers, and scuffed off down the corridor. Gresham opened the door of the green room and went inside. The lights were off; it was utterly still. She crept across the room relatively silently until she stubbed her toe on a large and unforgiving piece of ancient furniture.

'Ouch! Shit! Why am I creeping about anyway? Wake up, you selfish toad!'

There was some grunting and humphing in the bed and a small bedside light was switched on. Gresham stared at a man she'd never seen before.

'Who the hell are you?' she said with genuine alarm.

'Ah, you're Gresham, aren't you,' said the man, handsome and rugged, slightly too well manicured.

'Who are you?'

'Steve. Sorry, we've not been introduced. I'm a friend of Stan's.'

'Where is Stanhope?' asked Gresham. She couldn't bear the thought of marrying someone called Stan.

'Oh, golly,' said Steve. 'As far as I know, the red room. I think that's where he said he was going.'

'The red room! Why don't they just have numbers? What is it with this family, with this awful house? What am I marrying into? You know what happened to me? Eh? I don't care if you don't care, I'll tell you anyway. Stanhope left me sleeping in the car, that's what. I couldn't get into the house!'

'Oh God, I thought I heard something,' said Steven.

'It was me hammering on the door. I could have died of exposure.'

'That's terrible,' said Steve. 'Mind you, this place is so big the IRA could blow up the west wing and as long as you were in the east wing you'd never know.'

He was being too nice. Gresham had sensed it immediately he switched the light on. He should have been angry, being woken in the middle of the night by a stranger. He also didn't have that look, the one she was so used to with men. He looked at her kindly and openly, but with no lust, and lust was a language Gresham was fluent in.

'Yeah,' she said. 'Okay, I'm off to the red room. G'night.'

'Sleep well,' said Steve with a well-cared-for smile.

As Gresham's head hit the Liberty's linen pillowcase, Stanhope De Courcey, one day to be the 18th Duke of Weymouth, elder son of the family and theoretically in line to inherit a fortune estimated to be near one hundred million pounds, entered from the small bathroom and collapsed next to her.

'Sorry, sweet,' he muttered as he curled up with his back to her. 'Must have been something I ate.'

'Oh, are you okay?' she asked, ready to tear him off, but there was no reply, just a deep snore.

The conservatory at Landgate House was, as the old duke constantly reminded his guests, one of the largest private glasshouses in the country. Gresham entered at 8.30, fresh out of the bath and looking ravishing in a simple white suit. It was the first piece of non-black clothing she had worn for three years. It felt good.

'Oh, out of mourning at last, dear,' said her mother, not quite kissing either cheek. Gresham's mother, the painfully thin Alice Hollingford, was, despite her appearance, as strong as an ox.

Her father, Sir Roger Hollingford, was reading the *Independent*. He was deeply engrossed, as he had always been. She bent down to kiss him. 'Hello, Daddy.' He dropped the paper on his lap and looked up.

'Just been reading about you, you clever girl,' he said warmly. 'This film of yours is getting a hell of a lot of publicity.'

'I just hope it's all worth it,' said Alice.

'Of course it's worth it, Mummy. It's called hype.'

'Oh, goodness.'

'It means that all the punters have heard about the movie before it hits the screen and then, when it's a smash, I might finally get some recognition in this stupid industry.'

'I just hope you're right, dear,' said her mother. 'Have you had any breakfast?'

'No. Have you seen Stanhope?' said Gresham as she peered under the silver tureens of kedgeree and bacon. She piled food on to a plate and sat down next to her father.

'I don't know how you keep your figure if you eat like that, dear,' said her mother. 'You're not on drugs, are you?'

'Yes, Mummy, I'm a junkie,' said Gresham, sitting down and stuffing toast in her mouth. 'I sell my body on the streets to pay for rocks of crack cocaine. Now where's Stanhope?'

'I think he's gone out shooting with his pal,' said her father. 'I saw them heading off this morning, car full of dogs and guns. Never appealed to me, to be frank. He'll be back soon, I'm sure. What time is lunch?'

'God knows. Some old servant will come and tell us. It's like being in a bloody hotel here, a deserted one.' Gresham took another mouthful of kedgeree. She looked at her parents; they looked uncomfortable and a little tense.

'Look,' she said, almost feeling sorry for them, 'this is really terrific of you. I know it's a bore but it has to happen. You know. Tradition and everything.'

'This is what's so surprising, dear, you of all people wanting a traditional wedding.'

'Well, I can't see the point of faffing about. If you're going to bother you may as well go the whole hog.'

'Hear hear,' said her father. 'I've met old De Courcey. He's a charming fellow. Bit doddery now. Are they actually here, darling?'

'I don't know,' said Gresham, pouring herself some coffee. 'I got here pretty late last night. Didn't see anyone.'

'Neither did we,' said Alice. 'Still, it's a lovely house.'

A woman entered the room wearing a black dress with a white apron.

'I say,' said Sir Roger with a charming smile, 'are the duke and duchess anywhere to be found this morning?'

'They're still in their rooms, Sir Roger. I expect they'll be down presently.'

The woman delivered a fresh coffee- and teapot and walked away with no more than the rustling of synthetic cloth to mark her passage.

'What a perfectly odd family,' said Alice. 'They invite us here for the weekend, then utterly ignore us and leave us to rattle around in this glorious old house. It really makes no sense at all.'

Sir Roger smiled and turned to his radiant daughter. 'So, Gresh, do tell, how's it all going?'

'Oh God!' said Gresham, throwing her head back. 'You don't

want to know. Some prick at Channel Four is asking for final cut and they only put in a million. The distributors are kicking up a stink about the merchandising and they've only landed me in it by bringing the premiere forward to May, and we haven't even started a primary dub. I mean, it stinks, doesn't it? Allied Fountain are going down the pan. I'd sell my shares now while the going's good.'

'D'you know what she's talking about, dear?' asked her mother.

'Not a clue, but doesn't it sound exciting. And how's your, um, how's Eupheme?' Her father cast a glance at his wife.

'Fine. Prattling on about the underclasses as usual,' said Gresham, not wishing to talk about the boring Eupheme.

'Now, now, dear. That's not very nice,' said Alice.

'Well, she is a prattler, always having a go at me. Jealous as all hell basically, but what can you do?'

'Try and be nice, dear, she's not as lucky as you.'

It was one of Gresham's lifelong sub-skin grits that her own mother always defended her annoying half-sister. Eupheme and Alice hardly ever met. Alice didn't have a clue what Eupheme did and wasn't interested, but she would always remind Gresham how lucky she was and how she should be nice to Eupheme.

'I think she's fallen in love with a train-spotter,' said Gresham with some pleasure.

'Really? What on earth is that?' asked Alice.

'A saddo, an anorak, a puke merchant who writes down the numbers of trains.'

'D'you know what she's talking about, dear?'

'Haven't got a clue.'

'A man who plays with himself in public, Mummy.'

'Oh, good heavens above,' said Alice, looking away as though she were going to vomit.

'I thought she was in love with this sculptor fellow in Italy,' said Sir Roger. 'The drunk one with the hair.'

'Oh, Richard,' said Gresham. 'No, I think he's been given the old Spanish.'

'Who's the old Spanish?' asked Alice.

'Spanish archer. Oh, come on, Mummy. Raise your game. El bow.'

'El bow. Oh, Spanish archer. I see. That's terribly clever, dear. Is that in your film?'

'No, Mother. That would be very naff.'

'Oh, I see. I think.'

Stanhope entered the conservatory at a pace wearing a green shooting coat, mud-spattered corduroy trousers, yellow socks and a collar and tie. He was a little over six foot, dark-haired and devilishly handsome. Two glistening blue eyes surveyed the room with speed.

'Bloody hell, aren't Ma and Pa down yet?'

'No sign of them, Stanhope. Good to see you, young man,' said Sir Roger, standing and shaking hands with him.

'Yeah, great,' said Stanhope. He spun on his heel and held on to his thick mop of expensively cut hair. 'Bloody hell, I'm really sorry, I'd never have gone shooting if I'd known they were going to be such a bunch of wankers. Has anyone seen Piers?'

'Has anyone seen Gresham?' said Gresham.

'Bloody hell, Gresh. Didn't see you. God, you look gorgeous. Sorry about the car and all that last night.'

'Oh, what happened?' asked Gresham's mother, who, owing to her distant Italian ancestry, was never one to miss a bit of drama.

'I drove Gresh out here last night. She crashed in the car,' said Stanhope.

Gresham's mother drew an involuntary breath.

'He means fell asleep, Mum,' said Gresham, picking up on this. 'Stanhope still lives in the Seventies. It's a wonder he doesn't call this house a pad.'

'Yah,' laughed Stanhope quickly. 'So I really didn't want to wake her when we got here so I thought I'd make sure her room was warm and everything, then come back and carry the wee damsel across the old threshold.'

'Only you forgot and left me to freeze to death outside.'

'I don't know what happened. I was talking to Piers and Steven and then I woke up and it was this morning. I was utterly shagged. Same as you, darling. I'm truly sorry.'

'What an adventure,' said Alice Hollingford with a fixed smile.

'Very funny, though. You caused a right old rumpus when May let you in.'

'Is that Mrs Tifford?' asked Gresham, covering her mouth with mock embarrassment. 'Was it the swearing?'

'Oh, fuck, no, she's used to that. I think you just frightened her to death when you stormed through the door. Ghosts and what have you.'

'Good for you, girl,' said Alice.

'You're lucky I didn't beat the shit out of you, you great lanky wazzock,' said Gresham. She slid her arms around Stanhope's long neck, pulled herself up his awkward frame and kissed him.

Lunch was in the long gallery, 120 foot by 40, with a high and impossible-to-heat hammer beam roof. It was a cold, uncomfortable but impressive experience eating there.

The meal was a formal affair. It was officially a family gathering to allow the Hollingfords and the De Courceys to become acquainted, and as the engagement party was to be at Sir Roger and Lady Alice's London home the families had decided to spend the weekend together at Landgate.

They sat around an enormous table, ancient and polished to a mirror finish. Huge silver and porcelain pieces loaded with slightly overcooked vegetables were spread formally along its length. Bottles of wine and water, candelabras and small silver serving dishes made the table look cluttered and busy.

Three servants waited on the seated party, dishing up a very traditional lunch of thin soup, cold meats, new potatoes and greens followed by a hot steamed pudding and custard.

Gresham hated every minute, and during a particularly noisy anecdote told by the goofy Piers, she leaned towards Stanhope, smelling his dusty shoulder and delighting in it.

'Stanhope, you know when we're married and we come here at the weekend.'

'Yes, darling.'

'Can we try not to recreate the school canteen? Can we try and use something crude and nouveau and terribly down-market called imagination when it comes to eating? If I have another mouthful of British stodge I'm going to puke all over your mum.'

Stanhope laughed into his napkin, and slid his hand along the length of her thigh.

Gresham smiled. This little intimacy did much to reassure her. She was sitting opposite Steven, the clean man she'd met the night before in the green bedroom. He was delightful and charming but terribly discreet. She found out nothing about him during lunch.

Stanhope's mother, the Duchess of Weymouth, did not truly possess the grand appearance her title indicated. She was a short, grey-haired old lady rather than a duchess. She wouldn't have looked that out of place sitting in Row 7 of the coach on a Darby and Joan outing to Bournemouth

The duke, on the other hand, was a chip off the old block, see the family resemblance, strong genes, don't you know. Marvellous. Gresham pondered her role in all this. She didn't like the idea that her job was to carry on the genetic line of this awful family, even if she did feel rather attached to one of them. It was as if the women were just pots the next generation grew in. She could almost picture a baby Stanhope, like his dad in every respect from day one. The paintings on the walls of the house helped underline it. Continuity, certainty of position, clarity of background. No scrabbling around the birth, marriage and death registers of far-flung churches for this family. Their history surrounded them, very real, solidly built and still worth a fortune.

The old mother stood outside this wonderful legacy to the nation. It was as if she'd been brought in merely to serve a function. She had little input into the gene pool; she was a carrier for the future generations of the family. Neither of the sons looked anything like her and they were both almost mirror images of their father. Would that be Gresham in forty years' time? She was quietly chilled by the prospect.

'Well, I'd like to say a few words,' said the duke, standing up at the end of the table. His teeth were also protuberant, but not to the degree of young Piers.

'Oh, bloody hell,' said Stanhope. 'Don't go on too long, Pa. We want to try the new Range Rover through the mud, don't we, Piers.'

'Yah. Rather,' said Piers.

'What perfectly dreadful boys you are,' said the duke with little feeling. 'I do hope y'know what you're marrying, m'dear.'

He smiled kindly at Gresham. She smiled back.

'Well, we're all here today for a little celebration of our own. I know you'll be having a very grand ball next month in town, but I just wanted a little family tête-à-tête this weekend. I know I'm speaking for Grace when I say we are delighted to have been blessed with such a stunningly beautiful daughter-in-law. Stan's a lucky fellow and no mistake, so here's the very best to you both, and let's hope this whole affair doesn't go the way of the bloody awful royals.'

To a subdued cheer of approval, the company raised their glasses and toasted the couple, Gresham Alice Oriel Hollingford and Stanhope Vivien Seston Osall Hubert De Courcey.

'Hear hear.'

Chapter Eleven

'Up in the front with the judge's cup,' said Ian, staring into the mirror carefully. The average English-born ear would detect the slight regional variation in delivery with little difficulty. Not quite London cockney, not quite Birmingham, a slightly sharp vowel sound, which *in extremis* would make 'hello' sound like 'allow'. Ian almost said 'Ap in the frant with the jadge's cap', but not quite.

'Up, up, up,' said Cicily, craning her neck, making it even longer than it had appeared at first sight, which was uncannily long. To the same English ear, which at this time belonged to Eupheme Betterment, Cicily's voice defined her with the utterance of one simple word. Up.

Her 'up' said everything about her — the care with which she'd been raised, the expense of her dental work, the time she'd had at her disposal to perfect her diction. 'Up, up, up,' she said perfectly, 'up at the front ...'

'Up at the front,' said Ian. His 'up' still had a tinge of 'oop' about it.

'Better,' said Cicily. Eupheme smiled. She was making a difference. Ian was improving. She was so lucky to know all these wonderful people. She and Cicily had shared a dormitory together at Bedales. Cicily always longed to be an actress — she was wonderful in the school production of *Hedda Gabler*. She got into the Central School of Speech and Drama, fell in love with an American student, went to New York, had her heart broken, came back, fell in love with an Australian ballet dancer, went to Sydney, had her heart broken. This pattern was repeated another dozen times to Eupheme's knowledge, until Cicily gave up and started teaching voice at Central and the RADA. Through her contacts she became a voice teacher and dialect coach to actors the world over. She continued to fall in love with the very worst men, but no longer allowed it to ruin her life.

'Now listen, try saying it as though you were chewing toffee.'

'Come again?' said Ian.

'No, don't say come again, say, I'm sorry?' said Cicily. 'Did you hear how I said that, back in the throat, back, back, back. Far back. I'm sorry?'

'I'm sorry?' said Ian, imitating her better than Eupheme would have imagined possible.

'He's got a good ear, darling,' said Cicily, turning to her. 'But his monothongs are terribly sloppy. Pit, pet, pat, pot. All those are terrible. He needs to keep a pen on his tongue while he's practising.'

'How do we do that?' asked Eupheme. Cicily reached up and held Ian's jaw open, then placed a ballpoint pen on his tongue. 'Right, now when you speak, you'll feel your tongue trying to move. I want you to become aware of when it moves, and try and move it more. D'you understand?'

Ian nodded without making a sound. He did look rather tragic, Eupheme thought, standing almost to attention, doing everything the ravishing Cicily told him.

'After me, say articulatory agility is a desirable ability.'

'Aaahh,' said Ian, who then coughed rather violently.

'You see, the tongue is almost dead, just a great slab lying there. This is what we've got to work on, Ian. Did you hear how I said that?'

'What? I mean, I'm sorry?' said Ian.

'How I said Ian. You'd say Ee-yun.' she wrote it down on a pad of paper resting precariously on the crowded table. 'Ee-yun.'

'I s'pose so.'

'Well, in RP, that's received pronunciation, posh talk, you'd say iYaan.' She wrote "iYaan" on the sheet. 'Now say, Hello, my name's iYaan.'

'Hello, my name's eeYaaan.'

'Better. Did you hear that, Pheme?'

'Wonderful,' said Eupheme, beaming with pride. Ian was standing up straight, although he'd been told to relax, in the small front room of Cicily's tiny cottage on Flask Walk in Hampstead. The room was decorated in the Laura Ashley bomb blast school. Heavily patterned cloth and wallpaper were splattered about the place like blood, bone shard and brain tissue on the inside of an Alfa Romeo after a Mafia hit. Eupheme didn't feel comfortable there. The room was cramped and stuffy. She was wearing a cream skirt and boxy jacket from Nicole Farhi, plain and cool. She liked to think of herself as plain and cool, not fussy and chintzy as Cicily had always been. She knew her flat was in a worse mess, and it wasn't even her flat, and she hadn't paid the gas bill, the electricity bill, her mobile phone bill or the council tax bill. She knew that although Cicily never threw anything away and lived in a jungle of mess, she always paid her bills.

Eupheme felt a wave of depression approaching as she reflected momentarily on the never-ending chaos of her life, then glanced around the room again, looking for escape. The room was frankly a nightmare. Cicily was wearing great sweeping drifts of cloth which were clearly meant to be a sort of all-in-one dress. Her eccentricity always had been at the limit of Eupheme's tolerance.

'After me,' said Cicily, her eyes locked on to Ian's. 'Articulatory agility is a desirable ability manipulating with dexterity the tongue, the palette and the lips.'

Ian took a deep breath, concentrated on his tongue and dived in. 'Articulatory agility is a desirable ability manipulating with dexterity the tongue, the palette and the lips.'

'Marvellous, much better,' said Cicily. 'Could you hear the difference, Pheme?'

'Yes, but it all sounds a bit forced,' said Eupheme.

'Oh, it will for a bit,' said Cicily. 'It's all about tongue-tip muscularity, that's where the secret of RP lies, and then, once he's got it, he's got to let it go. Ee-yan, yah, oaky,' she added in a very far-back, county sort of way. 'It's no good if you use the minor tones, smunching all your words together.' She repeated his exercise phrase, running all the words together sloppily and imitating his accent with amazing accuracy. Ian laughed; he was clearly charmed by her. Eupheme noticed herself experience a moment of jealousy. She pushed it to one side by concentrating on the problems at hand. She wanted to know everything so she could continue Ian's training at every opportunity.

'He's so good. Such a hard worker. I wish some of my awful actors were half as dedicated. Plenty of time in front of the mirror, Ian, lip-rounding and lip-spreading.' She showed him what she meant in the reflection of the enormous gilded mirror that hung over the crowded fireplace.

'You think he'll improve once he relaxes a bit?' asked Eupheme.

'Oh yah, definitely,' said Ian, using a surprisingly good, far-back and plummy voice. The two women laughed, not looking at Ian but at each other as if to congratulate themselves on training a puppy to sit.

As Cicily showed them to the tiny rose-bedecked door when their hour was up, Ian stood out in the bright sun, looking at the passing crowds as they paraded along Flask Walk. Cicily held Eupheme's forearm and smiled broadly.

'Where did you find him?' she asked slyly.

'Ian?'

'Yes, he's a dreamboat!'

THE MAN ON PLATFORM FIVE

'D'you think so?' Eupheme noticed her mood lighten. It could have been the sun on the back of her neck. It could have been the fact that someone else had agreed with her at last about Ian's good looks.

'Oh God, Pheme! Come on. He's gorgeous, and so charming.'

'Charming! Ciss, if only you knew!' said Eupheme.

It had been a painful hour for Eupheme. For a start she was supposed to be at work, and listening to Ian's awful accent in that confined room had made her realise how hopeless the absurd task she'd set herself was. She desperately needed to talk about what she was doing with someone. Cicily stood there, so gentle, so trustworthy, so unlike Gresham.

'Look,' she said, 'you can keep a secret, can't you?' She checked to see if Ian was near. He seemed absorbed, staring into a small bow-fronted shop on the other side of the street.

'You know I can,' said Cicily.

'Okay, Ian's a train-spotter.'

'A what whatter?'

'A train-spotter. He's a nerd. An anorak, an autograph hunter.'

'I wish I knew what you were talking about,' said Cicily.

'Look,' said Eupheme, brushing her hand through her hair like her half-sister, 'you know I had that thing with Nigel Planer a few years ago.'

'Lovely voice. Naturally funny,' said Cicily.

'Well, I met him in the Pacific a couple of weeks back and Ian asked for his autograph.'

'Oh, that's so sweet.'

'Ciss, it's not sweet. It's bloody awful. But listen, that's not the half of it. Oh, I don't know where to start.' She took a big breath, 'The whole reason behind all this ... Look, you must swear not to tell. Okay? I'm having a wager with Gresh, and you must keep this quiet, but I'm having a wager that I can pass him off at her engagement party as a PLU.'

'I don't believe it. That's so exciting!' said Cicily. Not the reaction Eupheme had been expecting at all. It left her without words. Cicily jumped into the silence with a broad smile.

'Oh, Pheme, you're so brave. Only you would even think of doing that. I don't claim to understand why really, but it's so exciting. He looks wonderful. I'm sure you'll win.'

'You should have seen what he used to look like. I've spent hundreds of pounds on that. Thousands, actually.'

'Oh, Pheme. Brilliant. Is the bet for absolutely stacks?'

Eupheme paused for a moment, confused. It made perfect sense that the bet should be for a fortune, but it was for nothing. She ran her hand through her hair again as another wave of disbelief-based panic swept through her. What was she doing? Finally she said, 'I'm not doing it for the money, Ciss. The wager is Gresh will pay me all my expenses if I pull it off. If she thinks he's okay by the time of her party. It's the principle, Cicily. Gresh says that there's no hope of changing people. You know how she is – foul-mouthed fascist bitch, basically.'

'Pheme, she's not!' said Cicily with a shocked laugh. 'And anyway, she's your half-sister.'

Cicily knew both girls well, had always felt sorry for Eupheme, who on the surface seemed the softer, more sensitive one. Gresham, however, as Cicily knew, was very scared and far more fragile.

'Gresham's a hope vacuum,' said Eupheme. 'She always has been. She said he was useless.' She pointed at Ian, who had now turned and was looking at them quizzically.

'She said he was just another punter whose only role was to consume her films and her telly adverts and all her awful friends' rubbish. It's not right, Ciss, and it's got to change. There's still such a big feeling that people are born into their position and that's how it's got to be. It's hopeless if you believe in that. You don't, do you? You teach people to change.'

'Well, if you mean dialect coaching, on the surface I

suppose, but it doesn't change inside. I don't know if you can change that.'

Eupheme grabbed her arm harder than would be expected in their circles. 'You can, with the right stimulus, I know you can,' she said. 'He has changed, Ciss, honestly. He doesn't talk about taxi turning circles any more, or train timetables. He says he'll arrive at about eight as opposed to he'll pull in at Platform Five at oh eight hundred hours. He's changed in so many ways. His outlook has changed because I've shown him other ways to be.'

Cicily and Eupheme hugged, Cicily looking over Eupheme's shoulder at Ian, who stood watching. She smiled her sexiest smile at him. He smiled back, no embarrassment, no shyness, just honest open contact.

'She's very nice,' he said as they walked down Hampstead High Street together. His voice did sound different; he seemed to be doing the exercises Cicily had shown him as he was walking.

'Ian, please don't use "nice",' said Eupheme. 'Please say wonderful, fantastic, amazing, weird, dull, but not nice. Cicily is not nice, she's a very talented and wonderful woman, although she is a bit of a dippy old hippie.'

'She's very kind, she's very gentle,' said Ian, searching for words. 'I really liked her. I suppose most of the women I know are a bit on the boring side.'

'Please don't say "a bit on the boring side, or a bit on the interesting side",' snapped Eupheme. 'Say boring or interesting. Or say a little dull, actually.'

'What, I can say actually?'

'Yes, actually, you can actually.'

'Okay, I was going to say, actually, that most women I meet are either totally dull or really, really bossy.'

'Never use bossy.'

'Oh, right, bossy's bad, is it?'

'Naff.'

'Naff, okay. Some women I know are really ...'

'Dominant?' suggested Eupheme.

Ian nodded. 'Dominant. Yes, dominant. Socially, I mean. Not dominant in a kinky way – you know, sort of 0898 leather basque, down on your knees and lick my kinky boots. Hu hu.'

'Sorry?' said Eupheme, utterly confused.

'Well, dominant at work and that. You know, lady boss and all. I've had them, and I don't mind that, but every now and then ...' He paused to see if Eupheme would pick him up on that; she didn't. 'Every now and then, you meet someone who is a little more sympathetic to you. Naturally when this happens you feel attracted to them.'

'What? Did you fancy Cicily?' snapped Eupheme.

'Well, I don't like using the word fancy,' said Ian, smiling broadly, 'but I haven't finished.'

'What are you talking about?' Eupheme was very short with him.

'Okay. Actually, Eupheme, some people might interpret my attraction to a sympathetic woman as being a reaction against dominant women, but I don't think that's the case. I think that at some time a very dominant woman will meet a partner who fits in with them, and then she, whoever she is, won't be ever so dominating with that particular person any more because they'll see they don't really need to be.'

Eupheme had listened to what he said. She stopped and turned around, looking back up the hill. She had walked past the Nicole Farhi shop without looking in. She had listened to Ian talking and it was interesting.

'Please don't say ever so,' she said quietly as she stared into his eyes.

'Okay. Ever so is out.'

'Thank you,' said Eupheme. She put a hand on Ian's neck,

pulled at him a little. He bent down slightly and she kissed him softly on the cheek.

'That was brilliant,' she said.

Ian stood up straight and threw his shoulders back. 'Jolly good,' he said. 'Let's have some lunch, actually.'

Chapter Twelve

Ian spent nearly two hours getting to Reading; train from Northampton to Banbury, change for Oxford, train to Oxford, change to the main London line stopping at Reading. Then a taxi ride to the large Besco administrative headquarters at the entrance to Hambourne development park, a greenfield site outside the town.

On the journey he read *GQ*, *Time Out*, *Esquire*, *Premiere*, *Loaded* and *What PC*. The first five had been given to him by Eupheme to study and memorise. He bought *What PC* in the station thinking he wouldn't spend that long reading all the other magazines. As it turned out, he didn't touch *What PC*. He rapidly became engrossed in all the media gossip and reports on new films, interviews with really famous people, pictures of stars at glamorous parties. Pictures of stunning-looking women who made films, were in films, who took their clothes off for money. Rich people who laughed at the camera and enjoyed their lives.

Ian thought of the pictures of him in the old red cloth-bound family photo album that rested on the thin pine shelf above the television in the front room. He wasn't laughing in any of them; smiling politely, but never laughing. It wasn't that he didn't laugh; he did, but it seemed rude to do so when someone was pointing a camera at you. He wondered how all famous people seemed to know how important it was to laugh when being photographed. They looked good when they laughed. They looked strong and happy, maybe even laughing at everyone else who had jobs and died of diseases. Laughing at mere mortals.

As he gazed at the computer-enhanced layout, he knew that although he had met someone who seemed to inhabit this world, he would never play a part in it. He might be allowed to see it for some time, peek in through the door, but he was born on the outside and felt happy there. It wasn't a sad feeling, it was a very realistic and reassuring feeling. What it was, however, was undeniably a feeling.

Ian Ringfold was aware that he was having feelings for the first time he could remember. It wasn't that he'd never had them before. Ian knew he wasn't a robot, much as he'd like to be one occasionally. It was just that spending time with Eupheme had tickled him into realising that many feelings were in there, waiting to be felt. She had somehow made them less scary. When his father died and the world was inverted and went nauseous for a while, Ian searched around desperately for things that would take the feelings away. Anything outside would do, anything outside him. Model railways, *Men Only* magazine, computer magazines, remote-control model off-road cars, mountain bikes. Anything but the Aunts, the strange people with posh accents who came to talk to him, his mum making breakfast as normal and then the two of them sitting there in the small living room with the empty chair. It wasn't suddenly quiet, as his father had rarely spoken, but his absence was colossal. Ian read his magazines. Now, after all these years, Eupheme had arrived, out of the InterCity, and had lifted a blanket from him, a warm, safe, unchanging blanket, but as she did so new feelings had come up which seemed to make his shoulders expand, his mind reach out and want to embrace the world, not protect himself from it.

'Ian Ringfold, to see Mr Farthing,' he said to the smart receptionist. The entrance lobby reminded him of a large building society, very new and clean. He noted that the woman was using an Epson 2300, linked to the company mainframe. A huge and super-powerful computer; he briefly imagined a flight simulator that fully utilised the power and graphic-detailing abilities of such hardware. Would that he had the funds.

As he was shown into Mr Farthing's office, it briefly occurred to him that he might now, owing to promotion, have the funds, but hand in hand with this realisation came a more shocking one. Did he really need a new computer? Did he need one at all?

The office was overlooking a small ornamental pond and rock garden that sat in the centre of the building. Dull windows looked on to this rather sad and remote spot; there didn't appear to be any doors giving access to it.

'Ian, hi, John Farthing, sit you down, sit you down,' said Mr Farthing, who, to Ian's surprise, was possibly younger than he. 'Great to have you on the team. Glowing record. Well done, mate.' he continued, sitting back rather grandly in his red high-backed office chair. 'Really, I'm just here to help, you know. I'm always on the end of the line if you get in a log-jam or whatever. So, you're going to be area distribution manager for . . .'

'Northampton north,' said Ian, trying to be on the ball and helpful. 'Try and be on the ball, love,' his mother had said, and he was. He was wearing his best Next shirt and his Donna Karan suit, his Tricker's shoes and for some reason a pair of yellow socks that Eupheme had bought for him from the Gap store on Hampstead High Street. He had questioned yellow, wondering if it was a good colour for a classy man to wear. Eupheme insisted she knew best when it came to yellow socks.

'That's the place. Now, car. We can only, I'm afraid, offer the one point four Fiesta at this stage, but it's the new model, top of the range, goes like shit off a shovel, so I've been told.'

'That's wonderful,' said Ian. 'It's a very economic model

which is a big tick on the old plus side in my book any day of the week.'

'Absolut-omento,' said Mr Farthing. 'Now, your main task is to see that the total delivery package is running smoothly. You've got how many stores in the area?' He was tapping his keyboard and moving his mouse.

'Um, four, I think,' said Ian.

'Spot on. Right, with a combined average turnover of, what ... one point two million a week. So we're looking at a very healthy area. What's the competition like?'

Farthing clicked his mouse. Ian racked his brains.

'Well, there's a big Sainsbury's. There's two Asdas, three Safeway's and a massive new Tesco.'

'So, Marketing have clearly been doing a great job. With competition like that, we clearly haven't been sitting on our backsides. But you know, Ian, how important it is that we keep the products on the shelves. People have only got to find that there's no reduced-sugar strawberry jam one week and they'll go round saying, "Oh, they never have what I want at Besco's".'

'It's a side of the business which has always held a great interest for me, Mr Farthing.'

'Call me John, please,' Farthing said with a slight wince, as though Ian should have known better.

Ian nodded. 'Stock control and product display. Multi-containerised delivery systems. Sending a message out by computer and seeing a lorry-load of reduced-sugar jam arrive just in time to restock those shelves. That's what it's all about really. I'm fascinated by systems and love the struggle to improve them.' Ian had been rehearsing this line on the journey.

'Well, this is what we thought, Ian. Yes indeed. We said to ourselves, Let's be frank, Ringfold is not a people manager, he's a systems manager, which is in effect what you are now. That's not to denigrate what you do in any way, shape or form. No way, José. So we said to ourselves, For goodness' sake, let's not waste this talent, let's put it to good use. Up the old wages and pension package, throw in the car, set our Mr Ringfold on the fast track to achieving his goals. So now, everybody's happy.'

'That's great,' said Ian, wondering why they had decided he was no good for people management. He thought he got on very well with people; maybe he needed to hone his people skills. Suddenly he heard another voice in his head. The term 'hone people skills', which he had used without thought, suddenly sounded 'naff'. He realised the voice in his head was Eupheme's and it was, as he had always experienced it, critical and unforgiving. But he felt uncomfortable; something had changed. The engulfing, protecting reassurance he had always felt from being accepted within the corporate structure had started to slip away.

Mr Farthing handed him a large glossy brochure. 'Besco Superstores, Internal Ordering and Distribution Systems. A Technical Breakdown.'

'Thanks, that's great,' said Ian, feeling, for some inexplicable reason, a lump in his throat. Technical breakdowns were Ian's bread and butter. Understanding how systems operated, especially ones as complex and carefully managed as Besco's, was something that had always occupied the greater part of Ian's worktime thought. He shook himself a little, trying to throw off the feeling.

'Is there any chance,' he asked, 'I could have a look-see at the old AMDAHL five double nine five?'

'Not a problemo, Ian, my friend,' said Mr Farthing. 'It's in the basement. Not a great deal to look at from what I recall, but I expect you'll understand a hell of a sight more than yours truly.'

'It's just that I've been pumping data down the old ISDN line for so long now, I'd love to see where it gets crunched.'

'Follow me,' said Mr Farthing, and they walked from his office, along a corridor that absorbed all noise as far as Ian could make out, through some double doors and down a stairwell.

At the base of the stairs was another set of doors, very

substantial ones. A card swipe was attached to the wall to one side. Mr Farthing pulled a card from his shirt pocket and swiped it. The door thudded open and immediately Ian could hear the low rumble of a hundred cooling fans. They entered a brightly lit room where the noise level was quite high. A man was sitting at a desk with a large screen in front of him. The screen was so heavily strewn with dialogue boxes that Ian couldn't make out what programme he was running.

'Ian wants to see the old AMDAHL,' said Mr Farthing.

'There it is,' said the man, pointing to a box only a little larger than a domestic washing machine.

'Blimey O'Reilly,' said Ian. 'Two hundred and sixteen million instructions a second. Amazing.'

'There's faster,' said the man at the desk.

'No way, José,' said Ian.

'Yes indeed. In Denver there's a commercial computer used by some mail order giant, running at damn close to five hundred MIPS.'

'Stone me. Think of the power,' said Ian.

'Pretty soon there'll be a machine this powerful in every store, linked up by fibre optics. I reckon by the time someone touches product on the shelf, it'll be reordered.'

'Fantastic,' said Ian.

'What field are you in?' asked the man.

'Oh, just a humble old area distribution manager,' said Ian.

'Nothing humble about that,' said the man. 'I used to be one myself. Gives you a great grasp of the whole system. No point sitting here if you don't know a can of peas can still fall off a lorry, no matter how fast you've reordered it.'

'Absolutomento,' said Mr Farthing. 'Okee diddly doodly, we'd better get a shift on. Bit of a seminar upstairs, by all accounts.'

'Nice to meet you,' said Ian, shaking hands with the man.

'Good luck,' the man said with a friendly smile, and then

turned back to his monster computer. Would that he had the chance to work there, thought Ian.

Lost in a confused haze, Ian followed Mr Farthing through the plush, quiet corridors of head office and into a seminar room. There were ten other successful applicants to the company's internal promotion scheme already seated. They looked up and smiled at him. Ian smiled back but felt hugely uncomfortable.

A woman in an unpleasant-looking light blue suit entered and took up a position next to a wall-mounted wipe-clean chart.

'Good morning, everybody, I'm Janet Dailey. I'm an independent systems consultant, seconded to Besco's for the duration, and I'm here to give you the rundown on how we keep this show on the road.'

Ian picked up something about her voice. Her vowels had a sharpness that jumped out to the English ear. New Zealand, that was where she was from, although he could tell she was trying to cover it up. She talked for hours, using, he noticed, an Apple Powerbook 3400c laptop computer linked into a video projector to give computer-generated visual demonstrations of how the system worked.

Everything that happened in the small airless room was, as he would have put it, right up his street. However, all the way through the seminar the lump in Ian's throat got bigger and bigger. He didn't feel sorry for himself, he didn't hate the woman giving the seminar, he didn't hate the company. He just felt sorry for everyone, making all this effort, and for what? To finally, at the end of the day, when all was said and done, put a jar of marmalade on a shelf. He choked back a sob and ground his new teeth.

Chapter Thirteen

'The Ocean restaurant, Albemarle Street,' said Eupheme, throwing herself into the seat. The taxi pulled out into Upper Street's clogged traffic.

'Bit of a hold-up at the Angel,' said the driver.

'Fuck,' said Eupheme. She was determined to get to the restaurant before Ian to watch him and see how he coped with the slightly haughty staff. She had one week to go before the party. She was living on a knife-edge at work as Ian was taking up every available spare moment. Her flat, Geoffrey's flat, always a disastrous tip, was becoming positively dangerous. So much rubbish and mess; she had barely spent any time awake there in six weeks. She arrived late, bathed and slept and left before breakfast. Mountains of laundry littered the hall and she'd just had an e-mail at work from Geoffrey to say he was returning from Washington for a three-week stay.

Everything was going wrong.

Griff Rhys-Jones had pulled out of the benefit owing to filming commitments. She only had Hugh Laurie and Eddie Izzard confirmed; she still didn't have a definite booking for a band, although Robson and Jerome looked hopeful. She'd had interest from a Channel 4 production company who wanted to film everything, but that had gone quiet. The International Children's Trust was in a state of crisis. Apart from the fact that it had minuscule funds to help the many projects it had started around the globe, it had absolutely nothing in the bank to pay the staff. To Eupheme personally this wasn't such a huge worry; she had a private income, a discreet but adequate fourteen thousand a year from a trust fund set up by her father. However, Kevin and Christine had no such fortune behind them and were very anxious about the future.

All these worries crowded Eupheme's head as she sat in a stationary taxi, watching the little red figures slowly mount on the meter.

She tried to think positively. She started listing her achievements, imagining her mother, in one of her more sober moments, sitting at the kitchen table in Hove, writing out the list in her elegant longhand.

'You see, darling, it's not so bad,' she would say, and take a quick nip from a whisky glass.

In the previous five weeks she had indeed transformed Ian from train-spotter to minor hunk. This was the only thing that gave her hope. Her secret project was going ahead well. Although, of course, it was not so secret with all the office gossip and Ian's endless stream of pointless, badly typed e-mails. That was the problem with e-mail. As Eupheme saw it, anyone could read it, and she knew Kevin did. She also knew he was so scared of her he would never mention it to anyone. The latest message had read:

Eupheme. i could video your show if you like, with my sony 3 ccd camera i can work in low light situations no probs. broadcast quality with the right edit equipment, would that i had the funds. see you at the jim love ian.

He had started putting 'love Ian' at the end of his messages. What did he mean? Christine was fascinated and wanted to see the transformation with her own eyes.

'He does look pretty amazing,' Eupheme had said in the office, looking over her shoulder surreptitiously to make sure Kevin Waslick wasn't in earshot. She always had to check his e-mail account during the rare moments when he was out of the room. She had become quite a dab hand at going on-line, grabbing her mail and leaving.

'You've got to let me see him,' Christine said. 'I can't believe you've really gone and done it.'

'No one can see him until he's ready,' said Eupheme. 'At the party, that's where he's being unveiled.'

'That's not fair. There's no way I can go to the party.'

'Of course you can,' said Eupheme. 'I'll make sure you're invited.'

'Oh my God,' squealed Christine. 'Brilliant! D'you really think she'll let me?'

'She's got no choice,' said Eupheme emphatically.

She proceeded to spend a week leaving messages and sending faxes to Gresham, who had disappeared off the planet into her editing room. Eventually she received a very ugly-looking hand-scrawled fax which said simply: 'Bring who you fucking like!'

She had seen Ian on three occasions a week, usually two mornings and one evening to fit in with his work schedule. They went to the gym twice and out to a film or play in the evening. She gave him a large carrier bag of material to read – paperback books, glossy magazines, articles she'd clipped from newspapers, all with one thing in mind. To make this man interesting.

He seemed to absorb it all with little difficulty, just as she had suspected. He wasn't 'thick' or born to consume dross, as Gresham would have it. With only a little encouragement he had blossomed beyond her expectations.

She also knew that there was some part of him, a large part of him, that she never got near. He seemed completely self-contained, never asked for anything, not even his train fare.

He always offered to go halves when they ate out, offered to pay his fees at the gym. She never let him. She enjoyed his company, and now he was beginning to sound right, to look right; in fact, to look very good indeed. There was no point denying it, Eupheme was beginning to like him.

After half an hour and an £18 fare she got out of the taxi in front of the Ocean restaurant.

One glance through the window told her that Ian was already there, sitting at a table reading *Palimpsest* by Gore Vidal. He looked gorgeous, looked like he belonged. His clothes fitted him well. His body had changed from a sagging second-hand plastic bag to well-built, chunky boy meat. He was lightly tanned and well cared for. His hair glistened with Paul Masson hair gel; his shirt, £68 from Thomas Pink, fitted him well. It was all stuff she had bought him, but he looked right in it.

He was oblivious of her, sitting engrossed in the book. She looked around the large interior of the restaurant – it was busy but she didn't spot anyone she knew. Suddenly her eyes fell on two women eating together. One of them was looking at Ian with that look. The look Eupheme knew so well. The 'he would do' look. The woman nudged her friend and nodded in Ian's direction. Her friend turned a little and stared, her eyebrows raised momentarily. They fancied him. They thought her train-spotter was a bit of all right. She had done it.

'Hi, sorry I'm late,' she said as she sat down next to him. He leant forward and kissed her on the cheek. She was taken aback, but pleased. She smiled to herself as she flashed back to a few weeks previously. He'd never have kissed her; if she'd kissed him he'd have assumed she immediately wanted sex. He was bound to have done. And she'd have been hugely embarrassed if he had tried to kiss her in public. People would have looked at her and wondered what she was doing hanging with a nerd.

'No problem,' said Ian, carefully placing his book on the

table and taking a sip from a tall glass of sparkling mineral water. 'But I do have something to tell you.'

'Wait. Little test!' said Eupheme. 'Who wrote *My Beautiful Laundrette?*'

'Hanif Kureishi,' said Ian instantly.

'Who starred in *One Flew Over the Cuckoo's Nest?*'

'Jack Nicholson, based on a book of the same title by, um ...'

'Come on, quick-quick, like you were born with this information in your head.'

'By, um, an American writer. Now what was his damn name.' Ian sounded different, confident; his voice was deeper. 'Ken Kesey.'

'Correct. Who directed the film *Casino* and who was in it?'

'*Casino,*' said Ian, rubbing his chin thoughtfully. 'Fantastic Scorsese film, starring De Niro and Sharon Stone, very well made with a simple but dazzling style. A story of greed and drug-induced madness. Tragic and heroic. Naturally a very Hollywood picture but powerful nonetheless.'

'Excellent,' said Eupheme. Cicily's work had paid off. He sounded wonderful – confident, good tonal quality to the voice. Plus the information was perfect. The hours studying *Premiere* magazine, old copies of *Time Out*, the hundreds of movie reviews Ian had downloaded from the Internet – all this new information Eupheme had demanded he cram into his head had finally had an effect. He was sitting well; although she had only managed to get him to three Alexander lessons, his posture was so much more becoming.

'Now, what did you have to tell me?' she asked. 'And it had better not be about a computer or a railway train.'

'I've resigned. I've left Besco's. I couldn't do it any more. I don't have a job.'

'Oh,' said Eupheme, trying to assimilate this information. 'Can I ask why?'

'I started to get a lump in the throat.'

'Are you sick?' asked Eupheme, suddenly genuinely alarmed.

'No. I got a lump in the throat from being unhappy. A sort of emotional reaction, actually. I got promotion, a greatly improved pension package and a car. The Fiesta one point four, in-car stereo, CD player and digital mobile phone. I didn't want it. I wanted to go back to trolley supervision, which is where I started, but you can't go back. You've shown me that. You can't go back.'

'No, I don't suppose you can,' said Eupheme, trying to work out what to do.

'I've basically destroyed my life. I don't know what to do. I haven't even told my mum. I've got eight hundred and seventy eight pounds in a savings account, with the Woolwich, high-interest jobbie.'

'Don't say jobbie, Ian.'

'Sorry. I've got about two hundred in my NatWest current account, and I've got a Visa card that stands at zero, with a seven-hundred-and-fifty-pound credit limit. I just thought I'd tell you so you know what sort of position I'm in.'

'I see,' said Eupheme.

'I suppose I'll have to sign on,' said Ian.

'No, you don't have to do that.' Eupheme did some rapid mental arithmetic. 'I'll make sure you're all right, until the party.'

'Next week.'

'Yeah.'

'But I'm not saying this so you'll give me money. I don't want charity, thank you very much indeed.'

'Try not to say thank you very much indeed like that, and anyway, I'm sure you'll find another job soon. I'll help if I can.'

'D'you think I'm ready for the party?' asked Ian, smiling as best he could.

Eupheme looked to her left. The two women she had spied from outside the restaurant quickly turned away. They had been checking out Eupheme to see what was going on.

'Yes, Ian, I think you are.'

Chapter Fourteen

According to the three hundred and fifty gilt-edged invitations Gresham and her mother had sent out, the party started at eight. At 7.30 a fairly large number of what Gresham would term the sadder elements of the family were already in attendance. Her father's more distant relatives did stretch to what Gresham saw as the distinctly low-rent sector. Aunts and uncles, badly dressed and lumpy, old Grandma Serafino, who sounded horribly like Beryl Reid. She hoped no one important spoke to them. She was tense and uncomfortable, sitting on the huge blue sofa in the elegantly and very modernly decorated house in The Boltons where her mother and father had lived all her life.

She looked at Stanhope in the corner, on his mobile phone talking to one of his dreadful business people. He never stopped working; she hardly ever saw him. He was usually on the phone when she was with him. She knew he worked in the City but she didn't really know what he did. She scanned the room scornfully, smiling to herself when she remembered how she had discovered at around the age of fourteen that if she was as rude to people as she felt like being, nine times out of ten they came back for more and gave her what she wanted.

She spied her cousin Janet. Her father's side, no class, bottom drawer. Gresham laughed to herself as she said her cousin's name quietly. Janet. Janet was a secretary in the City.

She even had permed hair and she worshipped the ground Gresham walked on, which for Gresham meant the self-same ground immediately lost its value. At her father's birthday party the previous December, Janet met Stanhope and flirted with him quite tragically. Gresham found this behaviour particularly pathetic, although Stanhope responded politely.

Steven, Stanhope's friend and business colleague, was also there, looking a little odd in his very fitted evening dress with his bright yellow patterned cummerbund. His hair slightly too neat, too short, his body somehow more on display than the other men's. He was obviously gay, which was fine – half the people Gresham worked with were gay, but they were out, outrageous and obvious. It wasn't clear what Steve was into. She knew Stanhope had known him since they were children and Steve's father was someone somewhere, but it sounded dull and to do with banks. Maybe he was a Coutts or Hoare's or something. She couldn't remember. The room was filling.

Piers arrived early too, in the company of a very pretty young debutante called Helena, and two lanky lads with sweaty foreheads and eager grins.

'Fantastic to meet you, Gresh,' said one of them as he shook her hand. 'God, we've heard so much about you from Piers. I really loved "*Down on Me*," by the way.'

'When did you see that?' snapped Gresham quickly.

'Piers had it at school,' said the young man. 'We all watched it. Brilliant film, Gresh. What's your new one like?'

Gresham ignored the overly confident seventeen-year-old and looked around for Piers. He was nowhere to be seen, and the entrance hall was filling up with arriving guests.

'If you see Piers,' said Gresham, holding the young man's arm fiercely, 'tell him he's dead.'

'Fantastic,' said the boy with a wide-eyed smile.

Gresham found herself standing next to Stanhope in the entrance hall for nearly an hour as people poured through the large front door. She knew she looked utterly stunning in a skin-tight black minidress that showed off her figure to a staggering degree. She had spent half an hour in a complete panic trying to prepare herself for the evening. She'd been in the edit suite all day, grabbed a taxi back and threw herself in the bath as soon as she got home. She'd managed to have a haircut the day before. She'd had it cut very short – she knew it suited her and it was less trouble. However, as she stood in the doorway surrounded by adoration and social excitement, she was trying to come up with a way to re-edit the disastrous final scene of her film.

'Gresham, darling,' said Ruby Wax as they embraced. 'You bitch, look at you. Gorgeous.'

'You look dazzling too, dear,' said Gresham genuinely.

'Oh yeah, dazzling like a twisted, demented gargoyle,' said Ruby with her glittering smile. 'Where's that husband of yours?'

'Not my husband yet, darling,' said Gresham grandly.

'Oh, he will be, he's got no chance. You know Eddie.' Ruby gestured to a tall slim man with a beard. 'Eddie thought he had a chance, but I got him.'

'It's true,' said Eddie.

'Your Stanhope is almost taller than my Eddie,' said Ruby. 'I don't think I like that. I like to have the tallest husband. It says something about a woman, don't you think?'

'Definitely,' said Gresham. 'Coats over there, booze in the drawing room, food out in the garden.'

'Fantastic,' said Ruby. 'I've always wanted to see your dad's house.'

Ruby and Eddie disappeared into the throng. Gresham turned and saw her half-sister Eupheme, looking very well prepared. Not like her to make the effort, and surely standing there arm in arm with her was a very handsome, very attractive, very good-looking young man. He was over six foot, a lovely thick mop of slightly curly dark hair, wonderful eyes which seemed to look right into her. A quiet smile that made something tweak in Gresham, a mouth to die for. He licked his lips slightly as she looked at him and the tweak became a twinge. He was gorgeous.

Not like Eupheme at all to be with someone so yummy. She was normally dragging round some grey-haired no-hoper, a socialist historian or an overweight, sexually dubious comedian in a crappy suit the wrong colour for the occasion. The two women hugged.

'Hello, Pheme,' said Gresham. 'Glad you made it.'

'Congratulations, Gresh,' said Eupheme genuinely. 'You got him at last. Well done, honestly. I'm really, really pleased for you.'

They held each other at arm's length. Gresham was almost moved. She had known Eupheme all her life, and yet this was one of the very few times there had been genuine affection between them.

Eupheme introduced the man beside her. 'This is Ian, by the way.'

'Hi.' Ian shook hands with Gresham. Good strong hand-shake, nice big hands. The tan looked a bit fake but who cared.

'Hello, I'm Gresham,' she said to the big-handed man. 'It's my party. I'm marrying that.' She pointed at Stanhope, lanky and laughing as he listened to Ruby Wax's hectic banter. She looked carefully at Ian as she said this, watching for a hint of disappointment on his face. She got one, she was sure of it. He minded that she was marrying someone else. He was definitely interesting, she thought. The first man who'd done anything for her since Damen the cameraman. Other than Stanhope, of course, who was different.

'Very ... good to be here,' said Ian. Gresham noticed he seemed to have a little trouble speaking. Was he foreign? It somehow made him all the more attractive. She fancied him, instantly. She wanted to know more about him.

Janista Torrens, a minor actress Gresham had used in

her film, was pushing towards her; she had to delay her inquisition.

'There's drinks through there. Someone will look after your coat,' she said. She gave Janista a quick peck on the cheek and then spotted Piers De Courcey wandering around on his own. She moved away quickly, trailing what was meant to be a friendly arm in her wake, and zeroed in on the hapless Piers.

'You little oik, have you got a copy of my film?' She pinned him against the wall. It looked like fun but her grip was for real.

'Oh, Gresh,' said Piers, pushing back his thick forelock of curly hair. 'Yah, I meant to tell you, it's fantastic.' He looked at her and smiled.

'I don't want anyone to see that film!' she hissed. 'It's rubbish, I did it when I was a student. If that got out now it could really do a lot of damage to my work. You bloody idiot! Where is it?'

'Under my bed, in a locked chest. Gresh, it's totally safe.'

'What, under your bed at home?'

'No, at school.'

'For Christ's sake, Piers. You moron! I want it back and I want it back bloody soon, or so help me, I'll break your legs. I mean, actually break them with a lump hammer when you're asleep. All right?'

'No probs,' said Piers, smiling and revealing his stupendous teeth. 'By the way, super party.'

Gresham shoved Piers against the wall as if they were children playing. His head hit the bottom of a framed print of a large Victorian building. He winced and rubbed his head, the smile still managing to stay on his face. Gresham stormed down the bustling hallway, constantly ignoring men in dinner jackets trying to get her attention.

'I say, Gresh old thing . . .'

'Gresham, you must meet my brother . . .'

'Gresham, we're having a party next weekend. Do come!'

In the conservatory at the back of the house, people were standing around eating off plates balanced precariously on palms of hands, wineglasses barely gripped by fingertips while heads listened earnestly to myriad conversations. People laughing, talking, scoping the room to see who was there. Gresham entered and all eyes were upon her, not something she relished. Actors must be weird people, she thought, actually wanting this experience of exposure again and again. Gresham found it distinctly uncomfortable. She didn't mind one man looking at her, a man she liked, she was used to it, but huge crowds ... How could actors do it?

She spotted Eupheme and her partner near the buffet table. The man stood out, tall and lean. Thank heavens she didn't bring the train-spotter.

'Hi, Pheme,' she said as lightly and happily as she could. 'Sorry I couldn't talk more out there. It's bloody mad, isn't it? Half these people are Stanhope's dreadful City friends. Well, ghastly acquaintances, I should say. Bankers, and I use the word advisedly, and everyone a bore. Christ, you're not a banker, are you, Ian?'

'No, I'm presently unemployed,' said Ian.

'Oh, brilliant. That makes a change. We don't have to talk about your dreadful boring work. I thought for a moment you might be a lawyer or a doctor or something staggeringly dull like that and we'd all have to talk about court cases or lumbago.'

Gresham could feel her pulse racing. She was flirting; she hadn't flirted since she was a teenager, never got the chance. Every man she ever met always wanted to have sex with her, marry her or run away with her as soon as she spoke to them.

'No, not at all.' Ian smiled. A tiny bead of sweat ran down his cheek. He took the handkerchief from his breast pocket and mopped his face.

'Bit on the warm side in here,' he said.

'It's bloody boiling,' said Eupheme quickly.

'The doors to the garden are open,' said Gresham. They followed her through the crowded room. Normally a pair of huge sliding glass doors separated the garden from the conservatory; with them fully open the family had a social gathering space close to the size of a football pitch.

'What a garden,' said Ian, looking up at the floodlit trees billowing above their heads.

'Yes, Dad's quite good at this sort of stuff, isn't he, Pheme?' said Gresham. Eupheme nodded and started to say something. Gresham jumped in. She wanted to keep Ian's attention a bit longer. 'He is an architect. It'd be a bit sad if he lived in a shit-hole.'

She watched him laugh. He had a lovely smile. His eyes wrinkled as he looked at her, his head slightly to one side. She felt her heart flutter and wanted to put her hand on her chest but knew it would look naff.

She stood back and smiled painfully. The dreadful Christine Hanks grabbed Eupheme by the arm as she passed. She was wearing a huge yellow frock. She'd had her hair done, wore more make-up than Gresham had ever seen, and she was still managing to blush through it. A small mountain of food was piled on to her plate, which slowly fell off on to the patio as she talked.

'Eupheme. Hi!' she said. Eupheme gave her a kiss on both cheeks.

'Hello, Christine. You know Gresham.'

'Hi, Gresham, it's so nice of you to invite me. It's a lovely house. You're ever so lucky to live here.'

'Thanks,' said Gresham flatly.

'This is my friend Ian,' said Eupheme, introducing Christine to the tall man.

'Oh my God! I mean, hi there,' said Christine as she shook his hand. More food tumbled on to the floor. 'Oh, look at me, butter-fingers!'

'Hello,' said Ian graciously. Gresham looked at him from the side; he looked good. Strong chin.

'I've heard so much about you,' said Christine. She turned to Eupheme and said, 'He's bloody gorgeous.'

'All right, Christine, you can go now,' said Eupheme with a slightly strained laugh.

'Sorry. I'm a bit on the sozzled side,' said Christine. 'I've just met an absolutely dishy millionaire banker. I'll see you later.' Her large hips cut a swathe through the garden as she headed back inside the house.

'So glad you brought her,' said Gresham flatly. 'She brings so much to a party like this.'

'Oh, she's all right. Leave her alone, you stroppy bitch,' said Eupheme as lightly as possible.

'My half-sister,' said Gresham, turning towards Ian, 'is what one would classify as the clichéd bleeding-heart liberal.'

'Is that so?' said Ian with a gentle attentive smile.

'Yes. She surrounds herself with no-hopers, present company the obvious exception.'

'Thank you,' said Ian.

'Lovely ladies like Christine or sad old alcoholic sculptors, I suppose it's so she can feel better about her own lowly position in the world.'

'I don't think she holds such a lowly position,' said Ian. 'With all her marvellous charity work.'

How romantic. He was standing up for her. She'd soon show him. Gresham felt a huge need to embarrass her half-sister, who was standing there looking smugger than she'd ever seen before, and 'smug' was Eupheme's middle name.

'You'll never guess what she did ... well, tried to do,' said Gresham with a laugh.

'What?' asked Ian.

'She saw some tragic case, I mean a pitiful sight on a train station somewhere like Leicester.'

'Gresh,' said Eupheme quietly.

'I know you're bloody embarrassed about it, Eupheme, and so you should be,' Gresham said, momentarily acknowledging her half-sister. She turned back to the big-handed man. He stared at her with a slight frown across his forehead. 'She'd forced me, Ian, me, to catch a bloody train! So I was stuck with her and the lovely Christine and, oh my God, if she didn't start one of her numbers.'

'Gresh, I'm sure Ian doesn't want to hear this.'

'She saw a train-spotter, Ian,' said Gresham, forcefully ignoring Eupheme. 'A tosser, a tragic anorak. Ugly as sin, a spot-ridden hopeless case, pebble glasses, bugger's handles, the works. You know, BO to generate electricity with, a hand-shandy expert *par excellence* as my future husband would say. And Pheme, bless her, my dotty, demented, New Labour half-sister, claimed she could nurture him, this sad act, she could sort of educate him and reconstruct him into someone I would fancy. As if!' she said, impersonating a Californian Valley Girl. 'I mean, as if!'

'I see,' said Ian. He turned to Eupheme, who seemed to have gone very pale. 'Is this true?' he asked.

'Sort of,' said Eupheme, wringing her hands together nervously. 'I mean, it's more complicated than that.'

'Seems like an odd thing to do,' said Ian, with, as Gresham noticed, a slightly different accent.

'Well,' said Gresham with a laugh, 'we're both a bit crazy, aren't we, Pheme? We agree about nothing, but for some perverse reason, we get on.'

'Yes, it's very perverse,' said Eupheme. 'Ian, could you get me a drink, please? I'm parched.'

Ian stood staring at Eupheme for a moment, then nodded quietly and walked off.

As soon as he was out of earshot Gresham grabbed Eupheme's arm and said, 'Pheme, who is he? Jesus, girl, seeing you with a half-decent man is a shock, but this one's a dreamboat. Where did you find him?'

'Milton Keynes train station,' said Eupheme angrily.

'Oh yes. Like hell. No, really, he doesn't work for your charity thing, does he? Is he a doctor?'

'A doctor! D'you really think he could be a doctor?' squeaked Eupheme.

'I don't know. Tell me, who the hell is he?'

'He's Ian Ringfold. He's the train-spotter, the tosser. He's the man on the platform in Milton Keynes.'

'Bollocks,' said Gresham after a moment's reflection.

'I've won the wager, Gresh. I did it. You fancy him. He's the train-spotter.' Eupheme opened her small evening purse and pulled out a printed sheet. She danced around in a small circle, punching the air. She looked very stupid.

'I've done it. I've done it,' she said. She held the paper in front of Gresham. 'Here are my expenses. I'd be very grateful if you'd settle up soon as you can. See, I've run up quite a bill.'

Gresham took the bill and glanced at it. An A4 sheet with a closely typed list. She didn't bother to check the total, it was all too annoying.

'Oh, bollocks, Pheme. D'you think I came down with yesterday's rain? That's some bloke you know who you've just ... Bollocks. He doesn't look anything like the saddo on the platform.'

'Not that you'd remember anyway,' said Eupheme. 'He was too dull for you to look at. Look, I don't care what you think. You can ask him when he comes back. I didn't actually intend to reveal it in front of him because he doesn't know what's going on, but what the hell. I've won!' Eupheme repeated her annoying little circular dance. People standing near them turned and smiled at the odd spectacle. Gresham smiled at them fiercely. Eupheme stopped dancing and gave Gresham a hug. 'I'm sorry, Gresh, I shouldn't gloat, but it's been a really tough time for me. It's such a relief. Really.'

'Oh, Pheme,' said Gresham, now just beginning to wonder

if what she was saying was true. 'You can't expect me to fall for that. Look, if you're that broke I'll pay you anyway. What the hell. But that man was not the train-spotter.'

Christine Hanks came walking across the garden at quite a lick.

'Look out,' Gresham whispered unkindly, 'she might run us over.'

'Hi!' Christine said loudly. 'He's left, then.'

'Who?' asked Gresham.

'Ian,' said Christine. 'I just saw him slip out of the front door.'

'Oh, shit,' said Eupheme.

'Very convenient,' said Gresham. She turned and smiled at Christine. 'She expects me to believe he was the sad act from the train station.'

'He was,' said Christine.

'Yes, of course, you would say that. Have you really gone to all this trouble, hired some male model . . .'

'Male model!' said Eupheme and Christine in unison.

'Well, whatever, just to try and show me up. It's pathetic, Pheme. It really is. Look, the bloke on that station platform was about five foot five, a fat, ugly bastard with pebble glasses. He was a dirty old wanker and you expect me to believe, for one second, that the dish you came with was the same bloke. People don't change that much, Eupheme. They really don't.' Gresham pulled her chin in and laughed patronisingly.

'It was him!' hissed Eupheme. 'It was the same man.'

'It was, honest, Gresham,' said Christine.

'He's been to the gym, he's had a haircut,' said Eupheme enthusiastically. 'He never wore pebble glasses. That's just you stereotyping like mad. You don't even see people, not really see them, you just see a series of comfortable clichés, and you call yourself a film-maker. Ha! You're a bigot, a narrow-minded bigot, which is great, actually, because you're marrying another one, so you should be very happy.' Eupheme stood looking at

Gresham. A huge red blush had spread across her chest and neck; she was breathing deeply. 'Now, I want my expenses and I want them now.'

'I'm not paying. It wasn't him so I've won.'

'You have not!'

'It really was him. Honest,' said Chrstine. 'Eupheme's spent ages with him. He's had elocution lessons, he's learned how to talk, he mustn't say "ever so" and all sorts of other things. He's learned to talk about films and books, he's learned how to stand up straight with Alexander something.'

'Technique. Alexander technique,' corrected the fuming Eupheme.

'Yeah. He doesn't wear an anorak any more and he knows not to ask famous people for autographs. Oh, that reminds me, actually he did ask someone for an autograph just before he left.'

'Did he? Oh no. Who?' said Eupheme quickly.

'That nice one who's in the adverts with the odd-looking one. He's doing the benefit.'

'Hugh Laurie,' said Gresham.

'Did Ian ask for his autograph?' spat Eupheme.

'Yes,' said Christine. 'I told you. By the front door.'

'Right, let's ask Hugh,' said Gresham.

'Okay, ask him!' said Eupheme. 'I'm not kidding, Gresh. It's him. You're going to have to admit I've won.'

The three women walked swiftly through the crowd, Gresham in the lead with Eupheme very close behind. Christine stumbled after them, spreading 'excuse me's' and 'ever so sorry's' around like cheap confetti.

Gresham saw Hugh pouring himself a drink by the bar.

'Hugh!' she said, and embraced him, kissed him on both cheeks and held his arm.

'Hello, old girl, I . . .'

'Shut up, Hugh,' said Gresham flatly. His face was frozen in a smile. He turned to Eupheme.

'Hello, Eupheme, you look splendid.'

'Shut up, Hugh,' said Eupheme. 'Did a man just ...'

'I'll ask him,' interrupted Gresham. 'Hugh, has anything untoward happened since you've been at this party?'

Hugh looked up at the ceiling. 'Um, well, the delightful hostess and her splendid half-sister told me to shut up in as rude a way as I've come to expect of them.'

'But you haven't been asked for anything?' questioned Gresham carefully.

'Asked for anything? No. Oh, well, some chap wanted the old moniker, for his son apparently. By the front door when I arrived.'

'For his son!' said Eupheme.

'That's what he said,' said Hugh with a smile. 'He wanted an autograph for his son. He's a diplomat or something, lives in Egypt ... or somewhere. His son's a big Jeeves and Wooster fan.'

'A diplomat!' said Eupheme.

'So he wasn't a train-spotter?' asked Gresham.

'Don't think so, but then how can you tell?' said Hugh. 'Train-spotters are so fearfully fashionable these days.'

'Indeed,' said Gresham.

'It can't have been him,' said Eupheme.

'It was, I saw him,' said Christine. 'I'm Christine Hanks, by the way.' She held out her hand and Hugh shook it.

'Hi,' he said. 'So, this is all terribly intriguing. What are you two fighting about now?'

'Was he about six foot, dark hair, blue eyes with one front tooth slightly out of kilter?' asked Eupheme.

'Yes. I would say so, though I hardly glanced at him,' said Hugh.

'Shit,' said Eupheme.

'The bill is all yours, honey,' said Gresham.

'I've not finished yet. It was him. I want another try.'

'Oh, for Christ's sake,' said Gresham.

'Don't be silly,' said Christine.

'I've spent over seven grand,' said Eupheme. 'I'm not stopping now.'

'Seven grand! What on?' screamed Gresham.

'Clothes, lessons, travel, gym fees. My personal fitness trainer isn't cheap. It's all on my invoice.'

'What are you on, girl?' said Gresham, again adopting the Californian Valley Girl accent. 'I'm not paying seven grand for some saddo who still collects autographs.'

'You bloody will when I prove it to you. We've got a deal.'

'Face it. You lost,' said Gresham.

'I did not, you did. You know you did. You fancied him and when you found out who he was you looked like a ghost. He was the train-spotter and you thought he was a doctor. Admit it, Gresh.'

'No,' said Gresham. 'Even if it was him it was a naff thing to do. I can't believe you've been to all that trouble. You're cracked. You know that, don't you.'

'So, are you going back on your promise?' asked Eupheme, her voice shaking with rage.

Gresham stared at her. People were watching; she desperately wanted to humiliate her half-sister as much as possible, but she felt exposed. Now wasn't the time.

'No, I'm not. If it's him, and you can really prove it, I'll pay the seven grand, okay? Is that good enough for you?'

'Yes,' said Eupheme. The two women shook hands.

'Oh no,' said Christine. 'This is awful.'

'I've got the sneakiest suspicion,' said Hugh Laurie, 'that even if you explained exactly what all this was about, I wouldn't understand.'

Chapter Fifteen

'Christine, it's Pheme,' said Eupheme as the early morning sunlight filtered through the slimline blinds into the kitchen of her Clapham Common North Side apartment.

'Oh God,' said Christine Hanks, obliterated in darkness, voice heavy with morning fugginess. 'What time is it?'

'Seven thirty,' said Eupheme. 'I'm sorry, Chris, I know this is outrageous, you must absolutely hate me and I can understand why, but I really need your help.'

'Oh, Pheme,' said Christine hoarsely.

'I just had to ring you. I woke up so angry. Angry at myself mostly. Oh, this is terrible. Shall I ring you back later?'

'What?' mumbled Christine.

'Look, I'll be quick, then you can go back to sleep, poor thing. I need to ask you a huge, really big favour. Could you cover for me today, in the office?'

'Oh, Eupheme,' said Christine, her voice almost cracking with the pain she felt at being woken so early. 'I suppose so. I don't know what to say. I'm still asleep.'

'I'm sorry, Chris, but if I'm going to do anything about it, I've got to act now.'

'Anything about what?' asked Christine breathly.

'I'm going up to Northampton to get Ian and drag the poor man kicking and screaming to Gresham's place,' said Eupheme, the telephone cord now wrapped eight times around her slender fingers. 'I've spent seven thousand pounds making him what you saw last night, although it's not about the money. You know that, don't you? You saw him. He was wonderful, wasn't he? I'm not about to let it all slip. Gresham's not getting away with it this time.'

'But, Pheme,' said Christine with a yawn, 'There's a board meeting at twelve thirty today, isn't there?'

'I know, I know, it's irresponsible,' said Eupheme, her voice low and guilt-ridden. 'I'm torn in two. The trust and Ian, they are both equally important to me. Tell them I'm working on getting the Spice Girls to do the benefit. It's almost true, I met their manager a while ago. Anything, just cover for me, okay ... Chris?'

'Yeah, sorry, I nodded off. Yeah, don't worry. I'll do my best, but you know what it's like when they all get together. It's a bit on the intimidating side.'

'I'm sure you'll manage. You're brilliant, Christine,' said Eupheme, straining to see if her toast had popped out of the toaster. 'A really good friend.'

'He *was* gorgeous, though,' said Christine with a yawn. 'It's amazing what you've done.'

'I know. He's actually rather dishy, isn't he.'

'I couldn't believe it, almost dropped my meal,' said Christine, finally sounding as if she was conscious. 'It's his teeth especially. He's completely different, but the same, if you know what I mean. It was hard to believe he could look so posh and smart.'

'Thanks, Chris,' said Eupheme, relaxing a little. 'You can see I've got to do it, can't you? I'm very aware of all the wrong reasons why I could be doing this, but it is to prove to everyone that this snobbish attitude holds us all back. It's not to do with all the garbage she comes out with about me being the poorer, less good-looking half-sister with thick ankles.'

'Would that I had your ankles,' said Christine sadly.

'But it's not about me, it's about Ian, and about men, and about there being hope that men can change some of their, well, you know what they're like, some of their more negative things, not that I want to judge, but you know, Chris.'

'I know,' said Christine. 'Don't worry, Eupheme, you did win. There's no argument.'

'I didn't win! It's not about winning,' Eupheme almost shouted. 'It's about, well, it's about moving forward, as men and women. It's about growing, moving on to the next level, beyond the antagonism.'

'Sorry,' said Christine.

'Oh God, go back to sleep, you poor thing.'

Eupheme sat on the train alone. It was pulling its way through the grey, wet flatlands of Buckinghamshire – a cement works, the Ovaltine factory, grim-looking brickworks. The mandatory rail-side attractions slid past damply. Eupheme found the silence she was sitting in unnerving – time in which she had to think had come upon her as an unpleasant surprise. She knew why she was doing what she was doing – she had to win the debate. An open debate about everything that separated her from her half-sister. Eupheme knew she had chosen the harder path, the one that was not complacent about the way things were. The path that said things are bad and let's change them, not things are bad because people are stupid and deserve to suffer and be exploited. Her sister had relegated the majority of the human race to the bin marked 'consumer', and Eupheme knew in her guts, in her DNA, that this was wrong.

Ian had already proved her point beyond anything even she had imagined, and working with him had started her thinking along much grander lines. She cheered up as she imagined being dubbed 'the man whisperer' by the press, the woman who changed awful men into wonderful men, not by bludgeoning them with criticism and guilt, sneering at them and deriding them, as Gresham seemed to get great pleasure from doing, but by helping them love themselves and find their real and important position in the world. The world that had changed beyond anything their fathers could have foreseen when one woman burnt one bra on an American university campus in the early 1960s.

After all, that was what socialism was really about, not levelling everyone down, but lifting everyone up. That was the clever trick the Tories had played for all those years, allowing everyone to make a virtue of their stupidity, their crassness and their narrow world-view. Make a virtue and make money out of it – she understood that, was guilty of it herself, but that didn't mean that what she had experienced through Ian wasn't true. People could improve themselves given the right environment.

She could write a paper on it. Maybe she should get in touch with the legion of Labour MPs she knew, half of whom had worked in charities in one guise or another during the bleak years and most of whom were women. Maybe she could get a powerful job in the education department, then she could really change things. Go on *Newsnight* with Kirsty, write bestselling books about men-whispering, so that women all over the world could do the same thing.

The train pulled to a halt in Northampton station. A few people got off and Eupheme blindly followed the crowd through the low early seventies station building. Half the concession stalls were closed down; the place had the air of a disused toilet. On the ugly station forecourt three taxis stood waiting. Eupheme walked to the first. She was the only passenger to take one.

'Seventy-six Cyril Street,' she said, and the taxi pulled out. After a brief journey of which Eupheme took no notice it turned off the main road past a corner adult bookshop with shuttered windows and some feminist graffiti daubed violently across its fascia.

The taxi pulled to a halt and the Indian driver sat motionless. Eupheme got out. She was on a long, low redbrick terraced street. Each house had a front door and one upstairs and one downstairs window. The street was tidy – no litter, only a few cars. She thought she heard a cockerel crow. It was a good, old-fashioned working-class street, like Coronation Street. Everyone would know everyone else. There would be a sense of community in a place like this. Not like London.

She looked around and saw number 76, a light blue door with the paint flaking slightly along the bottom. The windows had impenetrable net curtains hanging in them. Eupheme chewed her lip. This was going to be tough, but she had to do it.

'That's one pound seventy,' said the driver.

Eupheme, who had already withdrawn a twenty-pound note, faltered for a moment.

'I'm sorry, how much?' she asked,

'One pound seventy,' said the driver. 'From the station to hereabouts, it's generally about that.'

'Okay, okay, sorry,' said Eupheme. She gave the man two pound coins. He started to look for her change until she blurted out, 'No, no, keep the change, please.'

'Oh, thank you, miss,' said the cabbie, and without fuss he drove off. As the cab turned the corner, the street was eerily quiet. She looked down the far end and could see a busy main road, but the traffic noise barely penetrated as far as where she was standing. She could hear birdsong; it was almost like being in the country.

She knocked on the door of 76. Nothing. She knocked again. A noise from within. Expecting someone to open it, she stood back from the door out of politeness. Her eye caught a flicker from a curtain in the upstairs window. She looked up but saw nothing. She smiled flatly and waited. Nothing. She was just about to knock again when the letterbox opened.

'Who is it?' came a thin old voice.

'Oh, hello, my name's Eupheme Betterment. I'm looking for Ian Ringfold.'

'He's not here,' said the voice. There was a silence, then Eupheme bent over to see if she could see through the letterbox. She smiled as sweetly as she could when she saw an old pair of eyes staring at her.

'Does he live here, though? Have I got the right address?'

'What's your name again?' said the eyes.

'Eupheme Betterment. Ian may have mentioned me. I'm from London.'

'I can tell that,' said the eyes. 'Hang on.' The letterbox flipped shut. Eupheme stood up, very confused as to what to do.

The door opened a crack, a stout security chain clearly in place. A wizened, liver-spotted hand held the door delicately and Ian's mother's face appeared. Eupheme's eyebrows raised involuntarily as she saw the obvious beauty this face had once borne. No wonder Ian had something special about him if this was what his mother looked like. 'Yes, well, what d'you want with him?' asked the woman, her accent not matching what Eupheme saw. It was similar to Ian's only stronger and with an angry edge. Eupheme couldn't tell whether it was aimed at her or the world in general.

'I just need to see him, have a quick word about a project I'm working on.'

'Making a fool of him, I'll be bound,' said Ian's mother.

'Not at all, far from it,' said Eupheme. 'I didn't think I'd get the opportunity to say this, Mrs Ringfold, but Ian is an extraordinary man, very kind and considerate. I just wish there were more like him.'

'Yes, I'll bet you do,' she said. Eupheme was now sure that most of this old woman's venom was aimed at her.

'Could I ask where Ian is at the moment?' she said. 'Is it possible to see him?'

'He's at work, where he should be.'

'Oh, where's that?'

'Up at Besco's, where else?' said Mrs Ringfold.

'I thought he'd resigned,' said Eupheme.

'I hope not. Goodness me, things are hard enough already without him gallivanting off at all hours.'

'I'm sorry,' said Eupheme. 'I don't mean to be any bother.'

'He looked terrible this morning. I had to give him a damn good shaking to get him up. Coming in at all hours. Goodness only knows what you get up to.' Her frail hand came up to stop Eupheme. 'I don't want to know,' she said. 'I just know you're all up to no good.'

'Mrs Ringfold, I assure you nothing ...'

'No good will come of it.'

'Well, can I ask where the supermarket is?' said Eupheme with a broad smile, the sort she imagined social workers used when faced with a difficult client.

'Wellingborough Road. The big new Besco's, you can't miss it. Huge, it is.'

'Oh, thank you,' said Eupheme. 'And which way is that?' She gestured down the street.

'Up the top, turn right then left on to Wellingborough Road, then it's about a twenty-minute walk.'

'Is there anywhere round here I can get a cab?' asked Eupheme without a thought.

'A what? Sorry?' said Mrs Ringfold.

'A cab, a taxi.'

'What d'you want one of them for?'

'Oh, I see. Well, I thought I might take a taxi. I'm a little pushed for time.'

'The number forty-seven bus goes up the Wellingborough Road, if you want to wait for it. Be quicker walking. What's wrong with you? You look fit enough.'

'Of course. No, sorry, you're right, I'm just being lazy, I'll walk.' Eupheme was backing away, smiling for all she was worth.

'What's your name again?'

'Eupheme, Eupheme Betterment.'

'It's an odd name, isn't it. Quite pretty, I suppose.'

'Thank you,' said Eupheme, suddenly feeling more cheerful. 'Thank you for your help.'

'He'll be busy, mind. They work him off his feet up there.'

Eupheme was now walking up the street backwards. 'I won't keep him long.' She smiled. Mrs Ringfold kept the door open, looking at Eupheme as if she were a strange native encountered in the jungle. Eupheme had felt a desperate need for the old woman to like her. It appeared hopeless. She was clearly seen as a brazen harlot from the big city, and although she would happily have explained why she was doing what she was doing, nothing could be done to change Mrs Ringfold's mind.

She waved at the still-open door when she reached the corner of Cyril Street, then turned and found her way on to the Wellingborough Road. As she walked past the drab shops Eupheme wondered, as she often did when confronted with the uglier side of man's creations, what it was that drove people to build a city like Northampton.

She tried to establish whether it was her own blinkered, privileged, cosseted view of the world. She decided it was and she had no right to judge Northampton in such terms. The dull grey clouds chose that moment to release themselves over the town, and what had appeared to Eupheme as a miserable redbrick maze was now wet, miserable and darker red brick.

She completed the journey that Mrs Ringfold had estimated would take twenty minutes in about thirteen, but that was because for the last three she ran as fast as she could, getting steadily more and more soaked in the sudden miserably cold downpour. Just as she finally saw the Besco sign and the large carpark, a number 47 bus sped past her and the resulting wave from its huge tyres hitting a puddle drenched her completely.

She walked into the store through the huge circular doors which seemed to sense her presence and turn accordingly. She was immediately welcomed by warmth and the smell of freshly baked bread. The store was brightly lit and busy, like any other Besco supermarket; in fact like any other supermarket anywhere in the developed world. Eupheme was not interested in its decor, but she did notice the inhabitants.

They looked somehow different, more lumpy, worse dressed, less well looked after, with more out-of-fashion hair than she was used to in London. Her supermarket, Sainsbury's on Clapham High Street, was full of trendy young people, not all good-looking or healthy by any means, but hip, categorisable. To Eupheme the shoppers in the Wellingborough Road Besco's in Northampton were a sorry breed, not altogether unlike the people she'd seen on Milton Keynes train station when she first met Ian. She walked up to what looked like an information desk. She stood waiting while the woman in front of her talked on the phone. The woman put the receiver down and said with a similar accent to Mrs Ringfold's 'Hello, can I help you?'

'Yes. I'm looking for Ian Ringfold.'

'Oh, right, yes, he's here somewhere. Just a moment, madam. Can I say who it is to see him?'

'Eupheme Betterment.'

The woman picked up a phone, pressed some keys and suddenly Eupheme heard the public address system click into life, not what she had wanted at all.

'Mr Ringfold to contact customer services please.' The lilt went up a notch. 'Mr Ringfold to contact customer services please.' The lilt went down, followed by a rapidly added, 'Thank you.'

'Thank you,' said Eupheme, feeling her cheeks flush horribly. The phone rang and the woman picked it up with a well-practised flourish.

'Yes, Ian, there's Philomeena Better ... sorry, what name

is it?' said the woman, looking at Eupheme with a wide-open face.

'Just say Eupheme.'

The woman was about to say something when clearly Ian said something himself on the other end of the line.

'He's on his way,' said the woman as she put the phone down. Her attention was immediately somewhere else as the chaos of the supermarket engulfed her. Eupheme looked around for Ian. She couldn't see him. There was a young man stacking vegetables but he had a badly dyed blond short back and sides.

'Eupheme, what are you doing here?' said Ian, who was suddenly standing beside her. She stood back a little. He was closer than he needed to be. He looked very different, wearing a white shirt, dark tie and a Besco badge with his name on it. 'Ian Ringfold. Deputy Manager.'

'Hi. I wanted to talk to you, to explain,' she said, the words tumbling out.

'So you came here, while I was working, and I'm already in trouble.'

'Oh, I'm sorry,' said Eupheme.

'You have no idea, do you. Look, by not taking the offered promotion package I've completely blown it.'

'I thought you'd resigned.'

'Well, I wrote the letter, I was going to post it, but then by the time I got here this morning I was bloody glad I hadn't. I've got to see Mrs Philips later. She's not going to be well pleased, I can tell you.'

'Mrs Philips?'

'My boss. The good lady who actually tried to get me promotion as opposed to get me to look a fool at some swanky party.'

'Ian, please listen,' said Eupheme, touching his forearm. 'Is there somewhere we can go?'

'Not while I'm on duty. I've just had my tea break.' He

glanced at his watch. 'I don't get lunch break for another one hour, fifty-seven and a half minutes.'

'Well, I'm soaked through,' said Eupheme, trying to elicit some sympathy from him. 'I've walked here all the way from your mother's house.'

'Huh, that's nothing, I do that twice a day every day,' said Ian.

'I know. You're very fit.'

'Wait a minute. Did you see my mum?' said Ian, looking worried.

'Yes. She was very nice.'

'Oh Christ. You didn't tell her anything, did you?'

'Like what?' asked Eupheme, already feeling guilty.

'About me resigning. She doesn't know anything about all this.'

'I don't think I mentioned it,' said Eupheme, feeling her toes curl up in her damp shoes.

'Oh God. I'm for it now,' said Ian, looking up to the ceiling.

'I just want to try and explain to you what's going on. About what happened last night.'

'I'm well clear on what happened last night, thank you very much indeed.'

Suddenly Eupheme sensed a lump building in her throat and her eyes began to fill with tears. She hadn't expected to be this upset. She looked at Ian; she could feel a tear running down her cheek. Ian chewed his lips and walked away. She was going to sob. Her lungs filled jerkily; there seemed to be nothing she could do. Ian turned and put his finger to his lips, telling her to be quiet. She knew her face must look awful. She covered her mouth with her hand. Ian disappeared behind a stack of Bran Flakes boxes.

He returned a few seconds later with a trolley. 'I'm just showing this young lady to the tinned produce section,

Joyce,' he said jauntily to the woman behind the customer services counter.

'All right, Ian,' said Joyce as she flicked through a mass of dockets on a clipboard.

Ian walked off briskly and Eupheme followed him in her squelchy shoes.

'The only way we can talk is if I show you around the store, and anyway, there's something I would actually like to show you,' said Ian. 'It's the tinned vegetable section, my pride and joy and, interestingly, a display system that senior management have picked on and are introducing into certain select stores all around the country. There's actually been an article about me in *Foresight* magazine, the in-house staff rag they sell us each month.'

'Ian, please, will you listen to me.'

'No,' said Ian, casting a sudden vengeful look in her direction. 'You've come into my store, this is where I work, I didn't invite you, so you listen to me and come and see what I want to show you. Okay?'

'Okay,' said Eupheme quickly. She was frightened. Ian had displayed real anger for the first time. She followed him as he worked his way through the scattered shoppers. He turned up an aisle that bore the sign 'Canned Goods'. He stood with one arm out, gesturing to the shelves. Eupheme looked at them. They had rows of cans, hundreds of them, thousands, stretching into the distance. She shook her head very slightly, desperately trying to think of the correct response. She knew 'very nice' would be offensive. She decided to play dumb.

'What?' she said with a slight smile.

'This is my display system. Stand here.' He took hold of her shoulders and moved her solidly but gently to the side of the shelving unit so that her head was right next to the cans. 'Look along,' he said. She did. She blinked. What she was looking at wasn't a random collection of cans, it was an amazing blend of colours, the intensity of which defied the brain. Sweeping

from the bright reds and crimson of chopped tomato and red
kidney beans, the colours moved through diced-carrot orange,
slowly blending into sweetcorn with red peppers, then fading
into the subtle variants of green of the peas and sliced beans.
It was a mélange of intense colour which completely held her
attention for at least ten seconds. She was suddenly aware of
an old woman in a mauve coat looking at her.

'Is she all right?' asked the elderly shopper.

'Yes, she's just admiring my display,' said Ian proudly. The
woman raised her eyebrows disapprovingly and shuffled off.

'It's brilliant, Ian. I really can't believe what I'm seeing. You've made something beautiful out of something so
mundane.'

'There's nothing mundane about canned goods,' said Ian.
'Blimey, canning organic products is a highly complex procedure
that's taken generations to perfect.'

'I'm sure. No, really. It's wonderful, such intense colours.
And yet when you stand and look at it from here, it's so
normal-looking.'

'That's the skill, you see. Because it's colour-coded, you
just follow your eye. It takes you to very near exactly what
you're looking for. See if you can find haricot beans.' Ian stood
back with his arms folded.

Eupheme laughed and then started walking along Ian's
colour-coded shelves. She was standing near baked beans, a
dull orange. She looked along the shelves and saw a beige
colouring and walked towards it. It was tinned new potatoes
in salted water. Then suddenly she realised. Right next to
potatoes were haricot beans in salted water. A similar colour;
she hadn't even thought where they'd be and when she saw
potatoes she had prematurely decided she was wrong. Then the
haricot beans just emerged from the shelf. It was incredible. She
picked up the can and held it above her head triumphantly. She
turned and saw Ian with a broad grin on his face.

'There you go. That's what I do, Eupheme,' he said flatly.

ROBERT LLEWELLYN

'I don't run charities or make films, I don't hobnob with top people or celebrities. I just help run a big store. That's what I do.'

'I know. I know, and it's brilliant,' said Eupheme, brandishing the tin of haricot beans as proof. 'That's the whole point of what I'm doing, Ian, don't you see?'

'No. I see two spoilt ladies who've had a bit of a set-to in the old ego department and have decided to use some poor old muggins, namely yours truly, thank you very much, as a sort of pawn in the old game of life. I was just a joke to be paraded at a top party. Well, I got Hugh Laurie's autograph and he was very nice about it. I've packed your suit and shoes and shirts up and they will be snail-mailed to you at the soonest convenience. Would that I could give you the haircut back, but there we diddly oh. Okay, now I must get back to work. It was nice meeting you. Bye-bye.'

Ian turned and started walking away. Eupheme followed him and grabbed his sleeve. He spun and twisted his arm, breaking her grip.

'Please, Ms Betterment, I have to work. Now either do your shopping like any normal customer or leave the store.'

'Ian, please. I need you. I need you to help me, please.' Eupheme was again surprised by the force of her emotion. Ian stopped moving away and looked at her, his face set hard against her. Eupheme took a big breath. She knew she could win him round, but she had to tread carefully.

'We won the wager, that's the thing. This is what I wanted to tell you. We won — well, you won. Not that the whole project was about winning, it's not, it's about growing, as men and women. It's about understanding each other better. Now listen, Ian, Gresham thought you were a doctor, don't you see? Her horrible snobbism was turned in on itself. When she saw you on the train station she called you a tosser, a sad no-hoper, she argued that nothing could ever change you, that you were born to be a saddo and a tragic anorak. That's what she said. You heard her last night at the party. She's vile, she's a snob, she's beautiful and she fancied you. You, Ian, she really thought you were cute. She called you a dreamboat and, what's more, she doesn't think you are Ian Ringfold who works in Sainsbury's.'

'Besco.'

'Besco, Besco, sorry. She won't believe me and she won't keep her side of the bargain and it's just not fair. Yes, it may seem to be a stupid wager, but my sister is a powerful woman and she needs to learn some humility. She's always had everything she wanted, everyone she wanted. No one ever says no to her except me. She has always been horrible to me too. She says I have thick ankles.'

Eupheme paused, waiting for a response. There was none. She looked at her feet. All she wanted was for Ian to say that she didn't have thick ankles. Nothing. She took a deep breath.

'All I want you to do is come back to London with me, after your shift. I'm not asking you to miss work. I'll pay, we'll have a meal somewhere sprauntsy and we'll go and see Gresham. You don't even have to change. We'll see Gresham and show her that this is who you are.'

'A saddo.'

'No!'

'That's what you're saying, you want her to see me like I really am. A saddo. So you can both have a good laugh about it.' Ian then put on an alarmingly realistic Cheyne Walk accent. '"Oh, we managed to change a saddo into a cute doctor type. Aren't we clever, but really he's still a saddo." Well, if I am a saddo, I'm a very happy one. Maybe I'm a happo and actually, at the end of the day when the chips are all down, you and your sister are saddos. Really.'

'Half-sister.'

'Makes no difference. Actually,' said Ian with a snide leer. For a moment Eupheme stood rooted to the spot. She couldn't make herself or Ian budge. She had been so sure he'd come with her back to London, she hadn't taken into account the possibility that he might actually defy her so blatantly. No one had ever done that to her before, not when she really wanted them to do something. She hated herself when she put pressure on people to do things, but sometimes, because she was so convinced she was right, she couldn't help herself. Ian's defiance brought up all her greatest fears; it shook her to the basement of her confidence. Her pleading left her body like vomit – it was as if her need for him to obey her was a poison that had to be expelled.

'Please come, Ian,' she blurted. He shook his head. She looked at him, mystified. How could he want to stay there when she was saving him from this drudgery?

'No,' he said flatly. 'Now I really must go. I actually have some real customers to attend to, actually.'

'Please don't keep saying actually like that, Ian,' said Eupheme. She managed to smile although she could feel herself shaking. She decided not to give up; she couldn't give up. 'And please promise me you'll come after work. What time d'you finish?'

'I'm on until four thirty, but I'm not coming. I'm shooting some video for some friends tonight. A pal of mine who's in the RAF has a radio-controlled state-of-the-art sixteenth-scale petrol-engined Hum V all-terrain vehicle. Not that you'd know or care about such things. Scale speeds of over two hundred miles an hour have been achieved in off-road settings. Sounds brilliant. He wants me to shoot some footage for demonstration purposes.'

'Oh God, Ian, please,' said Eupheme, now completely desperate. 'It would be so easy for you just to come and see Gresham. Please. She owes me over seven thousand pounds.'

'I'm sorry, that's not my fault. Would that I had seven thousand pounds to be owed in the first place. I can assure you I wouldn't spend it on clothes, shoes and Alexandria lessons.'

'Alexander. But you look so different. Hasn't anyone commented?'

'Yes, everyone is always commenting,' he snapped angrily. '"Oh, you look nice, Ian" and "Are you married, Ian?" and "I'll have your children, Ian" all the wretched time.'

'Who says this?' said Eupheme, her face breaking into a smile.

'All the ladies here – checkout girls, delicatessen girls and fish counter girls, the ladies over in the bakery section. Doesn't matter where I go, they all chip in and give me their two-pennorth. I've had enough. I can't wait to get back to my old barber's so all the lady folk leave me well alone.'

'But that proves my point again. Oh, Ian, please try and see what we've done.'

'Made my life a misery.'

'I'm sure not,' she said emphatically.

'Oh, well, that's good, then. You're sure not. Well, thanks for nothing. I'm me, here, this is what I do. Now, listen up and listen good, Eupheme Betterment. Leave me alone.'

Ian walked away and was immediately accosted by a shopper, a very large woman with two small children who were both screaming their heads off in the shopping trolley. She wanted to know where they'd moved the washing powder and wanted to complain to the management that if they moved things it meant she couldn't find them which meant her kids cried and when were they getting a crèche like the one they had in Safeway's?

Eupheme was stumped. She stood on the spot until more and more passing shoppers started staring at her. A bedraggled-looking woman holding a can of haricot beans, her hair dank and still dripping, her shoes a broken-down and soggy excuse for footwear. She started to wander towards the exit, worrying mainly about how she would get back to her flat, have a bath and go back to bed. Her bed suddenly seemed a very long way away.

'Have you got a receipt for that, ma'am?' asked a man in a brown uniform with a cap bearing the badge 'Group 5 Securitas'.

'What? Oh, God. Sorry. I don't even want them,' said Eupheme. 'I, um, it was a mistake, honestly, I was just seeing a friend.'

'As you haven't actually left the premises, ma'am, I'll let you off this time, but we do suffer from a fairly high level of theft at this store and we come down on miscreants with the full force of the law.'

'No, of course, I understand. Yes. Truthfully, I had no intention of stealing anything.'

'You're a pal of Ian's, aren't you?' he asked as he gently removed the can from Eupheme's hand.

'Ian. Yes, that's right. Has he told you about me?' she said, suddenly flattered.

'He's mentioned you in passing. Yes. I was wondering, you see, seeing as how you've sort of done what you've done with Ian, I was wondering if you'd be interested in taking on, well, another new client as it were. Being an attractive lady, I'll scratch your back if you'll ... well, as it were.'

'I'm sorry,' said Eupheme, slowly realising what was happening. 'I don't think you've ...'

'I was just pondering as it were on the possibility of us spending a little social time together. A meal, maybe a club. I'm a little more used to the same kind of life as you ... well, a little more than Mr Super-Nerd over there.'

The security guard grinned broadly. His skin was shiny from shaving. The air around him bristled with deodorant and aftershave straight from the supermarket shelves. How could Ian have told this man anything? She was incensed.

'I see,' said Eupheme. 'You want to go out with me, have dinner, some dancing and hopefully some sex.' She stroked her chin and stared at the young man in as scientific way as she could muster. He flushed slightly and nodded, a baby-boy smile breaking out on what had been a stern authoritarian visage.

'No,' said Eupheme, suddenly enough to make him flinch. She turned on her heel and walked through the automatic doors. She heard a muffled 'Stuck-up bitch' just before the rain hit her. She ran for shelter under the awning that covered the rows and rows of supermarket trolleys.

A young black man was standing under the vast glass-and-steel structure that emanated from the side of the supermarket. He was pushing a long row of trolleys towards her. He had a huge rainproof coat on bearing the company logo, but his jeans were street-baggy and his trainers looked nine sizes too big.

'Excuse me, is there anywhere around here I can get a cab?' asked Eupheme.

'A what?'

'A cab.'

The young man pulled a small earphone from his ear and turned towards her. His eyes looked in two completely unrelated directions. 'Sorry? Come again.'

'I'm trying to get a taxi, a cab. Can you tell me the best place to go.'

The man flourished a card from deep within his enormous pockets. 'It's my uncle. He's got a kicking minicab firm. Well reliable. Bell him.'

'Thank you,' said Eupheme as she pulled out her mobile phone and started dialling the number on the card.

'Nikoia F one-fifty. Well nice phone,' said the young man as he passed.

'Is your name Eddie?' she asked.

'Yeah. Who's aksing?'

'You're a friend of Ian Ringfold's, aren't you?'

'Yeah, for me sins. You know what I'm saying?' said Eddie with a wide grin.

'Could you spare me a couple of minutes, d'you think?'

Chapter Sixteen

Gresham sat in the dark. In every respect Gresham was sitting in the dark. The thing about this film, she thought to herself, is it's shit. It's a brilliant story with a brilliant ending, with a brilliant lead actor, Richard, lovely Richard, and it's got this Nona Wilfred, piece of horse dung so-called actress who is so bad that the whole thing falls flat, which could mean that the original script was weak because the female character doesn't work, and maybe Nona isn't so weak after all, which was an even harder thing to admit to.

'It is her, isn't it?' she said suddenly. Simon Langham stopped the Foley machine for the thousandth time that day. The face of the actress froze in mid-sentence, a rather cruel image of her as her eyes were half closed in mid-blink, her mouth slightly open in mid-diphthong.

'Well, she's no Diana Rigg, she's no Emma Thompson, she's no ... well, she's just no bloody good. She'll look great on the poster in that wet-T-shirt shot. The punters will lap it up.'

'What are we going to do, Simon? She sinks it. It's made me want to rethink the whole film. We've cut her out as much as possible and it's still crap.'

'It isn't crap. The funny bits are very funny, the sad bits are very sad, her bits when he's not with her are unbearable, but you've got Keith Allen being fantastic.'

'He wipes her off the screen.'

'Which is just as well. And you have got her tits.'

'I know you like her tits.'

'Well, frankly, without that tit scene, I wouldn't have been able to sit here for the last three months.'

'Thanks for your support,' said Gresham. 'Cheque's in the post, honey.'

As she pulled on her coat, Gresham and Simon swapped stock phrases from their infuriating industry.

'There's no midpoint?'

'They'll pay for the re-edit from their discretionary fund.'

'Where's the Act Two climax?'

'We'll make the money back in *Uncle Roger* T-shirts alone.'

'Funny films just aren't funny.'

'The Brits are coming!'

They had spent five weeks cutting and recutting *Uncle Roger* until it looked like *Auntie Margaret*, and still it wasn't working.

'She's good but she doesn't make me come.'

'The big money walked out of the preview after four minutes.'

'Get me someone like Richard E. Grant.'

All the test screenings, with only the most trusted of friends, had proved their worst fears. No one understood why the love interest was there. It was obvious all the way through that the Richard E. Grant character would have nothing to do with the Nona Wilfred character. The whole story was utterly unconvincing and more or less everyone said, 'It was a pity you didn't get Emma Thompson or Kate Winslet.'

No one understood it except Stanhope, who had sat rapt through the whole thing and praised Gresham to the roof.

'Good God, you are a clever woman,' he said afterwards. 'It's a staggering achievement, keeping all those strands going all the way through. My advice is don't touch a thing. It's quite, quite perfect.'

To which Gresham replied, 'Well, that shows you know fuck-all about film-making, darling, because it's shit.'

Gresham thundered down the stairs at Allied Fountain and saw Graham Walker-Smith, the company boss, standing in reception. She didn't want to see the boss; she had enough going on as it was without having to face the king of old leches.

'Hearing great things about *Uncle Roger*, Gresh,' he said without turning his gaze away from the lovely receptionist, Sally. 'I've just asked Sally if she'll accompany me to the premiere and she seems a little reluctant.'

'No, it's not that,' said Sally, flushed with embarrassment. 'It's just that I've promised to go with Pete.'

'Pete is her boyfriend, Graham,' said Gresham. 'And he's the same age as her, unlike you, you perverted old shagger.'

'Damn, you saw right through me,' said Graham with a smile. 'I'll have to go with my fucking awful wife, then.'

'Sally, I'm going out for lunch. I won't be long.'

'So, Gresh, tell me,' said Graham, putting his arm creepily around her shoulders, 'how is *Uncle Roger* coming along really? Have we got to enter Turkey management mode?'

'I need more time and I needed an actress who could do her fucking job and I needed to have some control over casting and everything that's wrong with the film is not my fault, I just want to make that clear. Now I am late because I only have a very short lunch break because I have to spend the whole afternoon and evening and possibly night stuck in that edit suite trying to make the damn thing work.'

'It's a tough job, film-making. No one ever said it would be easy, darling.'

'You never said anything except "the American money is tied to that tragic Wilfred bitch who couldn't act to save her scrawny arse, so use her".'

'Did I say that?'

'Bye,' said Gresham, and ducked from beneath his hot and uncomfortable arm. She noticed as she dived into a cab in the rain outside that Graham had already made a move on Sally, sitting on the desk and beaming down at her.

The journey to the restaurant on top of the Oxo building on the south bank of the Thames took, as always, a lot longer than Gresham expected. She lurched out of the cab and in through the expansive glass doors, then took the lift to the top floor. She got out to be greeted by a panoramic view of the Thames and the City of London beyond. Her attention was held by this spectacle for less time than it was possible to register. She saw her sister's auburn hair burning across the vast expanse of tables and headed in that direction. She saw Eupheme's profile, her wonderful complexion which just seemed to be there, no matter what she did. It annoyed her that Eupheme wore virtually no make-up. She didn't need to – her features were strong enough, her eyes big and clearly defined, her dark eyebrows naturally drawing the eye and underlining the wonderfully composite beauty of her face. Gresham knew her half-sister was somehow more genuinely beautiful than anyone else she had ever met.

'Sorry I'm late,' she said as she air-kissed her half-sibling. 'Pervy Graham got me in reception. Feel like I need a shower.'

'Who's pervy Graham?' asked Eupheme, her eyes sparkling slightly more than usual. Had she been using drops? Was she in love?

'God, you just don't know who is powerful in this town, do you?' said Gresham with a knowing flick of her long hair.

'I know Tony Blair. Well, I met him once. He's quite powerful,' said Eupheme. She laughed and then added, 'He's a bit on the powerful side.'

'No, I mean powerful in the industry.'

'Which industry?'

'Film, you great wazzock. God, Pheme, where do you live?'

'In the charity industry,' said Eupheme in a mock media junkie voice.

'Oh, God. Okay, I feel guilty. I never do anything to help starving Africans. Next.'

'Okay, well who is this Graham anyway? Is he nice?'

'Graham Walker-Smith. Nice! He's a total creep. A slimy, sticky-fingered pervert.'

'How disgusting. Why d'you work with him, Gresh?'

'He practically owns Allied Fountain, for Christ's sake, and all their subsidiaries. He's known Dad for yonks. He's got shed-loads of dosh and he's a total, unrepentant shagger. He was all over me just now. Makes you feel sick. Mind you, I fucking tell him. Doesn't matter what I say to him – because he fancies me he won't fire me off the project. Anyway, I'm his "too hot to handle" protégée. He likes having his picture taken with me at premieres and all that old rot.'

'Talking of old rot, how's Stanhope?'

'Haven't seen him for yonks. He works all hours, so do I. I haven't had sex in ten days.'

'Oh, you poor thing. I haven't had any in ten weeks.'

'Yeah, well, you are sad.' Gresham picked up the menu. 'What are you having?'

'The fish.'

'I'll have the fish too.' She looked around for a waiter. There was one standing right behind her.

'We'll both have the fish, please,' said Gresham, 'and a big bottle of sparkling mineral water.'

'Can I have another vodka?' said Eupheme. Gresham cast her a surprised glance. She could only remember Eupheme drinking once before, at a party they'd had when they were both sixteen. Eupheme had vomited copiously in front of all her friends and caused major-league embarrassment all round.

'Pheme, are you pissed?' asked Gresham.

'Not exactly,' said Eupheme, revealing that she clearly was. 'I just had to wait so long for you I had a little drink.'

'How many voddies have you had?' asked Gresham, suddenly genuinely concerned.

'Not that many. I just needed a drink.'

'You never drink.'

'I know.'

'Then why are you drinking?'

'I don't know. Why don't you have a voddie, Gresh. I need to talk.'

'I don't drink at lunch-time. Everyone knows that.'

'What, everyone in the industry?' said Eupheme sullenly.

'What's up?' asked Gresham. 'Has Richard dumped you?'

'Richard! Bloody hell,' slurred Eupheme. 'A chance'd be a fine thing. Would that he made any decision. Useless great lump. No, everything's fine, really. Everything's going really well. We've got the huge big benefit on the fifth, so you must come to that.'

'Oh, fantastic, Pheme. Who's on?'

'Spice Girls, with a bit of luck, Hugh Laurie and Jonathan Ross compering, Jo Brand, Nigel Planer doing poetry, Eddie Izzard, might even get U2.'

'Blimey. Brilliant. When is it?'

'I said, didn't I? The fifth.'

'Of what?' said Gresham, now slightly alarmed.

'May, of course,' said Eupheme.

'I don't believe it!' squealed Gresham. 'How could you!'

'How could I what?'

'For Christ's sake, my own half-sister. How could you! You know that's the night of my premiere.'

'What?' said Eupheme hotly.

'That's the night of my sodding premiere. *Uncle Roger*, the film I've been slaving away on for the past three years. Christ, the one night of the year I would really have liked your support and you have to mess the whole thing up with some poxy charity gig. Mine's a charity gig anyway. All the proceeds are going to the Terrence Higgins Trust, or something Aidsy.'

'Gresham, you cow, you bloody awful cow. How could you?'

'What? I didn't choose that night anyway, it was Graham Walker-Smith. They said they checked, they said nothing else was happening that night.'

'In the industry.'

'In town, darling,' said Gresham. 'Christ, this always happens with us. What is it about you? You always try and fuck up everything I do. You always have!'

'Gresham. How can you say that!' said Eupheme, her eyes filling rapidly with tears. 'When I had my ninth birthday party and my mum got drunk, you didn't turn up because you got to play tennis with some awful lord's daughter.'

'Oh, yeah, Wendy. Who is now at the Department of Trade, by the way. I had lunch with her the other day. Very promising.'

'Yeah, but you've always screwed things up for me.'

'Oh, this really is a mess. Loads of people have responded to our mail-out,' said Gresham. 'The place is going to be packed. I mean, everyone is going to be at my thing. I've even invited Hugh.'

'Well, you can't have him. And you can't have Ben Elton either.'

'I've invited him.'

'Well, he's doing a ten-minute spot for me.'

'This is bloody ridiculous. Can't you move yours. Where is it on? Some bloody awful town hall in Hackney or something?'

'The Royal Albert Hall.'

'Oh, Pheme. How could you? You are a bloody nightmare.' Gresham held her head in her hands. Her expensively washed hair fell neatly over her long fingers; she could feel its smoothness. It didn't help. This was so typical of her half-sister. The waiter arrived with the fish dish.

'I don't feel like eating now,' said Gresham.

'Nor do I,' said Eupheme.

'Oh, bollocks. I may as well,' Gresham took a huge forkful. She chewed with swollen cheeks, watching Eupheme swig from her large vodka.

'So why are you drunk?'

'Just felt like it.'

'Oh God, here we go, I've got to bloody well guess. It's not because of Richard the pisshead. It's not because of my premiere utterly stealing the limelight from your little benefit. It must be that I'm more beautiful than you with a better-shaped arse and wonderful legs.'

Eupheme sobbed hopelessly, her mouth open like a down-facing cresent moon.

'Christ, girl,' said Gresham, now embarrassed by the spectacle of her sister sobbing. 'What's happened? Is your mum okay?'

'My who?' asked Eupheme between sobs.

'Your mum.'

'Yes. She's fine.' Eupheme blew her nose copiously into a napkin. A diner on a nearby table glanced over with a look of barely concealed disgust.

Eupheme took a huge breath and pushed her chair back from the table. She sat with her hands on her lap, chewed her lips and said, 'I'm sorry to dump all this on you, but I'm crying, Gresham, because I am broken. And broke. And because we had a wager and you, well, I don't like to say it, but you cheated really. You did, Gresh, and it hurts me to say that. You thought he was a doctor, though, but even then you wouldn't admit I'd won, even though it isn't about winning. And now I can't prove to you that I did win for really complex reasons. It's just all fallen apart. You always win. You've always been the stronger one even though I'm older and I bloody well know more than you.'

'What wager?' asked Gresham. 'You're not still on about that tosser, are you?'

'You know I am. You thought he was a doctor.'

'Oh, God help us,' said Gresham.

'A doctor, Gresh. And that's what I wanted to prove to you, of all people. And somehow fate intervened and you blurted out about seeing him on the platform in your rude way. Why are you always so rude? And why do you always get away with it? You are so wrong about people not being able to change. I even surprised myself. He changed so much.'

'Well, where is he, for Christ's sake?' said Gresham curtly.

'He's at work.'

'Where? Models One?'

'You see.' Eupheme spat. 'You did think he was good-looking.'

'Of course I did. I never denied the man I met was good-looking. I just said he wasn't the train-spotter.'

'He is, Gresham, he truly is. You know I've never told you a lie. You know that.' Eupheme started crying again.

'Oh, bloody hell, Pheme. This is ridiculous. The man you dragged to my party was a dreamboat. I'd fuck him tomorrow if it wasn't for Stanhope. Actually, the way things are going at the moment I'd fuck him tomorrow regardless.'

'You might be surprised,' said Eupheme. 'I know you've always had men falling at your feet, but Ian is different.'

'Hang on, hang on, what is this about? Pheme, you haven't fallen for this guy, have you?'

'No, of course not,' said Eupheme, wiping the tears from her eyes with the back of her hand. Her brow was furrowed; she sobbed quietly. 'No,' she said again.

'You have. Come on, there's no point lying, Pheme. It's me. I can tell.'

'Gresham, how can you say that! I know you're astute because you're a film-maker and everything, but I really don't think you can tell if I have fallen for someone. You're wrong. I'm not in love with Ian, nor he with me. We had a very professional relationship. I helped him develop and, in so doing, I learned a lot myself.'

Gresham sighed.

'Yes I did, Gresham. I'm not too proud to admit that I had something to learn from him. About what is important and what isn't.'

'And what isn't?' asked Gresham.

'What?'

'What isn't important, what is this great knowledge that he had to impart?'

'Status, snobbery, fashion,' said Eupheme. 'All the things that your life is completely anchored to.'

'Oh, and yours is totally different, is it? How come I seem to see you at every dreadful snobby, status-conscious fashionable party I go to?'

'Exactly. Well, I feel like changing things. In fact, I'm thinking I may take this whole project further.' She took another huge swig of vodka. It splashed past her face and spilled down her front.

'For God's sake, Pheme,' said Gresham, more and more embarrassed by her demi-sibling.

'I've been thinking about setting up some sort of foundation which helps people change their lives and their outlook. I've been thinking about the whole thing. It's really exciting, Gresh. I've started to call it man-whispering, like that chap with the horses, only I just gently suggest to men a different attitude, rather than criticising them or punishing them.'

'You are pissed out of your tiny mind,' said Gresham.

'I am not,' shouted Eupheme. 'I know what I have done works, and just because you cheated me doesn't mean I'm wrong.'

'Christ. Can't you hear yourself? You're waffling on like a bag lady. Man-whispering, I ask you. You're off your fucking trolley, Pheme. Really, you're losing it.'

'I want to help people the rest of society has written

off. Train-spotters, sad fucks, anorak-wearing tossers, as you call them. People who've slipped off your acceptable fashion bandwagon. I may try and help them get back on. Not that the bandwagon is a good thing in the first place, but at least it would remove the harsh judgment and allow them in the door.'

'I don't want them in my fucking door,' said Gresham, taking another mouthful of fish.

'Anyway, I'm broke.'

'What d'you mean you're broke? You've got a private income. And a job. How can you be broke?'

''Cos I spent so much on fixing Ian.'

'Remind me,' said Gresham. 'How much do you claim you spent on him?'

'Over seven thousand.'

'Christ.'

'That's why he looks so fabulous. That's why he looks like a doctor.'

'A fucking sack of potatoes would look pretty sprauntsy if you spent seven grand on it. Guilt doesn't work on me, Pheme, you know that. The way it appears to me is I'd look like a prat, wouldn't I. People would hear that I paid my batty half-sister seven grand because she brought a fucking male model to my party and I believed it was a train-spotter. It's not going to happen.'

'I think I'm going to be sick,' said Eupheme quietly, and she stood up, napkin over her mouth, and lurched towards the ladies'.

An hour later Gresham heaved Eupheme's semi-conscious body out of a taxi in front of her flat on Clapham Common North Side. It wasn't an area Gresham knew or liked to visit. She had been to a dinner party there once which was a disaster as usual because she got into a fight with one of Eupheme's New Labour friends.

She opened the door and hauled Eupheme up the large airy flight of stairs and into the flat. It was much larger than Gresham remembered. She pushed open a door and entered a long cream-painted room with floor-to-ceiling windows facing the park. Gresham thought that if the same flat was in Chelsea or Knightsbridge it would be worth a fortune and she'd want to live in it.

Not that Eupheme paid for it. As usual she had some weird guilt-ridden arrangement with some awful diplomat who was always in Australia or America or somewhere and who was gaga about her. When he came 'home', as he had done during Gresham's one and only previous visit, his eyes followed Eupheme around the room like a pathetic old Labrador.

She lay her half-sister's groaning form down on a massive sofa and threw a cover over her. She stood up and arched her back, the pain convincing her that dead drunk women are indeed very heavy to manoeuvre. She smiled a little as she stared down at Eupheme's beautiful face. How could someone raddled with guilt and double standards be so attractive, and still not know it? She lived in utter denial, her flimsy liberal hypocrisy draped over her like her dreadful full-length skirts. Gresham shook her head and ran her hand through her own thick hair. Still smooth; that was a good conditioner. Eighty-five pounds from Liberty's.

She turned and walked to the window. Cars rumbled slowly past on the main road; a young child ran with a dog in the park. It was the most miserable view she had ever seen. It would drive her mad. She imagined that Eupheme would have stood there for hours looking at people in the park and planning ways to improve their lives, whether they wanted them improved or not.

Her hand brushed against something. It was a sheet of paper dangling over the edge of a large table covered with a green chenille cloth. It was a computer print-out of an abysmally typed e-mail message with an address written in Eupheme's hand.

Ian Ringfold, 76 Cyril Street, Northampton.

Gresham picked up the sheet of paper and, as she stared at her sister, carefully folded it and put it in her pocket.

Chapter Seventeen

'I cannot believe you let a beanie like that slip between your fingers, guy!' said Eddie. 'She was well taut, you know what I am saying. She was a hard-body guy, she was ... well, I only ever seen a beanie like that on a video, giving it the executive poom-poom, you know.'

'I know exactly what you mean, Eduardomundo,' said Ian, smiling at Eddie's energetic rantings.

'I was there, right in front of her. She was giving it the wet T-shirt treatment, you know.'

'What d'you mean?' said Ian, slightly startled.

'It was raining. Her shirt was wet, roonies and all on display, I had me bread in the air. I was up for it, an' she spoke to me an aks me where she could get a cab an' everything, and you, Ringfold, my man, you of all people, let her slip through your fingers. She was gagging for it, guy!'

Eddie nearly fell over with the force of his own delivery. He held his half-shaven head in his hands as he spun on one Nike heel. 'Gagging for it!' He almost fell backwards into a pallet of kitchen rolls.

Ian sat motionless, his feet occasionally hitting the thousands of packets of Daz Ultra he was sitting on. They had both come into the delivery bay to help organise the latest pantechnicon of groceries. It was held up in traffic and an unusual window of free time had opened in their day.

'She was virtually on her knees begging for some bread. You know what I'm saying?'

'I'm not sure I do,' said Ian.

'Beggin' for bread,' said Eddie, grabbing his own groin and dragging himself around the floor with his own baggy jeans. 'I never seen a beanie so frothed up. Not unless she was bein' paid to. It's there for you, on a plate. Prime pussy meat.'

'Please, Eddie,' said Ian, finally reminded that there was a line of taste which Eddie occasionally crossed.

'But how can I not notice, guy? It's a dream come true, and what do you do about it? You tell her to go away!' The pain of this memory drove Eddie to pound his fists melodramatically on the kitchen rolls.

'Careful, Eddie, you'll break the wrapping,' said Ian.

'I don't believe it, guy. That's all I'm saying. I have never in my life seen a better-looking woman!' He made great play of the word woman, as though, under these special circumstances, he was prepared to go as far as being politically correct to get the depth of his feeling across.

Ian surprised himself by how unmoved he was. He knew Eupheme was very beautiful but that, he constantly reminded himself, wasn't enough. It was the way he felt she was always moving him around when he was with her, turning his head so that he saw what she wanted him to see, stopping him speaking, making him walk differently. It was all too intrusive and had made him forget who he really was.

He sighed. Things had changed and he was bored. He tried to pretend he wasn't, but his old job really was quite uninteresting. Dull even. Some of the things about it still pleased him – entering the store first thing in the morning before the customers arrived, its airy spaciousness, the smell of the bakery, the banter between all the shelf-stackers and delivery men, Eddie holding forth as he pushed the giant steel-wheeled pallets full of milk in from the cold store. That still made him feel good, but it changed once the store was open, and he spent his day in a constant state of damage limitation and mild frustration, endlessly showing people where things were, even though virtually every item on the shelves was clearly signposted. Calling the in-store cleaners on the public address system when yet another jar of marmalade or bag of sugar burst open on the floor of the checkout aisles. Eupheme had made a huge impression on his life. He was going to miss seeing her, miss his exciting trips to London, but he knew he had to make his own way.

'Eddie,' he said finally, 'it's not like it looks, okay? Fine, if she was just a pretty lady then maybe wedding bells would ring and we'd have a bonk-of-the-year show on our wedding night.'

'Weddin' bells! Where d'you live, guy, 1950? Wh'appen to your drive, guy? The beanie wants some poom-poom, now. No preliminaries. Straight in with the bread.'

'Eddie, please.'

'The oven is hot. Hot, you know what I'm saying?'

'But behind the luscious looks and curvy figure there's this other lady, a really bossy lady who is dead annoying when all is said and done, and any form of . . . well, you know.'

'Shagging,' said Eddie lasciviously.

'Well, okay, that would only make matters worse, and actually, at the end of the day, she has never given me the slightest idea that she wanted to do anything like that with me. Like most ladies, she seems very distant and hoity-toity. I can't imagine it really. She's just too posh to actually do it.'

'They love it, posh birds. My uncle is always givin' the hammer to some posh beanie. They can't get enough.'

'Well, Eupheme isn't like that,' said Ian, suddenly feeling the need to defend her. 'She's got lots of problems, I suppose. I don't think she's a very happy lady. Anyway, she's got a bit of a fiancé in Italy or somewhere.'

'They always go for foreign geezers,' said Eddie glumly. 'All your supermodels and top beanies, they always go out with Italian footballers or American baseball stars who've got serious disposable, you know. That's what it comes down to, havin' serious disposable and a nice motor. You know, like a Cosworth Sierra.'

'I still think the Golf VR6 is the better car,' said Ian.

'The Cosworth Sierra is a serious car, guy. It would leave a VR6 standing. You'd have to get out of your VR6 and wipe the windows, man, because of all the dust left by my Cossy. Big sound system. In fact I'd take out the back seats and have some super-woofers fitted so the whole car moved, guy. Even when it wasn't moving it would sway with the rhythm.'

'This is after you win the lottery?' asked Ian, stretching and standing up. He could hear the delivery lorry approaching.

'I can feel it. I am the sort of guy you see in the *Daily Mirror*, blonde beanie either side, me in the middle with a bottle of top-quality bubbly and a cheque for seven million. It's going to happen,' said Eddie. 'And I'll tell you what.' He was now laughing almost hysterically. 'I'll tell you what. I'd drive down to the smoke in my black Cosworth Sierra with low-profile tyres and mag alloy wheels with my sound system pushing other cars off the road, and I'd find that beautiful beanie of yours, an' I'd take her out on the town, no expense spared, guy. We'd go to Stringfellow's and we'd watch the lap dancers, and then she'd join in, drop her clothes and wow the guys with her bumping and grinding, and then we'd go back ...'

The hiss of air-brakes broke into Eddie's rapturous fantasy. He stood frozen to the spot, face turned down with misery until he finally snapped out of it and with a jaunty step climbed on to the fork-lift and started it up. Ian walked towards the back of the vast trailer with his clipboard. Eddie had made him think. It was strange that Eupheme had come all this way to see him. Maybe.

He shook his head with what he felt was a knowing grin.
She just wanted to win her bet. She just wanted her £7,000.

'You know what,' said Ian as they piled another pallet of
Kellogg's Sustain into the storage area. 'She lost some sort of
bet with her sister ... well, her half-sister. Seven thousand
pounds.'

'Seven K!' shouted Eddie. 'How come she lost?'

'Well, I suppose I lost.'

'What was the bet? That she could shag you?'

'No! No, it was to turn me from a tosser into a
tasty geezer.'

'You're kidding me!' said Eddie, his face alive with delight.
'What a job!'

'Well, thank you,' said Ian.

'Jesus, you was one sad-looking geezer before she met you.
Now you're the thin white duke, you know what I'm saying.
Seven K. That's serious money. She must be real mad at you.
No wonder she drag all the way up here and beg you to come
back. Jesus, I'd eat pussy for seven grand.'

'Eddie, will you stop being so disgusting!' Ian snapped
angrily.

Eddie put his hands up in surrender, then clasped them
together in prayer. 'Listen to me, man. Listen. Get your skinny
white arse back down to the big smoke and be cool. Tell her
you'll do it for half the money. Jesus, Ian, three and a half K, you
could put a deposit down on a Cosworth Sierra with that.'

'Or a VR6.'

'Waste of money, guy.'

'Anyway, it's irrelevant. I couldn't do it. I'm not in the
business of accepting charity.'

'It's not charity!' shouted Eddie. 'You've worked for it. Been
readin' all them magazines, pumping iron, havin' haircuts, suits,
shoes, everything. That takes time and dedication. Learning
to speak like a lord. Jesus, Ian, you worked for that money.
Don't talk to me about charity. See what's going on around

you, guy. You're being ripped off at every turn. You deserve more than half.'

'D'you think I could really suggest that?'

'Demand it, guy. Say, I'm not coming back for less than three point five, take it or leave it. The beanie will melt.'

'I'll think about it.'

Eddie shook his head and gunned the engine on the fork-lift. He drove back to the tail-lift of the delivery lorry which was now disgorging five pallets of eggs.

The wall-mounted phone rang. Ian answered. It was Mrs Philips.

'Bad news,' she said. 'I've been on to head office. They say that your erratic behaviour does not bode well at this point in time, and frankly, when all is said and done, Ian, I can see their point entirely.' There was a long pause. Ian couldn't manage a response.

'I for one am deeply disappointed that you let your personal life interfere with your workaday life. Not a good move at the best of times. I had a hysterectomy last year and no one knew about it. No one. I was back at work two days later, still bleeding copiously, but I kept it to myself.'

'Goodness,' said Ian.

'Exactly. Now your personal life I know nothing about, Ian, and the less said on that particular score the better. Looking at things from a fresh perspective, as it were, I don't see that we can keep you on here in your present position. It's completely messed up my management scheme for the next five years. You see, I have a plan, Ian. A five-year plan that is in a constant state of flux, that I'll grant you, but I have Doreen McAllister down to become Deputy Manager, Dry Goods. I've always known she would do that job when you moved on. Well, you did move on and now you've moved back again and it can't be done, Ian. The only way is up, to coin a phrase. Now, I know you're far too senior and experienced to be filling the boots of old Gilbert, but he's close to retirement so the only thing I can offer is Night Shift Manager. Greatly reduced pay and pension but that's about all I can do. It's a total take-it-or-leave-it package, I'm afraid.'

'I see,' said Ian.

'D'you get my drift, Ian?' she said after another long pause.

'You're saying really I haven't got a job here.'

'We never sack anyone, Ian. Not without good reason. But what can I do? It's night shift or bye-bye, I'm afraid.'

'Okay, when d'you want me to work until?'

'I'm sorry?' said Mrs Philips.

'Well, I'm not going to be Night Shift Manager so we can forget that.'

'Oh well, now you put it like that, clearly I'd like you to stay on ... well, into the afternoon. When does your shift finish, Ian?'

'Four thirty.'

'Well, I'd like you to stay on until at least then. Mr Franklin will sort out your wage packet, don't have any worries on that score. I'll have a word.'

'Thank you, Mrs Philips, sorry I let you down. Things just got on top of me.'

'I'd rather not know who got on top of you, Ian. It's your business what you do in your free time.'

'Yes, Mrs Philips.'

'All the best, then,' she said curtly, and hung up.

'Wh'appen?' asked Eddie, who had driven up behind him, a massive pile of eggs balanced on the fork-lift.

'Got the grand order of the boot-a-roochie,' said Ian, smiling flatly. 'Mrs Philipo just gave me the old marching orders.'

'Bitch,' whispered Eddie.

'No, it was my fault really, being given a promotion opportunity within the company and then throwing the whole thing away. You can't go back, Eddie.'

'Yeah, but it's a job, y'know what I'm sayin'.' Eddie spun

in a circle on his massive trainers and then pulled out his mobile phone from one of his huge pockets.

'Bell the beanie,' he said, offering it to Ian. 'That's how much I care. I'll let you run up points on my mobile. Come on, Ian, bell her.'

'No. What's the point?'

'What other offers you lookin' at, guy!' said Eddie. He looked around dramatically. 'I don't see no management headhunters formin' a queue, y'know what I'm sayin'. You are out on your skinny white arse, guy. Ring the beanie.'

'Okay, okay,' said Ian, taking the old-model Motorola from Eddie. 'But I want to pay for the call.'

'Accept help, just accept it with grace. Y'know, gimme the dignity to offer somethin'. Jesus, you are uptight.'

'Okay,' said Ian with a smile. He dialled the number. 'Thank you,' he added.

Eddie walked around in a circle, wringing his hands. He froze when Ian spoke. Ian turned and shielded his mouth. 'Can I speak to Eupheme Betterment, please. Yes, it's Ian Ringfold.' He stretched his neck out like a proud businessman. Eddie danced up and down in delight.

'Hello. Ian?' said Eupheme. She sounded soft and gentle, not what he was expecting. It seemed to make him weaker and he wanted to feel strong.

'Eupheme, it's me. Listen, I'll go through with it . . .'

'Oh, Ian,' said Eupheme, clearly delighted.

'If,' interrupted Ian, 'if you split the proceeds half and half.' He shut his eyes as Eupheme started to explain.

'Ian, what are you saying? You know this isn't about money. I'm really, really amazed that you think it is in any way connected with the money. This is the whole point of what I'm doing. It's to do with the morality of her attitudes, and what they represent in the wider world. I don't understand what you're saying . . .'

He was amazed that she could so rapidly start explaining

everything and making his demand sound so utterly wrong. He looked at Eddie, who was making punching movements. He nodded and cut her off. 'I don't care about you or your sister or the money, come to that. My position is simple. You either give me half of the proceeds or I do nothing. Do we have a deal?'

'I don't know how I can do that,' said Eupheme.

'I'll tell you how. You add up the whole lot, split the figure fifty-fifty and give me fifty per cent of it. Yes, you'll be somewhat out of pocket, but it's better than losing altogether. Take it or leave it.'

There was a pause. 'Eupheme?' said Ian, still trying to maintain his solid male pose in front of Eddie.

'Yes, I'm thinking,' she said. Then, 'Okay, fifty-fifty, but you must promise to do everything I say.'

'I'll go the whole hog,' said Ian. 'I'll give it my very best shot. You know we can win, Eupheme.'

'I know.'

'I'll call you later and discuss details.'

He switched off the phone.

'Well?' asked Eddie.

'We have a deal.' Ian smiled. They exchanged slightly misplaced high fives that ended up like high threes. Eddie walked around the loading area, whooping for joy.

'Ian, my man, you are well wicked, you know what I'm saying!'

Ian climbed up on to the fork-lift and started up the engine. He moved it forward three feet and then applied the brake very violently. Four thousand eggs teetered on the edge of oblivion and then collapsed in a massive damp yellow mountain of split boxes on to the smooth concrete floor.

'Oh, damn, what an awful accident to have on my last day,' said Ian with a smile. 'Let's get some mops.'

'Mops!' said Eddie. 'We need a fucking JCB digger, guy!'

Chapter Eighteen

Stanhope De Courcey answered the door to his mews house and Gresham Hollingford, young, beautiful and as usual with a dark cloud of anger rumbling over her head, walked in without hesitation.

'Hello, sweets!' said Stanhope, his big face clearly delighted to see her. She threw her bag on to an ornate chair in the tiny front room.

'Stanhope, I need to ask you a bit of a favour,' she stated, stretching out on the old sofa which filled the rest of the space.

'Anything,' said Stanhope. 'I've had a particularly good day on the foreign exchange, so I'm in a fearfully good mood.'

'Well, that makes a change,' said Gresham. She heard a noise in the kitchen, looked at Stanhope with her wonderful eyebrows raised a little.

'Who's here?'

'Oh, Steve came back with me. We were having a bit of a celebration, actually. D'you want to join us?'

Steve walked through from the kitchen carrying a tray with glasses and a bottle of champagne. He was dressed in an open-necked white shirt and immaculate white trousers with no shoes. Not what Gresham thought men who worked in the City wore. He was gay, it was painfully obvious to her now. It didn't mean Stanhope was, but it was weird. She felt uneasy.

'Hello, Gresham, how's things?' he said softly. He smiled. He was too perfect.

'Not bad, thanks. Actually, I'm in a bit of a bind. I've got to go and look at a location for a night shoot, and my car is off the road.'

'Oh no, what's wrong with it?' asked Stanhope.

Gresham knew there was nothing wrong with it. She toyed with the idea of making up a mechanical fault, then dismissed the idea in a millisecond. 'I don't bloody know. It won't start so they've taken it in. I need to borrow a car.'

'Take the Rangey,' said Stanhope without hesitation. He picked up his pin-stripe jacket which had been thrown on the floor and found the keys in the pocket. 'I've just filled it up so you're lucky. Blessed thing drinks juice.'

'Thanks,' said Gresham, taking the keys. She had wanted to have a quiet talk with Stanhope but this was clearly not going to be possible with the charming Steve smiling at her.

'Where have you got to go?' he asked. Gresham seethed, knowing that she would have to be polite to this creep.

'Somewhere outside Northampton, apparently. It's for my next project and, as always with my arsehole production manager, the only time I can see it is right now, today, when I really could do with a break.'

'Oh, darling, you poor, poor sausage,' said Stanhope. 'D'you want me to drive you?'

'Not at all,' snapped Gresham. 'I'm going to be out till God knows when. Is it okay if I come back here tonight, though?'

'Of course, darling,' said Stanhope, still smiling, still with eyes only for her. She flicked a glance at Steve. He didn't seem to be paying any attention.

'Okay, I'll see you later, then,' she said, giving Stanhope a kiss on the mouth. He held her tenderly, as he always did. It felt good.

She smiled at him sadly as he and Steve waved her off from the door of the twee mews house.

The sun was just going down and the sky was a bright red colour. It was quite warm and Gresham opened the driver's window slightly. Every now and then, as she stopped in traffic, she could hear birds singing, a thing that had always amazed her about London.

She had decided to borrow Stanhope's brand-new Range Rover for two reasons. One, she felt very safe in it, sitting up high with its massive black bodywork surrounding her like a giant carapace. Secondly, she wanted to create an impression and knew this monster would do it. Although her car, a new-model Audi A4 cabriolet, the same model Princess Di had used, was pretty flash, it didn't quite have the grandeur.

As she pulled on to the M1 and put her foot down, she realised she had also wanted to see Stanhope and monitor how she felt when she saw him. Her wedding had become such an event that considerations like her feelings were being pushed rather into the background.

Before she realised what was happening she was doing over 110 miles an hour and thought it would be embarrassing to get pulled up for speeding. She slowed down to a sensible ninety and clicked on the cruise control. The phone rang. She pressed the hands-free button on the steering wheel.

'Yes?'

'Are you okay, darling?' asked Stanhope.

'Yes, of course I am, all things considered.'

'What things, sweets?' he asked, almost like a little boy. This from a man in his late thirties who earned over three-quarters of a million pounds a year, after tax.

'The film, having to come up here tonight.'

'I know, I know, it's a very difficult period for you, but it's all going to go swimmingly once the film is released, isn't it.'

'I hope so.'

'Anything else . . . ?'

She cut him off mid-sentence. 'Who's Steve?'

'Steve?' said Stanhope.

'Yes, is he still there?'

'No, he just left.' That sounded genuine.

'Who is he, Stanhope?'

'Steve. You've met him before, at the house.'

'I know, but who is he?'

'Well, he works at Morgan Grenfell. I've known him for years.'

'Yes, I know all that, but he's a poof, Stanhope, I know he is.'

'Yes, Steve is as bent as a nine-bob note, darling. Always has been.'

'Then why was he in your kitchen in white trousers with no shoes on?'

'Well, he'd been to the gym.'

'Oh.'

'Why d'you ask? Oh, sweets, you don't think Steve and I do the nasty, do you? Me, bump uglies with Steve! Darling, please.'

'He just gives me the creeps.'

'Oh, darling, Steve is delightful. Poor man, how can you say that?' Stanhope's voice had become high-pitched but was still charming. His whole manner was always so full of joy, and so rich. Gresham relaxed a little.

'Okay, he's not a creep.'

'I'm sorry, pumpkin, I know you're under a lot of pressure. If Steve appears creepy, I'm really sorry. I'm sure he's only trying to be friendly. You know what we City fellows are like. Not terribly good at all the relationships with girls business.'

'Tell me about it,' said Gresham, warming more and more to her multimillionaire future husband.

'And especially Steve,' added Stanhope. 'He's so much more confident with young jockeys.'

Gresham laughed. 'Okay, pumpkin,' she said disparagingly,

knowing Stanhope would take it. 'I'll try not to hate him, and all your other ghastly chums. I'll see you in the morning.'

'Wake me when you get in.'

'No, I'll sleep in the spare room.'

'Oh, pumpkin. I'm off the list, am I?'

'We'll see,' said Gresham, feeling a glow of warmth spread from her loins. She heard a crashing sound and a voice in the background.

'What was that?' asked Gresham.

'Oh, blast, just my gin and tonic, darling,' said Stanhope. 'I'd better go and clear it up. Smooch you later, you vixen.' He hung up.

It didn't sound right. A chill went through her body. Was that Stanhope's voice, the shout she had heard? It was almost like a tape loop playing again and again. A small shout of dismay at a minor mishap. 'Ah!' That was all it was. 'Ah!' It played on her mind as she braked hard to take the Northampton South turn-off. Once off the motorway she switched on Stanhope's computerised Wayfinder map, a small box mounted on the copious dashboard of the car. She tried to operate it as she drove, but soon found herself swerving around rather alarmingly.

She pulled over under the bright awning of a garage and studied the contraption more carefully. She had always been single-minded in her determination not to be intimidated by technology. She knew how film cameras worked, she knew about light levels and focal lengths, so she was not about to be thrown by this box of tricks.

There was a small trackpad at the bottom which she used to move the map around on the screen. After a while she located Northampton, then she pressed the + button, zooming in to the town map. She found the M1 and then worked out where she was. Leigh service station. She double-clicked the cross hairs on that location, then shifted the map until she located Cyril Street. Again she double-clicked and the map disappeared momentarily until a red-outlined route was displayed for her. The fastest course from where she was to where she was going.

'This I have got to have,' she said to herself, tapping the small box. 'Okay, we're cooking with gas.' She started up the car and pulled out of the garage with a vengeance.

Twenty-three minutes later she pulled to a rumbling halt outside 76 Cyril Street. She dropped down from the car and walked towards the door. She looked around – a small, miserable low-rent street, litter on the pavement, tiny buildings smashed together like hen-houses. They looked like one up, one down hovels.

'God, this is a fucking poverty pit,' Gresham muttered to herself as she stood in front of the door. There was no bell. She hesitated a moment then gingerly touched the letterbox and let the flap drop. She could hear a television inside, what sounded like a game show. She took a deep breath and knocked on the door. She could hear movement from within.

'Who is it?' said an old woman's voice from behind the door.

'It's Gresham Hollingford. Is Ian here?' she said, sounding as grand as she could, which was very grand.

'He's upstairs. Hang on a minute, I'll fetch him down.'

No sign of the door opening, Gresham thought, as she scanned the street to check for approaching assailants. No one; Cyril Street was completely deserted. She heard footsteps approach the front door and stood back a little. The door opened and a man stood in front of her in cheap elastic-waisted stretch pants which had sagged at the knees, ghastly department-store slippers and a T-shirt that had a spaceship flying through a road sign printed on the front.

'Blimey,' said Ian. 'What are you doing here?'

'Hello, are you . . . ?' Gresham, for one of the very few times in her life, was literally speechless.

'I'm Ian. I met you at your party. It was a brilliant do, by the by. I never got the chance to say thanks. I know you didn't really want me there and everything, but I'll never forget it. Seeing that many celebrities in one place and sort of mingling in with them ... well. D'you want to come in, by the way?'

'Oh, no, no,' said Gresham, appalled at the idea. 'I was wondering, would you like to, well, come out?'

'Sorry?' said Ian.

'Well, I, um ...' Gresham flapped her hands around in semi-desperation. She had always been able to talk before. She took a deep breath. 'You see, the thing is, well, I was intrigued to find out who you were.'

'Oh, right,' said Ian. 'Did Eupheme send you, then?'

'No, no. This is the thing, you see. I thought, well, no, I'll start again.' She was talking to the worst-dressed man she had ever encountered in her life, and she was stumbling like a fourteen-year-old. ''Pheme doesn't know I'm here. She doesn't ... Look, I can explain. No, maybe I can't.' She started to back away. 'I'd rather not intrude. Maybe it was all a mistake.'

'What was?' asked Ian. His smile was so charming, so utterly charming, and he was real. This was what she saw; this ragged heap in front of her was everything. There was no wall of confidence between her and this man. She was thrown like she'd never been thrown before. She took yet another deep breath and said, 'I'm absolutely starving hungry. Is there anywhere we could go, you know, to get something to eat?'

'Oh, I see. Well, I've had my tea. I could cook something up for you, if you like. Fried-egg sarnie or something.'

Another suggestion more ghastly than she could imagine. 'Oh God, no! No, I couldn't put you to all that trouble.' She sounded like her mother, every phrase a thin lie. 'No, look, I've come in my car.' She pointed to Stanhope's Range Rover.

'Oh, wow,' said Ian. 'A four point six HSE new-model Rangey. Wow! Is that your car?'

'Well, yes,' said Gresham, pleased at the response. At last, she was gaining some ground.

'Blimey O'Reilly, that's brilliant,' said Ian, stepping out of the house. 'They cost a pretty packet, don't they? But what a classic piece of work. Did you know the latest London taxicabs use the same chassis and suspension?'

'No, I never did,' said Gresham, genuinely surprised.

'Well, it's so sturdily built, apparently. Of course, the taxi doesn't have the permanent four-wheel drive or the off-road capability of this machine. Or the engine, come to that. The four point six. Brilliant.' Ian now stood in the street, admiring the car. 'Would that my mate Eddie was here. He would really appreciate a look-see at a vehicle of this calibre.'

'Oh, right. Well, shall we go or ...'

'Oh, wow. Can I have a ride?'

'You can drive if you like,' said Gresham.

'Would that I had a licence,' said Ian with a strangely attractive Rik Mayallian laugh. 'Never bothered to apply, what with no chance of owning a car. Anyway, I'm a bit of a train man myself, on the side. In fact I was just surfing the old Net-a-roochie and I came across an amazing American on-line journal called *TrackTalk*. All about spotters in America. Wonderful evocative descriptions of train journeys running through the Rockies, et cetera, and of course a completely different set of rolling stock.'

'Yeah, trains are a gas in America,' said Gresham.

'Don't tell me you've been on a Stateside train trip?'

'When I was a film student. Yeah. Coast to coast on Amtrak, and way down south – New Mexico, Texas, Missisippi, all over.'

'Oh, wow. You were a film student?'

'Yes. National Film School.'

'What, the one in Beaconsfield?'

'Yes. D'you know it?' she asked.

'Only through the website. I'm very interested in film and video. In fact I'm working towards getting my own digital editing suite here, desktop jobbie.'

'Oh, great, yes. I've never used one of those. I use film so it's still a scissors-and-tape job.'

Ian smiled at her. He shook his head slightly and then said, 'Well, I'll go in and get changed. I've got a suit here that Eupheme bought me, I'll put that on. I've just had a bath so I'm covered in that department.'

'Oh, right,' said Gresham, and laughed for the first time that day.

'What's funny?' he asked.

'You are,' said Gresham. 'Pheme never said anything about you being funny.'

'Oh, right. Is that funny ha-ha or funny peculiar?' he asked.

'Both,' she said.

'Oh. Okay,' said Ian. He smiled again. She smiled back. 'Well,' he went on, 'd'you want to wait inside?'

'No. If it's okay, I'll sit in the car.'

Gresham opened the heavy black door and climbed back up into the driver's seat. The door shut with a low thunk. She watched Ian walk back into the house in the wing mirror. Her fingers automatically went to the ignition keys. She paused. Was she going to drive away now and admit she'd blown it? Pay Eupheme seven thousand pounds because she fancied the arse off this gorgeous funny man who lived in a hovel with his mum? Clearly everything Eupheme had said about him was true. She gripped the steering wheel so tightly her hands hurt. She felt helpless, almost, very close to, bordering on being, leaning over the precipice of, being defeated by life for the first time.

It wasn't just the film — stagnant, coiled in that distant editing room like a sick child; her father and mother, estranged beyond redemption but never admitting it, never showing it even to each other. Her half-sister, as far as Gresham could see, was a bitter, broken woman on the road to madness. It wasn't just Stanhope and his funny friends and the feeling that she had never truly known her future husband, never really touched him. Even thinking of him as her future husband meant the barrier was in place; they almost had a professional relationship. There was still a huge wall of privilege and class which, even from her exalted position, seemed impenetrable. She had made love with Stanhope on many occasions, always with her on top, looking magnificently sexy, Stanhope's beautiful hands on her sides as she rocked on him. But it was always the same thing, her fighting her way to a climax and Stanhope somehow merely watching. His head beautiful, resting on a pure goose-down linen-covered pillow. Everything always smelled nice. Stanhope was impeccably clean and Gresham liked that. But he was never really there. And his tantric sex thing, that was strange. He had come with her, once, and it was wonderful and almost, at that moment, almost, she felt she was with him. But usually he didn't come. He was erect, he was a careful and sensuous lover, but he didn't come. There was no real eagerness, not desperate, animal eagerness. Sex never got dirty with Stanhope.

Her fingers fiddled with the dangling Range Rover key fob when suddenly the passenger door opened, the interior light came on and Ian slid into the seat beside her.

'Oh, wow, talk about luxury. Brilliant,' he said, now looking completely transformed. He was wearing a loose-fitting linen suit. It looked like Issey Miyake.

'Nice suit,' she said. 'Where d'you get it?'

'This? Oh, Donna Karen,' said Ian. 'It's nice, isn't it.'

'You look ... not bad.'

'Thanks. You look utterly amazing yourself, as a matter of fact.'

'I know.'

She started the car.

'Oh, listen to that. As Jezzer Clarkson would say, "Music to mine ears, a four point six big-block V8, bee-autiful."'

'Another one of your friends?'

'Who?'

'Jezzer or whatever his name is.'

'Jeremy Clarkson, ha! Would that he was. He presents *Top Gear*, for goodness' sake. BBC2's top factual programme, been on for the best part of twenty years.'

'Oh, yeah, of course,' said Gresham, realising she should have known, feeling tripped up, caught out. It almost hurt her physically. She had always been right, she had always known everything, particularly on any media-related subject. She'd been to a dinner party with Jeremy Clarkson in attendance once.

She engaged drive and put her foot down. The car leapt forward with unnatural power.

'Oh, wow, I can't believe I'm actually riding in here,' said Ian, turning quickly to look at Gresham. 'This is just the best surprise I have ever, ever had in my whole life.'

'Not bad, is it?' said Gresham, swinging the car on to the Wellingborough Road. 'Where shall we go? I'm fucking starving.'

'Oh, scuse your French,' said Ian, laughing nervously. Gresham laughed too. Everything this man said seemed to make her laugh. Ian Ringfold was so utterly different to anyone she had ever met before.

'Well,' said Ian thoughtfully, 'we could go to the Moti Matal.'

'What the hell is that?' asked Gresham, deciding to modify her language somewhat.

'An Indian restaurant, in the centre of town. I've only been once. The old chicken korma is excellent, I hear say.'

'No, sorry, no way am I going to an Indian restaurant. Open the glove box. There's an RAC book in there.'

Ian opened the small hatch and a light came on inside.

'Oh, wow, such a high level of fittings,' he said, peering into the small compartment. He pulled the book out.

'Now, look up the nearest country hotel with the most crowns. I want somewhere stinking posh. Sprauntsy to the max.'

'Okay, okay,' said Ian, flicking through the thick volume. 'Aha, the Wallace Hotel, outside Pitsford. Five crowns, and it says, um, one of the finest Elizabethan houses in the country converted into a magnificent exclusive hotel, excellent cuisine.'

'D'you know where it is?'

'Roughly.'

'Use that gizmo on the dash,' said Gresham as she booted the engine harder to get her through a set of changing traffic lights.

'Oh, wow, a satellite navi comp. Blimey O'Rourke, that is absolutely top of the range.'

'What's the satellite bit?' asked Gresham.

'What? Don't you know how it works?' said Ian with an amusing sneer.

'Yeah, of course I do, that's how I found you,' she said, imitating him. Ian pulled himself forward in his seat and pressed a small button on the side of the box. It bleeped twice and then a small pinpoint of green light appeared on the screen. He then used the trackpad to bring up the map. Gresham gasped as she realised that the green dot represented them going along the road.

'There we have it, satellite pinpoint location data. Brilliant. These things cost a fortune.' Ian then spoke in a peculiar mid-atlantic accent. 'Now I'll just plot in the co-ordinates, Miss Kochanski, and we'll be there in no time.'

Half an hour later the Range Rover pulled to a halt on the gravel drive of an Elizabethan mansion that made even Stanhope's country pile look a little drab. Beautifully lit, the building glowed in the moonlight.

They entered the hotel and Gresham booked herself a double room. Ian stood back, staring at the ornate wooden ceiling. Gresham felt dizzy, not sure what she was doing but fearfully excited. No one in her life knew where she was; she had become completely anonymous.

'We'd like to eat first,' she said.

'I'm afraid the restaurant is closed, ma'am,' said the receptionist, 'but there is room service.'

'Okay,' said Gresham. 'Well, we've got no bags so toothpaste and toothbrushes, condoms, and laundry.'

'No problem. Someone will come to your room shortly.'

Gresham walked towards Ian, grabbed his hand and pulled him along with her.

'Where are we going?' he asked.

'To our room,' she said with the most wicked smile she could manage.

'Our room?' asked Ian.

She ignored him and pulled him as hard as she could up the magnificent oak staircase, past wonderful dark paintings and exquisite wall hangings. She opened the door and pushed Ian inside.

'Oh, wow. This is really heavy, man,' said Ian, now imitating a TV character Gresham remembered from her childhood, the *Young Ones* actor Eupheme went out with for a while.

She eyed the room. It was perfect. A massive four-poster bed, a huge mirror in a gilt frame on the opposite wall, and a very modern bathroom leading off to the side.

'Not bad for three hundred and fifty pounds a night.'

Ian sat down on a chair with his hands clasped on his lap. 'You're kidding,' he said.

'Well, I didn't book in advance or anything.' She jumped on the bed, kicked off her shoes and undid the first two buttons on her shirt. She picked up the phone and dialled room service.

'Your best steak, all the extras, a bottle of decent red wine and a couple of Irish whiskeys, please. Room eleven.' She put the phone down and rolled on the bed, twisting and writhing until she could see Ian sitting on the chair in front of the mirror.

'Oh, look, I should go,' said Ian, his face now flushed.

'Why?' asked Gresham, completely nonplussed and slightly affronted.

'Well, I hardly know you.'

'I know. Exciting, isn't it?'

'I mean, I don't know you at all. All I know is you thought I was a tosser when you saw me at Milton Keynes, and you had a bet over me and Eupheme lost and now she's gone a bit sad, and . . .'

'She always was a bit sad,' said Gresham. 'And anyway, I never had a bet, she did, and what's more, she's right, you are a handsome boy, and I fancy you and I want to have sex with you. Is that so very bad?'

'Oh, lawks a lumme,' said Ian. 'You're the first lady who's ever said that to me. In a bed situation.'

'A what?'

'Well, as opposed to one of the ladies behind the deli counter.'

'Deli counter? Oh, look, never mind all that. Ian, I fancy you. I'm unhappy.'

'Oh, Christ,' said Ian. 'I really don't think I should.'

'Why not?'

'Well, I've made a sort of promise to myself that I won't make love with a lady until after I'm married.'

Gresham's jaw dropped so far it was clear she had never had a filling in her life. Her perfect teeth were on display for many seconds. 'You're kidding,' she said finally.

'No, it's a bit on the serious side, actually,' said Ian.

'You're not a Christian, are you?'

'Not fully, I don't think. I mean, I sort of believe in a life after death, spirity type of thing, only more Dungeons and Dragons than angels with wings playing harps, et cetera . . .'

'Please, Ian, be quiet,' said Gresham. 'Are you really telling me that sitting over there, in a hotel room with me, you are going to say no?'

'Well, much as you are a top lady in terms of attractiveness, a veritable *Penthouse* pet, I just don't think it's right. Anyway, I thought you were getting married.'

'I am. What difference does that make?'

'In my book, a fair old bit, actually. What would future hubby think if he knew you were here with another chap?'

'You are a scream,' said Gresham, throwing her head back and laughing. 'Future hubby just doesn't need to know.'

'Oh, well, if I had a lady wife, I'd want us to be very honest with each other in the infidelity data exchange area.'

Gresham could see herself in the huge mirror behind Ian's head. She looked, by her own reckoning, pretty close to being the most sexually desirable woman on earth. 'But Ian, come on. Are you gay? What is it?'

'No, I'm not gay. Not that there's anything wrong with people who are. What they do in the privacy of their own bottoms is their own affair as far as I'm concerned. I'm just happy that on my wedding night I will be able to look my lady wife in the eye and say, "Darling, this is the first time I've had full sex".'

There was a pause. Gresham could see that Ian was checking her out constantly; his eyes scanned her body frenetically. Then, slowly, what he had just said crept into her consciousness.

'Full sex?' she asked.

'Yes.'

'What's the difference between full sex and half-full sex?'

'Oh, well, the old heavy petting, that's all right,' said Ian. 'That doesn't really count.'

'So let me get this straight,' said Gresham, undoing her shirt and letting it fall off her perfectly formed shoulders. 'What counts is penetrative, copulatory, fucking-type sex.'

''Scuse your French. Yes. All right, if you have to blurt it all out like that.'

'God, you are weird,' said Gresham. She smiled and let her skirt fall down her beautifully shaped legs. They looked so long in the mirror; she was lucky to have this good a body.

She looked at Ian. His eyes, now having lost all sense of social decorum, were firmly fixed on her wiggling torso. 'Who told you about the facts of life when you were a kid? The vicar?'

'My mum,' said Ian flatly. 'When she first noticed I had pubic hair. I was in the bath. She explained the whole kit and caboodle.'

There was a knock on the door. Gresham stood up and opened it. She was wearing only bra and pants, testing the discretion of the man in a smart uniform who walked in carrying a tray containing all the things Gresham had asked for. She gave him a ten-pound note and the man smiled, taking a quick glance at Ian before leaving. Ian smiled nervously.

'Thanks very much,' he said. Gresham burst out laughing. The man left discreetly.

'You are brilliant,' she said, grabbing his head and kissing him. He responded more than she had expected, and although she was hungry and the arrival of the steak had taken precedence, she soon found herself writhing on the bed with this delightful man who was saying no. As if a man could say no. It was a brave attempt and it certainly made him more attractive, but the way he was mauling her body showed that, at the end of the day, they just couldn't help themselves. He stared at her in between passionate and very lovely kisses. She loosened his shirt and ran her slender fingers over his hard torso. He really was very gorgeous, like a model in *Dazed and Confused* magazine, like Jarvis Cocker with a body. Absolutely honest eyes, she thought, as she ran her fingers through his hair. She felt his head slipping downwards. Was he going to get off? She strained to see what was happening. Slowly and gently he parted her legs. She lay back, a huge grin on her face.

Before long he had his head buried between her thighs and she slid and writhed on his tongue, delighting in the spears of pleasure that ran through her. Something that Stanhope had never done to her and somehow, because he was who he was, she'd been too embarrassed to ask. She felt her mouth salivate;

she needed something in there. Her hand reached over for the plate under the silver salver. She knocked it over. Ian didn't pay any attention.

Her fingers found it at last. She pulled it to her mouth and, breathing noisily through her saliva, she sank her teeth into the tender flesh. She ripped off a great, hot lump of steak and reached her momentous climax as she chewed through the luscious red meat.

Chapter Nineteen

'Richard, what on earth are you doing here!' said Eupheme from behind the pile of papers and empty coffee cups that was her desk.

'Just flew in this morning. Thought I'd keep it a surprise,' said Richard Markham, smiling through his wonderful tan. He looked so healthy, out of context amid the pallid greyness of a wet April morning in London. For the previous four years Eupheme had only ever seen him in his beloved Italy, arms brown and lean, covered in plaster dust. Now the arms were holding a huge bunch of flowers.

'For you,' he said. Clearly, without the usual slurred speech.

'Oh, Richard. How utterly romantic,' said Eupheme, breathing in the heady scent. She put the flowers on the desk and stood up to embrace him. He held her hard and for a long time.

'It's good to see you,' he whispered.

'It's good to see you too. Oh, goodness me, what a surprise. Oh, Richard, what a funny man you are. You never write, you never ring, you just show up out of the blue.'

'I know,' he said, with the smile that had always melted her. She paused for a moment. She wasn't melting with the speed she had in the past.

'Oh God, what am I going to do! I don't think I've ever been so busy. If only you'd rung. I had no idea ...'

'Then it wouldn't have been a surprise,' said Richard, brushing Eupheme's hair out of her face. 'I've come to see a gallery owner. They want to exhibit my fist collection.'

'Oh, wonderful news.'

'There's more. They're going to tour it – here, New York, Los Angeles and Sydney. I've finally got the big show, I'm an international sculptor, Pheme. I'm going to sell my work for a fortune.'

'This is the best news I've heard all year!' said Eupheme, delighted at what appeared to have happened to Richard. He was in London, successful, rich, attractive, with that wonderful smell. Then she was brought back to earth.

'I'm going to buy Castello del Largo,' he said, referring to the medieval Umbrian hovel he rented. 'And do it up. Put in heating for the winter and a pool for the summer.'

'Oh, right,' she said, trying to maintain her smile. 'So you want to stay there?'

'Oh God, yes. It's so beautiful, Pheme, you know what it's like. I couldn't live anywhere else. I always forget just how filthy and disgusting London is when I'm away. I don't know how I lived here so long.'

'I'm so pleased for you,' said Eupheme, ignoring his negative evaluation of her beloved city.

'And there's something a lot more important.'

'Richard, look, can we ...'

'No, please, just listen to this, then I'll go and let you get on. Listen. I have stopped drinking.'

He stood motionless, looking her right in the eye. Not a flicker.

'I have completely stopped drinking,' he continued. 'I've been going to an AA group in Umbertide for English-speaking alcoholics. I've faced the truth and I'm dealing with it day by day.'

'Oh, Richard,' said Eupheme, her heart now melting rapidly. 'Oh, Richard.' She fell into his arms and squeezed him hard. She was so desperate to say 'I love you', but somehow the words wouldn't come out. She had been hurt by this man so many times that it was impossible to really trust him. She knew that, but if he really did stop drinking? Maybe.

'How long?' she asked, holding him at arm's length and looking into his dark eyes.

'Five weeks, three days. Not a drop. Nothing. Nada. It's totally changed my outlook. I wake up in the morning and I want to work, I want to breathe, and eat and live. And make love.'

They held each other tight, Eupheme picturing them in Castello del Largo but finding it hard to get the picture in focus. Their togetherness was interrupted when the door opened and Christine walked in carrying lunch in a big paper carrier bag. Kevin Waslick was right behind.

'Richard!' squealed Christine, dropping the bag and forcing her way through the small office towards him. He greeted her with open arms and held on to her for a surprising amount of time.

'You look wonderful,' he said finally.

'Oh, you say that to all the girls,' said Christine, flushed bright red. 'God, it seems like another life when we stayed with you. How's the house? How's the sculpture? Oh wow, you're here!'

Richard smiled at her. Eupheme's eyes quickly scanned the handsome profile before her. He was gorgeous.

Christine sat down and covered her embarrassment by rapidly sorting out everyone's sandwiches like a woman in a village hall bring-and-buy. 'I haven't got anything for you. It's awful,' she said. 'You should have rung.'

'I'm Kevin,' said Kevin Waslick to Richard. 'I take it you are the infamous Richard from Italy.'

'That's right. Nice to meet you.' The two men shook

hands. Eupheme felt a wave of pride as she watched 'her man' responding so well in a social situation, not being rude to people, not being embarrassing as he so often had in the past. The memories of awkward exits from restaurants and parties were many and unpleasant.

'Richard's got a whole string of exhibitions lined up, all around the world,' said Eupheme proudly.

'Oh, Richard.' Christine's hands were clasped to her bosom in ecstatic adoration. 'You are so talented.'

'Nonsense,' said Richard with a wicked smile. 'Just very lucky. And even more lucky to have Eupheme.'

Eupheme's eyes flashed at the assumption that Richard thought he had her. He had nothing of the sort. She assumed that no one would notice this reaction. She saw immediately that Christine had.

'There's one more thing,' said Richard, turning to face Eupheme. 'I have a little something here.' He put his elegant hand in his linen jacket pocket and extracted a small box. Eupheme's heart slipped a gear as a rush of adrenalin hit her stomach. Twenty-nine years old and no one had ever asked her to marry them before.

Richard opened the box, took Eupheme's hand and placed it there. She looked down, her eyes filling with tears. It was a small, discreet but very beautiful diamond ring.

'I want to marry you,' he said softly.

Eupheme looked up at Kevin and Christine, who both stood in rapt silence, waiting to hear what she was going to say. Richard looked at her with such adoration it was painful. Eupheme was desperate to blow her nose.

'Oh, Richard,' she said.

Chapter Twenty

Sitting in traffic jams had never been so relaxing, and as the sun streamed in through the Range Rover windows, the massive tailback of traffic on the M1 didn't seem so bad. Gresham pushed herself back in the comfortable driving seat.

'This is a lovely piece of music,' said Ian, sitting in the passenger seat wearing a pair of Dolce e Gabbana sunglasses and a dishevelled suit.

'It's by Howard Goodall. Brilliant man. I'm using it in my film,' said Gresham.

'Brilliant,' said Ian, 'and when do we, the lucky old general public, get to see this masterpiece?'

'How about this morning?' said Gresham. 'You know a thing or two about editing, don't you?'

'When all's said and done, I can cut things together with the best of them,' said Ian with his peculiar laugh. 'Not.'

'Why don't you come and see the rough cut, tell me what you think?'

'Oh, brilliant,' said Ian. 'Actually see a professional's work in progress. I can't wait to tell the lads and lassies at the video club. Would that I had my Hi8 with me. Could have knocked together some sort of fly-on-the-wall thingy. Got a few shots of the unfinished work.'

'If you did I'd have to have you arrested,' said Gresham with a sly smile. 'The people who put the money up for the film might get a bit miffed if there was a bootleg copy doing the rounds.'

'Blimey O'Reilly,' said Ian with his special laugh. 'Just as well I'm camera-free.'

'Ian,' she said as they crawled forward, 'will you do something for me.'

'In the sexual department?' he asked in disbelief. 'Is that a good idea while you're driving?'

Gresham laughed. This from a man who had made her come three times in one night, and all she had to do was touch his rather nice cock for about a minute before he thanked her profusely as he came in a tissue he was holding. No nasty mess, no awkward moments, and the best night's sleep she'd had in yonks. And he was still offering more.

'No,' she said. 'I was actually referring to the discretion department. I want you to promise that you'll never tell anyone about what happened with the two of us. Not even your mum.'

'Don't worry on that old score,' said Ian, laughing again in his peculiarly attractive way. 'I'll go to the grave with our little secret locked in my heart.'

'That's sweet,' said Gresham, then snapped, 'But most of all, don't tell Eupheme.' She looked at Ian. He smiled and shrugged.

''Course not,' he said.

'It would really upset her, I think. She's ditzy enough as it is. No point pushing her over the edge.'

'That's very true,' said Ian. 'And talking of your half-sister, I've got a bit of an idea.'

'Oh yes?' said Gresham with a sly grin, her eyebrows popping up and down suggestively.

'Well, the wager with her. It's all a bit on the old academic side now, I know, but if you were to win, if it was still plain for all to see that I was a tosser *par excellence*, a loser *royale*, you would save yourself a few grand, wouldn't you?'

'Oh, Ian, you fucking genius.'

'Well, wait, there's more, as they say in the trade.' Ian worried his hands together nervously. His long legs were crossed an almost inhuman number of times, twisted together like rope. 'If you would split the savings in a fifty-fifty-type way, passing half of said funds in my general direction in the form of a cheque, cash or money order — would that I had a card swipe — then I could be looking at an off-line edit suite with all the trimmings and I could go into business on my own account, what with being presently jobless, et cetera.'

'I'm not sure I understood everything you said,' Gresham replied after a pause for thought, 'but you're saying if I win the wager with Pheme, you want me to pay you half of the money I win, which I haven't won because she won't give me money because she's already spent it on you?'

'I think that's what I'm saying.'

'It seems like a pretty shit deal to me.'

'But you will have full satisfaction in that you've proved your sister is not much to write home about in the brain department.'

'True, but I get that just by watching her walk into a room.' Gresham suddenly saw herself sitting in the car in the sun, feeling warm and attractive, playing this gentle game with this lovely gentle man. She felt happy for the first time since she had first shouted 'Action' and seen a huge crowd of people doing her bidding. 'Okay, Ian, if you can look like you do, but be a complete nerdy computer bore, if you can make people puke with the tedium of your company, I'll do a deal.'

'No problemo, Ms Hollingford.'

'But not fifty per cent. I'll give you twenty.'

'Twenty? Blimey. You drive a hard bargain. Let's try and push it all the way up to thirty.'

'I couldn't do that.'

'I may have to embarrass you at your wedding.'

'If you're invited,' said Gresham with a smile.

'I will be,' said Ian with a return smile.

'Twenty-five per cent and that's my final offer,' said Gresham. She held out her right hand to shake on the deal. 'And you'd better be Mr Super-Nerd on the big day.'

'You're a hard woman, but I love my women hard. Ha ha,' said Ian, laughing like a lech and shaking her hand. She pulled his hand and placed it gently between her legs. By the time the great mass of traffic on the M1 pulled itself slowly southward again, she had attained another orgasm.

Sally the receptionist looked up with an eyebrow raised as Gresham and Ian walked into the offices of Allied Fountain.

'This is my friend Ian Ringfold. Film theorist.'

'Oh, right,' said Sally, clearly not believing a word.

'I want him to have a look at the rough cut. Is anyone here?' asked Gresham.

'No one important,' said Sally quietly.

'Is Simon in?'

'No. He went out about an hour ago. He said he couldn't be bothered to wait any more.'

'Didn't you tell him I was going to be late?' snapped Gresham angrily.

'Of course I did,' said Sally. 'He just got impatient.'

'Wanker,' said Gresham, then looked at Sally, who was clearly mortified. 'I don't mean you, I mean Simon, you great pillock.'

Sally smiled flatly. The phone rang and she answered it in her practised singsong. 'Good morning, Allied Fountain, can I help you?'

Gresham turned to see Ian still standing by the door with his dark glasses on. 'Sorry, Ian, completely forgot you were there,' she said honestly. 'Come on, let's have a look-see at the old film-a-roochie.'

She and Ian walked up the stairs to the third floor and entered the edit suite. She turned on the machine.

'A classic old Steenbeck,' said Ian, looking over the machine with keen interest. 'Wow, the full monty, so to speak. I've only ever seen these in pictures. This is so grade-one exciting, you know, Gresham.'

'Take a seat and watch, then tell me what you think,' she said, pulling down the heavy blinds and pitching the room into darkness.

She looked at Ian as the film wound through the complex of gear sprockets and rollers. He watched the film avidly, his brows occasionally shifting down, the skin by his eyes creasing beautifully. She knew the film so well, frame by blasted frame, that she could tell from his expression that some of the big set-pieces worked, the love scenes were a disaster and, to her annoyance, as the film entered its third reel, he started to lose interest. He kept glancing at her during scene changes that had long run-ins owing to the unfinished nature of the film.

The spooling wheel ran out of film and the tail-end flicked loudly as *Uncle Roger* came to an end. They sat in the glow of the Steenbeck screen.

'Well?' she said.

'Eupheme, I . . .'

'I'm Gresham,' she said curtly.

'Sorry, Gresham,' said Ian, laughing with his odd sneer. 'Sorry, Gresham. I mean, what a movie. It's major-league brilliant. Richard E. Grant is so funny. Really funny. You know, people will just laugh their jolly old socks off when this is on the big screen.'

'You didn't laugh,' said Gresham, still smarting from being called Eupheme.

'I did,' said Ian, scratching his head, trying to remember. 'Didn't I?'

'No, you didn't. Look, be honest with me.'

'No, I really, really liked it. It was excellent. He's her uncle, but he doesn't know. I mean, it's so funny.'

'And?' said Gresham after a short silence.

'Sorry?'

'And why doesn't it work?'

'Oh, well, you've got the scene where she gets in the little plane on the windy airfield in the wrong place. That should come earlier so you know she knows Richard E. Grant's her uncle and he doesn't know she's his niece.'

'Say that again,' said Gresham.

'Well, when she gets in the plane, right,' said Ian, counting the scenes off on his fingers, 'she sees ...'

'... the picture of Richard on the book cover! Yes, of course,' said Gresham. She sat there, again with her mouth wide open. She slapped her forehead with the palm of her hand. 'Of course she does. Of course. You fucking idiot.'

'Did I say something wrong?' said Ian with a look of guilt.

'No, you great dork-brain. That's it. That's it!'

She dived on him and buried her tongue in his mouth. She ripped at his shirt, the buttons flying off and hitting the walls with the energy of her movements.

She moved him until he was lying on the floor, then sat above him, gradually moving up until his beautiful mouth made contact with her aching sex.

Simon Langham walked in eating a Pret à Manger feta cheese and Greek salad sandwich. His mouth hung open, revealing what happens to Greek salad when you've been chewing it for some time. Without any real embarrassment, Gresham stood up, leaving Ian sprawled on the floor.

'We've worked it out,' said Gresham. 'Ian and I have worked out what's wrong with the fucking film!'

Chapter Twenty-One

Ian Ringfold had a series of small problems in his life which he quite enjoyed thinking about. He ruminated that there were always problems in life, but they were mostly dull and tedious. Tax bills to pay, work rotas to agree, orders for tartare sauce to check.

Now everything had changed. He sat back in his seat on the 3.15 to Northampton and opened the brightly printed box beside him. He lifted up the slim plastic object inside and sniffed it. Nothing, he thought, smelt quite as exciting and special as brand-new electronic items. A sharp chemical smell that lasted only a couple of weeks. Electronics factories must reek of it. Would that he had a chance to visit one.

Ian had decided to walk from Gresham's edit suite to Euston station. He wasn't in a rush and he had nowhere to go particularly. The home help was visiting his mum, the weather was nice, and he felt very warm and relaxed. He had walked up the Tottenham Court Road checking on the various electronic innovations in cluttered displays in the windows. He stood outside Micro Anvika and looked at the Psion P3 palmtop computer. The latest breakthrough in miniature electronics, an amazingly powerful computer housed in a tiny case. Word processor, diary, address database, world map, calculator, the whole caboodle. He entered the store, pulled his Access credit card from the small red leather purse his auntie had given him and purchased the Psion. He didn't ask for any literature, he didn't ask to try one, he just walked in and bought it. Something he'd never done before, but he wanted to be different.

After a successful purchasing experience, he continued walking up Tottenham Court Road until he saw a Pret à Manger takeaway coffee shop. He'd noticed that Gresham and Eupheme and anyone connected with them always seemed to buy their food at one of these places. He went in and bought a chicken tikka and salad sandwich, fresh orange and a cappuccino to go. Fairly weird as sandwiches went. Ian was used to Heinz sandwich spread, or at the most exotic cheese and pickle of the mango variety. As he chewed, he started to get a taste for the eclectic flavours. Everything, he decided, was brilliant.

He walked the rest of the way to Euston and sailed on to Platform 5 feeling like a man who knew how to deal with the world. He found a front-facing seat with a table and sat down.

'I'm sorted,' he said, imitating Ben Elton's 'got to get a double seat' comedy routine.

He inserted the batteries into the rear of the palmtop, pressed the 'on' key and the thing came to life.

'One serious bit of kit,' he muttered as the screen started to show him what it could do. He checked the time in Calcutta and Sydney and then opened a word-processing document.

He listed his problems in twelve-point Helvetica, bullet indentations, ranged left.

- No job
- Gresham
- The Wager
- Mum
- Full-scale professional Macintosh-based edit suite.

He sighed deeply and pressed the cursor key, watching it descend and ascend the list. No job. Well, somehow that didn't feel as bad as he'd expected. He had some money and now the chance of making a bit more. After that, who knew, but this fresh feeling of freedom was so intoxicating. He could go back home now and surf the Net without the slightest concern for time. No night shift, no day shift, just no shift. His time was his own for the first time in his life. He rewrote his list.

- Time, as much as I need
- Gresham
- Mum
- Spondulicks and the lack thereof

Those were his main concerns. He pondered on the possibility that he could easily fall in love with a very beautiful lady if he wasn't very careful. A lady ... no, a woman whose taste he knew he would never forget. If this was falling in love it really wasn't like anything he had imagined. He knew it was an impossible love and that nothing he could ever do or say, or earn for that matter, would come close to seriously wooing the lovely Gresham Hollingford. She was top-drawer material without a doubt; he was barely drawer-worthy at all, even in his borrowed Ermenegildo Zegna suit.

Then there was his mum. Even if Gresham threw all caution to the winds and wanted to elope with him, he couldn't just up and leave his old mother. She could barely move. Her hips were now so bad she was virtually bedridden. He had noticed that the iller she became the more tolerant and sweet she seemed to be. A lot of her old crabbiness seemed to evaporate; it was as if she supported everything Ian was doing. No longer chipping away at him and trying to keep him at home.

'I'll look after you, Mum,' he said to himself, feeling very soulful. He gazed at the screen, trying to understand what was happening to his life.

He suddenly realised what he had done. He'd written a list

of problems without Eupheme's name attached. The biggest problem of all. He quickly added her name to his bullet list, changed the font to bold and underlined it.

Charging into his life with her strange clothes and constant desire to control him. And she'd succeeded. He realised she'd completely changed the way he saw the world. She was right, she really had won the wager, and yet ironically he felt more relaxed with her dreaded half-sister, who had seemingly started the whole thing off.

His life had become so utterly entwined with these two women. Now he was playing them off against each other for all he was worth, which he knew wasn't much. It was Eddie's fault to start with, encouraging him to try to make money out of the situation, but once he had taken the first step, there was no stopping him. He found it absurdly exciting to be tricking both women, so no matter what happened he would get a couple of grand.

Computer Warehouse here I come, he thought.

He wiped the entire list except for their two names.

- Gresham
- Eupheme

Ian liked Eupheme. He thought she was interesting, fascinating even, but she wasn't safe. He felt safe with Gresham. She might seem dangerous when first encountered, but she was so clear about what she wanted there would never be a time when he wasn't sure. If she wanted his head between her legs, that's what she got. If she didn't, the thought of putting his head there wouldn't occur to him.

With Eupheme it was very difficult, if not impossible, to understand what she wanted. Sometimes he thought she might want him sexually – she would look at him in the same way Gresham did. But then, without anything happening that Ian was aware of, she would change and look at him as if he were a dead rat. Eupheme, Ian decided, was very unclear about what she wanted in life and was therefore a little on the dangerous side.

He laughed to himself. Although he felt guilty about splitting the proceeds whichever way the wager went, the fact that he'd thought of it at all gave him a warm feeling in his stomach. Ian realised, for the first time in his thirty-two years on the planet, that he liked himself. He was sure it was wrong and egotistical, but he did think that Ian Ringfold, ex assistant manager dry goods and shelf-assembly designer, was okay really. Really, really okay, actually.

Maybe it was that he felt he belonged somewhere, even if it was between two warring half-sisters. It was his role to be there and he felt good about it. He looked down at his Psion P3 screen again. He wanted to add something to his list, but couldn't decide quite what it was.

Finally he wrote.

- I belong

That seemed enough.

Chapter Twenty-Two

Eupheme and Richard climbed out of the small red Alfa Romeo outside the NatWest bank on Shepperton High Street. Richard had driven from Clapham in a calm and tranquil way, almost sedate in his gear changes and gentle braking. Eupheme noticed there was none of the blaring horn, foot hard down and to hell with the other guy approach that she had put up with on her visits to Italy. The drives up the mountain after another delirious night of drinking in the Bar Centrale, Umbertide had been burned for ever into her memory.

Richard had borrowed the car from his brother, who ran a fine-art restoring business in Battersea.

'I haven't told you,' he said as the car locks beeped in the quiet suburban air, 'I've actually lost my licence.'

'Oh, Richard,' said Eupheme sadly.

'I got stopped outside Mercetale. I was way over the limit. My name's Richard and I'm an alcoholic. I'm driving extra-carefully at the moment because I don't really want to get pulled over.'

'Oh, Richard,' said Eupheme again. 'It's really wonderful you can tell me this. It's brilliant you've faced this problem.'

'I know,' he said.

'I'll drive back, though. It's highly dangerous. You're not covered by insurance, are you.'

'No, but I just wanted to show that I could be responsible. I have so much to make up for. I've been so hopeless for so long. God, Pheme, I love you so much it hurts.'

She smiled pitifully at him and they embraced gently.

'Oh, Richard,' she said, then broke the embrace. She allowed a thought to bubble up, He's lost his licence and he drove me here completely uninsured, she said to herself. How could he? She couldn't let it out; she had to hold it, put it away somewhere, but she was furious. Maybe that's what marriage is about, she thought, being furious with your partner and doing and saying nothing about it. She sighed and started walking past the side of the bank to an entrance door set in a high brick wall. She pressed the bell. Christine's voice cracked on the line.

'Come up. Third floor.'

Richard and Eupheme had agreed to go to Christine's for dinner under some pressure. Eupheme wasn't ready for formal acknowledgments of her possible engagement.

'Come in, come in,' said Christine as she opened the door to her flat. 'Scuse the mess, it's awful. Filkins and Tonto have been absolute terrors while I've been at work today. The mess they've made.'

'The cats?' asked Richard, offering Christine a bottle of sparkling herb-flavoured mineral water. Christine had discreetly whispered to Eupheme that she was very happy to have an alcohol-free meal.

Christine dashed into the kitchen. 'Go into the front room and make yourselves at home. This is all ready.'

Eupheme followed Richard into the small front room which was cluttered with knick-knacks, pictures of cats, posters for the benefit, corn dollies and old armchairs with brightly coloured cloth thrown over them.

'It looks so much nicer,' said Eupheme, looking around. 'She's just decorated,' she whispered to Richard.

'Oh, it's all right, not a patch on your place, Richard,' shouted Christine from the kitchen.

'This is very nice,' said Richard. 'Lovely tree out of the window.'

'My tree,' said Christine. 'Yes, it's beautiful, isn't it? Never get bored of looking at that, and my thrush lives in there.'

'Such a lovely song,' said Eupheme helpfully.

'I do miss the song of the thrush,' said Richard. 'In Italy, that's one thing about this awful country I actually do miss.'

Christine entered with a tray containing a large earthenware pot, three plates and all the trimmings.

'It's my world-famous Guinness stew,' she said, lowering the heavy tray on to a glass-topped table. 'It's been cooking for three days now, on a slow cooker. It's a brilliant thing. Just throw it all in and leave it.'

'Wonderful,' said Eupheme, who didn't feel the least bit hungry.

'Oh no!' squealed Christine so loudly that it actually hurt Eupheme's ears. 'What have I done?'

'It's okay, I'm not that hungry,' said Richard.

'What's the matter?' asked Eupheme.

'Guinness stew. How could I have been so stupid? Oh no, Richard, I am so sorry.'

'Don't worry, it's fine, honestly.'

'No,' said Christine, holding both hands out to keep them quiet. 'I'll order a Chinese from across the road. They're brilliant. Not just any old Chinese, these are really special.'

'Don't bother.'

'Richard, be quiet, you're having a Chinese.'

Unfortunately for Eupheme, Christine's world-famous Guinness stew was not overly wonderful, and Richard's Chinese meal looked outstanding.

'Oh, this really reminds me of Castello del Largo,' said Christine.

Not me, thought Eupheme, who could remember only Richard's drunken lunging at her when she wanted to sleep.

'Christine, I'd really like it if you'd be involved in the wedding,' said Richard out of the blue.

'Oh, of course. I'd be thrilled to bits,' said Christine, wiping her mouth with a purple serviette.

'And whose wedding is this?' asked Eupheme with a pained smile.

'I know we haven't really talked about it, sweets, but as Christine is such a good friend of yours, and she's been so wonderful at tidying up the castle ... All that washing up you did,' said Richard with a smile.

'Oh, I don't mind,' said Christine.

'Richard, I ...' Eupheme found herself without the nerve to continue.

There was a silence

'What?'

'Well, I haven't ... well, I don't know yet. I haven't decided.'

'What haven't you decided?'

'Well, about marrying you.'

'What!' Richard was clearly shocked by this revelation.

'Oh, Pheme,' said Christine.

'I haven't actually said yes. I don't think I like you organising my friends for a wedding I haven't even agreed to. It's all been a bit sudden.'

'Oh, goodness. I thought it was all on,' said Christine.

'So did I,' said Richard. 'Why didn't you say?'

'I haven't had a chance.' Eupheme felt very uncomfortable. 'I've got so much on my plate at the moment I can't deal with marriage plans. I'm sorry.'

'But ...' Richard brushed his hands on his jacket, the way he did when he needed a drink.

'I haven't actually said no either,' said Eupheme. 'I just need a bit of quiet time to think about it. What with the benefit and Ian and everything.'

'Who's Ian?' asked Richard.

THE MAN ON PLATFORM FIVE

'Oh, it's not like that,' Christine reassured him.

'Like what?'

'She means I'm not having an affair with him,' said Eupheme.

'Who?' said Richard, his voice now getting louder.

'There's a man called Ian I've been doing a project with. It's been really interesting and very successful. It's nearly over now but it's very complicated.'

'Everything you say just makes it sound more weird,' said Richard. 'What project?'

'I can't really explain. It would sound daft, I know that. It is daft.'

'It isn't daft at all,' Christine reassured her. 'Can I explain?'

'Yes, maybe you'd better,' said Richard, his eyes now quite on fire with anger, hands working overtime on his jacket.

'Pheme had a bet with Gresham about . . .'

'It wasn't a bet,' snapped Eupheme.

'No, sorry, not a bet, a sort of thing, an argument,' said Christine.

'A political and philosophical disagreement,' said Eupheme.

Christine went on to explain the process as best she could. Eupheme listened passively. Hearing the story told by Christine made her feel strangely proud. She had achieved something profound with that man. At the end of the tale Richard turned and looked at her, all anger gone.

'I love you so much,' he said.

'Aaahh,' said Christine.

'You are so brave, you are such an artist. What a crazy thing to do. That's what I've always loved about you.'

Tears welled up in Eupheme's eyes without any warning. She had felt no lump in the throat, no warning, and also no desire to curry favour from Richard and Christine. She just started sobbing, spontaneously. Richard sat next to her on the sofa and comforted her gently.

ROBERT LLEWELLYN

'No one understands what I've been trying to do,' she said between sobs. 'It's been so hard, and Ian is so ... well, so ungrateful.'

'But you won, Pheme,' said Christine, her face also stained with tears. 'When I saw him at the engagement party I couldn't believe my own eyes. I know it's been hard for you, but you did show her.'

'But I didn't!' Eupheme wailed. 'That's the whole point. I just ended up making myself look a fool again. But anyway, it's all on again. I'm regrouping, I'm getting really prepared this time. She knows she's wrong now, and all I have to do is present her with the evidence. Just wait until the wedding.'

'Whose wedding?' asked Richard nervously.

'Gresh's, middle of next month, to Stanhope De Courcey.'

'What, the Duke of Weymouth's son? Bloody hell.'

'I told you about it when we were at your place,' said Eupheme.

'Sorry, darling. Can't remember a thing from before I was dry,' said Richard resignedly. 'But the De Courceys bought one of my pieces when I was at the Royal College of Art. I remember that. They are seriously stacked. Blimey, she certainly made a catch.'

'Exactly!' said Eupheme. 'She's marrying this awful man for his money. It's dreadful.'

'He seemed ever so nice to me,' said Christine. 'I met him at the engagement party. It was wonderful, so many people and Gresham's ... well, your dad's house is so lovely.'

'Anyway,' said Eupheme, barely covering her annoyance with Christine, 'it's been awful and I'll be glad when it's over and I can forget about the whole awful thing.'

'I can wait,' said Richard. 'I can wait till you're ready for me.'

'Aahh,' said Christine.

'Christine, do you mind?' pleaded Eupheme, suddenly angry again.

'Sorry,' said Christine, who started gathering plates, flushed bright red.

Chapter Twenty-Three

Ian's mum was asleep in the front room when he got in from the shops. He lugged the heavy carrier bags through the house and into the kitchen, being as quiet as the small space would allow. He loved the boiled cabbage and old polish smell of 76 Cyril Street. The familiar odour embraced him as he entered.

He put the shopping away in the old cupboards, feeling the now noticeably developed muscles in his arm and back as he heaved the heavy bags.

In the seventies his mother had lined the surfaces of these pre-war cupboards with sticky-backed plastic. He remembered that the trade name was Fablon, which sounded to the young Master Ringfold like a planet in *Star Wars*. This Fablon material was still there, scratched and faded but doing sterling service.

Ian had purchased groceries at Sainsbury's in town. He couldn't face going back to the Wellingborough Road Besco. True, he missed his discount, but he'd snipped up his loyalty card that morning without too much heartache.

He made a pot of tea, put some digestive biscuits on a plate and carried everything into the front room on a flower-motif laminated tray he'd got on discount from the household section on Aisle 14. He smiled resignedly as he realised that he no longer had to worry about Aisle 14 or any of the other aisles for that matter.

Although the sun was hot and bright outside, his mother managed to keep the small front room at an unchanging and fairly warm temperature all year round, and she never opened the curtains.

'Hello, Mum, cup of tea for you,' he said as he slid the tray on to a table he'd bought at MFI. It had come in flat-pack form and took him only two ticks to erect. Not bad for £24–99.

'That's sweet of you, son,' said his mother, her voice croaky with disuse. 'Did you have a nice time?'

'A nice time? At the shops, Mum?' said Ian with his Rick Mayall sneer. 'Oh yes, a very likely story, I don't think.'

'I thought you was with that young lady.'

'Oh,' said Ian, now confused. 'Well, that was last week some time. But yes, I had a very nice time, as a matter of fact.'

'Is she still here?'

'Who's that, Mum?' said Ian, pouring the rich-coloured tea.

'That nice-looking young lady?' she asked, immediately indicating to Ian that he needn't worry about explaining his whereabouts. It was ten days since Gresham had turned up at their front door.

'No, she's not here, Mum, that was ages ago.' He handed her a cup of tea with two digestive biscuits balanced on the saucer. 'Don't worry about it. I've got it all sorted.'

'Shouldn't you be at work, dear?' she asked, her voice now sounding anxious.

'I've got lots of new avenues to explore, Mater dearest. Loads and tons of new opportunities. However, there is a small fly-type problemette in the old ointment-a-roochie.'

'What's that, love?' she asked, in the same voice she used when he started talking about the baud rates on his latest modem.

'Well, the only slight drawback to the all new improved Ian Ringfold dot com is that I have to spend a night in old Londinium.'

He knew this would be a bombshell for his mother, but he thought it best to land the big one on her and then follow through with the gentler explanation. His mother said nothing. What colour remained in her cheeks fled as she stared at him, her cup of tea vibrating very slightly.

He had spent an hour on the phone to Eupheme the previous night and was quite tense about suggesting the plan to his mother. Eupheme had insisted that if they were going to win it would have to be a full-time commitment leading up to the wedding. That was where she was going to unveil him, so to speak. At Gresham's wedding, the social event of the decade. Before that, she wanted him to have a lot of dialect coaching from Cicily, she wanted him in the gym every day, he needed new clothes, a new haircut, his teeth still needed work. She wanted him to attend the benefit to get used to mixing with celebrities and to have a stock of good quality anecdotes, should he need them. There was far too much to do and she couldn't have him rushing off to catch trains all the time.

Ian insisted that he could manage all that but he couldn't leave his mother overnight and the benefit would run on past his return train time, therefore he really couldn't make it. Eupheme counter-insisted that he bring his mother with him as her flat was big enough for all of them and anyway she always felt guilty about all the space there not being used.

Ian got out his Psion P3 and flipped open the lid. He scrolled through a long document until he got to the part where he had made notes on the bus on the way home. He took a deep breath and started reading.

'Mum, the thing is, with my new job, I also have use of a rather nice flat in the Clapham area of South London. How would you feel about coming to stay the night there? I know you're going to say what about your friends and the aunts, et cetera, which is all well and good, but most of your friends have passed on or are dribbling in various homes and the aunts definitely live in a world of their own, to which, Mum, we do not, thank the old Lord above, have a key. And it's only for one night. For now, I mean. If it works out well, maybe we could increase it.'

'Oh, love, and I thought you were going to put me in a home,' said his mother.

Ian looked up from the screen to see that she was smiling. 'I'd never do that, Mum, don't worry. You can come with me. I'm going to arrange it all. Get everything sorted.'

His mother slowly sat up and drank some tea, her hands still shaking slightly. A stranger wouldn't notice, but Ian could see that she was really going downhill.

'What's your job?' his mother asked a few moments later, regaining her composure once the sugar had hit her bloodstream.

'Aha,' said Ian. He quickly scanned his Psion for an answer. He didn't have one. He was completely stumped as to what to say. Then he noticed a note at the bottom of his short speech. 'Keep it hazy.'

He smiled. 'Well, that would be telling, Mum. It's all a bit on the hush-hush side.'

'Nothing indecent, I hope,' she said.

Ian kept smiling at his mum and drank his sweet tea. 'Very hush-hush in point of fact,' he said, and started pondering various 'I've been recruited by MI5' storylines, but decided against this option and sat in silence.

Chapter Twenty-Four

To Ian, the block of two weeks between his conversation with his mother and the night of the benefit was a finite period of different-coloured days which ended with a black line. This image of time might have been influenced by the 'Claris Organiser' program he ran on his desktop computer, or it might have been that the men who designed the Claris organiser were like Ian, in that they saw time in neat-coloured blocks that had a start and a finish with a thick black line.

Unlike Ian, Eupheme never saw events taking place within specifically defined blocks of time. For her, time was like water, a huge lake of water that she could now see, as she was halfway through her twenty-ninth year, was beginning to develop beaches of dryness.

For Eupheme the two weeks had passed in a daze of arrangements, phone calls and frantic meetings. Her 'men-whispering' project had scarcely skimmed the lower reaches of her consciousness. With Richard's sudden arrival in her life and bed, and his heavily sleeping body left behind every morning, the International Children's Trust benefit and the fact that she hadn't paid a bill in the flat for nearly a year, she didn't feel as if she had a lot of free time for contemplating changing the world.

However, she could feel that the benefit would become

her crowning achievement in the world of fund-raising. The event was being hosted by Jonathan Ross and Hugh Laurie; the headline comics were Ben Elton, Hattie Hayridge, Eddie Izzard, Craig Charles and Jenny Eclair. Sir Paul McCartney was playing the finale with numerous musical guests. The event was sold out and already a huge amount of money had poured into the charity coffers. They had to call on volunteer staff to open envelopes, sort cheques and man the phones on the freephone credit card booking line they had set up, a service operated free for them by British Telecom. All this took place in the small one-room office which was a hive of frantic activity. The mess was almost unbearable, even for Eupheme, but every evening she and Christine walked down to the Holloway Road and paid many hundreds of thousands of pounds into the bank account of the International Children's Trust.

Eupheme was not only very popular in the office, she was very popular at home with her prospective husband. She still hadn't said yes, but it had become the next thing she was going to do. She would decide after the benefit, or certainly after Gresham's wedding. Whatever, before Christmas.

Eupheme's lake of time finally shape-shifted into 'the day of the benefit'. She should have been serene, she should have known everything was organised, accounted for and in order. Everyone knew what they were doing, where they should be, and what time they should be there. None of this information made any difference to her. At 3.15 on the afternoon of the great day, Eupheme was running around the office screaming.

'Christine, Christine! Have you got the box?'

'What? Sorry?' said Christine.

'The box of information leaflets? Oh God. I was relying on you.'

'Hang on a moment, please,' said Christine, who was trying to talk to someone on the phone. 'What leaflets?'

'The ones about us,' said Eupheme, tearing her way through the mess of her office. 'About our work, the trust. Oh God!'

'They're in the old dog-food box somewhere.'

'Well,' said Eupheme peevishly, 'did Kevin take them?'

'I don't know.' Christine was now quite openly angry. 'I wasn't here when he left. You were.'

Eupheme slapped her forehead. 'Yes, he's got them, I remember him carrying them out. What's wrong with me today?'

'You've got too many things on your plate.'

'Okay,' said Eupheme, clearly oblivious of Christine's concern. 'So is that everything?'

'Look, I'll call you tomorrow,' said Christine into the telephone. 'Everything's on hold until after the benefit. Sorry. Bye.' She put the receiver down. 'Now, what's the problem, Eupheme?'

'I know I've forgotten something. There's something I have to do. I've done the banner, I've done the leaflets, I've sold all the tickets. Everyone knows where they should be. What is it?'

'I can't think of anything. We all know what we're doing,' said Christine, standing up and brushing biscuit crumbs from her lap. 'I have to have a wee or I'm going to literally burst. Can you deal with the phones?'

'Christine, I've got to go!' wailed Eupheme.

'Just for ten seconds,' said Christine, darting out of the door.

The phone rang immediately. 'Shit!' said Eupheme, snatching it up. 'Yes.'

'Oh, hi, Pheme. You don't usually answer,' said the voice. 'It's usually the lovely Christine.'

'Who is this?' she asked.

'It's me, I'm at Euston. I thought you said you'd meet us. I printed out my e-mail just to be sure.'

'Ian!' Eupheme remembered what she had forgotten with an icy shiver. 'Shit.'

''Scuse your French.'

'Please don't say that.'

'Sorry.'

'Wait there, I'm getting a cab.'

Eupheme rushed out of the door just remembering to grab her huge D&G bag containing among the masses of objects that made up her daily life a heavy phone book. Leather-bound, not a Filofax or a Psion P3, as Ian had advised her to get, but a great big book with hundreds of yellow Post-it notes stuck with varying degrees of accuracy through its pages. Eupheme's phone book was legendary in fund-raising circles. It contained the addresses of all the leading show business players in London, not just their present addresses but all their previous ones, their old phone numbers, their fax and e-mail contacts, agents, friends and managers. All this information was jumbled in an amazing display of doodles, crossings-out and additions. Eupheme extracted the book as she stormed along under the broad-leafed trees fringing Highbury Fields. She wanted the number of the stage manager to check that everything was on schedule.

She found a taxi on Upper Street and headed for Euston, calling the stage manager on her mobile as the cab moved off. Everything was fine, everything was in place; the only problem the stage manager was having was that his mobile kept ringing during sound checks and could she please relax.

The cab driver waited on Eversholt Street as she dashed towards the Euston station concourse.

Her mind raced, her head throbbed with information overload as she stumbled through the crowds. How could she have forgotten Ian? All that work and yet somehow the memory had vanished. She tried to look into herself as she walked, tried to see why he had disappeared from her consciousness. Maybe it was because of the money – she had hated the way he had suddenly come back to her and promised to try to win against Gresham. For the money. It grated with her, and yet it was the only way. He had completely missed the point, but then maybe she was expecting too much of him. That then struck her as a dreadful thing to think, let alone say.

She stopped walking and clasped her hands to her chest. She knew it was no good. If he did it for the money, even if she did win, it wouldn't be true. She might as well hire an actor, as Gresham had suspected her of doing. The whole thing would be fake, and she really wanted Gresham to see that it was a real change. She would have to confront him with that. She would have to say the deal was off.

She started walking then paused again and turned around and around in a small circle. She had just had a flash of her half-sister's face, its expression showing that she had been caught out and made to see that she had finally blown it. Finally got it wrong. Even if Ian did only go through with the whole thing for the money, it would still be real. He had changed – it wasn't just 'an act'. She could see herself justifying what she had done in a seminar, people firing questions at her. She batted them back skilfully, often using the question to reveal the questioner's double standards or self-doubt. She started walking again, the crowds swimming before her, the panic rising inside as she asked herself what she was doing wandering around Euston station when she should be at the Royal Albert Hall.

Suddenly she froze. She looked through the mass of people to a still place. There was Ian, looking wonderful, hair perfect, teeth gleaming, and a careful loving hand helping an old woman walk slowly across the concourse.

It was his mother! She recognised her from the visit to Northampton. She walked up to them, all her previous worries wiped clean by a new monster cloud of anxiety.

'Ian, hi, um, Christ,' was all she could manage as she reached them.

'Shouldn't take the Lord's name in vain, love,' said Mrs Ringfold, looking up from her Zimmer with a surprisingly warm smile.

'God, sorry,' said Eupheme. 'Ian, um, look, it's just that I'm in a really huge hurry.'

'I know,' said Ian calmly. 'But we agreed Mum was coming.'

'Did we?' asked Eupheme, with a horrible sick feeling that he was right.

'It's okay,' said Ian, 'I'll put Mum in a cab.'

'What!' Eupheme snapped.

'I'll send her on to your place. She's fine, she can look after herself.'

'It's three flights up, Ian, it's not a house!'

'Okay, well I couldn't leave her. I told you.'

'Look, Ian, it's just really difficult today. I suppose I wasn't thinking when we spoke on the phone.'

'We'll be off first thing on the morrow.'

'Please don't say on the morrow.'

'Sorry,' said Ian. He ran his hands through his thick pelt of hair. 'Look, I'll go with Mum and make sure she's okay and then I'll join you at the benefit.'

Eupheme remembered the mess the flat was in — clothes everywhere, books strewn in piles, dirty dishes piled up in the sink. Rotting food in the fridge with the door that wouldn't shut. Richard asleep in her bed.

'Look, isn't there some other . . . ?'

Ian cut her off, not nastily, but firmly. 'I can always catch the train back home. No skin off the old nose-a-roochie. Just thought I'd throw in that "a-roochie" for good measure. Won't say it again. Don't worry.'

Eupheme looked at her watch. She wasn't really needed at the Albert Hall; Christine knew what was going on, Kevin was there, and she would only be a bit late. 'No, it's okay,' she said. 'We'll go in the same cab. This way.'

She started walking off briskly. Mrs Ringfold put her Zimmer frame in front of her and took a very short step forward. Eupheme smiled as sweetly as her temper would allow and joined the old lady, offering her an arm. She then experienced the vice-like Ringfold Senior grip and decided the old dear wasn't as frail as she looked. She walked as fast as she could, virtually dragging Mrs Ringfold along.

'Easy!' said Ian, grabbing his mother's arm and carrying the Zimmer frame. 'She not too steady in the old pin department.'

The two of them virtually carried her out to the waiting taxi and bundled her inside.

'This is the first time I been in one of these,' she said, running her liver-spotted old hand across the vinyl as if it were cut moquette.

Ian opened his mouth to speak but Eupheme put her hand up. 'Please don't start talking about taxis, Ian. Please.'

'Okay. Sorry, Eupheme. I'll be on my best behaviour from now on.'

It took seventy-five minutes of overheated discomfort to grind through the traffic and get to Clapham Common North Side. As soon as the cab pulled up outside Eupheme's building she jumped out and ran to the big front door. She wedged it open with a pile of old *Time Out*s that had been dumped in the hall and ran upstairs.

She went straight to the bedroom and found no sign of Richard. The bed was made; his bag had been put to one side, clothes folded neatly. However, the rest of the flat was an utter disgrace. Charging around, tidying as best she could, she threw dirty knickers and T-shirts, bras and half-washed tights into old carrier bags which she stuffed roughly beside the washing machine that leaked. She threw cups ringed with ten-day-old coffee mould into the sink, swept spilt muesli off the kitchen table and finally gave up.

Ian walked in with his mother.

'Bit of a climb there, wasn't it, Mum?' he said as he guided the exhausted woman to a chair. Eupheme rushed ahead of them and picked up a pile of unread faxes and unfinished letters she had put there a month before.

'Sorry it's such a mess,' she said. 'I've been fearfully busy lately.'

'Oh, it's a lovely place, dear,' said Mrs Ringfold. 'So much room. Wouldn't you have loved this much room when you was a kiddie, Ian?'

'I certainly would, Mum. I could have had some major battles with my toy soldiers in here.'

'He loved his soldiers, played with them for hours as a nipper.'

Eupheme smiled, automatically. She was completely uninterested but felt it would be rude to do what she wanted, which was to walk out and leave them to it.

Ian turned to Eupheme. 'Can you show Mum round, then?' he asked.

'Show her round?' said Eupheme, looking for the thousandth time that day at her watch. 'Of course. I'm sorry, Mrs Ringfold, it's just that I've been so rushed off my feet, today of all days, but of course. Let's see, where shall we start?'

'Well, she needs to know where she can put her things, her bags, et cetera. I'll have to pop down to the cab and get them. Can you show her the bedroom and where she should put her bits and bobs?'

Ian smiled and walked out of the door. Eupheme turned to Mrs Ringfold. She took a huge breath and helped the frail old woman up.

'The TV is there, here's the remote. Press any button for on, red one for off. Um, come this way to the kitchen.' She stood at the door as the old woman obligingly shuffled forward. Eupheme passed her and stood in the middle of the untidy kitchen.

'There's milk in the fridge, help yourself to anything, ring for a pizza if you want, number's on the fridge door. There's the kettle, there's clean cups in the cupboard over here.'

'Thank you, dear. I'll find my way around right enough. You go off and do your business. I know you don't want an old lady hanging around getting in the way.'

'Not at all. It's a pleasure to have you here,' lied Eupheme.

'Is your mother still with us?' asked Mrs Ringfold.

'Sorry?' said Eupheme.

'Your mother. Does she live near?'

'Oh, no, she lives in Hove,' said Eupheme. 'Near Brighton,' she added when Mrs Ringfold didn't respond.

'She must be very proud of you,' said Mrs Ringfold.

'Oh, yes. Well, no, she thinks I'm terribly untidy. Huh, that always drove her round the bend when I was young. "Tidy your room," she used to say to me. All the time. "Eupheme, tidy your room or you'll get no tea." I must have been terrible.'

'You see her much?' asked Mrs Ringfold.

'Not a lot, no,' said Eupheme, thinking of the drink-and-drugs binges that made her presence in the old Hove flat untenable. 'I suppose I'm always too busy.'

'Go and see your mum, that's my advice,' said Mrs Ringfold. 'It'll put everything into perspective.'

'Yes, you're right, I suppose. Yes,' Eupheme said.

'Ian was always a tidy little lad. He was never much trouble, which was just as well, because we was blessed with a child rather late in life.'

'I see,' said Eupheme sympathetically.

'You want children, love?'

'Well, I . . . yes. Some time.'

'Have 'em sooner than later. That's my advice. So you've still got a bit of energy when they're young.'

'Yes, I suppose you're right.'

Ian entered the kitchen carrying two huge bags.

'Goodness, what a lot of stuff,' said Eupheme.

'Yeah,' said Ian. 'Hope my mum hasn't been giving you her world-famous bits of advice.'

'Not at all. We've been having a lovely chat,' said Eupheme, glancing at her watch yet again. 'Come on, then. I'll show you your room.' She led the way down the long dusty corridor to the spare bedroom. She couldn't open the door because Geoffrey's bike had fallen over and blocked it.

'Goodness, what's been going on in here?' she laughed. 'Hang on a minute. I'll tidy it up.'

She shoulder-barged the door and managed to squeeze in. The room was not a room but an horrendous pile of disused domestic rubbish. 'Oh my God. Um, let's use the other spare room,' said Eupheme, opening the door opposite which led to Geoffrey's room. As she went inside she realised she hadn't opened the door for possibly a year; the air was musty and thick. Geoffrey's room was officially sacrosanct; she was allowed to have friends stay over as long as it wasn't in his bed, Geoffrey had always been very clear about that, and Eupheme had always respected his wishes. However, this was a highly serious emergency and she felt she could justify her invasion.

'I'll open a window,' she said.

'Don't you worry, love, you get on,' said Mrs Ringfold. 'I'll put me feet up for forty winks then I'll sort it all out. You get off to your shindig.'

'Are you sure?' said Eupheme pleadingly.

'Yes, I'm sure,' said Mrs Ringfold.

'See you later, then, Mum. You have a rest and a nice cup of the old Rosie Lee.'

Mrs Ringfold sat down on the bed and Ian bent down and carefully removed her grey plastic shoes from her twisted old feet.

'There you go, Mum. See you later.'

Ian and Eupheme left the flat and charged down the large stairs.

'Ian, I've got to say I'm not really totally happy about all this,' Eupheme said as they got outside and climbed back into the cab.

'What, about my mum?' asked Ian, smiling and looking out of the window at the passing sights of Clapham.

'Well, yes.'

'But you suggested it.'

'I know I did. I know it's my fault but it's very awkward having her there.'

'She's all right. Just ignore her. I do.'

'That's a terrible thing to say.'

'She's okay. I look after her.'

'She's your mother.'

'Yeah, but that doesn't alter the basic fact that she's really, really senile, actually.'

'She seems very on the ball to me.'

'What about your mum?' asked Ian.

'That's different.'

'Do you look after her?'

'She doesn't need looking after.'

'You never talk about her,' said Ian. 'D'you hate her or something?'

'No, of course not. She is, I admit, a very difficult woman, with a lot of problems, but of course I don't hate her. She's my mother.'

'Exactly,' said Ian. 'And I have to look after my mum. She's got no one else, so that's why, if I come and live in London to do the project, she comes with.'

'I know,' said Eupheme. 'But it's not just that. It's you, Ian. You've changed.'

'Of course I've changed. You changed me, or didn't you notice?'

'I didn't change you, you were already there.'

'Oh, wow, spiritual, man,' said Ian, adopting a silly voice.

'I just allowed what was there to come out.'

'Excuse me, Vicar.'

'You're different, more confident, in an annoying way.'

'Oh, sorry, I'm sure.'

'The whole thing about the money, that's very ugly, Ian.'

'What money?'

'About the wager with Gresham. I mean, I'm not doing this for the money, I never was. It's a point of principle.'

'I'm not doing it for the money either,' said Ian.

'Well, that's not what it looks like from where I'm sitting,' said Eupheme boldly. 'I'm not making money out of this, Ian, I'm just being paid my expenses. It's not like it's a seven-thousand-pound prize or something.'

'I know, but it's also a point of principle for me. I was duped, used and would have been dropped like old pants as soon as you'd won.'

'You would not!' said Eupheme. 'I would never have done that. I'm not like that. D'you really think I'm like that?'

Ian nodded. 'Look, you're not interested in me in any other way, are you? What would really have happened? Would we have stayed in touch? I don't think so. You've always kept me at arm's length. What would you have done if I'd kept hanging around? It would have been so embarrassing. We've got nothing in common. I'm not really interested in any of the stuff you think is interesting.'

Eupheme put her head as far back into the corner of the taxi interior as she could. She had never heard Ian speak like this before, articulate and piercing. She knew he was right but she couldn't bear to admit it to herself. She wouldn't really want him hanging around, and yet she wouldn't want him to disappear. She grabbed that thought and ran with it.

'What you say is . . . well, it's simply not true. I think we have, despite everything, become friends. Something, let me tell you, which would never have happened with Gresham.'

'Yes, you're probably right,' said Ian flatly.

'I am right, believe me,' said Eupheme. 'And as for keeping you at arm's length, I had to in order to keep an objective view on things. The whole reason I did this was because you are a very attractive man, Ian. I know you think you're nobody and unimportant, and I know you feel uncomfortable when you receive attentions from women, but it might be something you're going to have to get used to. All the women I know find you very attractive, which was my whole point. I was saying to Gresham that she was writing you off as uninteresting on such a superficial list of faults, faults which we, together, have rectified.'

Ian leant forward slowly and moved his lips to within centimetres of Eupheme's. He let her move slightly until their lips met and they kissed, softly at first and then passionately. Tears flooded from Eupheme's eyes as she held the hard body for the first time. Was this the man she loved? Her heart raced. She had never felt like this with Richard. Both men were beautiful, both men complicated and annoying, but only one did this to her. This kiss was the last thing she needed, but as she held the back of Ian's wonderful head, she realised it was the first thing she wanted.

Chapter Twenty-Five

Gresham Hollingford stood in the shower at her father's house and let the needles of water waste themselves against her exquisite skin.

To the casual observer, everything in Gresham Hollingford's life was perfect. She lived with her hyper-liberal mother and father in a beautiful, richly decorated house. She was highly attractive, fit, healthy, fertile, clever, witty and popular with famous people. She was about to marry one of the richest men in the country who, as an added bonus, didn't look like a fat Tory MP with dandruff, a body odour problem and a penchant for rubber-oriented domination.

As she stepped out of the shower and wrapped herself in an enormous and expensive bath towel her mother had bought in Paris the previous weekend, her face showed her mood. Not good.

It was the night of Gresham's film premiere. *Uncle Roger* was to get its first screening to hundreds of influential people at the Lumiere Cinema in St Martin's Lane. Not the Leicester Square Odeon, as she had hoped and dreamed, but the Lumiere. For that she blamed the useless people at Allied Fountain who hadn't booked anywhere early enough.

She hadn't been able to watch the film for three days without feeling physically sick. She had been present for the final dubbing, where the music and soundtrack were joined together with the images to form what everyone hoped would be a cohesive film.

She had only looked in from the doorway of the sound edit studio, endlessly stirring a Styrofoam cup of cold coffee with one of those little plastic stirrers that always broke.

The beginning of each showing was her favourite – it held such promise. She loved the opening credits, the skyline of London, beautifully photographed by Peter Morgan, her name in very large black letters across the Eurotunnel terminus at Waterloo. Then, as soon as the American actress appeared on the screen, riding a push-bike down Islington's Upper Street, utterly incongruous, Gresham turned away. It was as if the very image of the woman hurt her eyes. Simon Langham, her editor, constantly reassured her that she wasn't that bad and that Gresham was too close to the film.

Gresham thought he might be right as she turned, naked, in front of the huge mirror in her room. She growled at herself and stood close to the polished glass. She opened her mouth and checked her teeth. A small crumb of bread or potato was stuck between her two lower front teeth. She tried to wash it out with saliva but it just wouldn't budge. She tried to hook it out with the nail of her little finger and still had no luck. She walked back into her bathroom and found some mint-flavoured dental floss in her huge medicine cabinet, broke off a length and proceeded to floss the offending item away. She did it with such force that she badly cut the perfect gum between her perfect teeth, resulting in very heavy bleeding and not inconsiderable pain.

'Shit, fuck, bollocks!' she hissed as she washed copious amounts of blood out of her mouth with cold tap water. She looked in the mirror above the sink. It looked as if her whole mouth was bleeding. She took a bottle of antiseptic mouthwash from the medicine cabinet and rinsed vigorously, the cut stinging enough to bring tears to her eyes.

'Oh, fuck this!' she spat as blood and mouthwash sluiced down the sink. 'Fuck everything!'

She walked back into her bedroom and quickly got dressed – a new Versace one-piece with a transparent midriff. Even if the film was a flop she would still be a hit. She hoped. The party at the Guards Club after the premiere loomed like a dentist's appointment. Everyone she knew was going to be there. They'd all have an opinion; they'd all let her know what it was.

Gresham threw herself on the bed and lay very still. She didn't cry, she couldn't quite manage that, but she screamed into her pillow and ground her teeth in fury. When she lifted her head, the pillow was disfigured with blood.

'Oh, shit!' she said.

Stanhope picked her up outside the house at four o'clock. They sat together in silence for the entire length of the King's Road, Stanhope listening to financial news on the radio and occasionally talking to one of his city cronies on the hands-free. Finally he switched off the radio and phone and turned to Gresham.

'Tense?'

'As a naval recruit's arse,' said Gresham grimly.

Stanhope snorted a small laugh. 'Don't be. It's brilliant. Everything you've done, darling. I cannot tell you how proud I am. All I talk about at work, so I've been informed, is how talented you are.'

'Thanks, Stanners,' said Gresham. She put her hand on his neck, very smooth and warm.

'What have you done to your mouth?' he asked.

'Does it look bad?' she said, pulling down the sun visor and inspecting her mouth in the vanity mirror. 'Cut my sodding gum when I was flossing. Can you believe it?'

'My poor sausage,' said Stanhope. He put his hand on her neck as she'd done to him. Affectionate but not exactly passionate, she thought as she allowed her head to move in response to his touch.

Stanhope spent the remainder of the journey from Knightsbridge into the West End on his hands-free phone, talking to some awful loud woman in New York who threw huge figures around with such pride that Gresham was tempted to butt in and tell her she was dull.

The Range Rover pulled up outside the Lumiere Cinema and Gresham climbed out. As she did, to her utter amazement, what seemed like a thousand flashbulbs popped. She tried to smile and look nonchalant but she only just managed it. She and Stanhope had completely failed to notice the crush that had developed outside the cinema doors. They were so busy making arrangements for meeting up after the preview and making their way to the Guards Club on Horseferry Road.

Within seconds Stanhope was gone and she was surrounded by people — journalists and movie fans who'd come to the opening with the hope of talking to or at least seeing some stars.

'Are you pleased with the new film?' someone asked.

'Yes, very,' said Gresham.

'What was it like working with Nona Wilfred?' asked a male journalist she recognised.

'She's absolutely brilliant,' said Gresham. 'She's coming to my wedding next month, that's how close we are. She's my best friend in the whole world.'

'Is Richard E. Grant coming tonight?' shouted a voice from within the crowd.

'Definitely,' said Gresham. She finally managed to push her way into the cinema foyer, the door held for her by a very large security guard.

'Bloody hell, it's a nightmare out there,' she said, brushing her hair out of her eyes.

A man in a suit came up to her. 'Jake Hammond, I run Diamond Security. Sorry about that, Miss Hollingford, we didn't expect them here quite so soon. I'll have a team here any minute with some crush barriers so we'll soon have it sorted.'

'How exciting,' said Gresham. She went downstairs past stills from the film which made it look much better than she dared hope. The American actress looked unbearably attractive, Richard looked gaunt and hilarious, the still of Keith Allen in the nude looked shocking and alluring at one and the same time, and Jane Leeves looked amazing in the black floor-length rags she'd worn in her one, magnificent scene. The film, she decided, looked good. Her spirits started to lift. Maybe it wouldn't be such a disaster.

In the downstairs foyer a large group of people had already arrived; her agent, her mother and father, her editor, Simon, the managing director of the distribution company and the managing director of the film finance company, her producer, her casting director and a few of the minor actors who appeared in the film. They all clapped as she appeared and she did a small bow. As she passed her parents her mother gave her a tissue.

'I think you've bitten your lip, dear,' she said. 'There's blood simply gushing down your chin.'

'Shit,' said Gresham.

'Doors open in ten minutes,' said one of the ushers.

'Shit, shit, shit,' said Gresham.

Chapter Twenty-Six

The scene backstage at the Royal Albert Hall was chaotic but very exciting. Within ten seconds of walking through the stage door, Ian saw: Ben Elton eating a celery stick, Griff Rhys-Jones laughing, Craig Charles smoking, Emma Freud and Dawn French talking and Eddie Izzard walking down a corridor in very high-heeled boots. His heart was beating so fast he could hardly breathe. He had a small autograph book in his pocket which he squeezed with all his might, fighting the desire to proffer it to a passing constellation.

When he and Eupheme got out of the cab, whatever the magic that had held them together so passionately seemed to evaporate into the warm night air. He wanted to hold hands with her, he wanted to show her he cared. As soon as his fingertips touched hers she glanced at him, looking slightly amazed.

'Please, Ian, not now,' she said.

They entered a large dimly lit room that was full of noise and people. Ian watched Eupheme talking to people, being embraced by Jenny Eclair, knowing major celebrities personally. She looked absolutely ravishing, her long auburn hair tied up in a loose bun on the top of her head, her long, elegant neck so pale. Ian leant against the wall staring at her. He ruminated on how he was now in a room with more fame per square foot than he had ever known and yet he was quite happy simply to look at Eupheme.

'Are you performing here tonight?' asked a woman. Ian turned to her and smiled. Her face went through a minor spasm and she said, 'Oh, goodness, sorry, I thought you were ...'

'I'm just one of the volunteers,' said Ian. 'Who did you think I was?'

'Oh, well, I thought ... oh, you'll think I'm such a prat. I thought you were Ralph Fiennes for a moment.'

'He of *English Patient* fame,' said Ian with his thick eyebrows raised. 'Would that I was.'

'I'm really sorry. My name's Gemma. I work for Neil Reading, publicity. We did the PR on this show.'

'Oh, excellent,' said Ian, completely in the dark. 'It seems to be going very well.'

'Place is packed to the walls,' she said proudly. 'Mind you, brilliant line-up.' She smiled at him. He noticed she was slightly flushed around the neck. 'I hope you don't mind me asking,' she said, 'but are you Eupheme's husband?'

'Who, me?' said Ian with an explosive laugh. 'Not on your Dame Nelly. No, I'm Ian.'

'Oh, right. And what d'you do?'

'Video editing. Well, computer programming, writing code, general tech wizardry,' said Ian, hoping this would bore her.

'Oh God. I love techies,' she said. 'I'm so crap at everything like that and it's no longer something to be proud of, is it? I'm really ashamed of my ignorance, you know. I mean, I write on a computer at work, but I can't do anything clever with them.'

'Well, it's not that difficult once you get the hang of it.'

'So, are you mates with one of the comedians, then?' she asked.

'No,' said Ian with another laugh. 'I don't know anyone except Eupheme. This is all new to me.'

'I saw you walk in with her. She's amazing, isn't she?'

'Truly,' said Ian.

'The work she's done to organise this. It would have defeated me, I know that. She's so beautiful too, isn't she?'

'Yes, I think she probably is.'

'Oh God. You techies are so cool,' said Gemma. 'I suppose you can have better partners in cybersex.'

'Hell's bells, no way,' said Ian. 'That would be rather sad.'

He was just about to start explaining that cybersex was still in its infancy when Eupheme whisked him away and gave him a T-shirt.

'Put this on, you superstud,' she said with a sly grin. 'I'm going to be fighting women off you all night, I can see that.'

'I didn't do anything,' Ian said innocently.

'You don't have to. You're gorgeous. I'm so glad you've come, and I'm so glad you haven't asked for an autograph.'

'There's still plenty of time for that,' he teased.

Eupheme gave him a pile of leaflets to hand out to the audience as they entered the auditorium. She then pushed him through a door that led to a flight of stairs and into the red-plush magnificence of the hall.

'Blimey O'Reilly,' said Ian. 'It's brilliant, isn't it?'

'Can you come with, me young man?' He was shown to a doorway by a large woman in an International Children's Trust T-shirt. He stood by the door for about five minutes, just able to see people running about on the stage, the lights changing colour, the sound of a drummer playing each drum and cymbal again and again. A man kept saying 'One, two, one, two' into a microphone. A young woman stood on the opposite side of the door to Ian, also in the regulation T-shirt and with a handful of leaflets.

'Exciting, isn't it?' she said.

'Brilliant,' said Ian.

'I only came to see Ben Elton, couldn't afford the ticket. Student.'

'Oh, right,' said Ian.

'Are you a student?' she asked.

'Would that I was the age. Way past it, I'm afraid.'

'You don't look way past it,' said the young woman, a blush appearing on her throat.

Just then someone shouted 'Doors opening!' from within the hall, and moments later a flood of people started to pass between Ian and the young student. He handed out leaflets as fast as he could, concentrating on the chain of open hands that passed beneath his gaze. This chain was broken every once in a while by the dozens of people asking him directions to their seats, and before long he was showing them where to sit.

Ian realised during this heady period of expectation that his years of supermarket training had finally come in useful. It was a simple system that for some reason managed to elude the average member of the public. It took only a few moments for him to work out the seating arrangements and then within a breath of looking at someone's ticket he could direct them straight to their seat.

'It's really a very basic system, not that hard to understand,' he told the young student. 'Each row has a letter and each seat a number. It's amazing how few people can cope with that.'

'You're so good, though,' said the young woman, her eyes sparkling. 'The way you helped everyone. So few men would do that. You're very unusual.'

'Oh, I'm sure not,' Ian said over his shoulder as he started to guide another hapless group of goggle-eyed benefit-goers to their seats. The house was now filling up and he checked his watch. Seven thirty-five. He had to go.

He walked out into the great curved corridor outside the auditorium. He pulled off his T-shirt, folded it as best he could and stuffed it into his trouser pocket.

He then walked down the magnificent staircase and out on to the street. Finding a cab was very easy; there were hundreds dropping people off outside the hall.

'The Lumiere Cinema, St Martin's Lane, please,' he said as clearly as he could. The driver nodded very slightly and closed the sliding window between them. Ian pushed himself back into the seat, realising that this was the first time he'd actually been in a taxi on his own.

By the time he arrived at the Lumiere, the crowds were ten deep either side of a corridor held open by brawny bouncers. He cursed himself for not bringing an Epson PC500 digital camera with him. Thirty digital images before downloading and only nine seconds to store them. Would that he owned one.

He found the invitation Gresham had sent him in his back pocket and opened the door. He paid the driver, and as he turned to face the crowd a hundred flashbulbs went off at once. He smiled and waved, his heart in his mouth. He could see people behind the crush barriers turning to each other to ask who he was. They didn't seem to mind and took pictures anyway. Men standing on stepladders called out various names: 'Sean! Richard! Ralph! Rick!' Ian responded to all of them, waving at everyone as he approached the cinema entrance.

A massive bouncer greeted him at the door. Ian's heart momentarily sank, but then the blank wall of his terror and feelings of inadequacy was penetrated by a friendly face.

'Evening, Ian, you're looking very fit, mate.' It was Jake, his trainer from the gym.

'Blimey, hello there,' said Ian. They shook hands. 'What are you doing here?'

'Bit of a sideline,' said Jake. 'Got to pay the rent. Who you hanging with, then?'

'Anyone who'll have me,' said Ian with a big grin.

'Excellent. Way to go, my man,' said Jake, slapping him on the back and ushering him through the door.

Ian had never, in his entire thirty-one years and seven months, felt more excited and alive. To be allowed through the door; not only that, but to be on friendly terms with the gorilla who opened it. It was better than Doom, the ultimate computer game. In fact Doom seemed positively childish now he stood here, on the inside. He took a deep breath and worked his way down the stairs past the hundreds of people who were slowly meandering in the same direction. It seemed they all had to talk to each other for hours on the way into the cinema. There was a lot of kissing and neck-craning going on, but every time Ian followed someone's eyes to see who they were looking at he saw only more crowds. It took him some time to calm down enough to realise that the corridors were packed with quality constellations.

As his vision cleared, the faces emerged from the mass. He immediately saw Richard E. Grant, Ruby Wax, Rick Mayall, Jennifer Saunders and Ade Edmondson, Nick Hancock, Jane Horrocks, Chris Barrie, Jack Docherty, Tony Slattery and Danny John Jules. His head was spinning. The lads at the video club would never believe this.

He continued down the bustling stairway towards the door of the cinema, and then he saw her. Standing there, tall and elegant and beautiful, her shoulders bare, her neck long and unbearably kissable. Gresham Hollingford, looking as if she owned the place. Ian's heart skipped; the old butterflies started working overtime in his stomach. He stalled on the stairs momentarily, gazing at her without her knowledge. He couldn't believe that he had been so intimate with her and yet could still feel so removed. She flicked her hair back with her beautiful arm as she spoke to someone. Everything about her was utterly enchanting. He felt someone push him in the back gently, turned to see it was Chris Barrie.

'Sorry, old son,' said Chris. 'Bit of a crush coming down the old stairs.'

'That's okay, Mr Barrie,' said Ian as calmly as he could.

'Marvellous,' said Chris, who then waved to someone in the distance and merged with the throng.

'Brilliant,' said Ian.

'Evening, Ian, glad you could make it,' said Gresham quietly into his ear as they air-kissed. 'I may be calling on your services later.'

'Oh, I see,' said Ian.

'You've already seen the film, haven't you?' she said slightly accusingly.

'Yes,' said Ian.

'You don't want to see it again, do you?'

'Well, I haven't seen the ... well, the finished product, as it were.'

'The projection room is through that door, as it were,' said Gresham. 'I'll be in there as soon as everyone sits down.'

'Okee diddly doodly,' said Ian. He felt the hair on the back of his neck stand up as he left her. Everyone would have seen how friendly they were; he was one of them now. Special, privileged.

Gresham was immediately talking to someone else, so he moved on into the body of the cinema and stood to one side. Milling around in the crowd he saw Dave Allen surrounded by young people, Jane Leeves, the woman from the American sitcom *Frasier*, who was the one really funny actor in Gresham's film, he saw Lenny Henry and Mel Smith laughing together. He saw Brian Cox with a beautiful young woman and Jeremy Irons, the baddie from the third *Die Hard* movie, standing alone, smoking. He was with them, on the inside. It was so intoxicating. He belonged, he really belonged.

People eventually started taking their seats and the lights went down. He stood to one side as celebrity after celebrity passed within inches of him. He couldn't quite believe his eyes. He went back out through the doors as the ushers started to close them and into the now deserted corridor. He climbed the carpeted stairs up to the projection room door and gingerly opened it.

Inside, the projectionist, a bald man in his fifties, glanced at him but said nothing.

'I'm, er, meeting Gresham Hollingford in here,' he said. The projectionist didn't even register that he'd heard Ian, just kept adjusting a knob on the side of the machine.

Ian heard the familiar music of the opening credits coming through the small hole in the wall the vast projector was pointing through. The machinery made quite a noise as the huge spool of film ran its course. Ian was fascinated and wanted the projectionist to take him through the basic mechanism. He wanted to stand and watch as it whirred its way through Gresham's creation.

Then he felt an elegantly fingered hand gently grab his hair. He turned slowly to find Gresham standing right behind him. She looked up at him, eyes bright, cheeks slightly flushed, an utterly radiant beauty.

'I can't fucking bear it,' she said.

'Bear what?'

'They're going to hate it. I don't want to think about it. Come here. Do something to take my mind off it.'

'What happened to your mouth?' Ian asked, noticing blood caked at the side of her lips.

'Nothing,' said Gresham. 'Please don't ask. I just want to forget about the bloody film. Please, Ian, please.'

'What?' he asked, looking into her wonderful eyes.

'I want you.'

'What, you mean in a sexual way?'

Gresham pulled his head down and kissed him. Ian could taste blood. He pulled back without thinking.

'What is it?' she asked softly.

'Well, I mean,' said Ian, nodding his head in the direction of the projectionist. 'What about . . . ?'

Gresham took Ian by the hand and pulled him around the vast whirring projector. Up against the wall on the other side was a battered sofa covered in old magazines and empty soft drinks cans. There was a still from the film *Nikita* on the wall above the sofa, which was topped off with a huge mass of cables and wires hanging precariously from the ceiling.

Gresham pulled Ian down on to the sofa. 'Please, Ian,' she said into his ear. 'It's so exciting. My husband-to-be is just the other side of this wall, watching my movie along with everyone I know in the world. None of them know you. We can do anything and they'll never find out.'

'Blimey,' said Ian. 'I'm a bit on the nervous side if the truth be told.'

'Don't be,' she reassured him, kissing him again. The taste of blood was still there, which made Ian even more nervous. He put up with it out of politeness, and then she started to push him back on the sofa. She pinned him down by the shoulders and started to work her way up his body. She looked down at him, her beautiful hair hanging either side of her even more beautiful face. She pulled his limp hands up and put them on her breasts. They filled his hands with such a hugely satisfying weight he almost started to get lost in the heat. He could feel his mind slipping as the animal emerged. The need swam around in front of his eyes in the shape of Gresham Hollingford. She inched forward across his chest until her pubic bone was nudging his chin. He glanced down to see her small panties, an image he had stared at longingly for thousand of hours in pornographic magazines and on the Internet, and yet now it was strangely intrusive.

'Gresham, I ...' he started to say, but was stopped as she lifted herself, moved her hips and sat, literally sat, on his face.

Every *Loaded* reader's dream, the opening sequence of every cheap pornographic film, could not have bettered this moment, but it was wrong. Ian felt unhappy, awkward, uncomfortable, embarrassed, but most particularly he felt ugly. There was something about the way Gresham moved which made him think she thought he was ugly. Repugnant. And that somehow, through a thought process he couldn't for a moment comprehend, she found this sexually stimulating.

However, seven weeks of training with Jake had given Ian the lifting power needed to remove her without being violent. Just a steady upward force and she released him. He swung his legs off the sofa and stood up. He smiled as best he could. Gresham stayed where she was, kneeling on the sofa, looking up at him in resolute disbelief.

'Fuck off,' she said angrily and slowly, softly almost, as if Ian had been making unwanted advances towards her.

'I'm sorry,' he said, 'but I'm just not like that.'

'Fuck right off.' Still that singsong delivery which made it seem that everything that had just taken place was at his instigation alone. How did she do that? Almost force him into sexual activity then, when he wasn't so keen, make it all his fault. Women were definitely clever in this department, he thought. He didn't know how to react to Gresham at all but guessed that being polite and kind was the best bet. Rules he'd learned from his mother.

'Gresham, I really like you more than any woman I've ever known. I just can't sort of ... well, jump to it on demand.'

'Yeah, and ...' she snapped.

'Well, I just mean to say that it's got nothing to do with your attractiveness, in terms of you being a woman, et cetera. I mean, clearly in the being-a-woman department, you're top-drawer material, I mean, in terms of drawers being to do with beauty, not where you keep your nudie magazines. Sorry.'

Gresham's face turned the nearest he'd seen it to tears, her bottom lip quivered, her face folded into a different shape, her forehead shrank, lines appeared where none had been. Something warned him not to be too sure it was a genuine display of the old waterworks. However, he did feel very sorry for her.

'I was relying on you,' she said. 'The only thing that's kept me going all day is the thought that I could have a session with you. In here. And now even that has fucked up. This is the worst sodding day of my entire fucking awful life.' She threw herself full length on the grubby-looking sofa and wailed into the cushions.

'I have to go,' said Ian, suddenly desperate to get back to the benefit. Gresham was right about this night all going wrong. 'It's all gone wrong for me too,' he said, worrying that this was the wrong thing to say. 'If that's any consolation. Probably not. Huh. I'm really sorry, Gresham, I have to go.'

He suddenly realised he wanted to be with Eupheme. He knew she would never make him feel this wretched. He even wanted to tell Gresham how much he wanted to be with Eupheme, but he knew that would be unpopular to the power of ten. He stood for a moment, looking at Gresham's beautiful body lying on the sofa, her expensive dress hoiked up her thighs, her white pants barely covering the luscious curve of her tanned and perfect buttocks. Everything, in theory at least, drawing him to her. But, to his astonishment, he was desperate to walk away. He hadn't got this far just to fall for the first babe-type woman who threw herself at him.

As he climbed the silent stairs of the Lumiere Cinema he wondered if it was because Gresham was so sexually dominant. Maybe it frightened him. He had never been particularly turned on by the dominatrix pictures he had seen in various magazines over the years, but then Gresham didn't look like that. She was an ordinary woman in her dress style; she didn't wear a leather bodice or naff over-knee plastic spiky-heeled boots. She didn't call him slave and crack a pathetic whip, but she did have this huge sex drive which Ian hadn't expected. His mother and pornography had been his best guide as far as women's sexual drives were concerned. He'd always imagined women as silent in the sexual arena, doing it either for love or money. His mother had never spoken of sex as something she did, just something that got other people into trouble.

Ian's lifelong involvement with mild pornography had given him a peculiarly romantic vision of womanhood. After what had happened to his father he had wanted, from a very early age, to express sexuality firmly within the bounds of love. His father's death had been so lonely and secretive, and Ian really didn't want to die like that. He saw women as his salvation, but quickly discovered they were so fiendishly complicated that he had withdrawn and merely related to them visually. Before he met Gresham he saw women as essentially benign, loving, endlessly giving, soft and accepting. Not active, and definitely not as hyperactive and sexually hard as Gresham. If his mother was, in sexual terms, a low-powered Tiger Moth biplane, Gresham was an F18 Hornet fighter-bomber, laser targeting systems on and ready to rock.

'You off, then?' asked Jake, who was still standing by the door.

'Yeah, other fish to fry, me old pal,' said Ian, hoping it sounded right.

'Wey hey. All right, Ian, my man,' said Jake with a big grin.

Ian walked back out on to the now less crowded street. The crush barriers were still in position, some photographers were hanging around smoking, but most of the public had dispersed into the busy night.

'What's it like?' asked a man behind the crush barrier. Ian was thrown.

'What's what like?' he asked with a smile. The man was short, balding, with a face that looked like old fruit. Ian shrugged.

'The fucking film,' said the man. 'Is it shit? Is that why you walked out?'

'Oh, I see,' said Ian, 'No, it's really good. I did some work on it so I've seen it ten times before.'

'You worked on it, did you?' asked the man.

'Yes, bit of editing and suchlike activities.'

'Editor,' said the man.

'Oh no, that's a chappy called Simon. I just let them have the benefit of my humble opinion, that's all.'

'Can I have your autograph?' said the man.

'I beg your pardinium?' said Ian with a snorting laugh.

'Can I have your autograph?' said the man, holding out a pen and a notebook.

'Blimey O'Reilly, this is a bit of a first.'

'Get used to it, son. You're a media star now.'

'Am I?'

'Big-time film editor on a major movie like this. You know all the stars, their secrets an' everything. Don't you?'

'Oh, hardly,' said Ian. He signed the notebook very slowly. As he looked at the finished article he realised it wasn't a signature as such. Just a joined-up-writing version of his name. He put his website address below it.

'What's that?' asked the man when he looked at Ian's work.

'My website,' said Ian, about to explain to this sad fellow what that meant.

'See, got your own website. You must be a star, Ian.' The man looked closer at what Ian had written.

'Does that say Ringfold?'

'That's the one,' said Ian as coolly as he could.

'Is that your name? Bloody hell, did you make it up?'

'No, it's my name,' said Ian.

'You should change it if you want to make it in movies,' said the man.

'What to?'

'Something like Cruise, or Gibson or Reeves. You know, one of them cool names, mate. Ringfold, that's a toss-er's name.'

'Oh, right,' said Ian, suddenly feeling he was in the school playground again. He started walking away. 'I have to get going,' he said.

'Take care, Ian,' said the man, who turned and started talking to a group of people standing beside him.

Ian stood out on the road and leaned towards the slow stream of traffic that was battling its way towards Trafalgar Square. A taxi pulled up. 'The Royal Albert Hall, please,' he said, and climbed inside.

Chapter Twenty-Seven

Ben Elton did a storming set. He stunned the audience with his machinegun-style delivery and left them baying for more.

'Thanks, Ben, that was brilliant,' said Eupheme as he walked swiftly past her on his way backstage.

'Yes indeed,' said Ben, clearly pleased that it had gone so well. Hugh Laurie went on-stage and bumbled beautifully; the audience loved him too. The hardest job in the world, she had been told by the other comedians, was to be the compere, the master of ceremonies. Hugh was doing a lovely job, although he readily admitted it wasn't his favourite way to spend an evening.

Eddie Izzard appeared next to Eupheme, looking dazzling in Gaultier frock-coat, painted nails and a perfect amount of make-up.

'Are you Eupheme?' he whispered in her ear.

'Yes,' she said, smiling at him, thrilled that he knew.

'Hi, I'm Eddie,' he said.

'I know,' she said.

'Did you organise this?' he asked.

'More or less.'

'Well done. Brilliant night.'

'Thank you.'

'Am I on next?'

'Yes. Good luck, or break a leg or whatever it is you say to each other.'

'Fuck off is quite common,' said Eddie. 'Just wanted to say well done, lovely gig, lovely audience, really looking forward to it.'

'So without further mucking about, ladies and gentlemen,' said Hugh Laurie, 'please welcome on-stage the very lovely Eddie Izzard.'

Eddie walked up the few steps, shook hands with Hugh and took the stage. Gresham, standing beside and slightly below him, marvelled at that ability. She could no more climb those steps than fly.

The atmosphere in the Royal Albert Hall was exhilarating. Eupheme let her gaze wander around, staring at the thousands of people who were all there because of her. She had organised the whole thing from scratch, it was a sell-out, her position at the charity was assured, and everyone who had any connection to the International Children's Trust loved her.

She felt warm inside; she felt happy for the first time she could remember. Maybe this was a turning point for her – it felt special enough. Maybe her life would change now. All the potential was there for her to change. She was just resisting out of ... something. She contemplated this for a moment, feeling strangely at peace amidst the tension and chaos that surrounded her.

Her mother suddenly popped into her mind. She felt an enormous pang of longing to see her. Maybe it was her mother who had taught her she wasn't the centre of the universe, just a part of it, and that this was a good thing, a thing that would make her stronger and more resilient. Gresham had never learned that, and Eupheme had always been aware that one day, possibly, Gresham might find out, and the shock would be horrible. What was even stranger was the feeling Eupheme had that tonight she really was the centre of the universe. She felt it strongly. Anything that wasn't going on inside this hall was somehow irrelevant. She knew it was wrong and arrogant but that was what it felt like. This was so important – they were raising money to make children's lives bearable. They were alleviating suffering in a very real way by being there. This was without doubt a very large event, one that would go down in the history of such events as a major achievement to the benefit of the world. Like a mini-Band Aid.

She ejected these thoughts from her mind in embarrassment. Told herself to get a grip. It would all be over soon and the whole thing would be forgotten.

She sighed deeply, loud enough for the stage manager, who was talking quietly in his headphones beside her, to turn and smile.

'You okay?' he asked.

'Yes, Ned, I'm fine?' she said.

He spoke into the microphone that curved in front of his mouth. 'On cue seven, bring the house lights up full, just for two beats, okay?' He pulled the headphones down to his shoulders and turned to her.

'Is it a success?' asked Eupheme.

'What? This?' he said, shrugging. 'It's the best benefit I've ever done. Who organised it?' He smiled at her.

'Thanks,' said Eupheme.

'Hats off,' said Ned. 'It's running so well, such a good selection of artists. Brilliant, mate. Hats off. Hang on a minute.' He pulled his headphones back up and continued talking to a follow spot operator.

Eupheme visibly grew taller. A rough old hippie technician who had done more benefits and live shows than Eupheme had ever seen, wanted to see or know about had just praised her. If only Gresham could witness this, see her now, in her element. In control. Not only that, if only Gresham knew what an amazing position Eupheme was in with the two men in her life.

There was a handsome man backstage who wanted to be her husband, there was another handsome man in the auditorium who she couldn't quite seem to forget. And the kiss. It was so electric. She had no idea she could feel anything for Ian, and even less idea that he might feel anything for her. It was impossible, of course, but it was rather nice. She liked the idea of their intimacy even though it made no sense. Maybe it was a good thing; maybe it would make him even more convincing when the time came. But nothing serious could happen with her and Ian — he wasn't for her. What was wonderful about it was that now she was in complete control of all the parts of her life. She felt she had run a gauntlet of chaos and come out on top. She had Richard and Ian just where she wanted them, tidy and organised. Everyone knew where they stood and they all seemed happy. After Gresham's wedding then, maybe, if it felt right, she could, as far as this life and this world were concerned, retire. Pack up her belongings and move to Italy. Actually have children, give birth, hold a baby, breast-feed. In Italy, where people liked children. She could live on the hill with Richard. It suddenly seemed rather attractive for the first time in her life. Maybe it was age, hormones, all those biological-clock clichés.

'Eupheme, you're wanted backstage,' said Ned. She nodded and walked back towards the double doors that led from the auditorium. She was mildly annoyed that she was missing a bit of Eddie Izzard's increasingly weird but very funny piece of stand-up comedy.

She walked through the excited throng of people who had gathered in the green room. Faces from her life, people who cared about her and whom she cared about. If only life were always this intense and this exciting. She smiled at or embraced and received congratulations from Sir Peter Adelphi, the chairman of the board of the trust, Yoni Chiata Fairchild, and Carol Sarler, who were deep in conversation with Norman Lovett, Kevin Waslick and Christine Hanks. It was only when she saw Kevin and Christine that the smile was cruelly wiped off her face. They were both attending to the slumped form of someone she just couldn't quite pull into focus. The pain and annoyance consequent on what might be there was too intense for her. She felt faint, her heart raced, she felt sick.

Half slumped on a chair with vomit spattered down his trousers was the man who professed an undying love for her. Richard Markham was pissed out of his tiny mind.

'He's fine,' said Kevin anxiously, 'He's actually not that drunk, Pheme, he just lost his balance and fell on the food table. We just thought you'd know what to do.'

'D'you want me to take him home?' said Christine.

'Oh Christ. Oh God. I don't believe it,' said Eupheme, both hands to her mouth in utter horror. 'What's he been doing?'

'I've been fucking drinking, you thick bitch,' slurred Richard. 'I fucking love you, and this is all you do to me. You'd shag anyone, you would, you slag. Me drinking is all your fault, slag!'

Never before had she heard him use language like this. It was horrible. Then, to cap it all, he suddenly lunged towards her but collapsed on his knees as Kevin tried to hold him back. People in the room moved as far as they could from the scene, but they all watched.

Richard fell on to his face and wept loudly. It sounded so incongruous in the glamorous setting of the Royal Albert Hall green room. However, there was nothing else to do but engage him and get him out as rapidly as possible.

She knelt in front of him and held his flushed, foul-smelling cheeks. 'What has happened, Richard?' she asked, looking straight into his rheumy eyes. 'What are you saying?'

'It's your fucking train-spotter, your fancy man. You think I don't know! Fucking hell, why did I ever have to meet you? This is all your fault. I'd give you everything, that's how much I love you, and you do this to me.'

'What?' said Eupheme angrily. 'Do what?'

'Sleep with that tosser.' Richard spat the word out; dribble hung from his bottom lip. They stared at each other for a moment, Eupheme almost unable to resist gagging at the smell of his breath.

'I have never slept with him, never. Who told you I did?'

'Everyone knows, fucking everyone. Christine told me, but don't try and blame her! Fuck. They're all talking about it. I'm the bloody laughing-stock.'

He hung his head and groaned. Eupheme looked up to see that Kevin and Christine had been joined by Ian, standing between them wearing a very crumpled staff T-shirt.

'What's happened to you?' Eupheme asked.

'Nothing. I've been watching the show,' said Ian.

'Why is your T-shirt all crumpled?'

'I don't know,' said Ian. 'I put it in my pocket for a bit.'

'Why?' asked Eupheme.

'Um, I don't know,' said Ian. He smiled and looked rather pathetic.

'Why don't I take him home?' said Christine, bending down and putting a hand on Richard's shoulder.

'What did you say to him, Chris,' said Eupheme.

'I didn't say you slept with him, Eupheme, you know that. I said you'd spent time with him, but I couldn't really explain why. I'm so sorry, this is all my fault.'

'Oh God,' said Eupheme.

'Look, let me take him home. I don't mind. Really. I've been to enough parties for one life,' Christine said. She hooked Richard's right arm over her shoulders and helped him to his feet.

Richard's eyes wandered around the room with no particular object, but then locked on to Ian. Without saying anything, he lunged forward and smashed his large fist into Ian's face. Ian went flying backwards and landed heavily against Craig Charles.

Kevin Waslick grabbed Richard and manoeuvred him into the corner of the room. Ian lay curled up on the floor, holding his face. Eupheme stood up, halfway between the two men, and shook her head. She looked at Richard, who seemed to be almost unconscious, then at Ian, who was slowly being helped to his feet by Craig Charles.

'Hey, steady, steady,' said Craig. 'Almost spilt me Fanta. Unrumble, guys, come on.'

'Thank you, Craig. I'm so sorry about this,' said Eupheme.

'Don't worry about it. Bit of bother like that doesn't worry me, Eupheme, I'm a Scouser after all.' Craig grinned wildly at her. 'You okay, feller?' he asked Ian.

'Someone hit me,' said Ian.

'You don't say,' said Craig. 'Your eye is going to be the size of Swindon in the morning, I hate to tell you.'

'What's happening?' said Ian, holding his already swollen eye.

'Richard's going home with Christine, you're going to casualty with Kevin, I'm staying here,' Eupheme told him.

'That's the way to sort out problems,' said Craig. 'Send everybody else away and stay for the party.' He laughed loudly at this. Ian smiled at him.

'Can't I stay too?' he asked, even more pathetically, Eupheme thought.

'What a trooper. An eye like a baboon's arse and he still wants to get down. My kind of man,' laughed Craig, clearly enjoying the little drama. 'Who's the bloke that give you a clump, son?'

Eupheme intervened. 'His name's Richard. He's, well, he's . . .'

'An alcoholic,' said Craig brutally but truthfully. He then put on a Keith Richards stoned-out junkie voice. 'My name's Craig and I'm an alcoholic.' He laughed and gave Ian a friendly hug.

'He's going to AA meetings,' said Eupheme, wanting to defend Richard slightly.

'He bloody needs to,' said Ian sulkily. 'He's a nutter. He should be put away.'

'Should be put down, mate,' said Craig, still chuckling.

'He's just confused. He's an artist,' said Eupheme.

'I won't say anything,' laughed Craig.

'I'm going to look at my eye in the mirror,' said Ian. 'It really, really hurts ever so much.'

Eupheme swallowed hard. She didn't say anything, just watched Ian half hobble out of the room. She looked around, checked the crowd anxiously but saw that events had already moved on. Most of the people present had forgotten this little contretemps and were busy congratulating Eddie Izzard, who had left the stage to tumultuous, thundering, rapturous applause. Eupheme could hear it pouring in through the open door. She sighed deeply and crossed the room towards Kevin Waslick and Christine, who were still fussing over the slumped body of her future husband.

'Actually, can you take him home, Chris?' Eupheme asked, with a flat smile designed to hide the hurt.

'Of course,' said Christine. She touched Eupheme's forearm to reassure her. 'He can sleep it off at my place and I'll spend hours talking to him tomorrow about what he's done and all that. He's going to be ever so depressed, I know it. Is Ian all right?'

'Gone off in a bit of a sulk, I think.'

'Not surprising, really.'

'Richard really hit him hard,' said Kevin. 'I'm surprised he had the ability.'

'All that sculpting,' said Christine. 'He's got ever such strong arms.'

Eupheme looked at the heavens. 'Just get him out of here before he does any more damage.'

Chapter Twenty-Eight

Ian tried to turn over in his sleep and the realisation that he couldn't, that he was in fact trapped, brought him swiftly awake. He opened one eye; the other one just wouldn't budge. He managed to extricate his right arm from the tangled mass of bedding that surrounded him and his hand automatically went up to rub his eye. The resulting jab of intense pain caused him to wince and jerk his head. He was utterly confused and very uncomfortable. He slowly craned his neck and looked around him. He was in a strange room with a high ceiling that was bathed in early morning sunlight. It was a very beautiful old room, like Ian imagined you'd see in an old Russian palace. Motes of dust floated through the thick air; he could just hear the muffled rumble of traffic outside. He moved his head a little. The room was a mess, a mess of truly enormous proportions. He could just about tell that, under the piles of clothes, plates with unfinished food, cups with mould growing out of them, newspapers, magazines, faxes, books and piles and piles of paper, there was potentially a beautiful room. A large picture hung above the fireplace. It seemed to be a print of a huge Victorian-looking swimming pool. Ian tried to focus but couldn't manage with one eye. He lifted his head and saw that he was lying on a sofa. The memory of where he was came back gently, like a sunny patch floating over a field on a cloudy day. He was at Eupheme's flat. On her sofa, in her front room, in Clapham, in London.

Ian sniffed; something smelled. He buried his head under the covers again and decided not to bother getting up. It was all too painful and there was nothing to do except survive for another day, which didn't seem too attractive. Then his bladder got the better of him and he knew he had to get up. He lay still for a while as he tried to remember where the toilet was. He didn't want to barge into the wrong room. He imagined finding Eupheme in bed with Richard, and Richard getting out of bed, naked and huge, and punching him in the other eye. Ian's heart raced. His bladder reminded him again that it really was way past emptying time. He rolled himself off the long, low sofa and stood up.

He was only wearing his white 2(x)ist underpants and a *Red Dwarf* T-shirt he had packed in his small Donna Karan carrier bag which he acquired when Eupheme bought him a shirt. He stretched his calves a little by leaning against the wall behind the sofa with both hands and pushing his bare feet flat down on the old rug on the floor. It was an exercise Jake had shown him, and it always felt good to do in the morning. He noticed a photograph hanging on the opposite wall, framed properly with glass in front. Gresham and Eupheme, both looking younger, sitting on a low stone wall in a beautiful rural setting. They were wearing walking gear – posh red-and-blue Gore-Tex anoraks that looked as if they had cost a pretty penny and bright socks, heavy boots and good-quality thick corduroy trousers. They had a healthy flush to their faces and looked, basically, when all was said and done, ravishing. Their hair, unkempt and wild, was hanging in rain-washed rats' tails from their lovely heads. He smiled at the picture and reflected on the journey that had brought him to this point. This very point in time, one pixel wide by one pixel high. A nanomoment, almost indefinable it was so small, but it felt really special. Waking in the strange front room of a lovely woman who had taken over his life, introduced him to the first really semi-full-sex lover he'd ever had, taken him to parties, introduced him to more celebrity names than he could remember. A nanosecond of time, standing there, leaning against a wall over a big sofa, looking at a picture of these two wonderful women, half in pleasure, half in pain, with a full bladder and no idea where to go to relieve it.

He moved. The moment had gone and he knew he would forget it soon. He tried to remember to remember it, to hold it like a jewel as he had various golden moments from his childhood. He knew it would never work; he had received so many new memories in the previous eight weeks he couldn't possibly retain them all. He opened the door into the long, dimly lit corridor that ran the length of the apartment and was confronted by a stronger version of the smell he had first noticed in bed. He wasn't sure if it was his nose malfunctioning or if there really was an unpleasant smell. It wasn't a smell he thought would belong in Eupheme's flat; it felt wrong. He walked along the corridor as quietly as he could. He had no idea what the time was, but the sun was up and he assumed it was late. One door was open with a light on inside. He peered in; it was a toilet. He darted inside and relieved himself, breathing a huge sigh of relief as the discomfort dissipated.

He flushed and returned to the corridor, scratching his head and wondering what to do. He decided it was very difficult to know what to do in other people's houses when they were still asleep. You couldn't just wander around and nose about in case they woke up.

As he crept down the corridor he heard a sound, a key turning in a lock. The front door opened at the far end and a tall man entered wearing a smart suit. He was carrying three very large bags, festooned with flight labels.

'Hello,' he said in a deep and to Ian's ear very posh voice.

'Oh, hi, hello, hi there,' said Ian, feeling completely naked.

'I'm Geoffrey,' said the man. He smiled, a little.

'Oh, sorry, yeah, sorry. I'm Ian.'

'Hello, Ian. Nasty black eye you've got there.'

'Yeah. Sorry. I'm a friend of Eupheme's. Sorry, we got back quite late last night.'

'Did you? Okay, right, fine,' said Geoffrey, looking worried.

'Sorry,' said Ian sheepishly.

'What's that smell?' asked Geoffrey, now sounding a little more angry, Ian thought.

'I don't know. Bit on the old pongy side, isn't it.'

'Where is Eupheme?' Geoffrey was now on the border of visible aggression.

'I think she's still asleep,' said Ian. He smiled; he got no response.

'Right,' said Geoffrey, who barged past Ian and dragged his enormous bags down the corridor. 'Bloody hell. What a smell!' he said. He dropped the bags and opened a door to his left. He gasped and immediately took one step back, tripping slightly over his bags and half collapsing against the opposite wall.

'Oh my God,' he said.

Ian walked up the corridor and looked into the kitchen. He was now experiencing a special moment, one he would never forget.

There, only five feet in front of him, on the floor of a nicely decorated kitchen, was the half-burned corpse of his mother. The scene took a few seconds to come into focus. Ian tried to keep looking, but what he was seeing did not make sense. His mother, what was left of her, was lying next to the oven. It was a gas oven and the door was open. His mother's left hand was holding a closed box of household matches. Her right hand was a line of charred material which stretched into the oven. She had sort of half burnt, like a damp tea towel that was hanging too near the fire. Her head and upper body were completely burned, her legs, left arm and lower body were untouched. It was a bizarre and disturbing sight and it devastated the two men who were staring at it.

'Oh my fucking God,' said Geoffrey.

'Mum,' said Ian faintly.

'Oh my, oh fuck, oh fucking hell. I ... Jesus,' spluttered Geoffrey, frozen to the spot, holding his raincoat and leaning at an absurd angle against the wall.

'Mum,' said Ian, still half expecting her to change back to normal and get up. 'What happened?' he asked her. She didn't respond.

'Oh fucking hell,' said Geoffrey. 'What happened?'

'Mum,' said Ian. He realised he wasn't going to be able to say much else for a while.

'Is she ... I mean, was she your mother?'

'She's my mum,' said Ian.

'What happened?' asked Geoffrey.

'It's my mum,' said Ian. 'She's on fire.'

'Is she burning?' asked Geoffrey.

'I don't know. I think she's gone out,' said Ian.

'Jesus. Jesus. What shall we do?'

'Mum,' said Ian faintly. Things were going noticeably wobbly by this time. The edge of his vision was blurred and red. Sounds became the same as when you listen to them through a new drainage pipe on a building site. Stretched and weird.

A door opened. Ian turned away from his mother's smouldering remains at last and looked towards the sound. He could hear an echo. It was weird, as if he had a res-edit system built into his ears. Eupheme suddenly appeared through the door, but she didn't seem to be walking; she looked like a ghost. She seemed to float towards him. Her lips were moving but he couldn't hear anything, just a ringing in his ears. As she got nearer her speech became semi-apparent, blurred but just about discernible.

'What's going on? Geoffrey, what are you doing here? What's that bloody awful smell. Shit!'

Eupheme fell past Ian on to Geoffrey's bags. Ian felt something hot and wet on his foot. He tried to look down but it all became too strange. The red in his vision increased, the hissing white noise in his ears reached fever pitch. There was a smell of vomit, burned flesh and perfume. His vision pixellated, went black and white and then closed down.

Chapter Twenty-Nine

'Gresham, darling. Wakey-wakey time,' said Stanhope De Courcey softly. He leant across the large bed and gently shook her shoulder. Gresham groaned and pulled a pillow over her head.

'Darling, it's not the morning, you know. I've just come back from the office to check that you were okay. It's nearly two thirty.'

Gresham mumbled something from beneath the cushion. Stanhope stood up, resplendent in full City pin-stripe. He opened the curtain and let in the blazing sun of a hot London day.

'It's beautiful out, so rare these days. You should get up, darling. I'll run a bath for you.'

Gresham peeped out from beneath her pillow and saw Stanhope disappear into the bathroom. She heard him turn on the taps as he sang softly to himself. He was singing the theme tune to her film. The night before hit her like ice water. Her film, they'd all seen her film. She groaned again, in a mixture of anger and self-pity, burying the noise in the pillow. She felt Stanhope stroke her bare forearm. He sat on the bed and his weight shifted the bedclothes slightly.

'What are you doing back here?' she asked.

'Well, the publicity people from Allied called me at the

office. They'd tried to get hold of you, wanted to give you something. They couldn't get a reply, so I got worried and came back.'

'I'm okay,' said Gresham.

'I know. I know, darling. I've got the coffee on downstairs.'

Gresham knew what was coming. Everyone had decided to be nice to her, as if that was going to soften the blow. They were all feeling sympathetic, an emotion she had never partaken of.

'Go on, then, tell me,' she said, finally flinging the pillow to the floor.

'Tell you what?' said Stanhope, his face full of sympathy.

'What have they said?'

'Who?'

'The papers, the reviews!' she said incredulously.

'About *Uncle Roger*?' asked Stanhope slowly.

'Yes, yes! I can't bear it!' she shouted. 'I can't bear to look. What have they said?'

Stanhope took a deep breath, clasped his hands together on his lap and said, 'Well, they are mixed, darling. I think that's the term, isn't it? Mixed, and not everyone has run their review yet so we don't really know what the full verdict is, and it is a risky business, darling, you've always known that.'

'They hate it, don't they?' she said, now hugging another pillow for safety.

'They don't hate it,' said Stanhope, returning to the bath and turning off the taps. He re-entered the bedroom carrying a large pile of newspapers. 'They really don't hate it. They think Nona is very good. There's a big picture of her in the *Guardian*.'

'They think she's good!' squealed Gresham. 'How could they think she's any fucking good!' She grabbed the paper from his hand and started reading it.

'Well, I say good. I think they think she's been ... well,

sort of let down by the film, as it were. It's all a bit highfalutin for me.'

'Shut up, Stanhope. Please, let me read,' said Gresham, gripping the paper tenaciously.

After a promising start this romantic comedy sees Roger (Richard E. Grant) in a role that stretches him and a story that leaves him static. Candy (Nona Wilfred) is likewise left stranded, doing her best with weak material and hazy direction. The editing, the music, the support cast all do their level best with what is, after all is said and done, a fairly plodding rewrite of *All's Well that Ends Well*, not exactly a Shakespearean masterpiece in the first place. After glowing successes with clever reworkings of the classics, like Amy Heckerling's *Emma* rework *Clueless* and Baz Luhrmann's brilliant *Romeo and Juliet*, I suppose we were bound to be landed with a turkey eventually. It's a pity it had to be a British film after all the success our industry has been having. Interest certainly starts high; the opening is marvellous and there are certainly flashes of genius here. The scene where Candy realises who she is while preparing for a parachute jump is beautifully placed and exquisitely performed, but from there, like a skydiver with a broken ripcord, the film plummets to its doom. Gresham Hollingford, who helmed this £6 million Allied Fountain film, has not delivered after the early promise she exhibited. Wait for the video release, which, judging by last night's audience reaction, won't be long in coming.

Gresham threw the paper across the bedroom in disgust. She chewed on the knuckles of both fists and screamed. Then she threw her hair back and smiled at Stanhope.

'Okay, that was dreadful, but I'm still here. Where are the good ones?'

'Oh, I see.'

'What d'you mean?' she snapped.

'I said they were mixed, not that there were any particularly good ones.'

'You mean ... shit. Surely the *Daily Mail* liked it?'

'Um, well, let me see,' said Stanhope, finding his way through the stack. He extracted the *Daily Mail* and passed it to her. She quickly tore through the newspaper looking for the review section. Her eye was caught by a big picture of Richard E. and Nona Wilfred in the airfield kiss scene. The headline read 'The Man from Uncle' for some reason Gresham couldn't fathom, and the review, while not picking the famous actress out for any particular praise, was equally damning.

She read the reviews in each of the daily papers, scanning each one for a sign of hope. There was none. She let her head flop back on to the pillow.

'That's it, then,' she said, feeling a hard lump in her throat. 'That's the end of it.'

'Not at all, darling,' said Stanhope. 'Everyone I spoke to last night loved it. Mum and Dad were hugely impressed. Your father loved it, everyone.'

'Well, they aren't going to slag it off, are they?' said Gresham, stumping out of bed, dropping her nightie as she walked and almost throwing herself into the deep bath. A tidal wave of hot water threw itself on the floor. Stanhope stood by the door of the bathroom and sighed, turning his tiny mobile phone over and over in his hand.

'Darling, the thing is, the company are right behind you. I had a little chat with Graham Walker-Smith this morning. He is completely dedicated to you. Now, after these reviews I think it takes a pretty brave sort of chap to say that.'

'So, you think they are bad reviews,' snapped Gresham.

'Not bad, just a little negative.'

'I just want to die,' she shouted, then slid under the water completely. The feeling of submersion was very relaxing. The sounds changed, the warm water engulfed her. Then came the shock — she suddenly felt Stanhope's hands on her sides and for one awful moment she thought he was going to try to drown her. However, he pulled her out with such force that she gulped a mouthful of water and started coughing uncontrollably. He held her wet, naked body to his suit until she regained her composure enough to push him away.

'I don't mean really kill myself,' she said between coughs. She sat back down in the bath, sending yet another tidal wave of water over the side.

'Careful, sweets,' said Stanhope, mopping his suit with a towel and then throwing it on the floor to soak up the ever-increasing flood.

'Bloody hell, Stanhope. I just mean everything has gone wrong. Everything.'

'It hasn't, darling,' said Stanhope.

'It has. All that work. The bloody film is a write-off. A tax loss, a disaster that's been waiting to happen for years. I didn't know it would come to this. I never knew it could be this hard. I never want to make another film again. Ever. It's complete shit anyway. Who cares if you make a good film or not? They're all forgotten as soon as they've been shown. This will be forgotten quicker than most. After all that work, all that time. I've grown old making that damn film and these bastards just write a couple of lines and kill it. It's so unfair!'

'I know,' said Stanhope, reaching out to reassure her.

'*Uncle Roger* is finished. That's it. And so am I! Shit!'

Chapter Thirty

Ian sat on the 10.03 from Euston, calling at all stations to Birmingham New Street. He was wearing his Calvin Klein jeans, his Tricker boots, his *Red Dwarf* Series 8 T-shirt and a rather nice dark brown jacket from Ermenigildo Zegna. To cover the still-enormous and swollen black eye he was wearing his Dolce e Gabbana dark glasses. All bought on Eupheme's Coutts gold Master Card.

His mother was dead. He had spent the morning in a hospital somewhere in South London. He not only had a black eye, he now had three stitches in his left ear where he had fallen against a door handle in Eupheme's flat when he fainted.

He had spent the afternoon with the police telling them what had happened and how his mother came to be alone in a strange flat. The policeman he had spoken to seemed unmoved by the whole affair, and after his initial paranoia that he or Eupheme might be charged with murder he relaxed when it was clear this wasn't considered to be an option.

He felt weak but not ill. He felt light, as if he hadn't eaten anything for weeks, which was almost true. He had lost a lot of weight, but this feeling of lightness was new. It was almost pleasant.

He looked out of the window, thinking about his mother,

her funny, almost comical, old legs. They had looked like startled legs, amazed at what had happened to the rest of the body they had moved around for the previous seventy-seven years.

The train started slowing. Ian looked up from his feet, tears welling in his eyes. He recognised the buildings that slid past. This was Milton Keynes.

As the train pulled into the platform he decided on the spur of the moment to get out. 'Think I'll jump ship,' he muttered to himself, and got up, picked up his small carrier bag and waited for the train to pull to a halt. He had been through the station three dozen times at least since he met Eupheme, and it had never occurred to him to get out before. He was always in a rush either to get to London or to get back to his mother. Now there was no rush.

The train stopped and he got out. The air was warm and friendly; there was a light summer breeze blowing through the mirrored glass canyon of Milton Keynes station. He took a deep breath, pushed his chest out, yawned and decided he didn't feel so bad after all. As the train pulled out, his spirits lifted. There on Platform 3 stood Graham, Nick and Fat Stan.

'Way up!' shouted Ian, still feeling the remnants of a sob in his throat. The three men looked over at him and started to converse with each other. Ian waved.

'It's me, Ian, Hotshoe!' he shouted. They still looked confused. 'Ringfold dot co. dot uk!'

'Bloody hell's bells, et cetera!' shouted Graham. 'Would that I could have recognised you.'

'Gone up in the old world or some such?' asked Nick, his missing teeth visible even at this distance.

'Yes indeedy doodly. What about you guys? Still immersed in the world of trains and their ilk?'

'Yeah,' said Nick, flatly. There was a moment's silence and the two rail tracks between them seemed like a universe. Ian felt bad. He hadn't meant it to be a put-down.

'Brilliant,' he said, hoping to sound genuine. He knew he

THE MAN ON PLATFORM FIVE

could repair any damage, even if they did think his dress code was a little over the old top. He walked along the platform and up over the bridge. As he descended the steps to join his long-unseen friends he felt an overwhelming urge to embrace them. They were so true, so easy to understand, so immediate and 'there'. He knew where he was again and he appreciated it, wanted to show it. Knew he couldn't. An embrace would be very poorly received. They might immediately assume he had been seduced into the other persuasion, as it were, become a bit of a Ben Doon dash Phil McCavity merchant.

'Hello, hello, hello, yes indeed,' said Ian when he finally reached them. 'Good afternoon, gentlemen.'

'Pretty smart in the clothes department,' said Graham, grinning and friendly. 'What's been happening to you? Been checking the old website. It's been static for months.'

Ian took off his dark glasses. He was under the shade of the bridge and could hardly see his old compadres.

'Ouch,' said Stan. 'A right old shiner there, my son.'

'Oh, yeah, caught the fist of a top-grade sculptor,' said Ian, trying to open his swollen eye. 'Bit of a disagreement over our friends "the ladies", as a matter of fact.'

'Wey hey the lads,' cheered Graham loudly. An old woman passenger standing a little way along the platform looked up in alarm. Graham cowered guiltily then made a few apologetic faces. 'Sorry,' he half shouted.

'Bit of a shiner there all right,' said Stan. This repetition reminded Ian of the many afternoons of tedium he had spent in this man's company. Stan would have to repeat every dull observation four or five times before he believed anyone had heard what he'd said.

'Yeah, I got a wallop, Stan,' said Ian kindly.

'So, the old website not good enough for you now?' asked Graham obscurely.

'No way, José. I've just been a little on the busy side. What with two top-drawer ladies battling over yours truly.'

'Never,' said Nick.

'Yes indeedly doodly, Nicky boy. Plus there's been my going to top parties up in the big smoke and then, to cap it all, going back to a very nice top London flat belonging to one of the aforementioned people of the lady-type gender last night only to find my dear old mum half immolated on the floor of the kitchen.' He didn't want to spoil the story by mentioning the fact that when he had arrived home, Eupheme had just said 'Couch' to him, to make it clear where he belonged.

'Spontaneous combustion!' said Graham.

'Don't think so,' said Ian. 'The old fire brigade bloke, the actual head honcho for South London, he said he thought Mum was trying to light the stove, put her head in the oven with the gas on, lit a match and phwoomph.'

'Don't tell me it was an autolight oven?' said Graham.

'Precisely,' said Ian.

'Damn,' said Graham, and stamped on the floor in fury. 'The amount of times I've told my mum, 'It's autolight, Mum, don't use matches.' And this is what can happen. It's crazy!'

'I know,' said Ian, the guilt of how he'd left his mother still surrounding him.

'You got a nasty old black eye there, son,' said Stan, still lagging.

'So, she's a total goner, then? Completely off-line?' said Graham sympathetically.

'What's left of her,' said Ian.

'What does immolated mean?' asked Nick.

'Burned up in a major way,' said Graham. 'Check it out on www dot spont dot combustion. Brilliant website. Gruesome graphics.'

'Bloody Ada,' said Nick. 'Is your mum completely dead?'

'Completely,' said Ian.

'Bloody Ada,' said Nick.

'Why did the sculptor bloke give you the shiner, then?' asked Fat Stan.

'So what happened?' asked Graham.

'She's down the morgue being processed. It's an unusual case, apparently, so they're flying in experts from all over the world.'

'Bloody Ada,' said Nick.

'If I was hearing this from anyone else,' said Graham, 'I wouldn't believe a bloody word of it. But you, Ian, me old mucker, never a truer man met.'

'Thanks. It is all true, actually,' said Ian, using the voice Eupheme had taught him.

'Why was your mum at this lady's flat, then?' asked Fat Stan, and everyone turned to look at him.

'Bloody hell, Stan old mate,' said Graham. 'That's the first sensible question you've asked this year.'

'Why was she there, then?' said Stan, his stare hard and glassy.

'Well,' said Ian, not knowing quite how to explain, 'I've, um ... been doing a project with this woman. I'm not allowed to call her a lady.'

'Bit of a slag, is she?' asked Nick, his lecherous sneer revealing a healthily rotting row of slightly oversized front teeth.

'No, she's really, really nice,' said Ian. 'She doesn't like the word lady, she prefers woman. She's called Eupheme.'

'She's on your web page!' shouted Graham. 'Blimey O'Reilly, she's gorgeous. We've all been keeping a lookout, haven't we?' The other two nodded obediently

'Yes, she's very nice, and she has a sister ... oh, it's all very complicated.'

'God, I bet it is,' said Nick, without a hint of envy or malice, just an oversized helping of fertile imagination.

'Anyway,' said Ian. 'Anyway.'

'What?' asked Nick.

'I don't know where to start, so much has happened. I've met so many people, been to so many places, bought so many clothes, I don't know where to start.'

'You are one lucky bloke,' said Graham with a tight smile. 'Would that I had your looks.'

'Oh, rubbish,' said Ian, looking at Graham's misshapen face, his funny eye, his wonky teeth and his discount one-pound-fifty-off-on-Tuesday haircut. 'It's just luck of the draw, mate. Just happened to be in the right place at the right time.'

'So why was your mum at this flat, then?' asked Fat Stan again.

'Oh, right,' said Ian. 'Well, she went down to London with me because I worked at this big show, like a stand-up comedy thing, for charity.'

'I love doing charity work,' said Graham, impersonating Harry Enfield impersonating Dave Lee Travis.

'Yeah, it was a bit like that,' said Ian, laughing patiently. 'Anyway, I couldn't leave Mum in N'thampton, so I took her with me. We took her to Eupheme's flat and left her there while we went out on the town.'

'You left her there!' said Graham.

'Yeah, well, she seemed fine. She'd had her tea, I showed her where her bed was and everything. So we went out and it was an amazing show, Eddie Izzard was brilliant, not that I could see much because I was in the back, in the celebrity green room.'

'You were in the celebrity backstage area, all-areas pass kind of thing?' said Graham, his mouth open in exaggerated surprise.

'Yeah. That's where I got punched,' said Ian. 'So I went back to Eupheme's flat, in a taxi, P40, nice new one, red-trimmed interior, computer-controlled booking system and digital payment meter. Got in the flat and went straight to sleep. Woke up this morning smelling something distinctly funny. Then a bloke turned up who turns out to be the man who owns the flat, very posh, like a foreign diplomat. He's just flown in from Washington DC and doesn't know who the blazes I am, asks what the smell is. We find the source of the smell which is my mum half burned on the kitchen floor. Okay, so I faint, split my ear open on a door handle. By the time I come round the ambulancemen are all over me, the fire brigade are all over the flat and the diplomat bloke is asking Eupheme to move out of his flat right there and then, so there's bulk tear spillage. It was all a bit much and clearly my mum was at the bottom of their "to do" list, so I had a word with the two men from the undertaker's who came to get her body, well, what was left of it, and they're going to bring it up to N'thampton when all is done and dusted. So here I am, no money, no mum, no job, a black eye and three stitches in my ear.'

Ian stood with his arms folded rather grandly, looking down the the line to London. He sensed all was not well and tried to work out why before anyone said anything. He dared not look at Nick, Graham and Fat Stan.

'Yes indeed,' he said at last, hoping that would break the ice. Maybe they were being quiet because they were so amazed by what he'd done. Or maybe they didn't believe him. He finally glanced at them. They all had their heads down, staring at the platform.

'I hear a rumble,' said Nick.

'Incoming,' shouted Graham.

'Yeah, that's a big baby,' said Fat Stan as though they were waiting for a tidal wave on a beach.

Ian breathed a sigh of relief. Saved by a train. 'What's due?' he asked, and as he asked he realised he wasn't really that interested, and to cap it all he didn't have his Hi8 with him.

'The four fifteen from Euston. Or a goods from Willesden Junction, that would be heavy.'

'Excellent,' said Ian. He watched them move off towards the far end of the platform. Fat Stan extracted an old still camera from the pocket of his overstretched green track-suit trousers. Graham and Nick still had traditional spotters' ring-bound notebooks. Ian remembered that in Nick's shed somewhere in Nuneaton he had a very neat shelf filled with hundreds of similar books, gathering dust.

Ian didn't move. He ran his hand through his hair, wondering what to do. He could feel the expensive Guy Laroche hair gel he had rubbed in the night before. He dropped his hand down and felt the material of his clothes. Not a quilted blue nylon anorak, but a pair of jeans that cost as much as a camcorder, beautifully made and well fitting, a jacket that cost as much as a second-hand Ford Fiesta. He didn't feel right any more; he felt very wrong and very lonely. His mum was dead; the men he had deluded himself were his old friends were very much set in their ways. It wasn't that they were wrong or anything – a little lost maybe, but not bad, or dangerous. Just not like him. Any more.

The next train to Northampton arrived on time and he jumped aboard, found a seat and tried to feel comfortable. He didn't manage it, and as it pulled away he could see Fat Stan standing at the end of Platform 5, looking utterly alone in the world. Ian felt tears stream down his cheeks. He didn't sob, his eyes just ran, and he felt as miserable as he'd ever felt.

Chapter Thirty-One

Gresham felt excited at the prospect of getting out of town, opening the sunroof and letting rip on the motorway. She'd locked herself up in the flat since *Uncle Roger* had hit the screens. Contrary to her expectations, which had fallen below zero, ticket sales were far in excess of what anyone in the business had predicted. The punters loved the film, loved Richard E. Grant and most of all loved Nona Wilfred. There were reports of people going again and again; it was seen as the quiet romantic hit of the summer. In their weekend summation articles some reviewers referred to the film again in far more positive ways, 'quirkily amusing' and 'wryly sardonic' appearing in more than one broadsheet. There was even a picture in the *Sunday Telegraph* review section of Gresham talking to Richard E. and Nona Wilfred on the set.

None of this had done anything to cheer her up. 'I don't give a shit what the public think,' she said to Stanhope during a long night of teeth-gnashing. 'I don't know the public. I know the fucking reviewers and go to the same restaurants and parties as the reviewers and I'm friends with the reviewers' wives, because of course they're all fucking men, so of course I care what they say about my film. I've got to be nice to them next time I meet them. I can't spit on them or slash their faces with a broken wineglass. I've got to be nice to them and ignore the choking desire I have to fucking kill them!'

Gresham walked down the mews wearing black, remembering the VW advert from the eighties in which the yuppie woman threw away all the gifts a rich man had given her but decided to keep the car. She was keeping everything, including the man, and his car was a black Range Rover. This time she hadn't even asked if she could borrow it, just assumed it would be fine.

The car started first time. She switched on the digital map and moved the cursor until she found her destination. She then clicked the 'route' button on the small control panel as Ian had shown her and the box buzzed.

She started to move off along the cobbled surface of Clabon Mews, turning on to Cadogan Square and then Sloane Street. She stopped at the lights outside Harvey Nichols and looked at the map. Her route had been chosen. She pushed herself back into the armchair-sized seat and glanced down at the small Datsun waiting in traffic beside her. It was very full – an Asian family, big fat dad driving, mum with a baby on her lap, too many children and aunties in the back to count. Poor people in a smaller, cheaper, rusty car. The sort of thing that used to make her pass a cruel comment and laugh. Now it didn't. She felt sorry for them. Nothing was working. She needed something to cheer her up. She was out to get something that would cheer her up, come what may.

By the time she got to the Wellingborough cemetery, what had started out as a beautiful English summer day had developed into standard grey British drizzle. She drove slowly through the gates. A low redbrick wall surrounded the cemetery which occupied a small hillside. She looked through the drizzle, trying to find a funeral. She could see nothing. A more miserable place she couldn't imagine – an obscure cemetery outside a small provincial town, in the rain. She bit her lip.

'Shit,' she said, and banged the steering wheel. She could feel the now-familiar bubble of misery building in her throat; she couldn't remember feeling so low, so wretched, unloved and unattractive. It was loathsome. She noticed something in the wing mirror. Headlights flashing. She pulled the Range Rover forward and up on to a grassy bank. A hearse pulled past her, three small wreaths of flowers resting on the lid, one of which read 'MUM'. The hearse was followed by a large black limousine. Ian Ringfold was sitting in the back in amongst a group of ancient-looking women in black hats. She slipped the car off the grassy bank and followed the small entourage along the narrow tarmac drive.

The hearse stopped by an open grave. Two workmen stood under the upturned bucket of a JCB digger which was parked near by. A mound of sticky red soil lay freshly exposed on the rarely mown grass. Gresham pulled the Range Rover to a halt fifty yards behind them, switched the engine off and sat in silence.

'Fuck, this is depressing,' she muttered finally. She sat in the car and watched the slow process take place. A vicar arrived in a light blue old-model Ford Fiesta as the four undertakers lifted the coffin and carried it on their shoulders to the hole in the ground. Ian stood under a large black umbrella, looking dreadful. He had two very old women standing either side of him, both with walking sticks. They both seemed to be talking constantly, but Gresham could hear nothing but soft rain hitting the roof of the car.

The vicar spoke and the coffin was lowered into the hole. The vicar threw some dirt on top and Ian followed suit. The old women seemed to be talking to each other through the whole ceremony, barely glancing at the proceedings.

Finally Ian broke away from the group and walked towards the two men standing by the digger. They talked animatedly for a while, then one of them climbed into the digger and started it up. The large bucket jerked a little, then smoothly picked up a grabful of earth and slowly, gently tipped it into the hole. Ian talked with the other workman, watching the digger's movements with a fascination Gresham found touching.

She got out of the car, pulled on a black Dolce e Gabanna quilted rainproof jacket, and walked the short distance to Ian's side.

'Hi,' she said softly. Ian turned rapidly. He had been completely unaware of her presence.

'Bloody Ada. What are you doing here?' he asked without smiling.

'I wanted to see you,' she said.

'Bloody Ada. It's my mum's funeral.'

'I know.'

'How d'you know?'

'I heard,' said Gresham. 'Christine, you know, that fat girl that works with Pheme, she told me. I asked the registry office where the funeral was taking place.'

'Bloody Ada,' said Ian again.

'Sorry about your mum,' said Gresham.

'Thanks. She didn't do so bad on the old innings front,' said Ian. 'She made it to seventy-seven.'

'I know, but it must have been terrible for you.' Gresham looked at his ear, the stitches. 'What happened?' she asked, her hand almost touching the wound.

'Fainted,' said Ian. 'Bit of a shock finding her like that.'

'I'm sure,' said Gresham.

'She was a nice lady, when all was said and done. Had me a bit on the late side which is always a bit worrying. Lots of Down's syndrome people get born late, don't they? Oft I've wondered if I'm a bit on the old Downy side.'

'I don't think so.'

'They're always such nice people, though, have you noticed? Down's syndrome. Really happy and loving, and yet everyone wants to abort them and have so-called normal babies who might easily grow up to be selfish, mean bullies who steal things, beat people up and make everyone's life a misery.'

'Yes, I suppose you're right.'

'Have you noticed that there's a lot of irony around, or is it just me?'

'No, it's not just you, Ian,' said Gresham. She was suffering from the effects of irony too. The irony of feeling so close to this man, the least 'suitable' she had ever met, someone her mother would be appalled by if she knew where he came from. Someone the complete opposite of everything that Stanhope stood for. Yet she wanted to put her arm through his, she wanted to rest her head against him, be held by him, here, in this rain-sodden grey cemetery.

'Well, um, what are you doing today?' asked Ian.

'Nothing,' said Gresham, the rain now running down her face.

'Me likewise, Kimosabe,' said Ian. 'As of now, I have nothing to do for the rest of my life. I should take the old aunts back to the home, I suppose.'

'Was that the two old ladies you were with?'

'Yes. One of them is nearly a hundred. Time she cashed her old chips in, but then where would we be without the oldies?'

'I don't know,' said Gresham. 'I know I want to be with you.' Her heart jumped as she said this. She felt a rush of excitement. No one else had ever had this effect on her.

'Still!' said Ian incredulously. 'Blimey, I'd have thought I was off your "be with" list many a long moon ago, after the projection room fiasco.'

'Sorry about that,' said Gresham, 'but the projection room fiasco has paled into insignificance after the *Uncle Roger* fiasco.'

'Right. I'm sorry, I was a bit on the rude side. I'd have been much better off if I'd stayed with you. Wouldn't have had a thump from Eupheme's sculptor chap.'

'Richard!' said Gresham, suddenly interested. 'Did he hit you?'

'Yes, after I left you. He was a bit on the pissed side. As Craig Charles said to me, he's completely legless but not completely armless.'

'Why did he hit you, though? Was he jealous or something?'

'Apparently, although he's got no real reason to be.'

'My God, have you and Pheme been at it?' asked Gresham.

'Eupheme and I,' said Ian. 'Although we have indulged in a portion of lip-to-lip contact we are strictly adhering to the non-shagging principle in male slash female business couplings.'

'What? Are you in business together?' asked Gresham, still smiling as all this fresh news poured in.

'Well, only in the sense that we're doing the old proving to you that I'm not a total, unrepentant tosser of the male variety.'

'But you are,' said Gresham with a laugh.

'I know,' said Ian. 'That's what's so funny.'

'She's such a sad act,' said Gresham.

'She's lovely,' said Ian.

'Oh, you like her?'

'Of course. Don't you?'

'Well, I don't know.'

'She's your sister.'

'Half.'

'Would that I had even a quarter-sibling of any variety,' said Ian. 'Being an only child hasn't been one long string of twinkling events, you know. I've had an excessively dull life which has only just started to brighten up in the last few weeks.'

'Since you met me.'

'Yes, all right,' said Ian, smiling at her. 'Since I met you. And your half-sister.'

Gresham felt an overwhelming urge to hold him. She threw

herself at him, arms around his neck, allowing her weight to be carried by him. He held her gently in return, not passionately, just kindly.

'Oh Christ, Ian,' she said. 'I want to ... to be with you. Come back to that hotel, Ian, right now. It can't be far away.' She stood right in front of him, looking up adoringly. She knew he wouldn't be able to resist. He smiled down at her, his lips thin and pale.

'I don't think it would be appropriate,' he said softly after a few moments' silence. 'Not on the day I buried my old mother.'

'Oh, but it is, it's the right thing to do.'

'I don't think so,' said Ian. 'Not that I'm not deeply honoured by the proposal, believe you me. Would that it were another day, and that you weren't getting married, and that I had an income in a high K bracket that would support you, and that we could tie the old knot.'

'Are you asking me to marry you?' asked Gresham quietly.

'No,' said Ian flatly. She couldn't hide her disappointment, and then he held her arms. 'Oh lawks a lumme, I don't mean ... Look, sorry, I mean it's just not going to happen, is it?'

'Isn't it?'

'What, are you saying you'd marry me?'

'Well, if you wanted me.'

'Blimey.'

'Well?'

'I can't believe this is happening.'

'I can't either, but I just have the feeling that it maybe should. All along I've had my life planned out for me. And it's not been bad,' said Gresham, feeling a wave of guilt as she imagined her family and Stanhope, and Stanhope's family, knowing what she was doing. 'I'm not saying that I've had no say, I have, but everything has been arranged and supported and organised, really well. My film – I only got that off the ground because Dad gave me two hundred thousand to get the cameras rolling, and Allied Fountain only came in because Dad owns part of the holding company and knows the boss. Like my marriage to Stanhope. I haven't really done anything about it, it's all been my mum, and his mum, and our dads talking. And Stanhope's done everything because he's such a traditionalist. Ascot, Henley, St Vincent for Christmas, mews house in Knightsbridge, country house in Oxfordshire, Range Rover in the garage.'

Ian looked over to where the Range Rover was parked.

'Is that his, then?' he asked.

'Yes.'

'I thought it was yours.'

'It costs as much as a house, for Christ's sake. Where would I get that kind of money? Anyway, I'm allowed to use it whenever I want.'

'And you want to marry me?' said Ian incredulously. 'I can't even afford to buy a tenth-scale radio-controlled model kit of a Range Rover, let alone the real McCoy.'

'I don't care,' said Gresham. 'For a start, I'm stacked anyway, and secondly, you'd make a fucking good editor and they can earn shed-loads at the drop of a hat.'

'Oh my God,' said Ian.

'What?'

'I just can't believe this is happening. You, the most beautiful woman I have ever seen either in flesh, printed pictorial or digital form, is asking me, Ian, the no-hope tosser, to marry you and presumably take part in a wedding night with the traditional full-sex scenario.'

'Am I?' said Gresham, trying to work out if that was what she really wanted. 'Yes, fuck it, I am.'

Ian put his arms around her and lifted her off her feet. They clung to each other with breath-excluding vigour. Gresham's face broke into a tear-stained smile. She kissed his neck, he kissed hers.

'Let's go,' she said, and, arms tight around each other's

waists, being scoped by Ian's two elderly aunts, they walked towards Stanhope De Courcey's Range Rover.

'Hang on,' said Ian. 'You wait in the car. I've just got to sort out the old aunts. If I don't make sure they get back to the home they'll be wandering about the cemetery all day.'

Chapter Thirty-Two

'Tickets, please, miss,' said a voice. Euphème looked up through a haze of heavy day-sleep. A bald ticket inspector was standing next to her seat. She had been fast asleep and couldn't remember where her tickets were. The inspector stood in silence as she went through the untidy pile of overstuffed bags on the seat next to her. Three of them, each packed full with clothes and papers, a radio cassette machine, a fax machine in a box tied up with string and a portable electric typewriter she had been meaning to get Kevin Waslick to fix for nearly two years.

'I'm sorry,' she said, running her hands through her hair. 'I know I've got one here somewhere.'

'Try your purse, ma'am,' said the inspector without a trace of humour, just the air of someone who had had to stand and wait for sleepy people to find their tickets on too many occasions.

Euphème tried her purse and found the ticket immediately. 'Oh, gosh. I'm terribly sorry,' she said, handing it to the man, who gave it a cursory glance, punched a hole in it and continued on his way.

Euphème looked out of the window. She was somewhere between London and Brighton, passing the backs of suburban houses. Always in the past she had privately derided these houses and their occupants for being boring and right-wing, desperately struggling after the ever-illusory concepts of safety and stability.

Now, however, they looked rather inviting. They were, after all, home for the people who lived there. People with somewhere to live, somewhere to put all their stuff. Eupheme had somehow, through a series of events she hadn't seen coming, managed to lose her place in the somewhere that for years she had considered home. She had never worried about it, it was just there. Now the guilt of that assumption and the regret at the loss were crushing. She had lived on Clapham Common North Side for seven years. In that time she had paid the majority of the phone and electricity bills and that was about it. No council tax, no rent, no maintenance costs. She hadn't decorated the flat, repaired anything; she barely tidied it, usually only in a frenzied panic when Geoffrey returned home. She had met him during a party on a houseboat moored at Cheyne Walk when she'd just left college. She was living with her mother then, and very unhappily catching this same train into town every day. Geoffrey, who she took to be a standard closeted gay public schoolboy type, offered her a room in his flat. He was about to go to Washington; it was all too good to be true. And it was. For seven years she never bothered about where she lived. She lived there, in the beautiful flat. It was clear to anyone who witnessed Eupheme and Geoffrey together that he had been infatuated with her for years. Geoffrey never said anything, although he did look at her oddly and she was always tense in his company.

Eupheme blocked the idea out of her head and never felt the need to return this affection. She found Geoffrey a rather sad man, overly tall with too much thick black hair, now combed over his balding pate like matting. She had always preferred to see herself as his house-sitter, gently avoiding his very subtle advances on the rare occasions he returned to London. The nearest he ever got to expressing his feelings was to say 'Oh, Eupheme' to her as she made coffee for him. She would turn around moments later to see him staring at her quite openly. She would always manage to turn the conversation to matters of international politics and the Third World debt crisis, subjects Geoffrey was more than qualified to discuss.

Before his appearance at the flat on the fateful morning he had sent a card, a fax, an e-mail and left no less than three telephone messages warning of his arrival. All of them had managed to slip through the chaos of Eupheme's existence. He was only stopping off in London for two nights. His Paris job started immediately and he wanted to check that Eupheme was all right and give her all his new contact numbers. He had told her that before his arrival at the disaster that was his flat he was in an amazingly good mood. He wanted Eupheme to be the first to know that he was getting married to an American woman called Winter Kimberly. Winter would follow him to Paris shortly.

However, Geoffrey never had the chance to tell anyone anything. As soon as he opened the door to his flat he found a half-naked man with a black eye, the charred remains of an old woman on the kitchen floor and Eupheme looking more ravaged and dishevelled than he thought possible. Add to this horror the fact that the flat was in a truly appalling state of disrepair — the mess was overwhelming, the toilet was blocked and the washing machine had leaked so much that the flat below were suing him for damage to their ceiling. He had to deal with the police and the fire brigade, he had to placate his neighbours, one of whom told him Eupheme was 'on the game without a doubt'. As they cleared the flat together, he and Eupheme filled no less than nineteen black rubbish sacks with rubbish, newspapers, unopened mail and takeaway food containers. He had to call the special council house clearance service to remove them.

The trauma seemed to open some valve in Geoffrey and, as they worked, Eupheme was the recipient of a torrent of emotion. He told her he had loved her for years, had been prepared to put up with anything, had admired her philosophy and the work she did. He had proudly told his friends of his association with her, but now the veil was lifted he could see she had abused his love, his trust and his generosity beyond what any normal person would consider tolerable. She had to leave there and then and he never wanted to see or hear from her again. Eupheme recalled with a chill how she had managed to persuade the now spiteful Geoffrey to allow her a few days to help clear up and pack her bags. She quietly assumed that, given a little time and a cleaner flat, she could talk him round. It became evident within hours that this was not to be the case. Two days of misery followed, not helped by the arrival of an alarmingly young, breast-enhanced, dark-haired American girl. It was Winter Kimberly, Geoffrey's bride-to-be. She could not have been more than nineteen, very happy-go-lucky; Eupheme was tempted to think of her as bubbly, even. She turned out to be a table dancer from Ohio, charming and quite bright. Winter explained that she was just a 'girl working her way through college', and table dancing was very lucrative and clean. Geoffrey was the only customer she had ever dated and she was going to marry him.

Eupheme looked out of the window again to see the familiar pattern of streets running up the hillside.

The train pulled into Brighton station. She sat still as the other passengers disembarked. It had been raining when she left London, but now the sun was out. She tried to smile, tried to look on the bright side. There was nothing there.

She stumbled off the train and literally dragged her heavy bags along the platform. A handsome young man offered to help her but she waved him off; she didn't want any help. This was her period for suffering. This was her Calvary. She had sinned — she had been slothful, selfish, cruel. She had been manipulative, proud. The tears welled up as she approached the taxi rank. She had done everything wrong, and everything had gone wrong. There was nothing left to do but go home. And what a home to have to go to.

The taxi drove through the hot Brighton streets and into the hotter Hove streets. She got out in front of the huge Georgian house on Brunswick Square and looked up at the third-floor window. Her mother, Grace Betterment, was looking down at her, a mop of grey hair surrounding her once-beautiful face.

By the time Eupheme had crashed and bumped her bags through the door, her mother had descended the stairs to greet her. Eupheme fell into her arms, her weeping now completely uncontrollable. Her mother held her gently; they hadn't seen each other for four years.

'Hello, dear,' she said softly. 'Well, well, you have been in the wars. Come on, let's get you upstairs.'

When Eupheme came out of the dirty bathroom where she had spent so much of her adolescence, she joined her mother in the kitchen and knew at once that everything was normal at 'home'. Her mother pushed a large tumbler of rum behind the toaster just a little too late. Eupheme ignored it as she had always done, then glanced up at the kitchen clock as she had always done and saw that it was only 10.30 in the morning, as it always seemed to be.

'Tea?' asked her mother with a slight waver in her voice.

'Thanks,' said Eupheme, sitting down at the kitchen table and leaning on the huge pile of old copies of the *Daily Express*, which somehow had also always been there.

'I always knew Geoffrey was a bastard,' said her mother.

'Oh, Mum, it's not that. I was awful.'

'No you weren't, darling. You looked after his house for years and what thanks do you get.' Her speech was slightly slurred. Her face bore the telltale burst blood vessels and puffy cheeks that only women alcoholics seem to bear.

'Mum, I behaved appallingly. It really is my fault. You should have seen the mess when he arrived. It was a bloody nightmare.'

'They're all the same,' said her mother. 'They come back expecting everything in perfect order, then when you've slaved for them for years they dump you for some young floozy with a big chest. It's so predicable.' Her mother's arms gesticulated with some remnants of grace.

'His wife is a bit of a shock, actually,' said Eupheme.

'Typical. I bet she's barely out of the cradle. What does she do?'

'Um, she's a dancer, I think,' said Eupheme, treading on thin ice. Her mother had been a dancer, a stunningly beautiful ballet dancer in her youth who, through lack of funds in the late sixties and early seventies, had resorted to the rougher arm of the trade. In Soho, displaying her magnificent body to what was still in those days the true dirty-mac brigade.

'A dancer. It's always a dancer,' said her mother without seeming to notice her own ironic position. Eupheme's father, while already engaged to Gresham's mother, had witnessed Grace Betterment at a private party in Chelsea. She had appeared out of a cardboard cake wearing nothing but nipple caps and a tasselled G-string. She had been paid twenty-five pounds cash, an enormous amount of money in those days, as she always told Eupheme.

She had danced beautifully and caught the eye of a young architect called Roger Hollingford. She ended up in bed with him. He was engaged to be married but said he loved Grace more than anything and would give up his life for her. He saw her every now and then for a couple of months, and then it all went quiet. However, Grace had become pregnant. She took no precautions because, as she had told Eupheme endlessly, it didn't seem romantic. She had been on the pill but kept forgetting to take the damn things so she gave up completely. Roger disappeared, as Grace claimed to have expected. Left in the lurch in the sixties, pregnant, with a trendy flat in Notting Hill she couldn't afford. When she was eight months' pregnant and just about to be evicted, Roger came back to see her, completely unannounced. He had married Alice and come into a lot of money. He admitted to being a swine, but he wasn't a pig, a quote that Grace Betterment had often repeated. He started paying her a small amount of money to keep her going, always promising more but never quite managing to deliver. Baby Eupheme was born just three months before his wife gave birth to Baby Gresham.

When Roger became Sir Roger and his company won a huge building contract in Abu Dhabi, then Sri Lanka, then Singapore, he created an endowment for five-year-old Eupheme. He promised Grace, by then only in contact through letter, that he would never let Eupheme suffer and that he was proud of his two daughters.

Alice discovered the secret other child when the girls were seven years old. A letter left in a suit pocket with a photograph. Roger collapsed and admitted everything. Alice started suing for divorce; Roger said life wouldn't be worth living without her and she could have everything. He turned all his assets over to her – all his money, his houses, even his share of the architecture company, by this time worth several million pounds. Alice relented and returned home, but she did not relinquish her control of the assets. Eupheme visited the Hollingford household for the first time when she was nearly eight. She barely remembered it, except that Gresham had the most wonderful doll's house she never played with. However difficult it was for the adults, the children got on with each other very well, and a lifelong friendship built of a heady mixture of love and hatred developed between the two bright girls. Everyone got on; everyone that is except Grace Betterment. She moved to a small flat in Hove, bought for her by Sir Roger. Eupheme attended Bedales school, not too far from Hove in the Hampshire countryside. Gresham attended Queensgate in Kensington.

Each summer Eupheme went on a summer holiday with her 'family', leaving her tearful mother in Hove with only rum for company. Each Christmas, even more painfully for Grace, Eupheme went skiing in the French Alps with her other family.

'A dancer.' said Grace Betterment, now haggard and rum-raddled, sitting in her dingy kitchen. 'I might have known.'

'Mum?' said Eupheme after a long silence.

'Yes, dear.'

'I've decided what I'm going to do.'

'What, dear?'

'I'm going to look after you.'

'Oh, don't be silly, darling.'

'No, listen, I need to. I'll still work in London. I've somehow managed to keep my job. I'll commute from here. I've neglected you so terribly. I'm just trying to regroup and sort everything out. Everything is such a mess. I haven't paid my tax in five years. I just can't seem to get things sorted out. If I stay here and look after you, and buy lots of those box files from Ryman's and just sit down every night and go through all my papers, I can start again.'

Eupheme knew it was pretty hopeless.

'Oh, that's very sweet, darling,' said her mother. 'But you really don't need to waste yourself looking after me. I'm fine, honestly. It'll all sort out, dear. You'll see.'

These words had a hollow ring to Eupheme. Her mother had managed to spend the previous thirty years waiting for things to sort themselves out. The pile of red bills, the unopened council tax demands and the disembowelled purse that were scattered on the kitchen table were testament to the failure of Grace Betterment's policy. All it did was remind Eupheme of her own life.

'I've lost everything,' she said, 'and it's all my fault. It must be genetic. It must be.' In between sobs she said, 'Gresham's right, we are born like this, we have to stay the same the whole of our lives. It's so unfair, all those little children dying, and all those rich people getting richer, and that's how it has to stay. It's so, so unfair. Richard will always be . . .' She paused for a moment and looked at her mother. Then the emotion was too much — the walls burst, the dams gave way and the flood erupted. She spoke through a curtain of saliva and tears that stretched across her mouth. 'He's an alcoholic. He's never going to get better. It's so sad, and so unfair.'

She had a coughing fit. Her mother's hand found the glass of rum and downed it in one swoop, then she walked to Eupheme's side and held her head softly with nicotine-stained fingers.

'And Ian,' said Eupheme between sobs. 'I helped Ian to be just the sort of man Gresham would like and ... and ... and he doesn't like me. Of course he doesn't. How could I be so stupid? I bet he dreams about her all the time. It's so unfair.'

Eupheme's wail echoed through the small flat, and although her mother held her head softly in her lap, she was inconsolable.

Chapter Thirty-Three

Ian awoke feeling hugely comfortable, luxuriously relaxed, refreshed and clean. After the sensual fuzz had spread through his warm body, his hearing came back on-line and he heard Gresham Hollingford's voice. She said, 'Yes, I'll hold,' and then went silent. He just wanted to hear her voice; he didn't want her to know he was awake so he didn't move. He slowly opened the eye that was nearest the pillow. He could see a huge room, a long window and, through the half-open curtains, a beautiful beech tree in full bloom, lit by a bright summer sun. He wanted to sigh, but refrained, just let the beautiful image swim in front of his eyes. This was the first morning of the new Ian, the man, not the mouse. He was no longer a virgin; he had at last, at the age of thirty-one, experienced full sex. Not only that, he had very nearly stuck to his old guns, his original promise to himself, because this beautiful lady lying next to him was none other than the future Mrs Ringfold. The wonderful Gresham Hollingford.

Just the sound of her soft breath was enough to encourage his flaccid penis to stiffen slightly. He smiled. Talk about full sex — sex had never been fuller. They had copulated for hours, sometimes warm and secretive and close and loving, other times outrageous and pornographic and dirty and violent. Always passionate, always noisy, always absolutely exhausting.

'Hi, Stanners,' said Gresham suddenly. She slipped out of bed and walked around carrying the phone's base unit, trailing the long cable. Ian shut his eyes as soon as her naked form came into view. She spoke quietly, but Ian could hear very well.

'Yes, I'm fine, I'm sorry about being away. I just had to find a way to stop worrying about the fucking film.'

There was another silence and Ian tried to work out what his future wife was saying and who she was saying it to. Probably one of her top-drawer chums that she'd go shopping with every now and then, a thing he'd have to get used to.

'I know, darling, I should have rung, but there was something about being hidden away from everyone that was really a help. You're the first person I've rung, honey buns. I miss you.'

There was another silence. Ian started to wonder. This was a strange conversation, that was for sure. He opened his other eye and slowly Gresham was pulled into focus. She was standing with her back to him, silhouetted against the window. He could just make out a hint of pubic hair between her legs, fuzzily back-lit in the morning sun. Her glorious buttocks, hard and round and delicious, were rigid and inviting. His hand slipped automatically to his penis, which was now complementing the rigidity of Gresham's rear. He wondered if he had morning breath and morning armpits. Gresham looked so perfect, he couldn't imagine she had morning anything.

'I know. I know, Stanhope, but I . . . please listen. Of course I love you. Yes. Madly. Yes, of course I want to marry you. Of course. This is nothing to do with us. I know. I love you for ever. I always have, Stanners, you know that. Okay. Okay, I'm coming back today. I'm sorry about the car. . . . No, it's fine, I mean I'm sorry I took it without asking. I love you too. Yes. Bye.'

She put the phone back down in the cradle and stood staring out of the window. Ian's hand froze on his quickly deflating penis. His heart sank like an inflatable rowing boat hit by an air-launched Exocet. It plummeted, it crashed into doom mode. He froze; he had no idea what to do. Should he confront her?

He couldn't see the point. Should he pretend he hadn't heard anything and see if he could have more full sex before she fled? Much as she was a lovely lady, a lovely lady whose heart was elsewhere was not the lady for him. He hadn't come all this way as an all-or-nothing merchant to suddenly turn the old coat and be an 'anything for a shag' merchant. That way true sadness lies, he thought as he felt a stretch and a yawn coming on. He decided to pretend to wake up then and play innocent. He yawned exaggeratedly and stretched luxuriously, feeling the soft Wallace Hotel pillows beneath his head. He raised his head and looked around the room as comically as he could. Gresham laughed as she put the phone down on the bedside table. She jumped on him and smothered his face with kisses. It was so delightful Ian was swept along with it. He slid his arms around her and felt her lithe body squirming on top of him. She was gorgeous, better to feel than to look at, if that was possible.

'God, it feels good to wake up with you,' he said, conscious that he would probably never experience this feeling again.

'I know, you lucky man,' she said, and kissed him on the nose. She pulled back and elegantly flipped off the bed. He watched her breasts bounce a little as she made contact with the floor. Everything about her was utterly enchanting, at the same time hugely erotic and yet somehow beautifully innocent and natural. There was no pretence in that body, no make-up, shaving, dying or augmenting. It was organic, not digital; it was love. He knew that, and he knew he had lost it.

'What's happening?'

'I've got work to do, big boy,' said Gresham. 'Can't laze about in bed all day with a stud.'

'Is that me?' said Ian with a smile.

'Is that you. Of course it's you, you great horse. Christ, I feel like I've been fucked by one.'

Ian felt waves, not ripples, waves of sadness and pride washing over him. Sadness, pride, sadness, pride, back to back, one after the other.

'What about me?' he asked rather more pathetically than he had intended.

'What about you?' said Gresham, who had already dressed in pants and bra and was pulling on expensive-looking trousers.

'Well, how do I get home?'

'Oh, diddums,' said Gresham. 'I'll drive the bu-bu home. Never mind, little bobble-head.' She laughed and, halfway through pulling on a shirt, jumped on him again, grinding against his thigh.

'Christ, you're a sexy man,' she said.

'Well,' said Ian, 'what do I do then?'

'What?' asked Gresham. Her smile seemed fixed.

'After I've gone home, what do I do? I don't mean I want you to look after me. I mean, about getting married, about us. Do I just forget it, Gresham? Please be honest with me.'

'Oh, I see,' she said. She climbed back off the bed, and to Ian it seemed as if she climbed out of his world. 'Well, I need time to think about it.'

'Okay.' Ian felt the rejection coming and tried to cover himself. 'You ring me when you're ready.'

Gresham seemed to deflate. Her shoulders fell, her head dropped. She sat down in one of the leather-buttoned armchairs that littered the enormous hotel bedroom. 'I don't know what to do,' she said. 'Okay, I'm engaged to Stanhope and I love you. I'm torn, okay? I want to see you again, that's all I know.'

'I love you too, Gresh,' said Ian.

'I know,' said Gresham.

'D'you want me to stay in my house in Northampton and be there for you whenever you get a chance to get away from your husband?'

Gresham smiled with embarrassment and nodded her head.

'That's okay,' said Ian. 'I don't mind. I think I love you enough to take that, and you're the only lady I've ever had full sex with. I intend to keep it that way.'

'Oh, Ian,' said Gresham. She launched herself on him again

and they proceeded to make love for nearly two hours. They seemed so close, Ian forgot that she would never be completely his; he felt totally at one with her. After they had both come, he lay on his side, breathing deeply, looking at the profile of her beautiful face. She was already gone, waiting for the polite moment to get up.

Ian bathed alone, quickly and without much enjoyment. He inspected his penis for signs of change. It felt comfortable and a little sore but there were no visible signs of virginity loss.

He walked out of the splendid old hotel, still wearing his hired black mourning suit. He didn't care what people thought. What did it matter? He stood waiting on the gravel drive feeling shattered, empty, pointless. The Range Rover pulled up, the engine rumbling its deep-noted expensive timbre, Gresham at the wheel, on the phone. He climbed in and watched the hotel recede as the car pulled him away.

Gresham talked to her film people all the way into Northampton. Evidently she had been asked to read some new scripts for another film. She seemed cheered by the news but didn't communicate any of this to Ian. He chewed his lip and watched the road disappear under the bulk of the bonnet. He said nothing.

'I'll call you,' she said as she dropped him off on the Wellingborough Road. She blew him a kiss and looked, for a moment, right into his eyes, right into him, then she was gone. He nodded and waved as he watched the powerful black car pull away. She didn't wave back.

He stood on the pavement feeling utterly lost and alone. There really was nothing left now; that was it. He had to live with this great block of love that Gresham had somehow given him. It completely filled him up.

'Yoh, Ian, my man, wass'appenin'?'

Ian spun around. Wall-eyed Eddie was pimp-rolling along the street towards him.

'Blimey, Eduardo, what a pleasant surprise.'

'Was that you got out the Rangey, my man?'

'Yes indeedly doodly,' said Ian. 'Dumped by a top beanie after a night of bread-baking, as you would have it, Eduardo, my old palaroochie.'

Eddie stood frozen to the spot, his grin as wide as his many wonderful teeth would allow. He lifted both palms. Ian put out his hands with a little hesitation. Eddie slapped them both hard.

'Ian, my man,' he said. He was delighted beyond the call of necessity. 'You've finally been there, man. Was it worth the wait?'

'Oh, yes,' said Ian, his smile almost painful. 'It was more than I ever expected, and I'm in love and it's hopeless.'

'Whoa, Ian, easy, man, easy. You're in love!'

'Yes, with the old top beanie who's about to get married to some duke-type chap.'

'Whoa!' said Eddie. 'This is a disgrace. D'you want me to have him topped?'

'Sorry?'

'I know people, man. I could have him taken out for a couple of grand.'

'Blimey, no thank you,' said Ian. Eddie laughed. Ian laughed. 'Mind you, it's not a bad idea. I might get her on the old rebound.'

'Yeah, but you're so honest you'd only go an' tell the beanie, probably right in the middle of a session.' Eddie started to mime lovemaking – groaning, throwing his head back in ecstasy, grimacing like a dog humping a leg. 'Oh, darlin',' he said between humps, 'I got to tell you, I killed your husband. Uhhhn.' He mimed an orgasm rather well, Ian thought. Passing shoppers gave the two men a wide berth.

'Have you got the day off or something?' asked Ian when the mime session finally abated.

'Night shift tonight,' said Eddie glumly. 'You working?'

'Nope. Nothing cooking in the old income department. That's a bit of a depression zone in point of fact.'

'They're looking for someone in Rixon's.'

'You're kidding,' said Ian.

'No. My big brother, Danny, he's left, guy. Got a job at the big Barclays gaff on the edge of town, computers and all that. So there's a vacancy.'

'Rixon's. Brilliant.'

'Bell them, guy,' said Eddie, offering his new mobile. It was an Ericsson EP30. 'Danny give it me,' said Eddie. 'Part of his leaving package type of thing.'

'A grade-one piece of mobile hardware,' said Ian. 'What's the number?'

'It's in the autodial,' said Eddie, taking the phone back. 'Like a one-touch system for frequent numbers.' The phone beeped reassuringly as Eddie fumblingly pressed the keys. 'There you go, guy.'

'Hello,' said Ian when the phone was answered, 'could I speak to the personnel department, please ... Yes, it's Ringfold. Ian Ringfold.'

Chapter Thirty-Four

Eupheme's return to the offices of the International Children's Trust was routine and low-key. She had spent a very long week-end with her mother, from Thursday night until Wednesday morning the following week. Apart from leaving a message for Christine on the office answer service, she had spoken to no one other than her mother.

She walked into the office to find Kevin Waslick on the phone, Christine Hanks busy typing and her own desk piled high with unopened mail.

'Eupheme!' said Christine as soon as she saw her. 'Long time no see.' The two women embraced. Eupheme pulled away as gently as she could. She had known she would have to go through this and had been dreading it all the way from Brighton. She smiled and walked to her desk.

'Hi, everyone,' she said as she sat down, knowing she was also due to hear the gossip from the benefit but feeling unusually uninterested. 'How's it all going?'

'Fine. Everything's really good,' said Christine.

Kevin put the phone down. 'Eupheme, daaarling,' he said, imitating a theatrical luvvie, 'marvellous to have you back. I've become so very theatrical since our night at the Royal Albert Hall. I rub shoulders with celebs so much now I barely notice.'

'It was good, wasn't it?' asked Eupheme genuinely.

'It was brilliant,' said Christine. 'D'you know what we raised?'

'No.'

'Hang on,' said Kevin. 'I've just been doing a spreadsheet for the meeting. I'll tell you exactly.' He moved his computer mouse and a table of figures appeared on the screen. 'From direct ticket sales, fifty-four thousand, from sponsorship, eighty thousand, from Channel Four, three hundred thousand, from sales of T-shirts, programmes and peripherals, twenty-eight thousand, which comes to a grand total of four hundred and sixty-two thousand pounds.'

'Oh my God!' said Eupheme, her hands covering her mouth.

'There's still some odds and ends to tie up, but even after all expenses are covered, we're looking at over four hundred grand clear, from one night!'

'We can do the children's centre in Kenya,' said Christine.

Eupheme nodded. The children's centre in Kenya had long been a project the International Children's Trust had wanted to fund. Now it was possible. This was what her job was about. Raising money, helping people, moving resources to where they were really needed. Changing people's lives, not accepting that this was the way things were and there was nothing she could do about it. Her eyes filled with tears for the thousandth time that week. She wiped them away with the back of her hand. Christine's face was a portrait of empathy as she swayed through the desks and embraced Eupheme awkwardly.

'You're so clever to do all that,' she said. 'It would never have happened without you. You're so strong and brave. Isn't she, Kevin?'

'Yes, you're the best there is, Eupheme,' said Kevin honestly.

'Now dry up those silly old tears and tell us what's been happening,' said Christine. She moved towards the shelf by the photocopier and put on the kettle. 'Where the blooming heck have you been?'

Over a cup of Fair Trade tea, Eupheme related the terrible account of the events that had taken place after the benefit, some of which Christine and Kevin had already heard. They nodded and listened in silence as Eupheme talked, solidly, for about an hour. As she did so the cloud that had enveloped her so completely started to lift. True, the loss of her flat was pretty damning, but she wasn't on the streets, and Christine and Kevin flooded her with offers of floor space. As Eupheme tried to picture herself at Christine's flat she suddenly remembered Richard.

'Oh, he's been staying with me,' said Christine, answering her enquiry. 'He's really dried out, but, well ...'

'What?' asked Eupheme, feeling there was something she was missing.

'Well, he thinks he's really blown it with you and he sort of understands that you'll ... well, that the marriage is sort of off.'

'Oh, is it?' Eupheme noted that she felt completely unmoved by this bombshell.

'He doesn't seem to know. I think he feels too scared to come and see you.'

'Too scared!' said Eupheme. 'Am I really that frightening?'

'Can be,' said Kevin. 'You scare the shit out of me.'

'I don't know what to do,' said Eupheme.

'D'you love him?' asked Christine.

'I don't know. I don't know what I feel. And what about Ian. Has anyone heard from him?'

'One e-mail. He's working in a Rixon's electronics store in Northampton,' said Kevin. 'He sent a picture of himself in the corporate shirt with the corporate badge. He looks okay.'

'Let me see,' said Eupheme, slightly too eagerly. Kevin got up and Eupheme sat in his chair. He bent down and moved his mouse swiftly. Boxes appeared and disappeared on the humming screen until one opened with a picture of Ian centred in its frame. He was wearing a white short-sleeved shirt with a tie and a small badge pinned on his lapel. His hair looked gorgeous. She read the letter.

> dear eupheme
> got a job at rixons, better pay and loads of discount, edit suite on horizon. This is digital jpeg of me, direct download from Samsung SSC41on taken by kevin who works here. 756*480 pixels and retailing at under £800. Not bad when all's done and dusted. best ian.

'What on earth does that mean?' asked Eupheme, trying to understand the message.

'I think it means he wants to see you again,' said Kevin.

'Does it?' asked Eupheme.

'What are you going to do?' asked Christine, who had read the message over her shoulder.

'God,' said Eupheme, putting her hands to her mouth again. 'I don't know. Richard thinks I hate him, Ian hates me, my sister hates everybody.'

'Oh, Eupheme! Ian doesn't hate you. You've got to go to the wedding,' said Christine. 'You've absolutely got to go, with Ian. After all you've done. I wish I could come, just to see her face when she finds out. She rang up the other day, as a matter of fact.'

'Did she!' Eupheme was amazed. She couldn't remember her sister ringing before. 'What did she want?'

'Wanted to hear how the benefit went. I told her it was brilliant and she tried to sound pleased. Then I told her what happened after. About Ian's mum and everything. She didn't seem that interested. All she talked about was her film mostly. Apparently they were horrid about it in the papers.'

'Yes, they weren't very kind. I read one review,' said Eupheme. 'I felt really sorry for her.'

'Oh, Eupheme, you're such a good person. You're so forgiving.'

'I'm not, I'm awful,' said Eupheme. 'I'm too bossy, too controlling.'

'You're not. Not really,' said Christine.

'I am, Chris, but I do actually feel for Gresh. She'll take it very badly. She's so used to success and getting her own way. That's the trouble if you've always had everything. When something goes wrong, it really hits you. Oh God. Am I really talking about myself and projecting on to her? I am, aren't I?'

'No, you're not,' said Christine. 'Gresham's still horrid to you most of the time. And she lied about not fancying Ian. I saw her, and anyway, he's a dreamboat. That's why Richard was so jealous. He could see how well you got on with Ian.'

'I don't fancy Ian,' asserted Eupheme. 'Everybody seems to think I do, but I genuinely don't.'

'Well, he fancies you,' said Kevin. 'But then, big deal, everyone fancies you.'

'He does not!' said Eupheme, warming to this shower of compliments. 'Does he?'

'Looked to me like a puppy in love,' said Kevin.

Eupheme looked at the picture of Ian on the computer screen again.

'Well, whatever. If we don't go to the wedding I lose the better part of eight thousand pounds so I suppose we've got to do it. I've run up a huge bill. I'm really in the shit. I'm so stupid.'

'You're not,' said Kevin and Christine together.

Eupheme looked at the horrendous pile on her desk. An expensive manila envelope stood out from the brown morass. An SW10 postmark, her stepmother's handwriting. She opened it. An invitation for her and Richard to the wedding, in Stanton Harcourt church in Oxfordshire, and later a reception in the grounds of Landgate House, just outside the village. She tapped the invitation on her nose for a while.

She scribbled a note on the back of the envelope and handed it to Kevin.

'Can you e-mail this to Mr Ringfold, please, Kevin?'

Chapter Thirty-Five

The Moss Bros hire department in Covent Garden was never particularly quiet, but on a Friday evening in summer it was a chaotic scrabble for social dignity through a strictly codified dress sense. Ian stood trouserless in a fitting room for over half an hour, waiting for someone to return with a pair of dress pants that might fit him. Eupheme had pre-ordered the suit but had misjudged Ian's stomach size. The trousers he first tried on looked like clown's pants, the waist many inches too big.

'Been very strict with the old diet,' he said, holding the waistband out in front of him. 'Down to a thirty-two in the old inch department, don't you know.'

Eupheme smiled and shrugged. As he walked past he noticed she peeped down inside his loose-fitting trousers. He smiled. He was wearing his 2(x)ist underpants which he thought looked good, almost as good as the model that appeared on the cover of the box, the picture of the lad with the old washboard stomach and big packet, a sure way to sell the product to men lacking in both departments.

Finally a flustered assistant handed Ian some trousers. He emerged to be judged by Christine and Eupheme, who were waiting outside.

'Spectacular,' said Eupheme.

'Really amazing,' said Christine.

'Lovely,' said Eupheme.

'Gorgeous,' said Christine.

'Thank you, ladies,' said Ian. 'Oops, sorry, I used the old L word.'

'Uh-uh,' said Eupheme, wagging her finger. 'In this sort of environment, and in this particular context, where 'ladies' can be used in a slightly ironical, postmodern way, it's perfectly acceptable, even slightly droll.'

'Is it?' said Ian.

'Yes, perfectly fine. It implies you know it's pretty naff, but as you're wearing a morning suit, you look ridiculous and charming, and you're using a dated and outmoded term, there's an implicit knowingness to the whole thing.'

'Okay, if you say so.'

'Well, I'd like it if you knew so, Ian. Please try,' pleaded Eupheme.

'I sort of understand,' said Ian. He thought for a moment. 'Well, I don't, but somehow, when you tell me, it sounds convincing. However, I am saving up all the old good mannerage for the morrow. I promise I won't say lady out of a postmodern context, or say ever so in any context whatsoever.'

'It's ever so difficult, isn't it?' said Christine sympathetically. 'It's really made me aware of how I talk as well. Sometimes I think I must sound really stupid and thick.'

'It doesn't matter at all, really,' said Eupheme. 'Anyone who thinks you're thick because of your accent or speech mannerisms is showing their own ignorance.'

'That's ever such a nice thought,' said Christine.

'Isn't it,' said Ian sarcastically.

'That's what I've been trying to show. All the silly manners that still exist, all the exclusive tricks that Gresham and her awful husband use to exclude people and put them down. I want to show that they can be learned by everyone, which means they're not exclusive, which I suppose means they're valueless.'

'I see,' said Ian, scratching his head. 'I think. Is that good, then, to make them valueless?'

'Yes,' said Eupheme. 'It brings them down to the level the rest of the world has to live in. That level of privilege is wrong, don't you think?'

'I've never thought about it,' said Ian, looking at himself in the mirror. He thought he looked rather rich.

'Doesn't it make you angry that some people are that rich, born into that much wealth?'

'Not much, no,' said Ian. 'Each to his own, as the old saying goes.'

'What does that mean?' asked Eupheme, now fired up on her subject.

'Go, Eupheme, go,' said Christine with delight.

'Oh God,' pleaded Ian. 'Do we have to?'

'Each to his own, except that someone like Stanhope owns everything already. He's so rich, Ian. You cannot imagine.'

'I can, with a Range Rover four point six HSE Vitesse with the old Kensington interior. I'm talking the full leather spec, eighteen-inch low-profile Pirelli Scorpion tyres, hands-free cellular phone built in, with radar navigation systems *et al*. Being one of only two hundred and fifty produced in the whole wide world, well, you're talking serious spondulick exchange to get hold of a piece of hardware of that quality.'

'How d'you know what sort of car Stanhope drives?' asked Eupheme suspiciously.

'Sorry?' said Ian, trying to cope with a vast surge of adrenalin in his gut.

'I think you heard me, Ian,' said Eupheme, her brow furrowed as she tried to work it out. Christine looked utterly confused.

'What, Stanhope De Courcey? Don't you know?' said Ian, his mind now racing at a speed he had never previously experienced.

'What?'

'No, you wouldn't, I suppose. He was only featured in the last issue of *What Car Electronics* magazine. His Range Rover is a top-of-the-range model where communications and navigation are concerned. Absolute shed-loads, it must have cost. Yes, indeed. I was reading about him. That lucky old half-sister of yours has landed herself the catch of the old decade, there's no doubt in that quarter whatsoever.'

'I see,' said Eupheme. She turned without giving Ian a clue what she was thinking and spoke to the assistant. 'We'll take it with us now.'

Ian duly removed the suit and got back into his Chevignon jeans, his R.M. Williams elastic-sided boots and his blue Thomas Pink shirt.

He had caught the 3.17 down from Northampton, feeling relieved to get out of the house. The chore of sorting through his mother and father's possessions was not one he relished, and there was no one to help him. All the aunts were too ancient and didn't have a clue what day it was anyway. The wedding was the only bright spot on the horizon, and that had come around so fast. He knew it would all soon be over and he would be back to his quiet life. His quiet life which had seemed less and less attractive as time had worn on.

His part-time job at Rixon's had initially been a heady delight – to be surrounded by so much hardware, particularly in a store where he had spent so much money and time over the years. He pored over the literature so that within three days of starting, he could describe the technical features of every video camera and digital piece of kit they stocked.

However, as time had worn on, it felt like just that, time wearing on. He stood behind the counter for hours dealing with enquiries from men roughly his own age whose inarticulate mumblings about S video cables and five-pin DIN sockets and bumbling fingers opening small packages of components drove him close to going completely mad. He found some solace in the fact that when he managed to help them, they seemed really delighted.

In the rare quiet moments when he could watch a classic electronics enthusiast eyebrow his way around the shop, he reflected on how Gresham would despise these men, how rude she would be about them, how little she would understand them. Then he thought about how Eupheme would try to get them to change and appreciate opera and polo and art films and weird books about lesbians in long dresses and all the other strange hobbies she considered important and, more to the point, normal.

'Let's get something to eat,' said Christine when they emerged into the hot evening sun and the busy streets of Covent Garden.

'I've booked a table at Belgo Centraal,' said Eupheme.

'Oh, brilliant!' said Christine. 'I've never been there. It looks fab.'

'It is fab,' said Eupheme.

'Do they do really massive sausages?' asked Christine.

'Truly gross ones,' said Eupheme.

'Oh, great. I can't wait. I'm starving hungry.'

'So am I,' said Ian glumly, 'but I can only eat salad and fruit. Got to keep my weight down apparently.'

'Only for one more day,' said Eupheme, and put her arm through his as they walked. 'Listen, Ian, I've invited some old friends to join us. They are all dying to meet you.'

'Oh, crumbs,' said Ian, trying to use the correct terms.

'It's nothing heavy. They just want to see if what I've said about you is true.'

'Oh, shit,' said Ian. 'Well, what have you said about me?'

'That you used to be a bore and now you're a really wonderful, lovely man.'

'Blimey, so it's a sort of test, then.'

'No, not at all. Honestly, I wouldn't do that to you.'

'Yes you would, you'd love to. You are so odd, Eupheme.

Really, I don't think I'll ever fully understand you, which is probably good.'

'I'm not odd.'

'I'll do my best, okay. I'll try and be as top drawer as possible.'

'You don't have to be top drawer, you just have to be you.'

'Okay. Blimey, you really know how to make a chap tense.'

Ian smiled at her. She glanced at him, smiled back and looked away. 'Thanks, Ian,' she said without looking at him. 'You've been a trooper, you really have. I feel so bad about everything that's happened, but we just had to go through with the whole thing, didn't we?'

'I suppose so, yes,' said Ian. 'Thank you too.'

'Why? I haven't done anything,' said Eupheme. 'I've been completely awful, I really have. I just want to apologise to the whole world for what I've done.'

'You've changed my life,' said Ian. 'Not all for the better, I'll grant you, but you've changed it, so you are right to win the wager.'

'Good. I'm glad you said that.'

'Aahhh,' said Christine.

Ian felt warm and safe with Eupheme. She was odd as hell but still lovely. He felt himself soften towards her strange mannerisms, her distant gaze that so rarely seemed to meet his. He knew that if he was ever in a position to make a choice between these two sisters he would be torn. Hot full sex with Gresham or a complex, painful and awkward relationship with Eupheme? The choice for a young man would be simple – go with Gresham, you only live once, 'shag while ye may', et cetera. But he also knew that was how she lived too and she would drop him, had dropped him and left him badly hurt.

He wanted to talk to Eupheme about it, but he knew he couldn't. He just had to hold a great big grab-bag of feelings inside, not let anyone see them. Not yet. He had never had so many feelings before; he didn't know there were so many feelings to be had. It was as if he'd been into the feelings superstore on the outskirts of town with a limitless credit card and had a splurge. He watched the warm breeze blow through Eupheme's recently trimmed auburn hair. She was stunning. What was he even thinking? She was the one. It was so difficult to sort out with this many feelings. He needed to separate them all and store them somewhere.

They walked the short distance to the restaurant, past some buskers in the Piazza whom Ian studiously ignored. They wound their way through the dense throng of people waiting for their dates outside Covent Garden Tube station.

Ian was very impressed with the cantilevered steel walkway that made up the entrance to the Belgo. He glanced over the side at the noisy chefs cooking vast pots of food in the boisterous metallic kitchen. The place was jumping. He felt alive. He spotted Harry Enfield at one of the tables and studiously ignored him too. Would that he could get his autograph in person and ask him to do Tim Nice-But-Dim, but he knew it wasn't worth it. He pondered the possibility of coming back to all these various haunts once Eupheme's project was over. Would that he could afford it.

Eupheme stopped in front of a table where three women were already sitting. They were talking amongst themselves but all stopped and looked at Ian as he joined her.

'Hi, everybody, so good of you to come,' said Eupheme as she air-kissed the women one by one.

'This is Ian,' she said, turning to him and smiling. He smiled at the women. Two of them made cowgirl whoops. All of them smiled at him. A row of glistening eyes and teeth.

'Who's he going to sit next to?' said the blonde woman.

'Not you, Annie, he wouldn't last two seconds,' said Eupheme.

'I'm Christine, by the way,' said Christine, gently pushing her way between Eupheme and Ian.

'Just thought I'd mention I was here,' she added. 'Who wants to sit next to me?'

'I do,' said Ian gallantly.

'Ahh, isn't that sweet,' said the blonde woman.

'I'm so sorry, Chris,' said Eupheme. 'I just get so preoccupied. Oh God. Look, let me introduce everyone.'

Ian and Christine sat on one side of the long table. Facing him, four women giggled and nudged each other. Ian suddenly saw Eupheme as a nervous teenage girl at her first disco. It was so unlike the Eupheme he knew and feared and made her yet more appealing. He checked himself to see if he wanted her to be a teenager. He didn't think he did; it was just a side of her character she had not previously revealed to him.

'This is Annie Pinnock. She's on the board,' said Eupheme, introducing the glamorous-looking blonde woman.

'The board?' asked Ian casually, then panicking. He started hoping the phrase 'on the board' wasn't a strange women's euphemism for something he shouldn't ask about.

'International Children's Trust, the charity where I work,' said Eupheme, slightly annoyed that she needed to explain.

'Sorry. Not completely au fait with all the terminology,' said Ian, hoping the use of the French would sound casual enough.

'Cicily you know,' Eupheme said, pointing to Cicily.

'Blimey,' he said, using his strongest Northampton accent. 'How are yaw muy duuck?'

She laughed. They shook hands and she twinkled at him.

'This is Kirsty Wark,' said Eupheme, introducing the journalist whom Ian recognised as the woman who often presented *Newsnight* on BBC2.

'Hello, Ian,' she said, smiling at him and laughing a little. 'This is a treat for all of us.'

'Thanks,' said Ian. 'It's a treat for me too.'

He sat down next to Christine and picked up the menu. The

food was Belgian and they carried over three hundred different types of beer. Would that Fat Stan were here, thought Ian, he'd love to try each one. On the other hand, if Fat Stan were there it would be very boring. Ian's desire to say 'Blimey O'Reilly, Belgian food. Must be really boring' was strong but he overcame it. He could have said it if Fat Stan had been opposite as opposed to the four staring women.

'Okay, Ian, now that you're here, tell us. Why?' said Annie, throwing her hands up as if waiting for manna from heaven.

'Why what?' asked Ian innocently.

'Why do you lot write down the numbers painted on the side of railway trains?'

'Annie, really,' said Eupheme. 'Be a bit generous.'

'No, fuck it. I want to know. I do not understand it,' said Annie. 'None of us do.'

'It is rather intriguing,' said Kirsty.

'Well,' said Ian, 'let me see. I for one don't actually indulge in what is known in the common parlance as train-spotting, not any more. I did do, for a while, when I was a ... young chap. It was a passing phase, an interest. It kept me out of trouble and appeared to harm no one.'

'Lovely voice,' said Cicily.

'Thank you,' said Ian. 'You gave it to me. Anyway, some people ...'

'Men,' said Annie.

'Yes, men, sorry, they like writing down the numbers of trains because ... it's interesting. Because there's a lot of trains about, because you can follow certain engines as they work their way around the country. Because it's a system and systems are fascinating. Some people are plane-spotters, standing on the roof at Heathrow or Birmingham international airport logging all the incoming and outgoing flights. They soon build up a very comprehensive picture of international flight systems. I think that's what held my attention, anyway. I mean, you could, if you so wished, take up articulated lorry-spotting and eventually work out the routing system used by, for instance, the supermarket chains.'

'Yes, okay, but why?' said Annie. 'That's what I want to know. Why would you want to do this?'

'Well, if you're interested in systems and system management, then it is very interesting. I suppose you could say that men like to understand systems, and if there's a group of you that like this sort of area, then you have a common language you can share. It's not everyone's cup of . . .' Ian saw the cliché, but too late. He followed Eupheme's instructions and tried to make an absurd joke out of it. 'Cup of mineral water.'

The women smiled. They didn't laugh as he'd hoped and tell him he was brilliant and funny.

'So why aren't you a systems manager?' asked Annie quite officiously.

'Would that I had . . . sorry, I don't have the necessary qualifications.'

'Okay, tell us about the Internet,' said Kirsty Wark. 'Do you just use it to look at porn?'

Ian coughed a little. The question was so up front. A woman had mentioned pornography as casually as another had train-spotting. He hadn't really liked to think that women even knew about such things, but then he realised the absurdity of such a notion, as women appeared in porn to a rather large degree. He glanced at Eupheme, decided to be as honest but as tactful as possible.

'The Internet is just millions of computers talking to each other. There's nothing to be frightened of. Yes, there is a large amount of pornography available, but that only makes up about two per cent of the total content.'

'So, d'you look at it?' asked Annie.

Ian glanced at Eupheme, who appeared to be very happy, sitting back and watching his inquisition. He shrugged. 'Yes, I have done.'

'I knew it,' said Annie, throwing up her hands and sitting back. 'All men are the same.'

'Are we?' asked Ian, this conversation feeling oddly familiar.

'All men are the same,' Cicily agreed, 'but some have nicer voices.'

'I don't think they're really all the same, Annie,' said Kirsty. 'That's a bit of a blanket generalisation.'

'They are,' said Christine.

'All the bloody same,' said Annie. 'All they want to do is dump their wives and shag scrawny sixteen-year-old supermodels. It's so predictable. All the men I've ever known have lusted after schoolgirls. Unless they're gay, in which case it was schoolboys. It's so obvious, they just want to be with younger women so they can dominate them, prove to themselves that they are a real big man.'

Ian noticed the women nodding less enthusiastically as Annie went on.

'So, Ian,' said Kirsty, smiling in what he took to be a friendly way. 'Tell us, you're a man, do you lust after schoolgirls?'

Ian remembered the various schoolgirl-styled layouts in the many adult-oriented publications he'd purchased over the years. He felt a hot wave of guilt, but then remembered that although they did have a certain charm, he was not unduly attracted to them.

'I don't think I've ever done that,' he said. 'Not obsessively. Not since I left school, anyway. I mean, far be it from me to contradict you, Annie, but most of the men I know have preferred older women. And all of the men I've known have been peculiarly different, and also, they tend to think women are all the same.'

'Oh, do they?' said Annie provocatively. 'Well, bully for them. That just proves that men are as stupid as I thought.'

'Annie,' said Eupheme at last, 'there's no need to be so nasty.'

'Blimey, you think I'm being nasty!' laughed Annie.

'Well, why are you so angry?' asked Eupheme. 'I'd be the last person to defend men *en masse*, but surely there's hope for us, isn't there? They can change.'

'Look, all men are tossers and they've shagged up my life. Of course I'm angry, all women are angry, and if they're not, they bloody well should be.'

Ian decided that Annie was best steered well clear of. The other two seemed more sympathetic, although, as they ordered their food and beer, the conversation seemed to hang around his gender's long list of inadequacies.

Ian was used to this. He had heard the women in the staffroom at the supermarket have similar if not as articulate conversations. Men were all the same, they all lusted after schoolgirls and left their wives for younger women. It was in the tabloids every day — supermodels and old film stars. All men watched football, farted all the time, always wanted sex at the most inappropriate times, were violent, bad-tempered and spoilt by their mothers. He'd also heard a lot of men deride women as being all the same, interested in interior décor and babies and knitting, never wanting sex unless there was money in it. He found these generalisations to be less and less true as he got to know more women. On the other hand, he would describe Annie as a ball-breaker to Eddie. He just felt as if he were in a data desert when it came to understanding women, and he needed to do something about it.

During a period where all the women except Eupheme seemed very busily engaged in an anecdote about a university lecturer who had been barred from office for sexually molesting one of his students, Ian leant towards Eupheme and asked, 'Would it be okay if I asked a few questions about women?'

'Of course,' said Eupheme, putting a gentle hand on his back. 'Everybody, Ian wants to ask us a question about women. About us.'

This was just what Ian didn't want. He had intended to slip

the question into the conversation, not have it landed on top with such grandeur. All the women stopped talking and looked at him. He felt his face flush with embarrassment.

'Um, well, um, okay. It's this. If all men are the same, and are on the whole, as you would have me believe, pretty awful, and by and large men are brought up by their mothers, primarily . . . well, I'm not saying it's the mother's fault, because mothers live in the same, um, society as the rest of us and are subject to the same forces and, um, other ideology, but as that is the case, and the problem is so, um, fundamental, don't we need to go back to the root cause, as it were, and look at the relationships between, um, mothers and their sons, and fathers and their sons come to that, although my dad died when I was a kid – sorry, child – so I'm not qualified to discuss that so much. Personally.' There was an eerie silence around the table. Ian looked at their faces. 'So, I mean, you made us like we are. I suppose that's what I'm saying.'

'So it's still our fault,' said Annie.

'Not at all,' said Ian. 'But why do men behave badly, to borrow a title, if they indeed do. Didn't they learn it from somewhere, or are we just born like that, in which case, we'll never change and so we're not worth worrying about.'

'He's got you there,' said Kirsty to Annie.

'He bloody hasn't. Look, by the time a man has grown up, it's his choice, he's not governed by his bloody mother. It's a crap argument. Men are children, they just don't grow up.'

'Because their mothers don't want them to, because the only time a woman truly has control over a man is when he's her son, and women don't want to give that up,' said Ian. He could see three female mouths ready to devour his argument. 'And I can understand why not, because all the other men in her life are so difficult, dangerous and disgusting. It makes sense, for goodness' sake.'

'Bollocks,' said Annie.

'Ovaries,' said Ian. The whole table erupted in laughter.

'The three-foot sausages?' asked the waiter, completely oblivious of the conversation. The arrival of the food broke the tension. Ian watched as the women downed their large glasses of light flavoured beer. They ate the vast Belgian sausages ravenously. Kirsty and Eupheme had mussels. The piles of potato salad and seared vegetables looked delicious. He glanced at their plates longingly as he munched his way through a fresh but unfilling side salad. They talked of husbands, of divorce, of children and schools, of nannies and second homes, of celebrity gossip and recent horrific murder cases. They talked of men they had fancied and people they worked with whom they considered stupid. The range of topics was so wide-ranging, they jumped from one to the other with such skill; the way their conversations overlapped was almost poetic. No one interrupted or talked over anyone else. However, Ian couldn't see the join between two people's sentences. It was a seamless song. He reflected on how five men in the same situation would converse. Not like this, he thought – there would be one who barely spoke and who, even if he did, would be ignored; there would be one who never shut up and dominated the conversation completely; there would be one to whom everything was a joke and who hid behind his humour. Then there would be him, sort of joining in, sort of listening. Then he thought of Gresham and how she wouldn't have joined in this women's song; she would either have dominated or sulked. It wasn't, he decided, one of her more attractive attributes.

'This man,' said Annie through a mouthful of sweet cabbage, 'is a fucking marvel.' She pointed at Ian with her fork. He hadn't followed the conversation for a few moments and was taken by surprise. He assumed they had been talking about men, and now the conversation had swung around to him in particular. 'He can sit down at a table with five stroppy women, hold his own, not start sulking, not try and dominate the conversation, not try and show off, look fucking gorgeous, only eat salad, and I'll swear he hasn't farted since he sat down.'

Ian tried to remember if he had. He didn't think so.

'Thank you,' said Eupheme. Ian looked at her. She smiled at everyone. He tried to work out why if someone complimented him Eupheme said thank you. It reminded him of being a little boy, his mother thanking an aunt when she clapped his antics.

'And you,' said Annie, looking at Eupheme, 'are a fucking mystery. I can't believe you've really done this.'

'It's quite an achievement,' said Cicily, 'but then you had good material to start with.' She smiled at Ian. 'Sorry, love, to talk about you like you were an exhibit, but we've all followed Eupheme's project with interest.'

'You might have. I only heard about it the other night,' said Annie. 'I didn't believe it until now. Bloody amazing, Pheme.'

'Yes, well done,' said Kirsty.

'It is ever so amazing,' said Christine, touching Ian's arm. 'He's such a lovely man.'

Ian had no idea what to feel. He glanced at Eupheme, who sat back in her chair and looked at him.

'Well, I couldn't have done it without Ian, he's been an inspiration, and I'm so glad you've all met him. I really think there's something here, about charm and manners and politeness. I really think it makes a difference.'

'No, it's not that,' said Annie. 'That's not what we need. That's going back in the closet.'

'No, I don't mean it like that, Annie,' said Eupheme pleadingly. 'I just mean that we've all masculinised our language and mannerisms in the last twenty years, and the idea of a man with manners, grace and wit isn't about snobbery, it's about raising everyone. Making society a nicer, friendlier place for all of us.'

'Listen,' said Annie, slamming down her beer glass, 'what Ian did was be honest. Yes, he's looked at porn, yes, he's fancied schoolgirls, he was a bit of a train-spotter but he's moved beyond that. I don't want some bloke telling me one thing and doing another. That's what women have had to put up with for years. The double standards, the two-timing, double-crossing, cheating, conniving bastards. This is different. Here's a toast to the honest man.'

She raised her glass, as did all the women.

'To the honest man,' they said, and laughed and drank. Ian sat passively, smiling charmingly, hoping his raised eyebrows and dipped chin would do for him what it once had for Princess Diana.

'And good luck for tomorrow,' said Kirsty Wark. 'Knock her dead. She deserves it.'

Clearly these women all knew Gresham and just as clearly they were not that fond of her. Ian could hear her description of them; she would loathe them too. He felt completely divided between them. He liked these women – funny, passionate, successful, interesting. However, he felt, against all better judgment, that he could actually love Gresham – powerful, mean, unspeakably sexy, prepared to get dirty to get what she wanted. He couldn't see these women in the same way.

He started to ponder about a database running on UNIX which would group and subgroup women into complex specifications. Not a simple one-box list, one type or the other, but a Java-based mass of cross-referenced modules that would throw up various multicoloured patterns which gave guidance through a woman's character.

As the group slowly left the restaurant, Ian walked by Eupheme's side. She'd been strangely quiet all evening. Eupheme, he felt sure, would have a blue centre; he made a mental note to work on her first.

When they reached the street she clung to his arm, the top of her head coming up only to his shoulder. She was a little shorter than Gresham – not less good-looking, just different. Was it more complex? What colour would Gresham's central area be? Red was a bit obvious.

'Thank, you Ian,' said Eupheme as they strolled through the hot night air. 'That truly was a wonderful display. You were brilliant.'

'I don't know about the honest-man bit,' he said. 'That's a bit of a responsibility.' The file of deceit and dishonesty regarding his dealings with the two half-sisters was already long enough. He glanced behind them. Christine and the other women were looking in a shop window, talking the women's song.

'No, that's you, you are an honest man,' Eupheme said. 'We can see, you know. Women, for all our failings, are very intuitive about things like that.'

'Are you?' said Ian flatly. He felt a huge desire to tell her about losing his virginity with Gresham.

'Yes, we are,' said Eupheme. 'A woman can always tell there's something going on behind the façade, even if she's not sure exactly what. You boys are very transparent, you know.'

Was she saying she knew about Gresham? Ian couldn't be sure. He looked at her carefully as they walked. Her long neck suddenly looking very inviting. He wanted to bite it, bury his head there and breathe in deeply. He surprised himself with his new-found sensual desires. Was he suddenly going to turn into a lust-besotted Lothario who never thought about anything but sex?

'We've shown them,' said Eupheme, pointing up the fact that she was not in the same mood. 'You even won Annie round, and let me tell you, very few men have ever done that.'

'She's a very beautiful la ... gir ... chi ... tar ... woman,' joked Ian.

'She used to be one of the most highly paid catwalk models in Britain, you know, but she always hated it. She's had a bit of a rotten time with men.'

'Yes, I guessed that might be the case,' said Ian.

The party regrouped in the Piazza. They stood around watching the activity. Annie smoked, Kirsty called her husband on a mobile phone, Christine complained.

'Oh, my legs ache so much. I need a sit-down.'

Cicily stood separated from the rest, looking up at the night sky. 'It's a special night,' she said. 'I can feel it. It's going to be a special day tomorrow.'

'Yes, I think you're right,' said Eupheme, and she squeezed Ian's arm. He smiled at her. These women are all mad, he thought, harmless but quite mad. Still, he could use them as templates for his Java applet women-spotting programme. His fingers were itching to get on his keyboard.

Chapter Thirty-Six

When Gresham turned around and looked at herself in the gilt-edged mirror of the green bedroom at Landgate House, she took her own breath away. She had certainly always been capable of appreciating her own beauty, but this was very special. She had opted for plain and simple. The dress, in white silk, was by Dior. Not Dior in London, Dior on the rue Saint Honoré in Paris. It had a classic, timeless, Jackie Kennedy feel to it. It had cost just over seventeen thousand pounds – worth every penny, her mother had assured her. One morning her father had started to tell her how much the wedding was costing him, but she had stopped him when it went over a hundred thousand. He had only got as far as the marquee, one of the biggest in the country, the staff, over two hundred; he hadn't even mentioned the catering, which was being provided by the River Café. Gresham didn't want to know. If they'd had to hire a castle or a stately home as well, it would have been more, but luckily she was marrying into a stately home so they didn't need to borrow one.

Gresham stood in the bedroom surrounded by bustle and clamour. No less than three dressers, all from the professional theatre, had been hired to help her through the day.

'Oh, darling, I have dreamt of this day for absolutely yonks,' said her mother. 'You look so gorgeous, darling.'

'I know. Isn't it just the most beautiful thing you've ever seen? I mean, the combination, me and this dress.'

'It's literally breathtaking. Oh, that Stanhope is a very, very lucky man.'

'I know,' said Gresham, feeling a tear sting her eye. She had started to dread the wedding day as she found herself becoming more and more emotional. She kept stopping and looking at nothing, realising she was wanting Ian and then stamping on the thought like a child stamping on a beetle.

'Ah, darling,' said her mother, embracing her in the way only the English know how, barely making any contact at all, 'it's such a wonderful day, and perfect weather. It's going to be the most perfect wedding.'

Gresham made her descent down the main stairs at Landgate House to have the first of the *Hello!* pictures taken. She had to stand for ages while the lights were adjusted and the wedding veil was arranged on the plush red stair carpet. Her father had paid for a new one as the De Courceys' old one was more than a little threadbare. Gresham knew it wasn't as though the De Courceys couldn't afford a new stair carpet; they actively didn't want one. She'd seen Old Man De Courcey look to the heavens when the fitters arrived with the huge roll of carpet. It underlined for her the fact that her father was, after all, 'new money'.

Once the photographer was satisfied, her father escorted her to the small church in Stanton Harcourt, less than half a mile away. Sir Roger was already half cut and taking discreet nips from a hip flask. They rode in a white Rolls-Royce, Gresham grinding her teeth, gripping her bouquet with a vengeance.

'Nervous?' asked her father.

'What a fucking clichéd question, Father,' said Gresham, eyes front. 'Sitting in a Rolls-Royce with your father, in a wedding dress, going to a church, and you ask if I'm bloody nervous. Of course I'm nervous, I'm so nervous I'm even having clichéd thoughts. I keep wondering if it's the right thing to do.

If this was a film I'd cut this scene, I'd cut the wedding. I'd cut you right out of it for a start.'

'Bloody hell, darling,' said Sir Roger, 'it's a bit late for that kind of talk.'

'Is it?' said Gresham, feeling even more alarmed.

'Well, you love Stanhope, don't you?'

'I don't know! How d'you tell?'

'He's bloody potty about you.'

'Is he?'

''Course he is. You can see it, the way his eyes follow you around the room.'

'He doesn't, not enough.'

'Anyway, it's not like you to be nervous. You always know exactly what you want. Like your bloody mother.'

'I am not like my bloody mother.'

'Well, no, you are your own person.'

'Oh, yuk, Father, please.'

'Sorry, darling, bit American, wasn't it. I've been spending too much time there.'

'Oh God, Dad. What have I done?'

'You're getting married. It's wonderful. I know you're going to be happy, and you've found a very rich man who doesn't mind you having a career. That is an unusual catch, believe me. He's utterly charming, rich beyond the dreams of avarice, handsome and he loves you.'

'Yes, yes. I know all that makes sense.'

'I never thought for a minute you'd ever get married, darling.'

'Why ever not?'

'Not the type, I suppose. When you told me you were getting married, I'll admit it, my heart sank.'

'Dad!' said Gresham, genuinely shocked.

'Yes it did. I thought you'd given up, like so many women do. I've seen it so many times. Young women full of ideas and creative energy, they get to a certain age and meet a man and just give up. Let it all go to waste. I couldn't bear to see that happen to you. You're such a strong driving force. It would be such a waste if you turned into a county airhead, driving the kids to school and painting watercolours in the Cotswolds or whatever. You're a player, darling, that's what I mean. Like me. You're not like the family you're marrying into. The county set who've not had an original idea since the Middle Ages.'

'Tell me about it.'

'But then I met Stanhope and saw he was from a different generation. I knew he'd let you pursue your art.'

'No one thinks it's art, Dad. Bloody hell.'

'Okay, but at least he's not expecting you to wear an Alice band and have four boys called Max, Jack, Tom and Hugo.'

'God forbid.'

'Anyway, I think it's marvellous, darling, and you know I wish the absolute best for you. Bloody hell, it's costing me enough!'

He laughed as he said this. However, the laugh turned into a cough and Sir Roger Hollingford turned a bright shade of puce. He took another nip from his silver hip flask. Gresham patted him on the back.

'Don't go and die on me now, Dad,' she said, barely looking at him. 'That'd be very embarrassing, getting out at the church and leaving you in here.'

'You'd bloody do it too,' said her father between breaths.

'Of course I would,' said Gresham. 'Wouldn't let a silly thing like that spoil the gig. Uh-oh.' They had slipped into the village of Stanton Harcourt without her noticing. The car slowed as they approached the church. Eupheme was waiting outside, looking rather annoyingly good in a simple cream-coloured dress and a small hat. She waved, gave a thumbs-up sign and ran into the chruch. Gresham thought she just caught sight of Ian Ringfold outside the church door. She wasn't sure, but it looked like his movements as whoever it was followed Eupheme inside. Could she have brought him? Was he there, actually at her fucking wedding?

'I don't fucking believe it,' she said.

'What?' asked her father, who had returned to his normal, still fairly ruddy colour.

Gresham was just about to explain when she remembered what it was she was going to explain. She hadn't seen or heard from Ian since the morning after his mother's funeral, but she had thought about him. Occasionally her body had forced her to. She had resisted the temptation to see him again with pure willpower, something of which she had an ample quantity, but that didn't remove the desire.

'Nothing,' she said, 'Just that Eupheme actually looks all right.'

'She looks lovely. I saw her at the house earlier on.'

The car pulled to a halt. A small gaggle of villagers waited on the narrow footpath around the gate to the church. They were intermingled with half a dozen hardened members of the paparazzi who had come to snap celebrities. The man from *Hello!* had pride of place, a huge camera on a tripod right by the gate.

'Be nice to him,' Sir Roger suggested. 'They've more or less paid for the champers.'

Sir Roger got out first and helped Gresham manoeuvre her train out of the car. Some of the old ladies watching oohed and ahhed as she stood up.

'Okee diddly doodly,' Gresham whispered to her father. 'Here we go.'

She felt like Princess Di, shy and pretty and coy and a virgin. She chewed her lip in annoyance at the feeling. She was torn between hating what was going on and loving it, but she felt strangely objective about the whole process, almost as if she were outside herself, watching the tried and tested custom of father and bride walking towards the pretty village church.

The music started as she approached the ancient wooden

doors. Her bridesmaids, who had followed in another car, gathered behind her. There were three, all cousins from her mother's side of the family. Two she had never even met before, twins of four years old. She couldn't remember any of their names, but they looked delightful.

She walked down the aisle with her father, the music drowning out her muttered curses as she spotted loathed family members on her side of the church. Stanhope's side was equally packed with some of the ugliest, dullest-looking people she had ever set eyes on. All clearly county airheads, as her father would describe them. Horsey, hunting, vowel-swallowing morons with nothing better to offer the world than lessons in snobbery.

Gresham decided that although her own family were pretty ghastly, they were more interesting. Her mother was wiping her eye with a handkerchief as Gresham spotted her rather gaudy hat over the sea of faces looking at her. There was her dreadful cousin Janet, the secretary, her hair newly permed and looking even worse. When Gresham saw Eupheme turning to smile at her she felt a small rush of excitement. Eupheme grinned wildly; Gresham smiled back sarcastically and Eupheme laughed a little. Gresham quickly scoped the man standing next to her. It was Ian! He was there, standing there in a morning suit looking, she had to admit it, gorgeous. He didn't look at her, kept his eyes to the front.

Gresham pulled her head around almost involuntarily and immediately saw Stanhope, who was looking at her with his lovely eyes. He smiled. He was clearly so happy, and he looked wonderful – so smart, so tall and handsome. How could any man look so good in a morning suit? How could she ever have doubted what she was doing? She was so lucky, and he was so rich.

Gresham Alice Oriel Hollingford and Stanhope Vivien Seston Osall Hubert De Courcey stood next to each other facing the vicar. The combining of two great houses – the Hollingford fortune in the region of eighty million, the De

Courcey fortune in the low billions. It was a match made in heaven, and Gresham could see that the vicar was very chipper. He had discovered that morning that he would get a new church roof out of it, and change, thanks to the Hollingford Foundation.

Chapter Thirty-Seven

Eupheme had felt quite tearful during the service. She had never been that keen on weddings, but this one was her half-sister's, someone she had known all her life. Seeing her looking so utterly radiant had made Eupheme proud to be connected to her rather than envious of her. She had always loathed and despised her envious feelings for her sister, but on this day she genuinely felt happy and relaxed to be in her company, to be in her world. She really didn't want to be her sister for once; she really wouldn't have wanted to marry Stanhope De Courcey. Not for all the money, the cachet of the family name, the undoubted beauty of Landgate House. She was happy for her sister, and also felt rather proud of what she had managed to do. She walked out of the church with Ian, shaking hands with the vicar at the door.

'That was a lovely sermon. Thank you very much,' she said.

'Thank you,' said the vicar. 'I'm glad you thought it appropriate.'

Eupheme breathed in the country air. She felt wonderful. Everywhere she looked people were being polite, people were deferring to each other, letting someone else go first, shaking hands with each other, kissing the air. It was utterly delightful to be standing in the warm summer sun, a light breeze blowing off a large, recently harvested field. Surrounded by ancient gravestones, one of which, Ian pointed out to her, was the burial plot for the De Courceys.

'We're doing photographs back at the house,' said her father when she joined him by the gate. 'Bit public here.' There was now a large gathering of the public waiting on the road outside the church, even a policeman trying to keep people from completely blocking the way. There was a smattering of celebrity faces at the occasion. Eupheme had kept a weather eye out for Ian to see how he reacted when he saw them. He had, thankfully, behaved impeccably.

'Who's the fellow you're with, darling? I've not met him before, have I?'

'Ian Ringfold, Father,' said Eupheme. 'He's a computer wizard, complete brainbox.'

'Oh, I see. The new beau, is he?'

'No, Father, he's just a friend.'

'What about that dreadful sculptor chappie?'

'Richard? Well, that's more or less all over.'

'More or less?'

'It's complicated.'

'I thought it might be. By the way, darling, you look gorgeous,' said her father. 'You really do.' He gave her a kiss on the cheek. Eupheme immediately smelt whisky. Her awareness of people's drinking habits had always been keen, but had been particularly heightened since she witnessed Richard's decline and had moved back in with her mother. She thanked herself that Ian didn't seem the slightest bit interested in alcohol.

'Thanks, Father. Are you okay?' she asked. 'This must be terribly stressful for you.'

'Me! Fine. About a hundred and eighty grand lighter after this lot have finished, but other than that, okee diddly doodly.'

Eupheme's ear caught the last odd phrase and repeated it. Where had she heard that before? More to the point, where had her father heard it before?

'Okee what?' she asked.

'Oh, it's something Gresh keeps saying. Sorry, it's a bit on the catching side.'

Eupheme laughed and shook her head. Then she stopped and turned around. Ian was talking to Richard E. Grant as though the two had been to school together. She could tell from Richard's stance that he wasn't bored or irritated with Ian's presence – far from it, he actually seemed to encourage it.

Suddenly Nona Wilfred walked up to her.

'Hi, are you Gresh's sister?'

'Yes, hello, very nice to meet you, Nona,' said Eupheme.

'Oh, wow, I've heard so much about you. She talks of you so fondly.'

'Oh, that's nice,' said Eupheme, barely covering her surprise.

'Isn't this just the most beautiful wedding? Just like the Hugh Grant movie, isn't it? I love the way you do weddings here, it's so traditional. Really. The vicar even looks a bit like Mr Bean. I love it.'

'Yes, it's a very traditional affair,' said Eupheme, feeling slightly embarrassed for her race. 'Not all weddings are like this, though. We do have some more imaginative ones as well. Stanhope's family are very ... well, they're very traditional.'

'I wouldn't wonder. They've lived here for about a thousand years,' Nona said. She stared at the crowd around the newlyweds. Eupheme could see that she really was a very beautiful woman, even close up and in real life. No wonder she was a star.

'Yes. That's true. It's amazing, isn't it?' said Eupheme.

'I really do feel like Andie,' said the American actress.

'Who's he, your husband?' asked Eupheme innocently.

'No, silly, Andie MacDowell. She's a close friend. I wonder if I'll meet a stiff Englishman today.'

'There's plenty of those here, the crème de la crème, stiff and thick,' said Eupheme.

'I like you,' said the actress. 'You're so rude.' She brushed her luxuriant hair out of her eyes and cast a glance in Ian and Richard's direction. 'Oh my God,' she said. 'Look at him!'

'Richard E. Grant? Yes, he's gorgeous, isn't he?' said Eupheme without thinking.

'No, not Richard. He's a dear, of course. I mean the other boy. He's delectable.'

'D'you think so?'

'So handsome. So intelligent-looking. He looks like he could be stiff if he needed to. D'you know him?'

'Well, yes, I do, but I don't think ...'

'Oh, is he yours?'

'Mine? Oh, heavens, no,' said Eupheme.

'Well, introduce me, then. I'm in a dream world, girl. Help me dream.'

'Oh, very well,' said Eupheme, trying not to chew her lip with anxiety. She and Nona walked the short distance across the sun-drenched graveyard to join Richard and Ian.

'Hi, darling,' said Richard, briefly kissing the actress on the cheek. 'Isn't this the most fucking ghastly wedding? The most shit people I have ever fucking laid my fucking eyes on. I have never seen so many arseholes outside a bowel cancer ward.'

'I love it,' said the actress without batting an eye.

'You would,' said Richard. 'You're having a fucking Andie MacDowell fantasy, aren't you?'

'I certainly am. Hello,' Nona said, offering her hand to Ian.

'Hi there,' said Ian.

'This is Ian Ringfold,' said Eupheme. 'Ian, this is Nona Wilfred.'

'Will you escort me to the reception, Ian?' Nona asked with a twinkle.

'Oh, you're fucked, mate,' said Richard with a dazzling smile. He patted Ian on the back. 'Go on, off you go. Good luck.'

'Richard, please,' said the actress. She put her arm through

Ian's and started to lead him away. Ian gave Eupheme a nervous glance over his shoulder and shrugged.

'Oh, fine,' said Eupheme.

'Hello, I'm Richard,' said Richard.

'Sorry, I'm Eupheme, Gresham's half-sister.'

'Of course, I've heard all about you. Let's follow Ian and that slack-thighed hussy and see if she actually shags him on the road in the middle of the village, or if she can wait until they're in a field or the back of a car or something equally ghastly.'

Eupheme felt a shock wave go through her. She didn't want this woman taking over Ian. Who knew what he might do, or say. The whole plan could be blown apart.

'Are you serious?' she said.

'Well, she was mortally offended when I didn't want anything to do with her. She's fairly fucking insistent, darling, you know what American women are like. Sort of the female equivalent of Italian men.'

'I must stop her,' said Eupheme, and she immediately ran after them. Gresham and Stanhope were drawing away in the huge Rolls-Royce; the crowd was cheering and waving and throwing rice. Ian and the actress couldn't get through the narrow gate at the entrance to the churchyard, but Eupheme could see that Nona had his ear and her arm firmly around his waist. She tapped him on the shoulder. He turned.

'Ian, sorry to barge in,' she said. 'I think it's best if we go to the reception together.' She turned to Nona. 'Ian doesn't know anyone here, you see, so it's sort of . . . not the done thing. You see, I am family so it's sort of okay if he comes with me. I hope you understand.'

'I do understand,' said the actress. 'The done thing, don't you know,' she added, trying to sound plummy and English and failing. Eupheme smiled at her, her face twisted with anxiety.

'Sure, if it's that important,' said Nona, making much of her unlinking from Ian.

'It is. Honestly. I'm really, really sorry.'

'Shame, though. We were getting on real well, weren't we, Ian?'

'Yes, we were,' said Ian, looking at Eupheme oddly.

'Sorry and everything,' said Eupheme. She walked through the crown pulling Ian's sleeve.

'What's the matter?' he asked once they had reached the road. They joined the long entourage of guests who were walking towards the lodge and entrance gates to Landgate House.

'I can't let you get off with that bloody awful woman,' said Eupheme when she felt they were out of earshot.

'Get off with her!' said Ian, sneering badly.

'Don't sneer like that. Please.'

'Sorry.'

'She was all over you. I've never seen anything like it. Who does she think she is? Just because she's been on telly a few times. She's quite dreadful.'

'Are you telling me you've never seen *In Daylight*, *Hendrix House Party*, *Teasing Tom*, *Push Me Over* and *Gambling Randy*?'

'Yes, and all I can remember is her breasts. In every scene in every film.'

'Eupheme,' said Ian with a bright smile, 'she has only ever appeared in one film naked. I've checked. Believe me, it's all on the Internet nude celebrity boob website, boob-perv dot celeb slash list slash query. You can download stills of nude celebrity babes. If you want to. I never bothered myself.'

'It's disgusting. She's so . . .'

'Are you jealous or something?' asked Ian.

'No, of course not,' said Eupheme. 'I just didn't want you to get into a compromising situation with her. I know you've kept your virginity up until now. I didn't want some flashy American witch taking it from you before you've had time to think it over.'

'Blimey,' said Ian. 'I've never heard you speak like this before. Are you okay? Have you been drinking or snorting lines of coke or something?'

'No, I have not,' said Eupheme. 'And anyway, what do you know about snorting lines of coke?'

'All your lot do it, don't they?' said Ian.

'No!'

'They do. They might not do it under your nose, so to speak, but they're all at it. They will be here today, I bet.'

They followed the other guests through the picturesque village where the police had stopped the traffic to allow the great and good a safe walk. The house was obscured by a ten-foot-high Cotswold stone wall bedecked with ivy and Kifsgate roses. An enchanting entrance was revealed as they rounded a corner. A low wooden door was set into the wall and all the guests from the church entered through this. Eupheme and Ian followed, their leather-soled shoes crunching the fine gravel with a satisfying wealthy sound.

Once inside there was a short walk across a very formal eighteenth-century garden with rows of clipped box plants, tidy yew trees and low hedges. Then through a high box hedge and on to the drive. The view was Agatha Christie classic. In fact the house had been used in three period films to Eupheme's knowledge, including *Sense and Sensibility*. Perched grandly on the side of a small valley, the twenty-bedroomed Elizabethan mansion held the eye. Across the lawns, which dropped away from one side of the house, stood a circus-sized marquee, complete with flags and bunting. The colourful speckles of the wedding guests milled about; large saloon and four-wheeled-drive cars hissed past them as they walked. The less-favoured guests who hadn't been invited to the wedding ceremony were arriving in droves.

'Oh, wow,' said Ian as a helicopter landed on a lawn to one side of the house. 'Now this is what I call capital P posh. Bloody hell.'

Even Eupheme was swept along with the excitement of the day. She had never visited the house before that morning, but even with her greater exposure to the lives of the rich and famous, this place took some beating.

'Please, Ian,' she said as they quickened their pace along the winding drive. 'Absolute top-of-the-range behaviour. You know how much is at stake here.'

'Okee diddly doodly,' said Ian, and once again Eupheme found her ears pricking up at the repetition of this phrase.

Chapter Thirty-Eight

Ian walked into the vast marquee and breathed in the heady atmosphere. It was utterly intoxicating. He thought the party at Gresham's mum and dad's house in London had been la-di-da, but it wasn't a patch on this shindig. Long tables were laid out before him, each place setting with an embossed name label on the plate. A vast wedding cake stood in one corner and a massive flower arrangement, looking like part of a rainforest, was in the other. A few wedding guests were milling around. Ian was checking for celebrities but there didn't seem to be many about. He had done well to get Richard E. Grant's autograph. It didn't seem that Eupheme had noticed. As for the famous American actress, he couldn't believe how nice she'd been. He'd read about her on an Internet movie gossip web page; she had sounded like a total nightmare. But in the flesh – and what flesh, wey hey the lads, he thought – she was really nice.

'Hello, are you Richard?' asked a man who was wearing a very colourful waistcoat and who smelt of the same aftershave as Jake the bodybuilder at the gym.

'No, I'm Ian, actually,' said Ian, and they shook hands. The man gripped his hand firmly and held on to it for a long time. 'I'm Steve,' he said. 'Colleague of Stanhope's. You don't work in the City, do you?'

'No, I don't, actually,' said Ian. The man still hadn't let go of his hand.

'I know I've seen you somewhere before. You're very good-looking.' The man smiled and studied Ian's face carefully. Ian felt it blush. He suddenly realised that this man, holding his hand and standing quite close to him, was actually a bona fide fully paid-up member of the Ben Doon and Phil McCavity brigade. He didn't know what to do.

'Are you gay ... or not?' asked Steve.

'Oh, I see,' said Ian. 'Well, as far as I know not, but I've got lots of friends who are.'

'I bet you have,' said Steve. 'I bet they love you. Can we just go somewhere together and get really dirty? Like the tack rooms. I love the smell of leather.'

'Blimey,' said Ian. 'I don't think so.'

Steve pulled his hand gently but insistently. 'Come on, Ian, how d'you know if you've never tried it?'

'No thanks, if that's all the same,' said Ian, and he twisted his hand free.

'What a shame, what a waste,' said Steve. 'Still, never mind. If you ever change your mind – you know, want to see if the grass really is greener this side of the fence – give me a call.' He pushed a business card into Ian's pocket, smiled, gave him the lightest peck on the cheek and walked away. Ian noticed as he left that Steve was wearing a peculiarly short jacket and very tight trousers. He was impeccably smart and clean-looking. Ian shook his head. That was a bit of a first, Ringfold, he thought to himself.

'I see you just had the old Steve Carson "let's go and get dirty" proposition,' said a young man with enormous buck teeth. His voice was so far back in his throat that Ian could barely make out what he was saying. His words tumbled together and seemed to catch each other up at the end of a sentence until they were just a mumble.

'Yes, he seemed a very nice chap, but a little homosex-ual, maybe.'

'A little!' laughed the buck-toothed man. 'He's a raving woof!'

'I prefer the term gay, actually,' said Ian.

'So does he. I'm Piers, by the way, Stan's brother.'

'How d'you do,' said Ian. 'Ringfold, Ian Ringfold.'

'Hi, Ian. So you're not gay, then?' asked Piers. Ian must have registered alarm because Piers immediately added, 'I'm not either. Don't worry old chap. Strictly a ladies' man myself.'

Ian smiled. Piers could barely have been eighteen and yet he was completely convincing when he referred to himself as a man.

'Yes, me too.'

'You're here with Eupheme, aren't you?'

'Yes, I am as a matter of fact.'

'If you ask me, between you, me and the marquee, I think she's by far the nicer of the two girls. Gresham's hard as nails, don't you think, or don't you know her?'

'Oh, I know her quite well,' said Ian, trying to keep up with the general air of confidence this alarmingly young man had. 'I'm not sure I'd agree with you.' He decided to try out some of his new theories, ones he wanted to apply to his computer programme. 'Gresham does, on the surface, appear very aggressive. Her choice of language is, I'll grant you, quite outspoken, but I believe she has an inner softness. I think she's quite an unhappy woman, socially able above her intelligence, which repeatedly puts her in the position of appearing stupid, which she is in constant fear of.'

'Bloody hell, are you some sort of shrink or something?' asked Piers.

'No. Why do you ask?'

'Well, you're going on with all the old sociological stuff. All that inner this and that business sounded marvellous.'

'Well,' said Ian, deciding to pitch his new idea and see if it skipped across this plummy youth's pond, 'I'm working on a programme which is designed to help chaps understand the

ladies.' He began to warm to his subject. 'You see, people see
Eupheme as being softer, more demure, less demanding, but
believe me, that woman has an iron grip on what's going on
around her.'

'Really?' said Piers. 'Are you in the telly business, then?'

'Sorry?'

'I'd rather like to work in TV, director or something.'

'Oh, I see. No, this is a hot-sauce-based intuitive programme,
for a computer.'

'Oh, yah. Of course, yah,' said Piers, who lit up an untipped
cigarette.

'Imagine a graph,' said Ian, 'where the horizontal axis was
a woman's height, and the vertical her weight. Any woman can
now be measured with a ruler and a set of scales and then reduced
to a single point on the graph. After measuring a few hundred
women I should get a clustered sort of a line, made up of many
points, that shows the general distribution of women height- and
weight-wise. This is called a "two-dimensional phase space".'

'Blimey,' said Piers.

'Okay, well, that's just the start,' continued Ian. 'But I
will categorise women by several hundred thousand different
attributes, things like country of origin, parental age at her birth,
number and gender of siblings, breast radius, eye colour, parents'
religion, how she feels about her height and weight, where her
menstrual cycle is situated on a yearly calendar. All this and
masses more data. I mean, I would have to stand here and talk
for a whole day to tell you all the data required.'

'No need for that,' said Piers with a toothy smile.

'However, after this data input any woman can be reduced
to a single point in an n-dimensional phase space. Phase space
is just the same as the height/weight graph I mentioned, except
that it has more than two dimensions.'

'You've lost me,' said Piers.

'Okay, a three-dimensional phase space is easy to imagine.
Just think of a fly in a room. Instead of locating the fly according

to its position in terms of length, breadth and height, we imagine the fly's position to represent something like mood, emotional stability and biological clock pressure. For instance, a man using my program might only want to have sex with women whose "virtual flies" were located in a complex polyhedral space somewhere in the middle of the room. The precise shape of this zone can only be modelled by computer software. On the other hand he might like to be friends with a woman who's virtual fly was spinning around on its back on the windowsill.'

'Fucking brilliant,' said Piers.

'Okay, well, listen,' said Ian, now thrilled to have what seemed like a genuinely interested audience. 'In a phase space it is possible to have "stable" points, but this is unlikely in a phase space that describes something as complex as woman since a stable, unchanging woman is something that probably does not exist. And rightly so. Who'd want that?'

'Indeed,' said Piers.

'Instead, I am going to focus on "attractors", which are pairs of points in phase space that a woman might oscillate between. Love and hate, compassion and revulsion, generosity and selfishness, horniness and frigidity. These are common features of almost any phase space. I have started to write an intelligent front end to the software. It's basically graphical, which displays a rotating three-dimensional representation of the male user's "acceptable female envelope", which is the region of female phase space he can cope with. This also features the sexually alluring female envelope which is a subset of the former, probably coloured red. The woman in question would be represented by a FlyCon, a moving dot that due to data input may or may not be located within the two critical envelopes. If it's in the red zone he's okay in terms of sex but possibly not in terms of emotional warmth and security. Failing that he needs it to be in the "acceptable envelope". If it falls outside both he's in trouble, so the software provides a number of graphical slider controls around the edge of the screen allowing the user to experiment with certain courses of action. Moving the "action slider" to "take her out for dinner" or "buy roses" may work, or it may backfire. It might only need the "listen to her" button clicking to the on position for the whole graphical interface to make a shift.'

'It sounds absolutely brilliant,' said Piers.

'I've used NeuroLogic's "NetModel" software for the phase space engine and the graphical "front end" in Java. It will probably be web-based although I haven't decided yet,' said Ian. 'It's not all to do with fancying women or not, just understanding them better. We don't communicate in the same way – men, I mean.'

'Fantastic,' said Piers. 'We've got loads of PCs at school. Would it run on those?'

'No problem,' said Ian. 'Here's my card. That's my website there, but it's in a wet-paint stage at the moment. You're better leaving it a little until I've got the new program up and running.'

'Excellent, Ian. Bloody hell, sounds brilliant, because I for one, and I don't say this with any pride, do not understand girls one fucking bit.'

'Join the old club, mate,' said Ian.

'I mean, Christ, one minute they get all prudish with a chap, and the next, wham bam. I mean to say, you should see the film Gresham made when she was at film school. It's bloody hard-core.'

'Is it?'

'I think so. All about a girl who finds her husband by trying out his fanny-licking skills. It's pretty much in your face.'

'I say,' said Ian, trying to resist a smile and failing, 'I'd love to see it.'

'I've got a copy up in my room. D'you want to have a quick gander? It's only nine minutes long. We've got time before lunch.'

'Fantastic,' said Ian, and he and Piers set off across the

luxurious lawn towards the massive front door of the old house. As they walked, three similar-aged young men tagged along, all wearing morning suits and wing collars, all with similar mop-top haircuts to Piers.

'Don't mind them, these are my posse from school.'

'Hi,' said a very tall one with a massive Adam's apple.

They entered the house and walked straight through the crowded hallway. Hundreds of people were gathered there, talking, smoking, drinking champagne. Small children ran around screaming, an old black Labrador shuffled about sniffing the floor. Ian followed Piers up the massive oak staircase, along a corridor and into a room with a mauve door.

The room itself was mauve, old-fashioned-looking mauve. There was an enormous bed, a desk in front of the windows and piles of books and clothes all over the floor. The walls were adorned with massive pictures of racing cars, Elle MacPherson standing thigh deep in the Pacific, the anatomy of a Magnum revolver, the picture of the tennis girl scratching her bottom and a photograph of Piers, looking a little younger, standing arm in arm with Arnold Schwarzenegger.

'Sorry, it's a bit of a mess,' said Piers. 'Only got back from school last night.'

'It's a fucking disgrace, De Courcey. Report to me at once,' said one of the other boys.

'Fuck off,' said Piers, and they all laughed. He fumbled through a beautiful leather holdall and pulled out a VHS tape.

'I've promised to give this back to Gresh, but I thought we could all have one last look,' he said as he pushed the tape into a Sony all-in-one TV/VCR.

'Brilliant,' said another of the lads. 'It's well horny.'

This last phrase amused Ian. The boy who uttered it had been born with a silver king-sized cutlery service in his mouth, but was using a phrase coined by working-class cockneys.

Ian turned his attention to the film. The title appeared.

Down on Me, by Gresham Hollingford. The screen went blank as music thundered up.

A shot of a girl walking along The Boltons, in Chelsea, where Gresham lived with her mum and dad. She talked on a mobile phone but the music of Alanis Morissette was playing so she could not be heard. The scene cut to an extreme close-up of two people kissing. It was the same girl and a rugged-looking young man.

'Lucky bastard,' said one of the boys.

'Shut up, Whittaker,' said Piers.

The film continued with the girl pushing the boy's head down until he disappeared. There were then some very shaky camera shots of a man performing cunnilingus, intercut with sunlight coming through trees and water running off a man's back. Then there was a close-up of the girl taking huge bites out of a piece of steak. Ian raised his eyebrows and shook his head in amazement.

He realised he meant nothing to her. He was an object, not necessarily of derision, but of fun, pleasure. A toy, and he wasn't even a boy. The whole thing with the steak was a sort of joke, he supposed, although he couldn't quite work out why. Whatever, his desire to have a romantic love affair with this woman suddenly seemed woefully naïve.

'Pretty incredible, isn't it?' said Piers. Ian nodded.

The scene cut to another man, and another similar adventure, and another and another.

Finally the picture faded into a list of credits written in chalk on a pavement, with an old Sheryl Crow song playing.

Piers ejected the tape. 'My new sister-in-law,' he said, his massive teeth glinting in the sunlight coming in through the long-shuttered windows.

'That is one very hot movie,' said the lad with the Adam's apple. 'Your brother is a lucky bastard, Piers, he really is.'

'I wouldn't think he's that bothered, actually,' said Piers.

'Oh, I say, he's not a woof, is he?'

'Fuck off, Whittaker,' said Piers. 'He's just so wrapped up in making massive piles of dosh I should think shagging is the last thing on his mind.'

'First thing on mine all the livelong day,' said the boy with the Adam's apple.

Ian sat on the bed, dealing with the sudden realisation that he had yet again fallen into a world totally alien to him and people seemed to accept him right away. True, they were all wearing very similar bib and tucker, Ian's haircut was nicer, his shoes were better, but if they could see where he lived, they'd probably choke on their own swallowed vowels.

'Looks like lunch is up,' said the Adam's apple boy, who was peering out of the window. 'I say, who's that lovely spot of totty?'

The boys fell over themselves in the hysterical scrabble to get to the window. Ian stood up and, almost against his will, strained to see over their thickly coiffed heads.

'That's my divine sister-in-law's half-sister,' said Piers. 'Eupheme Betterment. Get your filthy hands off her, the lot of you.'

'Bloody hell, the place is crawling with top totty,' said Whittaker.

'I'm fucking ravenous,' said Piers,

'I'm up for getting well pissed,' said the Adam's apple boy.

'Will you join us, Ringfold, old chap?' said Piers. 'We're off to the trough.'

Ian said nothing, just smiled and followed the noisy rabble along the wonderful old corridor, every available square inch of wall covered in what must have been seriously pricey works of top art. He saw into one bedroom where three men were busy kneeling on the floor snorting amazing amounts of cocaine through fifty-pound notes. They had laid a massive gilt-framed mirror on to the bed and lines of cocaine had been cut all over it. There must have been a thousand little rows, like tents in an army camp. Ian's eyebrows snapped up yet again. Everything he thought seemed to come true, everything he wanted to see he saw. He felt stoned without having taken anything.

Down the wide stairs again, and there, at the bottom, looking stunning in a full-length cream dress, was Gresham with her new husband. The two of them seemed to glow in the midst of the huge crowd which was slowly moving out of the front door. Ian felt a lump in his throat. There she was, there was the top of her head, the top of the head he had watched as she put his penis in her mouth, so tenderly and sweetly. He tried to reassure himself that it wasn't a pornographic memory but a romantic one.

He looked at her hand on Stanhope's back as they swayed through the crowd, accepting kisses and handshakes from everyone who could get near them. It seemed that everyone at this fantastic party was drawn to them. He stood motionless on the stairs for a long time, watching the wondrous couple slowly move outside. He took two steps down and his eye caught someone. It was Eupheme, standing in the corner next to a large bronze statue of a naked man with a sword. He smiled at her. She merely raised her eyes at him. He walked down the rest of the stairs and joined her.

'Where have you been?' she asked with a smile.

'Oh, just upstairs, with Piers, you know, Stan's younger brother.'

'Stan, is it now? Goodness,' she said, nudging him gently. 'And you're well in with Piers. What did you talk about?'

'Well, he showed me Gresham's first film, the one she made at film school.'

'I don't think I've ever seen it,' said Eupheme.

'I don't think you'd forget it if you did,' said Ian as he led her out into the hot summer sunshine. 'Lovely day for a wedding.'

'I've been thinking,' said Eupheme as they walked across the grass, 'I saw Gresham look at you in the church. She clearly remembers you and she looked utterly horrified. You must have made a very big impression on her.'

'Must have.'

'Now this time I don't want you skulking off when I confront her, so stay near me from now on. Is that okay? I'm sorry, Ian, but we've got to do this.'

'That's why I'm here,' said Ian. 'And it's amazing. It's just really, really amazing. This wedding must have cost so much money.'

'Yes, it's ridiculous, isn't it? My father is a very rich man and he does an awful lot for charity, but this is such a conspicuous display of wealth. If some of the children we help could see this, well, they'd die of shock. Oh no, what a terrible thing to say. How could I say that? Oh God. Anyway, now listen, Ian.' She pulled him a little closer as they approached the entrance to the marquee. 'You're sitting next to me in the tent, okay?'

'Okay, that's fine,' said Ian.

'We're right up on the front table, so she'll be able to see you all the way through the wedding breakfast. I want absolute top-table manners. I want complete charm and top accent all the way through. I know you can do it.'

''Course I can, darlin',' said Ian in his roughest Northampton accent. 'Don't yaw worry, muy doock.'

'Please, Ian, someone might hear you.'

They entered the tent and stood face to face with Richard Markham and Christine Hanks. Richard was looking slightly haggard in a fly-blown morning suit, Christine was wearing the same bright yellow frock she had worn to the engagement party.

'Surprise,' she said. Ian smiled broadly, glanced at Eupheme and saw the colour drain from her face.

'What are you doing here?' she asked finally.

'We got invited,' said Christine as grandly as she could. 'Well, Richard did.'

'Sorry, Pheme, it's all my fault,' said Richard.

'They've got one of Richard's pieces in the courtyard. You must have seen it, it's amazing,' said Christine.

'Yes, I remember it,' Eupheme said to Richard, who stood very still, clearly not drunk.

'I sort of rang them up and asked if I could bring someone as a sort of guest. I sort of explained that I wasn't coming with you. I had to do it, Pheme, I needed to see you.' Richard glanced at Ian and Ian stopped smiling at once. Christine nudged Richard slightly and he coughed and stood almost to attention. He faced Ian and looked right into his eyes.

'I'm deeply ashamed of what I've done,' he said, as if he'd learned the apology by rote. 'My name is Richard and I am an alcoholic. I can understand if you don't forgive me. What I did was totally wrong and unforgivable. I can only offer my most heartfelt and deepest shame at the pain and distress I have caused through my actions.'

'Oh, that's okay,' Ian said as cheerfully as he dared after hearing the dirge. 'It's all water under the old bridge.'

'That's ever so nice of you, Ian,' said Christine. 'You've been really worried about this moment, haven't you, Rich?'

'That, and other things,' said Richard quietly.

'Well, we've got to find our seats,' said Eupheme.

'You need to talk to Richard,' said Christine flatly.

'Can't we talk later?' objected Eupheme, now slightly annoyed.

'I really need to talk to you, Pheme,' said Richard. 'You see, I'm marrying Christine and we're having a baby.'

'Blimey O'Reilly,' said Ian.

'Please don't say that, Ian,' said Eupheme.

'Oh, this isn't how it was supposed to be,' moaned Christine.

'I beg your pardon?' said Eupheme, providing an excellent display of someone for whom the penny is dropping.

'Christine is pregnant with our baby, and we're getting married, in three weeks, in Italy.'

'Gordon H. Bennett,' said Ian. 'Um, congratulations are in order, I believe.' He kissed Christine on the cheek and shook hands with a very nervous and depressed-looking Richard.

'You're pregnant?' said Eupheme, now in a fully dropped coinage frame of mind.

'Yes. Twelve weeks,' said Christine. 'I didn't want to say anything until we were sure, but it's been confirmed by my doctor last week. Due on April the fifth next year. I want a boy.'

'You're pregnant!' said Eupheme.

'I know it's a shock, Eupheme. That's why I wanted Richard to tell you while you had your dinner.'

'It's lunch,' said Eupheme dismissively.

'Sorry, lunch.'

'Actually, if you're going to be picky, it's breakfast,' said Ian in an impeccable accent. 'Wedding breakfast. Actually.'

'What are you going to do?' asked Eupheme, looking at Richard for the first time.

'Get married,' said Richard.

'Oh my God!' said Eupheme. 'I don't believe it. I can't deal with this now. How could you do this to me! Oh my God, why did you tell me now. Here. Today.'

'Are you really angry?' asked Christine naïvely.

Eupheme put her hands to her head. All around them people filed into the huge tent. Someone tapped on a microphone, then a thunderous, plummy, born-into-power-and-wealth voice said, 'Hello, everybody, if you'd like to take your seats for the wedding breakfast, the glorious couple will join us soon.'

'Oh, that's him, isn't it?' said Christine, clutching her small bag to her now even more ample bosom.

'Duke of Weymouth,' said Richard quickly.

'It's so exciting, isn't it, Ian?'

'I should say so,' said Ian as poshly as he could manage.

'Ian, come with me. You two can sort yourselves out,' Eupheme said dismissively over her shoulder.

'Eupheme, come back,' said Richard. 'We've got to talk about it.'

'Fuck off, Richard,' said Eupheme, more loudly than Ian thought was polite. 'How d'you expect me to react!'

Ian followed her as best he could through the crowds of people looking for their names on the place settings. She stormed through the tables like a woman in a very bad mood, climbing the one grass-matting-covered step to the raised end table. She and Ian sat at one end, about thirty seats from the still-absent newlyweds.

'Fucking hell,' said Eupheme. 'Fucking bastard. Fucking fat-slag bitch. How could she do that to me? I don't believe it.'

Ian stared at her. He had never heard her swear before. It was very shocking. It was also very exciting. Although he had allowed a few fantasies about Eupheme to float through his imagination, they had always involved him pleading and her acquiescing like a vicar's wife. As though the whole business were a bit on the mucky side and she'd rather be flower arranging. But this fury he saw, that was someone else; in fact a lot more like her half-sister. He felt a stirring for her he'd never felt before. He decided to call it a reciprocal lust notion. Eupheme was angry and it showed. Her emotions had never really made an appearance before; she had always been so logical and careful, which was attractive, but in a distant, objective way. It didn't make Ian want to bury his face in her neck and say, I love you. Now she was really angry, which also might mean, and he imagined a linked 'hot-sauce' floating box in a strong shade of purple with yellow lettering, 'angry', click and glide through to 'passionate', click and glide through to 'sexy'. Wey hey the lads, as they said in the trade. If she got angry she might just get passionate. In other ways.

He watched Eupheme scan the room from their vantage point on the top table and followed her gaze. Richard was standing next to Christine and they were both talking to the man who had spoken into the microphone. The duke, Stanhope's dad.

So, Christine and Richard had made the old beast with two backs, and now she was up duffage. Richard looked a bit down in the old dumps, but then again, to go from Eupheme to Christine was a bit of a let-down in the old beauty stakes. Not that beauty meant everything and Christine seemed like a very nice lady, although a little on the broad side for Ian's taste.

The marquee filled. People took their seats. The place smelt of money – the perfume was so rich and thick you could almost see it wafting through the canvassed enclosure. That special light – Ian wondered how you could ever recreate the effect digitally. If his hot-sauce site had the background colouring of a marquee in the summer, it would really stand out.

Everyone stood as the bride and groom entered. There was a huge round of applause, shouts and bellows from the men in the room. Ian stood and clapped out of politeness. There was quite definitely a lump in his throat. For a man who held very strong romantic notions of love and marriage, the sight of the first woman he had slept with walking past him wearing a wonderful cream wedding dress was hard to take. She looked breathtakingly beautiful, heart-achingly so. However, he was not feeling as hurt as he'd feared owing simply to the fact that he knew he never could, and never wanted to, fill Stanhope De Courcey's shoes. He would never walk into a marquee and have five hundred people stand and cheer. It just wasn't going to happen, and that wasn't such a bad thing when all was said and done. He sat down slightly earlier than the rest of the gathering. He wanted to shrink and not be noticed and felt a little exposed up on the high table.

Gresham glanced at him as she stepped up on to the raised platform. She smiled at Eupheme. An usher tried to guide her around the long table so she would pass behind Eupheme and Ian. She gestured the other way and had a small discussion with the usher, who blushed and guided her in the direction he wanted to go in. She slowly made her way around the long table with her new husband.

The food arrived with great speed, the waiters and waitresses almost running while carrying armfuls of plates. The yellow and green salad-type product looked decidedly strange but tasted delicious. Ian had certainly never seen anything like it in Besco's very respectable series of cookery books. He swallowed, took a sip of water to freshen his mouth and decided to take the plunge with his neighbour.

'Quite a bit of organisation required for a feast of this scale,' he said to the very old lady beside him, who looked as if she could give his aunts a run for their money in the ancient monument stakes.

'Indeed. It must be. Are you a friend of the groom?'

'No, the bride, and her sister.'

'Half-sister,' said the old lady. She smiled softly and glanced at Eupheme, who was busy talking to her neighbour. 'I knew you weren't family.'

'Oh no. I'm not family.'

'You're a very striking-looking man. Was your father in the Green Jackets, by any chance?'

'I don't think so. No.'

'You look like a fellow I knew in India.'

'Do I really?' said Ian, 'Some people say I look like Matthew Modine. Some say I look a little like the young Robert Mitchum. Naturally, I can't see it myself, but then there are seventeen and a half billion people on the planet. We all do share the same basic set of facial characteristics, so I suppose we are bound to look a little like someone. You remind me of my Auntie Maud, actually.'

'How very intelligent of you. Are you engaged to Miss Betterment?'

'Goodness me, no. We are just good friends.'

'Pity. She's a lovely woman. The accident of her birth is certainly not her fault. She deserves a happy life but I fear it will always evade her. It's as if fate trails the cloak of joy just two feet in front of her. She's always been nearly happy.'

'That's terribly poetic,' said Ian. A hot-sauce website for old ladies. Of course. That was a massive market. Who understood them? Only other old ladies, and yet they had a vast store of knowledge that could help the whole of mankind, if it could only be translated into a form that the common man could understand.

'I'm an old woman and I can't be bothered with the niceties of life at my age, so tell me, are you a practising homosexual?'

'Goodness me. No, I'm not, as a matter of fact,' said Ian, trying his hardest not to say Blimey O'Reilly. 'What a perfectly extraordinary question.'

'I only ask because so many young men are these days. Don't worry, there's nothing new, there were plenty of them around in my day, only we called them pansies. Most of them were utterly charming. I only ask because you two make such a handsome couple, it seems to make sense that you should tie the knot.'

'Oh, I see. Well, I'll certainly think about it.'

'Especially as Gresham has finally wed. We've all waited long enough.'

'You seem to know them well,' said Ian.

'I'm their grandmother,' said the old lady.

'Oh, right, well, you would, then.'

'Are you okay, Grandma?' said Eupheme, almost leaning across Ian.

'I'm very fine, thank you, dear. I've just been talking to your delightful friend, Mr, er . . .'

'Ringfold,' said Ian.

'Mr Ringfold. Yes. He's utterly charming.'

'Thank you, Grandma,' said Eupheme, her smile returned and the delight back in her voice.

'You're not so bad yourself,' said Ian. Eupheme nudged him gently under the table.

'Thank you,' said the old woman. 'That's the first compliment I've had from a man since the early nineteen fifties.'

Ian turned and smiled at Eupheme. Someone banged a hammer on a table. Ian's plate, only half finished, was whooshed away as the speeches started. Those from the best man and the bride's father were all pretty much standard wedding speeches. Jokes about the individual's past went over Ian's head. He studied his hands throughout, thinking about Java applets and colour-coding systems, 360 degree retrieval platforms and floating data nodes. He heard some plates clattering outside the marquee, which reminded him he was quite interested to see the catering operation in action and would have loved to have slipped out of the tent to have a quick chinwag with the staff.

Suddenly, when he was miles away from the laughter and clapping in the huge marquee, Eupheme nudged him. He looked up. Eupheme and Gresham's father was speaking.

'And although it is a break with tradition, strictly speaking, I know that Gresh's sister Eupheme would dearly love to say a few words today, so, Eupheme.'

Eupheme pushed her chair back and stood up next to Ian.

'Well, I am very used to public speaking but this is still a terrifying moment,' she said, her hands clutching a small pile of three-by-five cards. 'However, when Gresham and I were twelve we were on holiday in Antibes and two awfully nice-looking French boys came up to us on the beach. I was rather interested in them and tried to talk to them in French. Gresham, you may not be surprised to learn, was utterly uninterested. She sneered at these poor boys with such disdain I thought they'd run off immediately. They didn't. They hung around for the following two weeks. It was only Daddy's intervention with a walking stick which kept them at bay. I was with Gresh when she met Stanhope for the first time, and she was so rude to him I fully expected never to see him again. He's stayed the course, which says more about him than anything I can say. I tried to learn from this. It hasn't worked for me yet, but I'm still being as rude as I can to all the men I most admire. You never know.'

The dinner guests 'aaahed' at this.

'But really,' Eupheme continued, 'all I want to say is I've known Gresham all my life, more or less.' A small laugh rippled through part of the audience. 'I think she's the most amazing woman I have ever met, the strongest, often the most annoying, but truly the most brave and courageous, intelligent and creative woman who has ever set foot on this earth. Stanhope, I wish you luck, but then I don't really need to because Gresham loves you, and let me assure you she has never loved another man. You're the only one.'

Ian was drinking from his water glass at this moment and thought about producing a huge stage cough. He didn't need to. Numerous men seated around the lower tables shouted out 'Lies! Damn lies!' much to the mirth of the gathering.

'Oh, I know, but I mean she's never been in love. When I knew Gresham had decided Stanhope was the one, I could tell she was really in love with him. She was so different, and although I don't know Stanhope well, I can tell by the gathering here that he is much loved and respected.'

'Rubbish, he's a wanker!' shouted a very plummy voice from the back, eliciting another huge laugh.

'I wish both of them all the luck in the world together,' said Eupheme, bravely talking over the noise. 'They deserve each other and I think it's safe to say all our hearts and thoughts are with them today. To Gresham and Stanhope.' She raised her glass.

'Gresham and Stanhope,' said the entire gathering, raising their glasses.

Eupheme sat down and Ian gave her a peck on the cheek. She looked at him, slightly shocked.

'Well done,' he said.

'Thank you,' she responded.

'You've been pretty awful to me, and I still like you very much indeed,' said Ian. 'So being horrible to men has worked on my account.'

'Oh, has it?' said Eupheme, a blush forming rapidly and enchantingly on her chest and neck. 'Oh. Right, then.'

The giant cake was carried into position by no less than four men in livery. Gresham and Stanhope stood up and

posed for the photographer as they held the knife ready
to cut it.

'So bloody traditional,' muttered Eupheme into Ian's ear.

'Your speech wasn't traditional,' said Ian.

'Daddy wanted me to do that. It was all his doing.'

'Anyway, I thought tradition was what weddings were all
about,' said Ian.

Everyone clapped and cheered again and the family closed
in around the married couple. The gathering was beginning to
disperse.

'Should we go and see Gresham?' asked Ian.

'Yes. I suppose we should.'

Most of the people in the marquee were already on their
feet. Groups milled around, clumps of people filed out on to
the lawn. Waiters appeared and scurried between the tables,
swiftly removing plates and glasses. Eupheme stood up and
started to move slowly through the crowd towards Gresham
and Stanhope. As she got nearer Ian saw her hand reach out
behind her and search blindly for his. He looked at her hand
momentarily. It was a beautiful hand; maybe she even had better
hands than Gresham. He made a mental note to build in a hands
subsection in his understanding women program, maybe with
GIF images of hand types on a drop-down menu which would
further colour the character build-up.

He moved his hand forward and allowed Eupheme to pull
him through the crowd of poshly spoken men and women. All
eyes were on the golden couple as they shook hands and kissed
their many admirers.

'Gresh, I'm so happy for you,' said Eupheme as they finally
reached their goal.

'Thanks, Pheme. That was a lovely speech. I'd completely
forgotten about those French wankers. Was I really that awful?'
The two women embraced.

'I was being kind,' said Eupheme. Gresham looked over
her half-sister's shoulder in Ian's direction. He really did feel

as if he was in the presence of a king and queen. They looked so magnificent, even bigger close up than they looked from a distance. Light seemed to glow from them, they were both so attractive.

'This is Ian,' said Eupheme as she stood back from Gresham. 'You remember. He was at your engagement party.'

Suddenly Ian found he was shaking hands with Stanhope De Courcey. 'Hello, Ian, so glad you could come. Have you had a good time?'

Ian was thrown. This huge, confident man seemed to know his name. His voice was like a talking Coutts cheque book; it almost smelled of leather and old money. He was looking at Ian. He looked interested; he looked as if he wanted to listen to what Ian had to say. Ian felt speechless.

'Ian, this is Stanhope,' said Eupheme finally.

'I've sort of worked that out, actually,' said Ian. 'Congratulations, Stanhope.'

Stanhope laughed; so did Gresham. Ian felt almost faint. He looked at Gresham. She was so perfectly serene. No one would ever have known. She was so supremely confident that Ian wasn't about to say to her husband, 'Actually, I have buried my tongue inside your wife so many times I can't remember. She has sat on my cock for hours and we have fucked each other senseless. She told me she loved me and said she always would.'

'Congratulations, both of you,' he somehow said, out loud. 'It's been a lovely wedding, really has. Been to loads. This is the best by a long chalk.'

'Thank you,' said Stanhope. 'Hope we get the chance to have a few words before play is over.'

'Yes indeedly doodly,' said Ian with a big grin. Eupheme glanced at him. A very fat man grabbed Stanhope's arm and pulled him to one side, breaking their magic circle.

'So, how are you feeling?' Eupheme asked Gresham, who had seemed momentarily out of the proceedings.

'Knackered. Hardly slept a wink last night.'

'Nerves,' said Eupheme. 'You poor thing.'

'Bollocks. I was on the fucking phone to Hollywood. I'm shooting a feature there in October.'

'Oh, Gresh!' said Eupheme. 'That's wonderful news. Did you hear that, Ian?'

'I did. Congratulations, Gresham,' said Ian.

'So you really are the train-spotter,' said Gresham. At last, there was a clue. Ian could see a small blemish, a flush, on her neck.

'Yes, if that's what you think I was doing. But yes, it actually was me on Milton Keynes station.'

'You win, Eupheme. This man is a certifiable dish,' said Gresham with the kindest smile Ian had ever seen on her perfect face. He turned to see that Eupheme's face was a picture of delight.

'You really mean that!' she said.

'Yes. I cannot deny that I am amazed at the transformation. Everything I said about people not being able to change is bollocks. There's the proof,' said Gresham, gesturing towards Ian. 'How much do I owe you?'

'Oh, we don't need to talk about that here and now. I'm just so happy you agree, but now of course I feel really, really guilty. Oh God, Gresh, I'm so sorry, I don't know how I could have done this. It is your wedding day, after all.'

'Eupheme,' said Gresham, 'I have been horrible to you so many times, the least I can do on my wedding day is admit I was wrong and pay up. We agreed. I really didn't think you could do it, but you did. Stanhope asked me who you were, Ian, during the meal. I said your name was Ian and that you were a public transport specialist. Was that all right?'

'Brilliant,' said Ian with a smile.

'I said you were Eupheme's latest boyfriend, and Stanhope said you looked like the most handsome man in the marquee. So, there you go.'

'Golly,' said Ian.

'Oh, Gresh,' said Eupheme, hands clasped to her cheeks and tears welling in her eyes. 'You're so amazing.'

'Oh, don't go soppy on us, Pheme,' said Gresham. She leant forward and touched Stanhope's arm. He turned his head away from his insistent noisy male admirers.

'I'm going outside, darling,' she said. 'Need a bit of air. I'm not feeling a hundred per cent.'

'Oh, darling, are you ...'

'Don't worry. I'm fine. This dress is extremely tight and I need a bit of fresh.'

'I'll be with you in two tics,' said Stanhope. 'Remember we've got to do a whole load more photos for the dreadful *Hello!* man.'

'Eupheme,' said Gresham, spinning to face her half-sister. 'Could you get me a glass of water?'

'Of course. Are you all right?'

'I'm fine.'

'Oh God, this is all my fault. I shouldn't have brought Ian. I'm so sorry.'

'On the contrary, sis,' said Gresham. 'I'm so glad you did. He can escort me as a special treat. We'll be ... somewhere outside, by the house.'

'Fantastic,' said Eupheme, and she nodded enthusiastically, smiled at Ian and almost skipped off through the mêlée.

Gresham took Ian's hand and walked through the crowd, accepting kisses and admiration from everyone they passed. Suddenly Ian was in Stanhope's place. It was very embarrassing. However, no one looked at him – they were still completely mesmerised by Gresham's beauty.

'You look stunning,' said Ian as soon as they had broken free of the marquee. He glanced away from her and realised they were in the catering enclosure. It was a far bigger operation than he had imagined. What seemed like hundreds of people were busy cleaning up and packing the thousands of plates, knives, forks, spoons, bowls and glasses. Huge glass dishes of fruit and ice cream were being prepared along one side of the canvas-fenced area. The guests could see none of this, and, Ian suddenly realised, could see nothing of him and Gresham.

'Come with me,' said Gresham. She led him through the admiring gazes of the waiters and waitresses, some of whom clapped briefly as they paused from their labours.

'Are you sure you're okay?' asked Ian. 'D'you want to sit down?'

'Are you kidding?' said Gresham with her smile. 'I feel brilliant. I just wanted to get you away from everyone for a moment.'

As they passed a large array of gas stoves which were propped up on hastily erected wooden pallets, Gresham paused. There was a pile of freshly cooked steaks in a metal oven dish at one end of the cooker. She picked one up and held it at arm's length. She continued walking, steak in one hand, Ian in the other.

'This is my brother,' she said with a delightful laugh. A small group of waiters who were sitting on some hay bales waved and smiled. 'We're just organising a bit of a surprise for my husband.'

She led him through another canvas flap and into a small area containing dozens of huge red propane gas cylinders. As soon as the flap was down Gresham slapped the steak down on a safety valve, pulled Ian towards her and kissed him with an almost violent passion. He was so stunned he couldn't respond.

'Bloody hell!' he mumbled from between her crazed lips. 'You've got to be fucking kidding!'

'Please, one more time. Please, Ian. Do me. Do me like you do.'

'I can't!' said Ian. 'You're married!'

'Please, Ian,' said Gresham. 'One last time. I just have to have you one last time.'

She held his hair with one hand, kissed him hotly and lifted her dress with the other. 'Please, Ian,' she said, her eyes only inches from his. 'Please do me again.'

'Blimey O'Reilly,' said Ian. 'You must be desperate.'

'I'll fly you to LA. I'll get you Tom Cruise's autograph, you can meet him. I can introduce you to Jodie Foster. Please, Ian.'

She pulled his hair downwards. He felt his knees bend. He felt the ground make contact with his knees. All he could see was cream silk, so smooth, so warm. His face slid over the perfect round of her belly. His body came to rest and his nose was pushing against the divine bulge of her pubic bone. Her long finger was tucked just inside the material of her thin silk panties. Ian shrugged, sighed and delved.

He glanced up, over the tightly gripped folds of silk that Gresham had in her left hand. She bit and chewed at the steak held in her right. She moved her pelvis in the way he had come to know so well. Suddenly she stopped. He hadn't heard her reach her normally quite convulsive and rapidly achieved climax. He glanced to one side when he felt something wet on his leg. He could see a pair of legs next to his. Someone standing on the lush lawns of Landgate House, right next to them in the propane gas section of the catering area. He glanced further up just to confirm what he already knew.

'Oh, oh, oh my God,' said Eupheme. She was holding a glass of water at such an angle that it was spilling on the grass and on Ian.

Gresham continued to chew her steak, looking at her half-sister with surly contempt. Ian discreetly wiped his face on his sleeve and stood between them.

'Oh, oh, oh,' said Eupheme. Ian felt sorry for her. She was so shocked she couldn't even cry. She was trapped by the horror of what she had seen.

'What?' asked Gresham.

'I . . . Oh.' Eupheme turned from them and was violently sick in the corner.

'Oh, that's nice, thank you,' said Gresham immediately. She pulled her wedding dress down angrily and threw the steak on to the grass beside her. Ian felt slightly sick as well. He couldn't help sneering a little as Gresham threw him a look.

'Let's go into the house. You can finish there.'

Ian's jaw dropped. He felt it go as if someone had cut a cable that held it in place. He looked at her, those beautiful blue eyes, cold and mean as a bullet. See through everything, rip through everything and take no prisoners.

'Gresham,' said Ian, pulling himself to his full height, 'I would sooner go down on a dead baboon by the grave of my mother than ever see you again.'

Gresham had started to leave before he could finish.

'I think you'd better both leave the wedding,' she said. 'Send me a bill, half-sister. I'll make sure you get your money.' Without looking at either of them she slipped out.

It was a moment, he knew that. It was a full-screen jpeg pixellated point in his history, a data node of outstanding height he would never be able to remove from his hard drive. He sighed deeply, just aware of the scent of Gresham on his lips.

He passed Eupheme his handkerchief. She was still bent over, sobbing quietly between coughs.

'You okay?' he asked her eventually.

Eupheme didn't answer. She stood up and wiped her eyes. She didn't look at Ian.

'I have to get out of here,' she said matter-of-factly.

'Okay,' said Ian. He pulled at the canvas wall where it was lashed together in one corner. He could see a small stretch of grass, then a thick clump of trees.

'If we go this way we don't need to see anyone,' he said as he started to undo the lacing. After a few moments the wall fell apart and they were free. Eupheme stepped through the gap.

'Thank you,' she said without glancing at him. They walked through the hot sun across the lawn until they reached the trees. The sound of a jazz band wafted across the grounds. Ian glanced back. In the distance, beyond the catering compound, the huge marquee stood grandly in front of the elegant house. Children in smart clothes chased each other across the vast expanse of lawn to the side of the marquee. Flags fluttered in the afternoon breeze. He raised his eyebrows. He knew this was the last time he'd ever be this close to such wealth.

They walked through the trees together in silence. Ian felt very relaxed with Eupheme. She seemed so delicate now, so vulnerable. Lost, really. He looked around them. The woodland seemed to be getting thicker and they were heading downhill.

'Where are we going?' he asked.

'I don't know,' said Eupheme. 'Away.'

'Well, the carpark is the other side of the house. We could work our way around, I'm sure.'

'We'll reach the wall soon. If we follow that around, we'll get to the carpark eventually, won't we?'

She spoke as if nothing had happened, but also as if she didn't really care what happened. He wanted to talk to her, to tell her everything, but she didn't seem to be there. He knew she wouldn't hear him.

They walked a little further until they were faced with an enormous stone wall.

'Left or right?' asked Eupheme. Ian knew from his brief glimpse of the geography of the estate that the shortest route was to the left. He turned that way and started walking. If there was nothing to say, and nothing to do, then his best bet was to get back home as soon as he could and start working on his program. He began to think of it again – the colours, the data input menus. He'd have to keep the program simple enough for anyone to use but complex enough for the job in hand. And women were fearfully complex. He only had to look at what had just happened to him to see that.

They reached the carpark after an invigorating twenty-minute walk. The sun was at its hottest and the last hundred yards or so, what with wearing the full wedding kit, were less than comfortable. It was only as they reached Eupheme's hire car, a Ford Ka, £39–95 a day from Budget, that Ian realised they hadn't spoken at all. He had barely been aware of her walking slightly behind him.

They climbed in, sitting next to each other in the cramped, stifling heat of the interior, and both a bit on the hot side from the exertion of the walk.

If she didn't talk soon it was going to be really, really uncomfortable. Ian opened the sunroof as Eupheme pulled out of the carpark, across the crushed dry grass, past the endless rows of Rolls-Royces, Bentleys and Range Rovers. A young man in a T-shirt waved at them as they pulled on to the drive, then down between the beautiful beech trees, past the old gatehouse, through the huge wrought-iron gate and on to the main road at the end.

'I never want to see you ever again,' said Eupheme once they had driven out of the village and had reached open country. 'I am sorry I have messed up your life. I will send you the share we agreed as soon as I receive it. I'm sure you'll be okay. You're a very resourceful young man.'

'Blimey, what have I done?' asked Ian.

'What d'you mean, what have you done!' said Eupheme, her eyes set on the road ahead.

'Well, that wasn't my idea, you know. Back there with your sister.'

'You looked like a very willing part of it, though.'

'Oh, bloody Ada,' said Ian. He felt angry now. How could he win her round? What could he say that would be right? If only he had a program that would help him. He could load in all the possible responses, see what the program kicked out. Should he tell her that really he loved her – that wouldn't sound very convincing, and did it mean that he did love her? There was some unbelievable need to stay with her that was boiling around in his brain. Could he tell her he'd much rather go down on her any day of the week? No, she'd take offence. He could ask her to marry him. That sounded like the least offensive option.

'You've seen her before, haven't you?' said Eupheme.

He hadn't expected this. 'What?' he said, trying to think.

'You've seen Gresham before. You've been having an affair with her. You're not a virgin, are you?'

She looked at him, her eyes on fire with anger.

'Yes, okay, I'm not, but she did promise to marry me.'

'I knew it!' screamed Eupheme. Her knuckles turned white as she gripped the steering wheel. 'I knew it! The bitch, she did it on purpose. She found you. I knew it. Why didn't I see it coming? Why didn't I believe my own judgment? She got everything again. The bitch.'

'She didn't,' said Ian, hoping to placate her, assuming that Eupheme wanted him in some way, although he couldn't quite work out which. 'She never got my heart,' he lied. 'I could never have loved Gresham. She's a nightmare.'

'She won. She might have lost the bet but she won again. I did the work, she got the man, she got everything she wanted and then just walked away, like she always has!' Tears were now streaming down Eupheme's cheeks. 'She's always had everything.' She was nearly screaming now. Ian felt nervous for the first time. He realised that the Ka was going rather fast. True, they were on a long straight road, but when something the size of a Ka is doing close to ninety-five miles an hour, engine screaming, wind roaring across the open sunroof, woman at the wheel with less than a full grip on the old marbles, tension can begin to mount in the old pant-seat department.

'She's won again!' screamed Eupheme. 'I just don't believe it! How could she! What drives her? What has she got? She's not human!'

The car started to lurch around rather violently. Ian gripped the sides of his seat in terror. He could hear the tyres screeching as they tried to grip the hot road surface. He glanced at Eupheme, who now also seemed suddenly genuinely scared.

'Shit!' she screamed. Ian instinctively grabbed the wheel. He had never driven in his life but he knew he had to do something. The car hit the bank and the wheel lurched violently. Ian pulled with all his might, amazed at the forces he was dealing with. The car was now heading for the other bank, and still it felt as if they were going faster and faster. He pulled the car clear of the opposite bank only to feel it lurch too far. He was fighting enormous centrifugal forces on the one hand and Eupheme Betterment gone loopy on the other. No mean opposition. He glanced down and saw the ignition keys. His hand grabbed and turned. The engine died, the car slowed, and he pulled on the handbrake with all his strength. The car started slewing around crazily. The rear wheels locked, screaming rubber filled the air. The car was heading for a field gate. Ian tried to steer, but the wheel wouldn't move. He pulled harder. Still nothing. The gate was on them, or they were on the gate. One last tug — nothing.

The car hit the gate at an angle, smashing it to matchwood. Something big and white popped into Ian's vision with an explosive hiss. The front bumper then caught the very solid old gatepost. The car spun around and slid sideways across a dusty, recently mown hayfield.

When it finally came to a stop, the silence was completely unexpected. Ian realised he was in pain. What he experienced really was leaning fairly heavily towards the intense agony end of the pain spectrum. He lifted his hand to rub his head, and it felt wet. He stared at his hand — blood, what looked like buckets of it. The shock was slow to materialise, but as he stared about him he realised he'd been in a fairly serious car crash. He quickly looked at Eupheme. She was more or less lying across the now slightly bent steering wheel. A deflated air bag half engulfed her head. She slowly sat back. Her face was crumpled, tears pouring down her cheeks. He wasn't sure what happened then — she was so still for such a long time. It was possible that time was being distorted by the intensity of the experience — maybe only a few seconds had passed. Then Eupheme sobbed, her face folded into despair and time started running at its usual pace.

'It's okay,' said Ian, moving his arm out to comfort her. 'We're both still alive. It's okay, Eupheme. Don't cry, please. There's no need.'

'I want to die,' she said.

'No you don't, you're too intelligent for that.'

'I'm not. I'm so stupid. I always have been. She's so clever, she deserves everything, that's why she gets it. I don't deserve anything.'

'Um, let's not worry about her for a moment. We've been in a bit of a crash. Let's worry about us.'

More sobs followed as Ian softly patted Eupheme on the back. He felt blood running down his neck and began to wonder if he should attempt to move and get medical help. They were facing the way they'd come. The remnants of the gate lay on the field in front of them; a hub-cap, a wing mirror and a shower of broken glass littered the entrance to the field. Large and beautiful mixed deciduous trees shielded them from the direct sunlight. It was actually a rather beautiful spot.

'Not a bad place to end up, really,' said Ian.

Eupheme looked up like a child distracted from a tantrum. She glanced around the field and then continued crying. Ian heard an engine. A yellow tractor pulled itself gingerly through the gate. A gentle-looking man with a shock of grey hair sat at the wheel. He pulled the huge tractor to a halt beside the car, turned off the engine and jumped down from the cab. Ian could hear a Spice Girls song playing on the tractor's powerful sound system.

'You all right?' he asked.

'Um, think so, more or less,' said Ian. 'No bones broken. I just got a bit of a glance on the old head.'

'Young lady okay, is she?' the man asked, peering into the car.

'Yes. Driver's air bag. She's a bit upset, but no serious injury.'

'Right. You been up at the De Courcey place, have you?'

'The wedding, yes,' said Ian, feeling rather proud that where he'd been was that well known.

'Okay, well, don't move, right,' said the man. 'Just to be on the safe side, like. I'll call an ambulance, all right.'

'Thanks,' said Ian.

The man stood back a pace and looked at the vehicle. 'Car's a bit of a mess, but it don't look dangerous. You turned it all off, have you?'

'Yes. It's all off.'

'Fine. You wait there,' said the man. He reached into the cab of the tractor and pulled out a mobile phone.

'I'm sorry,' said Eupheme, through a veil of tears. Ian turned to look at her. They held hands.

'It's okay. I'm sorry. Didn't realise pulling out the old key instigated a steering lock. Bit of a shock that. I'm clearly not up on the latest in 'in car' security systems or I would never have pulled a stunt like that.'

'I nearly killed you.'

'No, it's fine.'

'I'll never drive again. I shouldn't be allowed.'

'You will. You're fine. It's been a tough day, but you won your wager.'

'Oh, please.'

'You did,' said Ian. 'You changed my life. Like it or not, that's what you've done.'

'I've made your life a mess. I've given you a taste of a life you can never have.'

'Eupheme, don't misunderstand what you've done. I don't want that life, thank you very much. I've got my own. I won't miss not hanging around with the Stanhope De Courceys of this world. No way, José. But you've shown me wonderful things that have opened up new worlds to me. I was so blinkered before, because I was so scared of everything. Well, it is frightening, but it's also interesting. Would that I could tell you about my new program that I've been cooking up on the quiet, but you'd be bored by it and rightly so. Bit of a boys' package perhaps. I'd like to show it to you when it's done and dusted.'

'A program?'

'Computer program, not a Channel Four doco,' said Ian with a smile. 'I think you'll like it. It's not about trains or taxis. In fact it's not about any form of transportation.'

'What is it about, then?'

'Women,' said Ian. 'It's a program to help men understand women.'

'Really?' said Eupheme. She wiped her eyes with the back of her hand. 'How does it work?'

'Don't know. Haven't actually finished writing it yet, but it's going to run on Mac or PC platforms. It's a hot-sauce-based data display system with embedded Java applets and webbots. Should be very interesting.'

'It's a lovely idea. I think. It's not pornographic, is it?'

'No, it's not.'

'Good.'

'It's meant to help men understand how women operate, like a manual. Most of the men I know don't understand women, and traditional database designs just don't do justice to the complexities of mood and intuitive knowledge. So it runs as a three-hundred-and-sixty-degree finder. You'll sort of float through free-form data rather than have it confined to boxes.'

'I bet it'll be brilliant. Like your display of cans. You're so clever, Ian.'

'Thank you,' said Ian.

He saw the man from the tractor lean in through Eupheme's window. She didn't seem to notice him. She was looking at Ian in a way he'd never seen before.

'I wish I could kiss you, Ian, but you've just been doing something with your mouth that I don't want to get involved in.'

'I won't ask,' said the man softly. 'There's an ambulance on its way, coming from Witney. It's got to come along the A420 and there's roadworks outside Standlake, but it won't be long. It's best if you both sit tight, all right? I'll wait with you.'

'Who are you?' asked Eupheme.

'George Hemmings,' said the man with a bright smile. 'I was just working on a water main up the road a ways when you passed me like a screaming banshee. I thought my time had come, I tell you. Then you smashed through the gate and somehow didn't get killed. Bloody miracle, really, but there you go.'

'Thank you, George,' said Ian, who realised he was now looking at the world through a long tunnel. There was no pain, just a bit of buzzy nausea. He suddenly saw his mum's body in the oven at Eupheme's flat. His legs felt like lead. Everything went grey and misty, smelt of sick and sounded like feedback. Then nothing.

The next thing he knew he was being wheeled down a corridor in a hospital. He felt very nauseous and wondered where he could vomit without causing offence. He was lying on a gurney just like in *E.R.* only no one was running or shouting out his vitals. In fact no one seemed in any sort of panic, which of course could have been a time distortion thing on his part. A face appeared in his field of vision, pale and tense but familiar and very beautiful.

'Ian, you're okay. It's me, Eupheme, you just lost a bit of blood, you're fine. Honestly, you're fine. Oh my God, I'm so sorry. I'll wait for you. I promise I'll wait for you.'

'I'm so glad,' said Ian drowsily. 'I'm sorry if I hurt you. Back there.'

The stretcher was pushed into a little curtained-off area. A woman doctor appeared and took Ian's wrist.

'Hello, there, I'm Dr Westlake. Let's have a look at you.'

'It's all my fault,' said Eupheme, pounding her chest. 'I was driving. I nearly killed him.'

Ian reached up and grabbed her wrist to stop her hitting herself.

'It isn't your fault,' he said, now feeling a lump in his throat which wasn't a result of sudden vehicular impact. 'I was being disgusting, taking advantage of you and Gresham. I was just going along for the ride and I've ended up hurting you, which I now realise I really don't want to do.'

'Don't you?'

'No.'

'Oh, Ian. I'm so sorry. Please forgive me.'

She held his hand. He squeezed hers. She squeezed back. He watched a tear roll down her face. He felt he could hold her hand for ever.

'Have you finished?' asked the doctor eventually. 'Only I'd like to take an X-ray and put a few stitches in your head before it gets any steamier in here.'

'Sorry,' said Eupheme.

'I like cunnilingus, but Gresham made it into a chore,' said Ian, still feeling dizzy. 'I promise I'll never go down on your half-sister again.'

The doctor gently wiped the blood off Ian's forehead. 'You soon think you've heard everything in this job,' she said, 'but there's always something new. "I promise I'll never go down on your half-sister again." That's a classic. It's going in my notes.'

Epilogue

Five years later

'What's it like being married to someone so rich?' asked Jennifer Cornwell, the Australian journalist.

'Why d'you ask that?' said Gresham. The noise of the party made the interview a fairly difficult procedure.

'Oh, sorry,' said the journalist. 'It's just a bit of background. I'm doing this piece on women film-makers, you know, what motivates them, how they get to do what they do.'

'Right, and you think because I've got a rich husband I can afford to be dilettante and naff around making crap films all the time.'

'Not at all,' said the journalist. She was smiling as she spoke and Gresham could tell she was delighted with such a quote. 'But d'you think it makes a difference?'

'What?'

'Well, not having to worry about money all the time.'

'I don't know,' said Gresham flatly.

'Oh. Right.'

'I've never not had money so I don't know,' said Gresham. 'My dad is a bit on the rich side as well.'

'Right,' said Jennifer Cornwell. 'Now your first film was,

427

like, a commercial success, wasn't it, but were you disappointed with the press response that *Uncle Roger* got?'

'Yes,' said Gresham. She didn't want the interview to go on so she had decided to keep the remainder of her answers very short.

'Oh, right,' said Jennifer Cornwell. 'And you've just come back from Hollywood.'

'Yes.'

'What were you doing there?'

'Another movie.'

'Oh, right. Great. Did you shoot another movie?'

'No.'

'Oh, right. What, development?'

'Something like that.'

'Project dropped? Bummer, mate.'

'No, nothing was dropped, just a few changes here and there,' said Gresham, not wishing to say she was sacked but knowing the news would emerge sooner or later.

'Oh, right. I really liked *Uncle Roger*, by the way. I thought the critics were a bunch of sexist arseholes.'

'Thank you.'

'Don't mention it, mate. Thanks, anyway,' said Jennifer putting away her spiral-bound notepad. 'That was really helpful. The piece will be in *Elle* magazine, in the February issue.'

'Okay,' said Gresham, almost smiling at the departing journalist. She stood up and glanced around the room. She was at the Allied Fountain Christmas party which was being held in the Café Royal on Regent Street. It was packed with important people in the industry. It was a nightmare.

Most of the people she knew; most of them she hated with a tooth-grinding passion. She looked for Stanhope, saw him by the bar – immaculate suit, hair thick and luxurious, smile enchanting and fresh-looking in this sea of horror. He was leaning over someone, towering over them. Standing very close to them. She tried to see who it was — a young man with short hair.

Sally, the receptionist from the office, almost fell past her, wrapped around a large man.

'Salls, who's that bloke Stanhope's talking to?'

'I dunno, darling,' said Sally, very drunk, leering around the room. 'Which man?'

'Look, by the bar, next to Stanhope. Who's that funny little man he's talking to?'

'Bloody hell, where've you been?' asked the man Sally was attached to. 'It's Damen fucking Rooks.'

'Who's he?'

'Plays for Arsenal,' said Sally. 'Footballer. This place is full of footballers and hairdressers. I thought we were supposed to be a fucking film company.'

'Rent-a-celeb, mate,' said Sally's man.

'See you later,' said Sally, and she lunged at the man and disappeared into the seething crowd.

Gresham sat down again. She chewed her lip. She had been married for five years, had actually been with her husband for about six months in all that time. She had always known Stanhope was bisexual, had told herself she didn't mind. She told herself it was hip to have a bisexual husband. She'd told herself this so many times she really didn't mind, only when it was so obvious. Discretion was important; it was the cement that held marriages like hers together. And there was Stanhope with some pretty-boy footballer. She was angry. It felt like another kick in the teeth, and she'd had plenty of those. She'd been working in Hollywood, living in what they called 'development hell' and spending any free time she had either crying on her own in the Westwood apartment Stanhope had bought for her or fending off dull men in restaurants. She almost made a film, got sacked, almost made five others, shot eight promo videos for bands of varying success, got sacked again and came home. She had nothing to do, no projects to develop, no scripts to read. Then just as she felt she had hit the bottom she had been invited to the Allied Fountain party. It was only later she realised she'd been invited to the party but not to any meetings. Her arrival back in England wasn't exactly auspicious. In the ten weeks since she'd been back she had only been interviewed by *Elle* magazine and that wasn't even a profile piece. She noticed Maxine Tabac, a woman she'd known years before who produced commercials. Maybe she could start again. She was still young. She'd had some radical ideas about car commercials when she was in LA.

She suddenly caught a glimpse of the new girl standing in the middle of the Café Royal. Throwing her stupid hair back like a tart caught in headlights. Kristen Wallace. Couldn't have been more than twenty-one years old. Looking stunning in a red falling-off-her-tits floor-length dress. Surrounded by some of the most powerful men in the business. Drooling over her openly, trying to be witty. It was a pathetic sight. At least Stanhope didn't do that sort of thing. What had Kristen Wallace actually done? Made some shit-awful piece of crap, a low-budget film about some smelly old woman living alone on a council estate, and they all swarmed around her. Allied Fountain had already signed her up for a three-film deal, or so she'd heard.

'Fuck, I hate this business,' she said. No one heard.

Ian almost trotted the short distance from his office down the stairs, along the hall and up to the front door. He pulled it open to see Eddie in a huge quilted coat with the hood up, standing in the constant grey drizzle that had constituted the weather for as long as Ian could remember.

'Eduardo, me old pal-a-roochie,' he said. 'Come in, come in.'

'I'm well the soaked,' said Eddie. 'Walked here, guy. Wheels off the road.'

'Oh no. What's up?'

'Big end's gone, guy,' said Eddie, shedding his coat on to the floor. 'Me uncle said he fix it and now it's mash up bad. I'm not gonna aks him again.'

'Need to take it to an authorised dealer,' said Ian, trying to be helpful.

'It's a Cosworth Sierra,' said Eddie. 'Specialist vehicle, you know what I'm saying.'

'Eddie, I'm speaking to you as a mate, you know that, but your Cosworth Sierra has a plastic wing on the back and a sticker that says Cosworth, and that's about as near as Mr Cosworth ever got to the vehicle in question.'

'Oh, that's right, take the piss, Mr Moneybags. I'm telling you the power unit is genuine Cosworth.'

'Sorry, Ed. Want a coffee?' said Ian, going into the tiny Cyril Street kitchen and putting the kettle on.

'Five sugars and no milk,' said Eddie, who flopped down on the old sofa, the only piece of furniture in the back room. 'This place change a bit,' he commented.

'Oh, it's a bit of a mess. I spend most of my time up in the old office,' said Ian, pouring sugar into Eddie's mug straight from the packet. 'But I had to get rid of most of the old junk. Couldn't stand the sight of it. Front room's pretty much the same, I never go in there really.'

'Busy?' asked Eddie.

'Very,' said Ian, 'Feet barely touch the old ground from one day to the next. What about you?'

'Whatever happen in a supermarket? Nothing. People do shopping, you know that. That's no problem, I just in such a mess at home with the big beanie.'

'Marsha?' enquired Ian, referring to Eddie's partner of three years and the mother of his baby daughter.

'She bin mad as hell, I don't know what I done. Nothing seems right, you know what I mean.'

Ian passed Eddie the cup of steaming super-sweet coffee.

'You need a copy of WomanWizard.'

'Oh yeah, that's goin' to help me understand her, is it?'

'That's the idea, Eduardo.'

'It's stupid, guy. I understand her now, she's a ball-breaking baby mother. She got my seed in her fist and she's twisting. I don't need no 'puter program to tell me that.'

'Well, it might sort of throw some of the old light on to how best to approach her, you know, in terms of how not to blow it, when to make a move, et cetera.'

'I can't believe people have bought this thing.'

'In their droves, Eddie, but they wouldn't keep buying it if it didn't work.'

'How much'll that set me back, then?'

'Free, gratis and for nothing, my old mate. What system you on?'

'PC, innit,' said Eddie.

'No problemo, Windows compatible, needs about fifty megs of hard disk space and at least thirty-two of RAM.'

'Big fella.'

'Tell me about it. It's a complex program, Eddie, but a doddle to run. Have you ever seen it?'

''Course I have, in the shops an' that.'

'Come upstairs. I'll give you the old world-famous Ringfold run-through.'

'Kickin', guy!' said Eddie, who followed Ian up the narrow staircase and into what had once been Ian's parents' bedroom. It had been transformed into a brightly lit office with three massive computers humming away under the work surface. A series of awards were hung in silver frames on the wall opposite the two small windows. A steel shelving system housed more humming hardware and boxes of WomanWizard computer programs.

A young woman sat in front of a computer screen, speaking quietly into a telephone headset. Eddie nodded in her direction.

'Jasmin,' said Ian. 'She's here four days a week now, dealing with telephone enquiries. She's brilliant, keeps her databases very tidy, I'd be lost without her. No one processes a credit card payment faster.'

'You employ her?' asked Eddie, staring at the attractive young woman.

'Yes, but Eddie, only for secretarial purposes. I'm a family man now, no more playing the old field for yours truly.'

'Kickin',' said Eddie for no reason Ian could pinpoint. 'Giss a job, then.'

'Well, I had meant to ask. I don't know how permanent – who knows in the cut and thrust of software innovation? – but what about store manager?'

'That's me, guy,' said Eddie with a cheesy grin.

'Keeping tabs on the CDs and floppies going out of here is proving to be a little bit much for moi. I could do with an extra pair of hands or three.'

'Kickin',' said Eddie.

'First things first, though, my old pal-a-roochie,' said Ian as he guided the smiling Eddie to a chair. Sitting on the tidy white work surface in front of him stood three twenty-four-inch high-resolution colour screens. In front of each lay an extended keyboard and a mouse with a WomanWizard mousemat.

'This is totally kickin',' said Eddie, his eyes scanning the room independently. 'It's like mission control, you know what I'm saying.'

'Bit of a dream come true, n'est-ce pas,' said Ian, beaming with pride. He tapped one of the humming boxes under the work surface. 'This is my new baby, a five hundred and fifty megahertz multi-processor. This baby sings.'

'I'm tellin' you,' said Eddie.

'Anyway, have a look at the old WomanWizard, on the end monitor,' said Ian, pushing a swivel office chair towards Eddie. 'I've just got to reply to a load of e-mail.'

Eddie spent five minutes reading the screen and occasionally tapping keys as Ian pretended to reply to e-mail. He wanted to see how Eddie responded to his key question section, and was in fact monitoring his progress on his own screen.

'What do I do now?' asked Eddie when he had filled in the last box.

'Click start,' said Ian, and pushed his chair along to join Eddie. They watched as the screen started to build a mass of floating shapes, mostly oblong although some were rounded triangles, some spherical. The colours were subtle variants of blue and green.

'Very peaceful,' said Ian.

'Yeah, nice,' said Eddie. A little bell sounded, confirming that the program had loaded up and was ready to go.

'Let's fly,' said Ian. 'Just point the cursor at wher-ever you want to go and click. You'll get the hang of it pretty quick.'

Ian watched Eddie carefully as he moved the mouse and the shapes on the screen started to move with him. Eddie smiled, just as all the people who had tried the program for the first time had done before him, just as he had done when he had finally managed to make the horribly complicated thing work the first time.

Hesitantly at first, Eddie started to sail through the colourful floating, data that made up the woman he loved. Marsha. She was mostly blue and green, but as Eddie turned past the mountain that was her patience he came across a red shape that vibrated slightly. He continued to sail towards the shape which defined her anger, normally hidden, and suddenly the screen went red.

'Oh, man,' said Eddie.

'She's one passionate lady,' said Ian.

'Tell me about it.'

'Go through the anger shape, see what's there.'

Eddie moved the mouse and the anger shape filled the screen. As soon as the screen was red, another series of shapes appeared, some with question marks defining them as needing more data.

'It's not complete, obviously, you'd need her to fill in a few data packets first, but it's giving you a pretty good idea of what's going on, isn't it?'

'It's like bein' with the beanie herself, like stuff happens I don't expect, and in real life it's too late, but here I can, like, go back and try again.'

'Eddie, you are the best advert the program has ever had,' said Ian. He handed him a brand-new plastic-sealed copy of WomanWizard for Windows. 'Have fun.'

Eupheme Betterment felt a little tired. She was not one for prolonged train journeys when a flight would have been so much faster, but Ian and Jackson seemed to be enjoying themselves.

The previous day had started early with a train journey from Torontolla station to Florence, then changing for the express to Milan, changing again for Lugano. They had clambered off a slow train in the middle of the night in a little town called Chur, high in the Swiss Alps. They stayed in a beautiful wooden ski lodge, almost completely deserted as it was early June. Eupheme had a lie-in but felt guilty and got up anyway. When she looked out of the windows she was staggered by the sight that greeted her. A massive panorama of overwhelming mountains and forests, and in the distance below them a silver lake glistened in the morning sun.

Ian and Jackson had finished breakfast by the time she joined them, her son sitting demurely with his napkin tucked into his little Gap shirt.

'I've got my napkin on, Mum,' he said. 'And I didn't spill anything.'

'Good boy,' she replied, almost crying with the love she felt for him.

The three of them walked down the quiet road from the hotel. Their bags had been taken on ahead of them. Ian and Jackson stood waiting on the tiny station. The platform looked delightful, bedecked with summer flowers.

Jackson, who was now four and three-quarters, was dressed very smartly in a pair of lederhosen Ian had bought in a tourist shop.

'Look, I know it's a bit on the naff side, but they'll last for ages,' he had said to Eupheme. She shrugged. She felt so relaxed now; she had finally laid her past to rest. After all the ghastly tension of the journey down to Italy she felt a smile rest naturally on her face.

They had visited Richard and Christine Markham at Castello del Largo, the old farmhouse now chock full of children. Christine was on her fourth. She was more matronly than ever, able to manage a conversation, breast-feeding, filling a washing machine and cutting up ripe tomatoes at one and the same time. She was clearly ecstatically happy. Not only that, she seemed to have found a new lease of life, taking Italian lessons in the evenings and going to lectures on fine arts in the local town hall.

Richard, on the other hand, looked broken, balding, grey-haired and very thin. He admitted he was still drinking quite heavily but claimed to be coping. Somehow through all this chaos he was still creating his pieces; his work was still selling. He still travelled the globe every year to open an exhibition somewhere.

Castello del Largo looked like a wreck — four children, three boys and a baby girl could do serious damage to a home. Jackson seemed to enjoy their visit, joining in the rough-housing with the boys and picking up some Italian swear words in the chicken-filled farmyard outside.

Eupheme felt herself relax the minute she actually set eyes on the couple in the old farmhouse. It had been four years since they had seen each other, and then it had only been a brief meeting at the offices of the International Children's Trust where Eupheme was still working.

She still saw Gresham whenever she was in London, not very often. Strangely, since Ian's WomanWizard program had sold so well, she and Ian had seen Stanhope De Courcey for financial advice, all of which had proved to be very sound.

They had bought a roomy but nondescript house in Primrose Hill in London. Ian still worked in Northampton because he felt more comfortable there, and his mother's old house was a free office. Their holiday had been eagerly awaited as they had both been working very hard leading up to it.

Eupheme went into the ticket office and checked the times of the connection for Paris. They had another long day's train ride ahead of them; this really was going to have to be a one-off.

'Here it comes, Dad.' She heard Jackson through the open window of the ticket office. It was a steam train, of course, and Jackson was thrilled to bits to be going on it.

The sound of the engine filled the air as the narrow-gauge steam locomotive rounded the bend below the station, puffing hoarsely to climb the gradient.

Eupheme glanced out of the ticket office. She could just see Jackson standing with his legs slightly apart, like a goalie waiting for a penalty. It was only then that she noticed he was holding a small notebook, as was Ian. They both had stubby pencils poised.

The train pulled to a noisy, hissing halt. The rich smell of coal and steam filled the air. Eupheme took the tickets and walked out on to the platform. Ian and Jackson quickly pocketed their notebooks and pencils and stared at their feet as innocently as they could.

'Train's here, Mum,' said Jackson as nonchalantly as a four-year-old is able.

'I can see that, darling,' said Eupheme, pushing his hair

into place and kissing Ian on the cheek. 'What are you two boys up to?'

'Nothing,' they both replied in unison.

'Nothing at all,' said Ian.

FIONA WALKER

SNAP HAPPY

A budding stand-up comic, Juno is voluptuous, hedonistic, funny and terminally untidy. On her thirtieth birthday, she decides to have a wild one-night-stand to mark the occasion. But seducing her new flatmate before he's had a chance to unpack his belongings is not a wise move. Just over from New York, Jay Mulligan is intense, mysterious and, as Juno joyously discovers, far better than breakfast in bed. It's only when they both get out of that bed on the wrong side three days later that the problems start . . .

HODDER AND STOUGHTON PAPERBACKS

NANCY TURNER

THESE IS MY WORDS

Eighteen-year-old Sarah begins her diary in the summer of 1881, when he father decides to pick up the whole family, horses and all, and move them from Arizona Territory – hotter than the devil's frying pan – to greener pastures in Texas. Sarah's thirst for knowledge inspires her through the long days on the wagon trail, as she diligently keeps the diary that proves at times her greatest comfort.

The family travels through a land of rattlesnakes and Indians, hastily dug graves and unbearable loneliness. Full of fire and strength, with a spirit that cannot be broken even in the midst of fighting, sickness and death, Sarah turns out to be her family's greatest support. But she is tender as well as tough, and she yearns to be loved. In the harsh and unforgiving landscape of the West, Sarah meets the man who is to be her greatest passion.

Pioneer woman, free spirit, settler of America's Western frontier: Sarah Prine is all of these. She is also the most remarkable and lovable character in contemporary fiction.

HODDER AND STOUGHTON PAPERBACKS

MARC BLAKE

SUNSTROKE

Sex, drugs, guns and money – everything you ever wanted from a package holiday.

Summer on the Costa del Sol and it's hotter than a Merc in a Moss Side car park.

Mike Trent's holiday starts badly when his midnight swim in the hotel pool is interrupted by a falling corpse, pushed from a third floor window by a sinister Scotsman.

Sarah Rutherford, using her job as a travel rep as cover, is in town to investigate the mysterious death of her party-loving sister.

When the two join forces, they find themselves up against the criminal community: a pint-sized skinhead called Kevin, the demented brothers Esteban, a slavering wolf, a hunchback pornographer, and an ex-pat villain with more than once secret to hide.

Still, you can't make paella without peeling prawns.

HODDER AND STOUGHTON PAPERBACKS

A selection of bestsellers from
Hodder and Stoughton

Snap Happy	Fiona Walker	0 340 68227 2	£5.99	☐
These is my Words	Nancy Turner	0 340 71778 5	£6.99	☐
Sunstroke	Marc Blake	0 340 71772 6	£6.99	☐

All Hodder & Stoughton books are available at your local bookshop or newsagent, or can be ordered direct from the publisher. Just tick the titles you want and fill in the form below. Prices and availability subject to change without notice.

Hodder & Stoughton Books, Cash Sales Department, Bookpoint, 39 Milton Park, Abingdon, OXON, OX14 4TD, UK. E-mail address: order@bookpoint.co.uk. If you have a credit card you may order by telephone – (01235) 400414.

Please enclose a cheque or postal order made payable to Bookpoint Ltd to the value of the cover price and allow the following for postage and packing:
UK & BFPO – £1.00 for the first book, 50p for the second book, and 30p for each additional book ordered up to a maximum charge of £3.00.
OVERSEAS & EIRE – £2.00 for the first book, £1.00 for the second book, and 50p for each additional book.

Name _____

Address _____

_____

_____

If you would prefer to pay by credit card, please complete:
Please debit my Visa/Access/Diner's Card/American Express (delete as applicable) card no:

Signature _____

Expiry Date _____

If you would NOT like to receive further information on our products please tick the box. ☐